Wishi

CW00419498

T.G. Frost

ALSO BY THIS AUTHOR:

K – Block

I wrote most of this story before
my first baby was born.
I finished it after he arrived.
I dedicate this book to my partner,
who carried him with a smile.

PROLOGUE

< static >

"Hey everybody, welcome back to another episode of Travel Haunts. I'm HauntsWivHanna, taking you, as usual, to the country's most known and unknown haunted locations. Before we begin, don't forget to hit that Like button and please do subscribe and click the little bell to get notifications around the clock."

< static >

"Today I've come to- "

< static >

"-a peaceful town, but the locals haven't been very welcoming. So far, no one who's talked to me has attested to experiencing any paranormal activity- "

< static >

"I've been informed that the youngsters – meaning me, apparently – have a spot just inside the woods. There should be a bridge for me to cross, can't miss it they said."

< static >

"This looks like the place. It looks well lived-in by the local youngsters, and should actually serve as a decent base of operations. I can get everything prepped here. I have my usual bag of tricks with some new additions this week. And yes – I am sorry – I have brought a pack of cigarettes. I know you guys have been following my separate personal channel and whilst trying to give up the cancer sticks, dealing with the paranormal almost on a daily basis makes it tough."

< static >

"-enter the code on the website HAUNTSWIV98 to get a discount on your personalised Zippo- "

< static >

"Can you see me?"

< static >

"Okay, whilst I set up the camera, I'll fill you guys in. The town- "

< static >

"-kinda just popped up in members-only forums, rumours of a town people have passed through and felt bad vibes, like the kind you get when someone tells you a ghost story you know is true. That's this place, and I'll agree, this place has weird vibes. One of the unfriendly locals who talked a bit said there was, like, a residue here or something."

< static >

"-a great word for ectoplasm- "

< static >

"-leaving behind my second camera, microphone and voice recorder. I'm only taking camera one and ciggies for now. So let's head out and see what we can find. I don't know what to expect, but my mind is open. I was warned away from the deep woods, which means we have a starting point. Wish me luck!"

< static >

"It's starting to get dark. I haven't found or heard anything but guys, this place is so creepy. Like, I'm actually terrified right now, and I don't scare easy."

< static >

"-lighter's ran out of juice, the spare's in my rucksack- "

< static >

"Jesus, this is fucked up. Check this out. See these pillars? I swear I walked right by here a few minutes ago and they weren't there- "

< static >

"-like something is trying to lure me in- "

< static >

"-and now I'm out of cigarettes- "

< static >

"I'm heading back to base. Might even go back into the village. I don't know what I was thinking coming out here alone. I...constantly feel followed. Every time I hear a noise...there's nothing there. This is the most intense Travel Haunts yet."

< static >

"-should be here. This...this is where base camp should be. I...I made sure, I even marked tree trunks to...to find my way back- "

< static >

"HELLO?"

< static >

"Where am I? I...this isn't right."

< static >

"I'm whispering now because I'm hiding. I started hearing voices in the woods. Like chanting. I left behind the voice recorder for some stupid reason...and the camera one is low on battery- "

< static >

"They voices've stopped. If I just keep walking in the same direction I should...no..."

< static >

"-the fucking pillars again! Maybe I should go through. My gut is telling me no but...Jesus. I have to, don't I?"

< static >

"-nothing here, but I think something used to be. You can see the ruins. A church or house maybe? I'm going back, fuck this place- "

< static >

"Gotta leave! Gotta leave!"

< static >

"-voices, chasing me- "

< static >

< static >

HauntswivHanna was one of the most viewed ghost hunt channels on Youtube. After recording this footage, and narrowly – she believes – escaping with her life, the host, Hanna, doesn't upload the video and deletes her channel, losing a fanbase of over one million subscribers. She didn't see or find anything that night, and brought back no evidence of chanting voices, which were not captured on her camera. She did, however, attest in a police statement to a strange sensation, specifically using the word "residue."

When releasing a final video statement on her Twitter before deleting that too, she said "some things are more fucked up than ghosts."

She left her rucksack behind.

PART I

'The Price of Entry'

CHAPTER 1

Another night, another fight.

The floor is sticky, the air heavy with the smell of last night's stale popcorn. Cigarette smoke wafts under the hanging light fixtures. The social club is as dingy as its windows, and that's the way the owner likes it.

Tables have been pushed to the sides of the function room. Mismatched chairs set up around tonight's entertainment have already been shoved into disarray by the punters. About fifty in all. Not bad, not great. They're rowdy enough. Some have forgotten to not sit their pints literally at ringside.

Behind the bar at the back, Frank, the owner, watches disinterestedly. It's the fifth fight this week. He's drying a pint mug, the pawn shop gold weighing down his aged fingers tapping against the glass. At the foot of the bar are bronze screws where once an actual bar had been. The story went that Frank pulled it up to flog after Reg Kray stomped someone's head on it. Rumour had it the blood was still wet when money exchanged hands. The East End is built on legends.

In the ring, Nick takes a painful blow from his opponent, a shot to the ribs that pushes him back. The ring rattles, an antique in its own right, held together by blood, spit and duct tape. Mostly duct tape. Falling back against the ropes, Nick knows one of his ribs is fucked. That familiar sting. The crowd laughs and throws insults. Regular faces.

The opponent, who looks worse off, gestures with his gloved hands for Nick to come and get some more, grinning with blooded teeth. He's a Manc. They're always mad. He's lost count of how many 'Mad Mancs' he's fought, but credit where credit is due, they all lived up to the name.

Using the ropes, Nick springs himself forwards. His rib feels like hell, he should stop, but this isn't a garden-variety bout. No referee and only one round. First one to drop the other wins. Or one of them could submit, which is a fancy word for pussy out.

The punters cheer. They clasp notes in their fists. Smoke hovers above their heads like fog.

Nick throws a left hook that connects with the sweet spot on the Manc's chin. Like a sack of spuds, his opponent is down.

After the fight, Nick touches up his wounds in the dressing room mirror. The dressing room is a disused ladies toilet, the paint faded and flaking. The mirror itself is smeared with stains. To his left is a mounted vase with a long dead flower in it, one of Frank's ways to tart the place up a bit. "Birds' shit stinks too," he'd said.

Nick has a split in his bottom lip as well as the regular swelling over his face. It doesn't disrupt his rugged looks too much, gained from a life of getting punched in the mug. His jaw has always been made from anti-knockout material. At thirty-seven, he looks decent enough.

His rib hurts. The codeine he dry-swallowed after the fight has demoted it to an irritating throb. Tomorrow it won't look so hot, and breathing will be a pain in the arse.

He gets dressed, jeans and tee-shirt, faux leather jacket. He picks up the plastic bag holding his dirty gear and heads into the club to collect his pay.

Most of the punters have cleared out, winners and losers alike, leaving in their wake discarded balls of paper, roll-ups and germs. Only a stubborn few remain, hunched over pints they'll be nursing for at least another half hour.

Over by the doors Nick sees the Manc, one of his eyes puffed closed, chatting with friends. Probably from Manchester, supporting their mate and for a good piss-up.

Frank is standing at the bar, sleeves rolled up to reveal his tattooed Popeye forearms. He's counting through tonight's takings in the public eye, as always. He enjoys showing his position in the club as judge, jury and executioner. Nick goes over.

Frank doesn't look up from the cash. The never-ending cigarette in his mouth bobs up and down as he speaks.

"Good fight tonight, Nicky boy."

The East End is prominent in his accent. Frank is the only person who calls Nick, Nicky.

"Not bad I s'pose," Nick replies. "What's the take?"

Frank flicks through the crisp wad. He hands over four notes which Nick snatches, crumpling the money.

He narrows his eyes. "Seventy quid?"

"Take it or leave it, Nicky."

"This won't keep me in fucking cat food."

Frank looks up from his money, a ribbon of smoke drifts over his face. "You ain't got a cat."

"How d'you know I ain't got a cat?" Nick says, holding the notes up to the light.

"'Cause you 'ate 'em." Frank takes the cigarette from his mouth.

"Come on Frank, you know what I mean. I won. There should be more."

As Frank speaks, Nick pockets his money. "What can I tell ya mate? You saw what we had tonight. It's 'ard to get punters through the doors during the week."

"You don't seem to be out of pocket," Nick observes.

Frank jams a thumb against his chest, knocking cigarette ash to the carpet. "I *own* this gaff." He simmers. "Listen, Nicky, if you ain't 'appy with the pay, why don't you try something more official?"

Nick shakes his head. "You know I can't."

Frank does know. He's known for a while. He asks, "How about bouncin'? Any work there?"

Nick sighs, "Yeah, got a couple of gigs coming up. One's nothing special, the other pays better."

Frank puts the cigarette back in his mouth. Nick is sure it's replenished itself.

"There ya go then," he says. "Look to the future."

Nick scoffs. Some future he's got laid out ahead of him. He needs work, not hope. He looks over to the doors. The Manc and his pals are still floating around.

"You know I like ya, Nicky. If I could give ya more, I would. On my life."

Frank puts a hand over his heart. The wrong side.

Then why don't you? Nick thinks with bitterness.

A man appears behind the bar. Heavy-set, but not fat. A mean looking bloke with hangover eyes and a polo shirt. He taps Frank on the shoulder, there's something conspiratorial about it.

"Frank?" It comes out as *Fwank*.

At that, Nick begins to walk away. Club business isn't his. Frank grabs him by the arm, lowering his voice.

"Listen, I'm prob'ly gettin' myself into some shit 'ere Nicky, but I just want to let ya know that the Georges were 'ere yesterday askin' after ya."

"Both of 'em?" Nick asks, leaning in.

"Yeah. Said they wanted to have a chat."

"They always do," Nick says. "You tell them I was in tonight?"

"No, Nicky. Just told 'em ya wasn't about and that was it. They took off."

They'd only come in to make themselves known, leaving their mark in the same way a dog pisses on a post box. They'd know Nick was fighting tonight. Unlicensed fights were the Georges' bread and butter.

"Cheers for letting me know." Nick swaps his bag to his other hand.

"You be careful with them boys," Frank warns him.

Nick nods. "I'll see you next time, Frank."

Frank performs a half-arsed shadow box. "I'll try to get ya in for a Saturday spot, Nicky. More punters, more cash."

The man at the bar is insistent. "Frank?"

Frank waves the man off, mumbling his irritation.

Nick asks light-heartedly, "What're you up to now, Frank?"

"Just a bitta business, Nicky boy. Nothin' to worry about."

"Bit late for business, innit?" Nick smiles.

Frank smiles back, winks. "Money never sleeps."

They shake hands. Nick watches Frank disappear through a squeaky door behind the bar with the other man. Dodgy dealings going on back there, Nick thinks. Frank is a stand-up geezer for the most part, but his life is a trail of under-the-table crime.

Nick goes to leave, nodding his thanks as some of the pint nursers lift their glasses to him.

He's stopped by the Mad Manc, who's wearing a grin eerily like the one he wore in the ring, minus the blood. More than once a sore loser has tried it on after a loss. Nick braces himself for a post-game dust up. The Manc's taller than Nick thought. Some men have bad posture when they rumble.

"Good match that, mate. Proper good," the Manc says with jarring cheer. His jaw is red.

"I'm glad we both had fun." Nick untightens his leg muscles. Slightly.

"Me and the lads are poppin' out forra few bevvies. Wanna join?"

It's nearly one in the morning. That aside, Nick doesn't keep friends. Anyway, all he can think about is a hot shower and bed.

"No thanks, pal," Nick smiles, "but cheers for the offer."

The Manc shrugs. "No probs, mate. Maybe I'll see youse up near me sometime?"

Nick tells him that maybe he will, though he has no intention of going near Manchester any time soon.

He shakes hands with the Manc and his entourage, who are all surprisingly high-spirited, holding his smile for all of them. Nick is good at getting along with people without much effort. Be friendly without being a friend, that's the key.

When he leaves the social club, he is on his own in the street. His smile falls away. A police siren wails in the distance. That's the deal in

London: roadworks by day, sirens by night.

It's dark. The streetlamp up the road casts just enough orange-yellow light to see by.

To Nick's right is a minibus, the Manc's carriage, parked on double-yellows. Nick doubts it'll be moved. It tilts toward the social club. The road is convex, the markings gone. Potholes cover the tarmac like acne.

He looks up at the gently swinging social club sign, its lightbulb flickers. The picture, a dancing gypsy woman, is barely visible, though the green of her eyes still stands out. Frank says the gypsy is because of his heritage, but there's never been any solid proof of that. The cracked paint is sun-bleached, which has always struck Nick as strange because he can't remember the last time the sun touched this street.

Estelle's is as charming as it is deplorable.

Nick begins the hour-long journey home. He could take a taxi, but he likes the walk. If the Georges were prowling they'd have approached him already. At the end of the street he crosses the road into a dark alley. His footsteps echo. There's a smell of overflowing dustbins.

This part of the city is lonely this time of night. Nick likes the emptiness, he feels it suits him well.

§

By the time Nick gets home the codeine has worn off. He dumps his bag, coat and keys on the kitchen table – which has never been used to eat from – and goes into his small bathroom. He turns on the shower, the pipes groan. In this crumbling redbrick building, he doubts his is the only flat with shitty plumbing.

As the steam thickens, Nick removes his tee-shirt and takes himself to the mirror. Where the mirror has been screwed into the cabinet, there are rusty trails. It's one of the many things Nick has promised himself he'll get sorted.

Bruising has already started to show over his ribs. It hurts to prod. That damn Manc did a number on him. Tomorrow it will be the shape of a purple continent. If the rib is broken, he'll go see the doctor. He can take a beating, but a rib in the lung is punishment too much. He checks his split lip by licking it. It tastes metallic, the blood congealed. Turning his head to inspect for any unnoticed wounds, he sees his well and truly cauliflowered ear. *That's not going anywhere*, he thinks.

Nick moves away from the mirror when his reflection becomes a blur under the steam. In the shower, he places his palms on the tiles and lets the water rain onto his back. It soaks through his dark hair, massages his scalp, stings the scrapes on his knuckles.

Where the taps have been fitted are haloes of the same orange gunk that plagues the mirror. It, too, has left trails that run down the inside of the tub to the plughole. Nick closes his eyes, imagines himself somewhere better. For five deserved minutes he enjoys the heat.

Dressed in boxers, he comes back into the kitchen, straight to the water-spotted sink where a glass waits for him. He rinses it, figures a couple of paracetamol and ibuprofen will help before he goes to bed.

Looking up, he stares at his reflection in the window. The flat is a couple of floors up, there is no view, only another brick wall which has lost its red. Nick notices the podge he's put on. It's not a lot, his fighter's physique is still intact, but all the same he isn't happy about it. He has become complacent recently, not helped by the lack of work, meaning he can only afford junk food. Chinese takeaway boxes are stacked by the side of the bin.

Only now does he notice the second reflection coming into focus behind him. It speaks before he does.

"Good fight tonight, Nick?"

Nick doesn't turn. He answers the reflection. "I won, if that's what you mean?"

"For pennies, I assume."

"It's a living."

The reflection scoffs, smirks at the same time. "No it isn't."

Nick turns, leans against the counter, sets the glass aside. Seeing the man sat at his table, he no longer feels bad about his weight.

"What do you want, Harvey?" Nick asks.

"Straight to the point?"

"I'm tired."

"You look it," Harvey George observes, narrowing his beady eyes.

Nick hadn't heard any noise, no crack of a forced lock. It must've been whilst he was in the shower. The racket that thing makes, a rhino could sneak into his flat. Harvey George isn't far off.

"What do you want?" Nick repeats himself.

Harvey stands, the chair creaks under his mass. He holds a rosy-cheeked smile, makes a point of dusting off his grey-silver three-piece, giving extra attention to his arse. These suits don't come cheap, the gesture says.

Harvey walks closer. Nick crosses his arms, knuckles red from the fight, but doesn't steel himself. It isn't Harvey's nature to lash out. That's the *other* George.

"You haven't been avoiding us, have you Nick?" asks Harvey.

"No," Nick answers. "You just keep missing me."

"Aren't you going to pop the kettle on?"

Nick glances at his kettle. It's a plastic throwback that belongs on a building site. "Out of teabags."

"Coffee?"

"Need to do a shop."

"Lighten up, Nick." Harvey drums his hands on the table.

Harvey is a talker. If something can be dragged out, he'll trawl. Loves the sound of his own voice.

The Georges get about, see London as one big pie that they've firmly got their teeth into. By the looks of things, Harvey has taken many bites from many pies, though he is still lean under all that fat. A formidable figure.

Harvey looks over the kitchen. "Aren't you tired of living here?"

"It's a home," Nick says.

Harvey George sneers, "It's a shithole."

"What do you want, Harv?"

The last man who called Harvey that ended up with a smile he'd never get rid of. But Nick and the Georges have history. There's leniency. The only reason Nick chooses to use it is to cut Harvey short. If given the chance, Harvey will talk all night.

Harvey peers into Nick's plastic bag. His voice is playful when he says, "You still owe us, Nick."

Nick keeps his arms folded. He knows what Harvey is going to say. This isn't the first time this has happened. Two weeks ago, Harvey ambushed him in one of the local boozers, and a week before that it had been the pair of them as soon as Nick had stepped out of the ring after another poorly paid fight. This, however, is the first time one of them has entered into his home.

Harvey adopts a tone like he's talking to a teenager, "You remember what my brother and I did for you, yes?"

Nick replies, "Yeah."

"We want to call in that favour," Harvey shrugs. "As you well know."

"That was a long time ago, Harvey."

"Not that long."

Nick shakes his head. "I can't."

Harvey swipes a finger along the kitchen counter, rubs his thumb and index finger together, inspecting the dust. He fixes his eyes on Nick. "It's polite to return favours."

Nick goes to the cupboard above the builders kettle. He opens it, starts shifting things around to find the paracetamol and ibuprofen. "I don't want to get mixed up in that shit."

"Who said anything about shit?"

Nick closes the cupboard, no tablets. "*Your* shit, Harvey."

Harvey tuts, says, "Nick, we've known each other a long time. Why're you making this so difficult?"

"I'm not trying to make it difficult, mate. No's an easy word."

"Just," Harvey pauses for effect, he's always been one for drama, "hear me out."

Nick stares hard at him. It's like having a face-off with a Pitbull you know has a nasty bite. Nick doesn't want to be in the Georges' pockets more than he already is. It's a distant memory that he used to call this Pitbull a friend.

Harvey leans on the table, it creaks more than the chair did. He is smiling. "Don't you even want to know the kind of work I'm offering?"

Some curiosity floats around in Nick's head. Whatever the job is, it will pay well. He almost wants to ask. Some of the jobs he takes are already on the iffy side of the law, and he wants no part in what the Georges call business. Not again.

Nick rubs his forehead. "Harvey. Please."

Back in the so-called day, Harvey would always listen to and consider Nick's opinions. A fraction of that remains. He drums on the table again. "You know what? You're tired, it's late. Or early," he chuckles. "This was only a passing visit."

Harvey pulls his suit jacket flat, adjusts the Windsor knot of his tie which pushes into his neck fat.

"I don't want us to be enemies," says Nick.

"Nick," Harvey spreads his tree trunk arms as if inviting an embrace, "you could never be my enemy."

Nick wishes he could believe that.

"You're probably overqualified anyway," Harvey says. He goes into his pocket and pulls out two small bent up boxes, tosses them on the table. "There you go."

The paracetamol and ibuprofen from the cupboard.

"Those'll help," Harvey smiles, turning to leave.

"I'm sorry, Harvey," Nick says. He isn't.

Harvey turns to face Nick. "You're a tough purchase. Word of advice, Nick? One day you might need a favour yourself." He takes a couple of seconds to let the drama do its thing, then adds, "Don't go burning your last bridge."

Crossing his arms, Nick replies, "I'll be fine."

"I'm sure you will." Harvey smirks, gives the kitchen another distasteful once-over, then leaves. The overhead light shines momentarily on the bald spot at the back of his head. His footsteps make every floorboard protest under his weight.

Nick calls after him, "Will I need a new lock?"

He assumes Harvey broke in. There's a pause before Harvey calls back.

"No Nick, that won't be necessary."

Nick hears the front door of his flat open and close, then the sound of a key turning the lock. That was a threat. This whole visit has been a threat.

He thinks he'll get a new lock anyway.

CHAPTER 2

The next morning, elsewhere...

Duck Lane is a quiet stretch of unmarked country road. Banks of grass, wild flowers and nettles hide the edges of the tarmac. It's a couple of minutes past seven, and all the early birds are out catching worms.

A bicycle splashes through a puddle, splitting a buzz of midges. The water reaches up to tickle the rider's bare ankles. It feels nice and fresh. Morning fresh. The air rushing over her face is cold, a better charger than any energy drink.

Katy stands up on her peddles, taking deep gulps of country air, her cheeks red with the refreshing sting. She leans over the handlebars. Her braided ponytail flaps behind her helmet, whipping against her backpack. To her left are fields, to her right is woodland. She can smell both, colliding together like different oceans. This is her favourite bike route, and even better is the hour she gets to spend at the creek before school.

Hanging low, the sun pushes her shadow out in front. Looking for cars first, she manoeuvres through a natural opening that takes her into the trees, ducking her head under a loose tangle of brambles. The creek is less than a quarter-mile into the woods. It sits at the bottom of a shallow slope, a picturesque postcard of earthen colours and sounds. Katy lets gravity take her to the water's edge, tyres whispering through the leaf litter.

The brakes squeal. Katy dismounts before she's come to a complete stop and rests her bike on the ground, then removes her helmet. Excited and in a hurry, she opens up her backpack and retrieves the notepad with the pencil sheathed in the ring binding. Today is an important day at the creek.

Water burbles over the rocky riverbed. Katy swings herself around a tree, steps onto the first of a series of protruding stones, then the second, third, making a game of it. A few of the stones are slippery, and she laughs when she nearly loses her balance, leaning forward with her butt stuck out to keep it. Katy gets herself to the centre of the flowing water where there is a large flat rock shaped like a lily pad. These stepping stones have always been here. She thinks of them as having been placed just for her. She squats down, gazes into the water, the tip of her pencil already touching paper.

Nestled between two rocks, protected from the flow of the water, is a clump of frogspawn. Katy has been monitoring it meticulously, taking notes and sketching the progress of the froglets. This morning's page is fresh. Today is the day she believes the tadpoles will emerge. The thought makes her smile.

She checks her digital wristwatch (waterproof, of course). There's still a good amount of time left before she has to leave for school, which is good. In their little bubbles, the tadpoles are taking it easy.

It's quiet today, more so than most days. The treetops rustle together, yet the birds do not join in with the sway. Usually, the quiet doesn't bother Katy. It does now, though she is unsure why. Just a peculiar feeling in the pit of stomach, like after you eat a sandwich too quickly. She looks over her shoulder, nothing but woodland. Telling herself she's being silly, she returns her focus to the frogspawn.

Her striking blue eyes widen. The tadpoles are squirming frantically inside their jelly. It'll be any second now, and she nearly missed it! She jots down the time, writes some notes on their movements and makes a quick doodle that she will improve on at lunch.

Wind skates down the slope, rolling dead leaves into the water that immediately sail away. Using her notepad, Katy shields the frogspawn. Wearing only shorts and a tee-shirt, she hopes the wind isn't a precursor to a cold day. It isn't supposed to be.

Her braided ponytail hangs over her shoulder, almost touching the water. She whips it away, leans in closer as the first of the tadpoles breaks free from its gelatinous womb.

After the last one hatches, Katy watches them dance inside their wedge of calm water. She's already noted, with an underline, that on some of the tadpoles she can see tiny little eyes.

She wants to gently lower her hand into the slippery tumult, to feel the new-borns writhing around her fingers. The best way to learn is through touch, after all. She knows she shouldn't. Things are already confusing enough for the tadpoles without a giant prodding at them, and yet she lowers her hand anyway, smiling, biting her lip in anticipation of the sensation.

She isn't expecting a voice.

"Beautiful, aren't they?"

Like a hook, the voice rips Katy from her world. She gasps, yanks her hand away, almost falls into the water. She drops her notes on the lily pad stone, the corners of the paper becoming damp. Katy picks it up. Pinched between her thumb and index, she shakes the notepad, praying that her notes and drawings aren't ruined.

She turns to confront the voice, but there's no one there.

"Hello?" she says, raising the O to a higher pitch.

Only the trickling water answers her. With a surefootedness she wasn't aware she possessed, Katy takes herself over the wild bridge of river rocks onto dry land. The leaves crunch reassuringly beneath her feet. She hugs the notepad to her chest. Suddenly she feels cold, as if she *had* fallen into the water. She scans the top of the slope. No one. Peers into the deeper woodland where thick, shiny green poison ivy interwoven with brambles guards further mysteries.

Not a soul.

But the voice had been clear.

"H…Hello?" she tries again, a tremor in her voice.

A frantic flapping of wings pulls her attention upwards. She sees no birds, but the trees…have they grown taller? Are they stretching even now? They appear to spin before her eyes. Shafts of sunlight create a dizzying kaleidoscope.

Katy no longer cares about the important morning at the creek, or the disembodied voice. She's been taught the dangers of strangers, is aware of what happens to vulnerable girls caught unaware in isolated places.

She runs to her bike, picks it up. The bell chimes. That's as far as she gets before she gasps at the dark figure watching her from the top of the slope. It stands statuesque, appears to be made of shadow. Where its feet should be, soil rushes up to join its legs. Although its face is a smear of darkness, Katy feels it staring at her.

"Beautiful, aren't they?" The male voice says from somewhere else.

"Leave me alone," Katy answers.

The cloaked figure floats down the slope at speed, dead leaves billow up around it. Before Katy can scream, it's upon her.

Later, when people come searching for her, all they find is her bike, her backpack, and her notepad in the water, trapped in the same wedge where the tadpoles live. They are flailing over sketches of themselves.

CHAPTER 3

It's dark and cold out in the city.

Bitterly.

An aged homeless man in a long, natty overcoat trudges by on the pavement, moving with the fragility of discarded litter. A slight limp plagues his left foot. His arms are crossed against his body. Perhaps the grey-tinged beard strapped around his face aids in keeping him warm. He looks at the nightclub as he passes. The neon lights tease the glitz and glamour inside, a life he'll never know, or maybe once did. It's been so long. He scans the myriad faces in the queued up crowd, not one of them noticing him. They look like different versions of the same people.

Minding the nightclub door, Nick sees the homeless man, seemingly wary of the invisible borderline that separates him and the rest of society. The homeless man makes brief eye contact with Nick before disappearing up the street. And just like that, he is forgotten.

The entrance to the nightclub is a thick wooden slab of a door. Supposed to be soundproof, if they ever closed the fucking thing. Black paint peels away from it like eczema. Inside, lights flash between red, blue and pink. The beat of the music is muted, an atonal drone that seems to bleed into itself along with the chatter of the queue outside. A red velvet rope herds them close to the poster-ridden brick wall. Separate from the queuers, a red carpet, flanked on both sides by pyramidal fire lanterns, leads from the entrance to the roadside where expensive cars have been steadily dropping off their fares in conveyer belt fashion.

To look at it, the nightclub known as Tutt's is a worn down geriatric. Tufts of scrub sprout from its foundations, the façade is in need of a pressure wash, and a few licks of paint would go a long ways, but that's just for show, a pompous display of irony, for the inside is an opulent sideshow of Mummy and Daddy's money.

Nick mans the rope, wearing a black suit and tie – the only suit he owns – as per the club's stern request. It's bulky and uncomfortable, but tried and tested.

There's been zero trouble tonight. So far, anyway. It's rare that something doesn't kick off in these fancy clubs. Doesn't matter how swanky the gaff or its punters. Nick is taking advantage of the banter of some of the half-way pissed patrons waiting in line, embarrassments to themselves. By doing this, he makes an internal list of potential troublemakers. There are three at the moment, most notably some wanker with a ponytail.

It's the second night since the fight with the Manc. Nick did wind up going to the doctor's in the end, only to be turfed out with some painkillers and a come-back-if-and-when. The job last night – minding the door at some dive hosting a Ladies Night (one pound shots sealing the deal) – had been a struggle, but he feels much better tonight.

A smoky, Northern question comes his way, "That won't affect you if trouble starts tonight, will it?"

Nick answers, "No, Jan."

Jan, a tank of a woman, stands on the left side of the door, treating everyone with suspicion, as per. A prison tattoo, half covered by the collar of her hi-vis, stands out on the side of her neck, which is so thick it's one with her shoulders.

"I should hope not," she stresses without looking at him. "I don't need fuckin' patient."

Nick glances at her as she waves in a couple of slender blonde things who are glued to their smartphones. Jan runs a hand through her silver crew cut that makes her head look like the top of an anvil.

"How come you got out of wearing a suit?" Nick asks. He's worked with Jan before and knows to take her comments on the chin and move on.

"Told 'em it wasn't happening. I don't do suits."

It would be a pain for Jan to find a suit that would fit her powerlifter's frame. She's the lucky one. Nick would rather be wearing more suitable attire for the job. Jan surely has a stab vest on under her hi-vis.

He puts his hands in his pockets. "Any names in tonight?"

Jan checks her clipboard. "If there are I haven't heard've 'em." She slaps the clipboard against the chest of a man about to walk inside with his lady friend. "Need to check the girl's bag, sir."

The rich dickhead – his bare ankles on display at the bottoms of his Levis – who fancies himself eccentric but is actually just a prick gets smarmy immediately, asking Jan if she knows who he is before the woman in the little black dress he's with starts getting lippy, reverting in no time at all to calling Jan an ugly bitch. Jan is a pro, and despite the way she looks, she is calm.

She tells the couple that it's just the way it is, no entry without a check. Nick lets her handle it. Usually, punters on the defensive means they have something to hide. Jan'll sort it.

In the background, the muffled beat pulses. Nick swears the song hasn't changed for a couple of hours. His radio crackles. The voice at the other end lets Nick know he can let four more in. He unclips the rope, and the four that move inside throw the irate couple some judgemental looks, giggling just loud enough to know they'll be heard. Self-important, entitled people like this can't go without letting the world know how they feel, as if their opinion actually matters. Besides, the only difference between them and the angry couple is that the angry couple didn't hide whatever they're sneaking in.

Nick purchased a new lock for his door, but hasn't yet replaced it. DIY is a hassle at any time of day, month or year. But Nick knows the George brothers. After they've made their move they like to let things lie for a while, long enough to lull their targets into a false sense of security before pouncing. He won't wait until that deadline, but Nick figures he has time to prepare for the Georges' next pitch.

Unless the *other* George gets impatient. That bloke will be their downfall.

Things with Jan and the shitty couple are going as Nick expected. They are getting more confrontational, toying with physical. Jan is keeping her composure, but Nick hopes the couple push her to the limit. When Jan goes off it's quite a spectacle to behold.

Voices and music fade away when Nick sees the homeless man again, walking the opposite way this time. A Porsche blares its horn at him as it pulls up to let out its passengers. The homeless man is skittish, recoils, watches the two men who get out strut up the red carpet.

Nick thinks you could be forgiven for thinking the paparazzi were out photographing the rich and hopeless.

The men go into the club unchallenged, and without batting an eyelid at Jan's situation. Nick searches for the homeless man, but he's vanished.

"Look," Jan says, "you can either let me search the bag or leave, makes no difference to me."

The man hits her with a classic. "This is an infringement of our rights!"

"I don't rightly give a shit, mate. Rules is rules, take your pick."

"I've had enough of this, we're going in," the man declares.

He grabs his lady friend's arm and barges past Jan. As he does, Jan snatches the bag away with no care for its price tag.

"Hey!" The woman whines.

"I'll just conduct a quick search and then you can be on your way," Jan says.

The woman looks nervous, the man, too.

Nick gives Jan a quick look, and the look he receives back tells him she's handling it. It's a subtle technique, a nod or a flick of the eyes, but if you've been in the game long enough, you can read your colleagues expressions like a book.

Nick lets another couple into the club. He's aware and ready, standing by for the moment if it happens.

Jan dips her hand in the bag.

A Rolls-Royce pulls up to the curb. For the second that Nick can see its grill, the car is a snarling beast. It purrs as it idles. Racing green, almost black in this light. The streetlamps caress its curves, giving it a pearlescent sheen. It's a big car. A little too big, Nick thinks. He wouldn't be surprised to see the Georges step out, only Tutt's isn't one of their haunts. He can't see who's inside, the windows are tinted black.

Jan pulls a baggy out of the handbag. Inside are white pills.

"Fuck," the man sighs.

"A lot, isn't there?" says Jan, looking at the man and woman.

A few people in the queue notice, begin to whisper amongst themselves, enjoying the drama. One unseen punter sarcastically utters, "Uh-oh."

"More than a personal amount here, wouldn't you say?" Jan asks.

"Fine. Fuck," the woman pouts. "Just let us go, then."

"Oh is *that* how it goes, sweetheart?" Jan lowers the baggy. "Nick?"

Nick doesn't hear. He's watching the Rolls-Royce as its passenger steps out.

It's an old man, or…oldish. In his late-fifties. It's hard to tell as he steps onto the pavement, using the doorframe to keep himself steady. He's immaculately dressed in a grey suit, with shoes shinier than the car. The grey in the man's hair disappears, and Nick thinks that maybe the man isn't that old at all. Trick of the light. The man raises his head and the grey returns, silver just above his ears, and the wrinkles now tell Nick the old man is *older* than he first thought. The mercurial gentleman smiles as he surveys the club.

If he's a face, Nick has no idea who. The old geezer is a bit too old for Tutt's, the thought reinforced when a black cane is passed out to him.

Another man – a giant – gets out the other side, dressed just as well, but not so scene-stealing.

Jan shoves his shoulder. "Nick!"

He answers, irritated. "What?"

"I said what're we going to do about this shit?"

She holds up the baggy for him to see.

"Oh," Nick says.

"Oh," she repeats.

A number of the queuers have fished out their phones, already filming in case something juicy happens for them to plaster over social media. *This fucking generation*, Nick thinks.

"Call the cops," he says with a shrug. He'd rather not have the police floating around, and can confidently assume that everyone else here would agree.

"Don't think so," Jan replies. "They'll just complicate the evening. Management won't like that."

"So let us go?" the man interrupts, reaching for the pills.

Jan pushes him back with a firm hand, the same one holding the handbag. The girl seems more concerned with the handbag's safety than her boyfriend's.

"Not fuckin' likely," Jan snarls. "You had your chance."

A woman screams, followed by more. It comes from near the pavement. The smartphones move to see what's happening. Nick spies the homeless man. He's standing in front of the Rolls-Royce geezer, brandishing a kitchen knife with a price tag still dangling from its handle. The blade gleams under the lights. The geezer appears more angry than afraid, standing tall with both hands perched on his cane.

Nick races from his position at the rope, pushing a couple aside. Just as the homeless man is about to plunge the knife into the geezer's chest, Nick tackles him to the ground – ribs screaming for more drugs – just before the giant can. The knife clatters under the car, the only weapon left now is the smell of the homeless man's coat assaulting Nick's nostrils.

The homeless man screams. "He has to die! He has to die!"

He delivers weak blows against Nick's back before he gives up. He begins to cry, curling up into a foetal position. Nick keeps him pinned, conducts a quick search for any more concealed weapons. There are none.

Of all the too-rich-for-shit punters, only one calls the police. Inside the club, the music drones on. Those inside dance as if nothing has happened.

It takes six minutes for the police to arrive.

Jan was right. All they do is complicate what should have been a standard night working the door. An ambulance arrives, too.

The police take statements (Jan's is particularly cold and dismissive) from those involved before leading the homeless man away in cuffs. He's sobbing, babbling, his teeth yellowed to the point of orange. He has also urinated himself.

As he is tucked into the back of a police vehicle, so too are all the smartphones returned to pockets and handbags.

There's no sign of the couple who tried smuggling in the drugs. They must've scarpered at the sound of sirens.

Nick sits on the roadside, watches the homeless man get carted away. The sirens toot once as the car pulls away. He hopes there's some extra money for the night's trouble. Unlikely. There's still a few hours of the night left, and as far as Tutt's is concerned, the ordeal is over and forgotten. "It's part of your job," the manager will say, and that annoys Nick because, mostly, it's true, especially when your employment is cash in hand.

A pair of shiny shoes clack over. They stop next to Nick. He looks up and sees the geezer smiling down at him, leaning on his cane.

"Thank you for intervening, young man," he says.

The pain in his ribs has settled down, so Nick stands. The geezer is shorter. Behind is the giant bloke, a wide-shouldered brute who looks annoyed.

"Don't worry about it," Nick replies, smiling politely. He holds out his hand.

Without extending his own hand, the geezer adds, "You are not hurt, I hope?"

A brief hesitation, then Nick retracts his hand, rubs the back of his neck instead. "Uh…no. No, I'm alright."

The geezer's smile broadens. "Do not take offense. I am a germaphobe."

Nick shrugs. "None taken."

When the geezer – grey hair combed flat against his skull – doesn't move things along, Nick says, "I should be asking you the same."

"Ah," the geezer waves a dismissive hand. "No harm done."

"Still, coulda been bad."

"It never would have been." The geezer takes a moment before saying, "Because of you."

Nick looks to the line of young faces, the near-stabbing already used up as gossip. He's a stranger again, separate from the one-minute-hero version of himself burned into the electronic cloud. He says, "Listen, uh, don't wanna be cheeky, but, what're you doing here anyway? Bloke your age, this isn't exactly…fitting."

"You presume to know my age and locales of interest because of it?" The geezer quacks a laugh, places delicate fingers over the blue cravat puffing from his collar. "Age is but a number, young man. Youth comes from the heart, not digits."

Nick laughs, not sure how to answer. Is there one?

"What I am saying, is grab youth however you can." The geezer holds his chin high, ironing out the loose skin hanging around his neck. "Even if you must steal it, young man."

Cars are starting to form a queue behind the stationary Rolls-Royce, horns blaring. Jan is over by the door, glaring at Nick. She'll be doubly pissed off because of the drug couple getting away. It won't matter to her that he just saved an old boy's life. Her attitude is the same as the club's. The world has no time for heroes.

Nick sighs. "I should be getting back to it. Maybe you should take the rest of the night off."

He goes to pat the geezer on the shoulder. The old man grabs his wrist. It isn't painful, but Nick is surprised by the strength in it. The geezer, smiling, says, "I think I shall do just that, but just one more thing, young man, before you continue with your busy evening."

Nick waits for him to continue.

"My card. It would please me if you were to take it."

In his other bony, liver-spotted hand, the geezer is holding a business card.

"What for?" Nick asks.

"Must there always be a reason?"

"Look mate, I'm glad I could help and all but- "

"I might have an odd job or two for you. Nothing too strenuous, though someone such as yourself need not worry about that. Your physical prowess is in evidence this evening."

"So's his." Nick tips his head to the giant man.

After chuckling, the geezer gives the card a seductive wiggle. Nick doesn't want it. Any extra work is good work, but this is most likely low pay errand running, and he doesn't want to be caring for the guy, either.

He takes it anyway.

The geezer is pleased, releases Nick's wrist. "Thank you," he says, then taps his black cane on the pavement. "Yes. Splendid. Apollo?"

The big bloke behind him grunts.

"Let us take our leave, we can reschedule for another night. I believe we gained more than we came for, anyway." He winks at Nick.

The giant (did the geezer really call him *Apollo*?) helps the geezer back into the Rolls. Other drivers express themselves with harsh language poorly bleeped out by horns. Then the Rolls is rolling, reflections slipping from its curves as it leaves the red carpet.

Nick pockets the card without looking at it, returns to the door. An eager crowd waits behind the velvet rope. For a while he continues in auto-pilot.

He'd been correct in his assumption. Jan is doubly pissed, and remains so for the rest of the mostly trouble-free evening at Tutt's. Another assumption comes true. The guy with the ponytail *is* trouble. Nothing a chokehold can't remedy.

The walk home is quiet. Once again Nick is able to be one with the emptiness. He's the only person out at this time of morning. The moon is an oversized bulb in the sky, dimmed by the city's own artificial glow. In the dark streets that lead to Nick's flat, light twinkles on the road and buildings, making it appear as if each surface is covered in slime.

Rounding the corner of his building, he contemplates skipping his ritual shower and going straight to bed. The event with the homeless man is like a distant memory now, but an exhausting one.

He fishes for his keys in his coat pocket, stops when he sees two shining yellow orbs floating in the shadows outside his door.

He tugs his tie off his neck. If these orbs belong to who he suspects they might, he hasn't the energy to deal with it.

They shimmer, lower themselves.

Nick steps forward, prompting the automatic light to struggle on. The orbs lose their shine. A cat is revealed, hunkered down in the spot where a welcome mat should but would never be. It watches Nick. Black all over, any more detail than that – other than the yellow eyes – he cannot see. It must have been cozied up here for a while for the light to go off and stay that way.

He tries making a noise to scare it off. Unperturbed, it gazes at him. Nick makes a noise again, a hiss, stomps closer. It yawns, turns around and trots away with its long tail held down, past a couple of dustbins.

"Fucking things," Nick mutters to himself.

Before entering his building, Nick takes one more peep at the bins. He's being observed by the shining orbs again. Then they vanish.

He passes through the kitchen into his bedroom. It looks like the nest of a down-on-his-luck noir detective, the only thing missing is a fold-down bed. Nick flicks on the lamp, sits on the mattress. The springs tick under his weight.

He lets out a tired sigh, rubs the back of his neck and loosens the suit collar. A red groove is left in his skin where it has been digging in all night.

Nick undresses. The card given to him by the geezer falls from his pocket, taps face down on the floor. He picks it up, turns it over. An address he doesn't know, no phone number, no email. Not even a name. A shitty business card, he thinks.

Nick tosses the card into his bedside table draw, then he forgets it exists. For a while, he watches the darkness to make sure nothing is in it.

He sleeps a dreamless sleep, hoping that tomorrow will take its time to arrive, forgetting that it is already here.

CHAPTER 4

London is capped by a silver-grey sky, the same colour as the ocean before a storm. Nick is at the back of the number five bus to fucking nowhere. It's just gone nine o'clock. Contributors to society are already at work and the bus now holds only the slack-necked, the down-trodden, the heart-broken and the given-ups. Nick tells himself he isn't one of them, though it's getting harder to believe.

Each person looks miserable, gazing gormlessly out of the dirty windows upon a world of broken spirits and missed opportunities. Zombies. Nick tries to avoid contamination.

A woman, a few rows in front of him, looks at Nick over her shoulder, her red lips two shocking lines against her pale face. She doesn't look miserable, she looks…inquisitive.

Nick keeps making quick eye contact between bouts of staring out the window, watching the pedestrians and knock-off takeaways blur past. He only wants to see if she's still gawping. She is. Every time. She's an older woman, handpicked from the fifties, her hair rolled up, attractive in a classic way, but her grey sky eyes are unnerving. The lines running down from the corners of her mouth are like cracked porcelain.

The bus stops with a hiss and the doors swing open. The smells of diesel and fast food board the vehicle. This is, thank God, Nick's stop. He stands and sidesteps down the aisle. As he passes the woman he is tempted to say good morning. Even better, he'd like to call her out for staring, but he doesn't, having neither the energy or the care. A smile suffices, but isn't returned. All she does is look him up and down, her lips twitch to signify the passing of judgement. Condescending cow.

The bus pulls away before the doors finish closing, coughing acrid heat over Nick that isn't unpleasant this chilly morning. Nick is glad he's off the bus. Buses at this time are always a circus.

Shoulders hunched, collar up, he makes his way past graffiti-tagged shops to Cobble Road, the ironically cobble-less street where Estelle's is stuffed. Here, there are no pedestrians. The road looks worse during the day, because now you can *see* it. Filth and grime are duned up against the edges of the buildings. The less seen, the better.

Nick crosses the road, hopping over broken glass, to Estelle's main entrance. There's a sign in the window that says CLOSED. Nick knocks anyway.

Nothing.

He knocks harder, calling Frank. Rubbing his hands together, he blows into them.

Nothing.

He cups his hands round his mouth and calls up at a window with its curtains drawn.

Still nothing.

Nick peers into the window, wipes it with his forearm. The club is empty, chairs and stools upside down on tables. It's the only cleaning that's been done since his last fight, it seems. He pulls away from the window.

It's been four days since the fight with the Manc. Nick has tried to call Frank, but so far hasn't heard anything. It's not unlike Frank to disappear for a couple of days. To be unheard of for four is pushing it. Nick needs to hold Frank to that promise of a bigger prize fight. The job at Tutt's paid well enough to keep Nick in food for the week. Gas, electric, and of course, rent, still need to be covered.

He stands for a few seconds. Breath puffs out in front of him. There's nothing else Nick can do here. He'll have to keep calling Frank until he gets an answer.

Nick pays visits to various establishments he's worked at before, asking if any work is up for grabs. None of the clubs, not even the seedier ones, have anything for him. He even calls a couple of unlicensed fight promoters from what has to be Britain's last – and worst – phone box, which has been moonlighting as a toilet judging by the smell. The promoters have nothing for him either.

The day is getting on. Nick spares ninety-nine pence for a coffee. The café he goes to, Derek's, is a noisy little den with unmanned roadworks outside. Clattering is a constant form of muzak from the kitchen, challenged only by the sound of frying breakfast meats. He takes a sip from his drink, sets it down on the table, creating a new ring on the vinyl cover that resembles a crop of circles made by drunk aliens.

Nick's situation is looking worse than it's ever been. Gazing out the window through peeling letter decals, he thinks about before it all went tits up, back when he could afford coffee worth more than a quid and he didn't have to scrounge for work. Before the Georges had done the favour for him.

It'd been a stupid decision made under pressure, one that very nearly cost Nick literally everything. He often feels like it did, anyway. He can't blame the Georges. He'd been the one to say yes, and what happened, happened. The weight of it is still around his neck. He'd like to be rid of this guilt bridle, but doesn't know how to take it off. The worst thing is he can't get rid of the Georges. They've infected his life like a slow burning virus. If he can't atone for the past, he can at least hold it at arm's length.

He sips some coffee, feels coarse granules slide over his lips. He's still watching the world outside when he sees in his peripheral vision a dark figure sitting opposite him. When he turns to face it, it's gone. He's gotten used to the Figure, a remnant of the Georges' favour. He thought it had come to him the other night, expecting the yellow eyes to be connected to its dark skull. Finding a cat instead…was that better?

Before he finishes his coffee, Nick decides it's time to go home. It's near five o'clock by the time he gets back.

The cat is there when he returns, as is the stench of sewage that always fumigates this nook of the city when the daylight wanes. The cat was there the day before, too, has made its home by the bins.

It approaches Nick and sits down a few metres behind him as he unlocks his door, wrapping its tail neatly around itself. It observes him, the tip of its tailing tapping the ground like an impatient finger. Nick stomps his foot to scare it off. The attempt fails, and to show just how silly he'd been, the cat tilts its head questioningly.

"Still hanging around, huh?" Nick says.

The black cat, Nick has to admit, is handsome. Not like the other strays that stalk the alleyways. Its fur is short, but lustrous, as if it receives professional grooming.

Nick kicks a puddle. None of the drops touch the cat and it continues to watch him with its brilliant yellow eyes.

"Go play with the traffic," Nick tells it.

It stays put, twitches its tall, pointy ears, blinks slowly, licks around its mouth. It must be recently stray for it to look this healthy, hasn't lived rough long enough for its fur to go scraggly. And it *must* be stray, no one living here would risk a cat like this one getting pinched. Whatever it was, the animal had made a bad decision and is now paying for it.

Like Nick.

It becomes bored, turns around, struts away with its bushy tail floating high.

On the other side of the door is a letter hanging from the post slot. It's shaken loose when the door closes. Nick picks it up. It doesn't carry his name, referring to him instead as the tenant. It looks official, marked by various stamps. Inside is a fuck-you and Nick knows it.

Upstairs, he flicks the kettle on. It screeches as it begins to boil yesterday's water. Nick goes to the table to open the letter. It starts with complicated words and doesn't let up. He discards it before the kettle has time to finish.

Who'd have thought there'd be so many ways to spell eviction?

Suddenly, he doesn't fancy a cuppa. Suddenly, Harvey George's offer of a job doesn't seem so uninviting anymore.

But he can't get in with their shit. Not again.

Sitting on the bed, he drops his head into his hands, massaging the headache brewing inside his skull. In his palms he feels the vein running down his forehead throbbing.

He lifts his head and says, "Fuck."

The flat isn't much, not the kind of place he'd invite friends to – if he had or desired any – for beers and a takeaway. The floors are uncarpeted and uneven, every other floorboard moans when stood on. The wallpaper is dull, and in a few corners of the flat there are brown shockwaves where damp has slowly exploded, which has tainted the flat with the accompanying smell. The electrics are dodgy (the kettle knows this), the heating is sporadic, though only to one or the other extreme. The pipes in the flat above rattle as Nick's upstairs neighbour finishes on the toilet. Nick has unwillingly learnt Mr and Mrs Spencer's toilet timetable.

It's a shithole, Harv hadn't been wrong on that one, but it's Nick's shithole. To lose it would be to leave him with literally nothing.

"Fuckfuckfuck." He sighs it as one word.

He looks at the bedside table. The drawer is shut, but the card the geezer handed him sits on top, white enough to shimmer. As if by magic.

Picking up the card, he slides open the drawer, meaning to put it away and give Frank another call in the morning. As the thought of Harvey's offer tempts him over his mental horizon, Nick finds he cannot drop the card, either because he doesn't want to or his fingers won't let him. Perhaps there *is* another option.

Nick wonders how much collecting an old man's shopping pays.

CHAPTER 5

The slat at the bottom of a metal door slides open. A tray is shoved inside, then the slat closes, clanging loudly. On the tray are overcooked vegetables, a sippy cup of water and questionable meat. Katy, holding her legs to her chest, doesn't leave the single cot that has been her bed for days, now. She stares at the tray from over her knees.

The sterile grey-green room is no bigger than a single cell. There is only the wiry cot that has become her sanctuary, the sink opposite in the corner, and the metal toilet that sits disgustingly close to her pillow. At night, if she does sleep, she sleeps with her head closest to the door. When sleep doesn't come, she stares at the ceiling until it finds her. There's certainly no wild bridge to guide her away.

The emptiness is sickening. There are no windows. A solitary bulb. She doesn't know exactly how long she's been here, only that it hasn't been long enough for her to starve. She hasn't touched any of the food given to her, but looking now at the fresh tray, veg spilling over, her stomach groans for her to give in. She salivates. The colourless meat is starting to look like a ribeye.

"You'd best eat, dear," a voice from the other side of the door says.

Katy jerks her head up to look at the door that stares coldly back at her. This is the first time she's heard a voice since the day at the creek. It's a woman.

"You'll get sick if you don't," the woman adds. She sounds nice, has a warm voice that makes Katy think of Grandma.

Katy glances at the food again, bites her dirty nails. She licks her lips, can't help being suspicious of the meal. It might be poisoned.

"It's safe," says the woman.

Katy looks to the door again. She hasn't talked since being taken.

"Y…You're the f-first person to…to talk to m-me."

Her cell echoes like an empty water tank.

"Oh, dear. That just won't do," the woman replies, her concern sounds sincere. "What's your name?"

Katy is reluctant, but is more scared of the quiet, wants to hear something other than the blood pulse in her head. She answers, "K…Katy."

"Katy what, my dear?"

"Robbins."

The woman laughs softly. "Katy Robbins. That's a pretty name."

Katy cannot help but be drawn into this woman's friendliness. This person might be the only friend she has here, a buoy in a dark sea. She rests her legs, letting them lay flat on the bed, her knees, still crusty with woodland mud, are immediately grateful.

The woman persists. "And what sorts of things do you like, Katy Robbins?"

"What do you m-mean?"

"Every young girl has their hobbies, dear. I'll bet you're no different."

"I like animals," Katy answers. It feels good to talk, the cobwebs are clearing from her throat. She's surprised to not see them floating out from her mouth.

"Me too," the woman replies. "You can trust animals with *anything*. You probably wanted to be a vet, or a zoologist?"

Wanted. There's something very final about that word.

"Dear?" from the woman.

Katy asks, "What's…*your* name?"

The woman doesn't reply. Katy asks again. The silence is stronger. She starts to hear her blood pulsing around her body. It sounds like Pacman.

Afraid of the Pacman thump in her ears, she speaks again. Her voice slaps back at her from the cell walls. "W-Where am I? What is this place?"

"Just eat up, dear," the woman encourages her with a lack of enthusiasm.

"I want my mum and dad." Just mentioning them causes Katy's eyes to well up. They've been in all her thoughts.

"I want, doesn't get."

Katy had heard that saying before from her mum, back when she'd been a little girl.

Katy sobs, "Why are you doing this to me?"

"My dear," the woman sounds shocked, "nothing is being done to you."

Katy wipes her eyes, desperately wishes this was a dream, that this cell was her bedroom disguised by sleep and behind the grey-green paint were her violet walls covered in posters. She closes her eyes, imagines her room, the smell of it, the feel of her quilt, the warmth of it, the voices of her parents downstairs.

They would be so worried about her.

On the other side of the door, reeling Katy from the safety of her imagination, the woman continues to speak.

"I would like to be your friend, Katy."

Katy hangs her head. "I want to go home."

"But you *are*, dear."

"No I'm not!"

It's a while before the woman speaks again.

"I am sorry, dear. I didn't mean to upset you."

"Just let me go," Katy says. "You said you wanted to be my friend, s-so…so let me go."

"I can't do that, dear."

"Then leave me alone. Just leave me alone," Katy cries.

"But- "

Katy lifts her head. "But what?"

"I have a present for you."

Again, Katy wipes her eyes, the soft skin around them is sore. She can't help herself. "What…is it?"

The slat at the bottom of the door scratches open, makes her jump. A notepad slides in. A pencil rolls in after it. The slat closes and Katy gazes at the notepad like a mouse contemplating cheese on a trap. Some mice get lucky.

"Thought you'd like a new one," the woman says.

Years of upbringing decide the next words that come out of Katy's mouth.

"Thank you."

"No need for that, dear. It is you who deserves thanks. You have no idea how important you are."

Katy doesn't know what she means. Doesn't ask. It scares her. She takes her braided ponytail – fraying now like an old rope – in her hands and begins to stroke it.

She uses the ponytail to mop up her tears before she gets off the bed to collect the notepad. She takes it, sheaths the pencil into the ring binding where it belongs. The cover is lime green with shooting stars. She might draw a picture of Mum and Dad, or a lion. She's good at lions.

"Try and eat, Katy Robbins," the woman suggests. "Don't make things worse for yourself. You must be starving."

Katy doesn't reply. She gets on her knees, gawks at the colourless meat for what feels like a long time. Eventually, she listens to her stomach, takes a shred of meat which, although grey on the outside, is pink in the middle. Juicy, actually.

Katy Robbins takes a bite, chews until her jaw hurts.

"Good girl," the woman whispers.

CHAPTER 6

Nick double-checks the card, inspects the building before him.

This is the place.

Apparently.

It's in the middle of a dead street with no cars or liveable accommodations. A renovation project waiting to happen. All the buildings are hemmed in tight, sealing in the moist air.

Definitely Victorian.

There is a faint oily odour, left over from the factories maybe, locked inside the bricks.

Bit dark, he tells himself.

He isn't sure what he's looking at. A house? Shop? Neither? A squat build compared to the rest, squeezed in at the last. Its large windows are soaped out, no open or closed sign, though there is an old shoebox of tatty paperbacks at the bottom of the front steps. Ten pence a pop. It doesn't look right, like a bad 2D prop.

Nick dry swallows some paracetamol for his ribs, ascends the steps under a discoloured green and white awning. The number on the door is 67, though reads as 97 because the 6 hangs loose. Nick knocks, rattling the glass. He looks inside, can only make out ghosts in the dust.

"Anybody home?" he asks himself, knocking again.

No one answers. Just like at Frank's yesterday.

He wonders if this is a joke. The geezer didn't come across that way, but you can never tell.

Stepping out from under the awning – noticing that it's fat with stagnant water – Nick looks up at the building, trying to see any sign of movement in the windows. There isn't. He almost expects to see gargoyles perched at the top.

Nick thinks he'll leave, isn't sure what he was thinking anyway. It's good to explore your options, but this one is too weird. He's surprised when he sees the wide-shouldered giant man filling out the now open doorway.

"Jesus," Nick scoffs. "You trying to give me a heart attack?"

The giant keeps a straight face behind tiny reading glasses, wearing a frown that must weigh a kilo. His white shirt is unbuttoned at the top and the sleeves are rolled up, revealing thick black hair in both areas.

"Erm...Apollo, right?" Nick asks.

The giant doesn't speak.

"I'm from the club, from the other night." Nick cocks a thumb over his shoulder. "Remember?"

The giant grumbles, walks back into the gloom, leaving the door open. It's *one* way to invite someone inside, Nicks thinks. He looks up and down the street. Still dead.

Inside it's as if the dust had existed only within the glass pane. The air has to be the cleanest in the city. There are rows of bookshelves, three aisles on both sides, crammed with antique hardbacks. Everything is immaculate. The dim, warm light in the room pulses. A small spiral staircase at the back-left leads to another level where, at a glance, it appears more books are kept. A tin sign fixed to the wall at the head of the staircase reads, The Orphanage.

Squeezing himself as best he can, the giant makes his way to the front desk, where there is another door beyond.

"Cosy," Nick says, trying to get something from the giant.

He follows, footsteps softened by the Afghan rug. Underneath it sounds hollow. He nearly stands on...bird shit? He peers up. Hanging above him is a chandelier with bulbs that could be candles, they even flicker as if...

They *are* candles.

Talk about being aberrant. That explains the pulsing light and the drops of wax he mistook for bird crap.

Past a ream of paintings stacked against the wall, Nick follows his guide into the back office, which is lit with electric light.

A grandfather clock ticks, its visible pendulum snatching the lamplight in the middle of every swing. There are hundreds of pictures hanging on the dark green and wood panel walls. All various shapes, sizes and styles. A desk at the back of the room exhibits a vaudeville of odd trinkets.

At the side of the room, the giant sits himself in a rickety wooden chair, crosses his legs and continues to read a book which might've come from the shoebox.

Content to forgo making idle chit-chat, Nick takes himself to one of the pictures, a black and white landscape that reminds him of old class photos. In it are about twenty men and women, all standing in a row, smartly dressed and smiling. A few unhappy children stand in front. Poor sods have been paraded for the camera in hideous tunics straight out of a period drama. They must be eight to twelve years of age. In the middle – he thinks – is the old geezer. His younger face is grainy, though the eyes are crystalline, defying the quality of the photograph.

"Nineteen-sixty-six."

Nick turns. The geezer is balancing on his cane just a few feet away in a white shirt and waistcoat complete with a pocket watch.

"Sorry, I didn't hear you," Nick says.

"And I am sorry I startled you," the geezer replies.

"You didn't."

Smiling warmly, the geezer hobbles closer, the cane knocking on the floorboards. Nick should have heard that.

"Sixty-six," the geezer continues, joining Nick. "Before I needed this old thing." He taps the cane on the floor again. "A successful year, if I do say so. Every year is. Unprecedented in most establishments."

Nick scans the room. "There's hundreds."

"Many years means many memories," the geezer speaks with affection. "I like to commemorate each one to ensure I never forget. They keep me encouraged."

With a grin, Nick jokes, "Mind going soft?"

The geezer holds his smile. Up close, his skin is like creased linen. He nudges Nick on the foot with the tip of his cane. "Not just yet." Then he adds, "I knew you would come. A little late, perhaps, but I knew all the same."

"I was beginning to think no one was in."

"I gave you my card, did I not? I do not surrender them to people lightly. What kind of a man would I be to send you to an empty residence?"

Sensing a sliver of hostility in the question, as if he might have caused offense, Nick avoids it with a new one. "So, what're they all for?"

"What are *what* all for?"

"The photos. Who're these people. What do you do?"

"Oh," the geezer lifts his chin, looks fondly at the class of '66. "Trading, mostly. Awfully dull, looking in from the outside."

The giant snorts.

"I thought this was a book shop or something."

"It is, and…other antiquities," the geezer rolls his hand.

Nick laughs. "Running things a little inconspicuously, aren't you?"

The geezer strokes the buttons of his waistcoat. "Young man, this is the way I intend it. Lots of valuable artifacts adorn my shelves, therefore I do not believe it is in my best interest to advertise them to the world. I deal strictly by appointment only."

"By handing out business cards to strangers?"

He winks. "Precisely. Then again, you are not a potential client. I do not think. Nor a man prone to heists. Now…come along."

They go to the desk. The grandfather clocks setting a marching pace. Nick sees a date on another picture goes back to the fifties.

"Would you care the hang your coat?" the geezer offers.

"I'm alright, thanks."

"Suit yourself." Before sitting the geezer points with his cane. "I believe you have already had the pleasure of meeting my assistant, Apollo?"

"Yeah," Nick replies, nodding at the giant.

"Excellent. He is a wonderful polisher, and has a great many more talents. You shall have to forgive his thriving hospitality skills."

"Forgiven." Nick has no interest in Apollo and his talents. Get along to move along, though. That's how you get hired.

Adjusting the sleeve garter choking his arm, the geezer announces, "My name is Ulysses Crane."

Crane sits in a high-backed red leather chair. Nick takes it as his signal to sit down, too.

"Nick Parker," he says.

"Nicholas," Crane replies. "What a strong name."

"Got nothing on Apollo."

"Quite," chuckles Crane. He lets out a ragged breath, then begins, "So. Why are you here?"

"Surely you know?" says Nick. "You said you knew I'd come."

"Knowing one thing does not mean knowing all things."

Nick clears his throat. "You mentioned that you might have work for me. I'm interested."

"Let us try again." Crane scratches his pockmarked nose, adjusts a crow statuette on his desk. "Tell me why you have come here."

"Well…I mean, work. Money," Nick answers, confused.

Crane laughs. "I did not ask why you are here. I asked *why*?"

Frowning, Nicks says, "I'm not sure I follow you."

"Yes you do. *Why* are you here now?"

"I told you. I need money."

Crane slaps the desk. "Again."

"I don't- "

"Again." Another slap.

"I have bills," Nick blurts, a twinge of agitation. "Rent, water, gas, electric, food. Things I need."

Crane says, "No, that is not it, but we are getting closer, I feel. If all you simply wanted was money for paying your various bills, a young man such as yourself could- "

"I ain't that young," Nick interrupts.

Crane draws a soft smile. "Look at me, *young man*. You are still healthy, strong, capable. I think I can attest to that myself. So if only for money, why not find yourself a normal job, with a wage and reliability?"

Nick's patience is running out. He didn't come here for this, yet there is something about Crane that implores him to answer. "It's not like I haven't tried. Jobs aren't exactly in abundance right now, especially not in my line of work, and whenever I land one I can't hold it down. I'm just not cut that way. I know it sounds like a cop-out, but…" Nick shrugs. "You can't rely on anyone else, can you? So here I am, taking odd jobs that I *am* cut out for and, like I said, trying to earn some money. Relying on myself."

He leaves out that it's been harder to find a job since the Georges' favour. If reputation is fur, scandal is shit.

"Surely you cannot rely on just yourself?" asks Crane.

"Yeah," Nick nods, "I can."

Crane steeples his fingers, listening carefully. Enjoying it, it seems.

"But what about fighting?" he says. "You still *rely* on someone to hand over your winnings."

Hang on. "How do you know I- "

"Answer the question, please."

"I rely on myself to win." Nick tightens his jaw.

"And working doors at nightclubs? Are you not relying on *them*?"

"I choose where to work. Fighting, bouncing. It's cash in hand. My name isn't on any document. I owe nobody. They hand me my money, but it's up to me where I get it."

Crane suggests, "They could withhold it from you. You rely on them to be honest people, and I am sure many you have encountered are questionable personalities. Not being on any document means you have no way to prove they even owe you money if they decided to swindle you."

Nick guardedly agrees. "It's possible."

"And what about me?" Crane touches his chest. "Are you not relying on *me*, now?"

Nicks counters, "You offered work, handed me your card. I'd say you're relying on me."

Crane opens his palms. "Therefore it strikes me that reliability, as a construct, is rather like a liquid, would you not agree? No one person can rely on just themselves. There has to be trust from at least two parties."

Crane has a point. An annoying one.

He continues, "And yet – the enigmas of reliability aside – it appears that you have chosen to be here over your usual sources. So I ask again, Nicholas Parker, why are you here? And please answer honestly or I shall have Apollo escort you to the door."

Apollo peaks over his reading glasses.

Nick stares into Crane's eyes. He's hooked in a hypnotist's lullaby, urging him to say the right thing.

Finally, with a sigh, Nick answers. "I'm desperate."

Crane claps. "There is the answer I wanted."

"You want me to be desperate?" Nick asks.

"Young man," Crane stops clapping. "I want you to be *you*. I just wanted to know who *you* is."

"Well now you do."

"Yes. Now I do, and all the better for it. Unlike my books, Nicholas, I want you to be constantly open. I want your spine to crack and your pages to crease and for all of your emotions to show their dog-eared edges. You have been open with me and I am glad. Openness is an admirable trait. Crucial, for myself. We have exposed the root, though there is more to the tree. I do not know the depths of you, why you cannot hold a *normal* job. Perhaps you have been through a wrongdoing."

You've got that *right*, Nick thinks.

"Maybe it is a punishment unto yourself," Crane goes on. "Why that is, I do not know. Something in your history, maybe. I shall pry no further, but I think that you have not yet been to the edges of desperation, though that is not to say that you are not a desperate man."

I've been over the edge, once. Nick recalls Harvey's visit, the offer of a job. He doesn't think he will ever get that desperate again.

"What are you?" Nick tries to lighten to mood. "A psychologist?"

"No, sir," says Crane. "Just an old man who is interested."

"In?"

"*Everything.*" Crane's eyes peel wider.

"How can you be interested in everything?" Nick asks.

"Easily," says Crane. "When everything is available, everything is addictive."

Nick snorts, "S'pose there's worse things to be addicted to."

"Perhaps."

Nick folds his arms. "So what now?"

Another slap on the desk from Crane. "What *now*?"

"Yeah, now that you've exposed me, what now?"

"I said I would have work for you, and I do."

Nick sits straight. "I'm hired?"

Crane flattens his palms together. "Yes."

"When do you want me to start?"

"Today?" Crane's bushy, caterpillar eyebrows raise themselves.

"Now?"

Crane winks. "Right now. Unless you are busy? Though in my experience, desperate men do not tend to be too leisurely."

"No, I guess not," Nick agrees.

"Excellent, because I need you to collect something for me."

I knew it, thinks Nick with an inward eyeroll. But it's a job, and it's money. "Okay. Where and what?"

"Eager, are we not? The what does not matter, the where, I have written down for you."

Crane passes Nick a folded square of paper from his waistcoat pocket. Maybe he won't be performing a meals-on-wheels service after all.

Nick says, "Nothing that could get me in hot water if I was stopped by an enthusiastic police officer, I hope?"

"Nothing like that, young man." Crane leans back in his chair, places his cane over his legs like a safety bar. "There shall be another driver to meet you. You might have to wait a while, but you must not leave without the package."

"You sure this package isn't prison-worthy?"

"Quite sure."

"How will I know who I'm meeting?" Nick asks.

"You will," Crane assures with a wink.

"How does payment work?"

"You shall receive your money when the package is safely delivered. I ask that you do not look at the item, not because it is" – Crane curdles his lips – "*dubious*, but because it is fragile."

Nick replies, "No worries." Whatever he's collecting, he doesn't give a shit what it is so long as it's harmless.

"I never had any," Crane smiles. "Now, I apologise if it seems like I am rushing you away, but…"

Both men stand. Nick goes to offer his hand before remembering that Ulysses Crane is a germaphobe.

"I have a scheduled luncheon in…" Crane checks his pocket watch and the grandfather clock. "A few minutes."

Nick replies, "Will I be needing a car?"

"Will you?"

"I don't have my own, so…"

"Not to worry, you can take one of mine." Crane turns to Apollo. "Apollo, will you kindly fetch the keys for Nicholas? He is champing at the bit to be on his way and I am loath to hold him any longer."

Apollo closes his book, takes it with him as he squeezes into the front of the shop.

"Nicholas?" says Crane.

When Nick turns, Crane is sterilising his desk with a wet wipe, lifting an animal skull to get under it.

"You can rely on me, you know. Never doubt it. And I hope I can rely on you."

"Sure." Nick puts his hands in his pockets. There's something about Crane that he trusts. "You giving me the Rolls?"

Crane laughs. "Young man," he answers. "Not on your life."

§

Before Nick leaves, Apollo hands him a parcel. Whatever's inside is heavy, thumping against the cardboard sides.

"What's this?" asks Nick.

"Delivery," Apollo grunts. He's South African, his accent sharp.

"He speaks. Who's it for?"

"Same person you're meeting now. Make sure they get it."

Apollo stomps away before Nick can ask anything else. There's no name on the parcel, no clue as to what it could be. When Nick leaves, the car is already outside waiting for him.

CHAPTER 7

The smell of smoke is a feature that comes with the car. It's starting to give Nick a headache.

Crane loaned him a Mercedes, a good motor, certainly fancier than anything Nick has driven before. It's an older model, still expensive enough to have the honour of a hood ornament. It looks out of place parked in this rat den under a bridge. Nick has kept the car close to the wall. Separating both sides of the bridge is a narrow canal.

Nick switches off the radio. He's been waiting for hours, watching the silver sky become a deep blue, now with a rind of moon. The only light he has is the bulb inside the car, which doesn't show him much of the outside. He'd seen enough when he'd first arrived. An art gallery of bad graffiti and a row of crumpled boxes where even the sewer bums have decided to move out.

Occasionally, a car or something bigger will pass overhead. A few times he has considered driving back to Crane, telling him that the other person never showed up, but Crane had been adamant about waiting and Nick doesn't want to fuck this job up.

He looks at his watch. Nearly eight o'clock. That puts his waiting time at almost four hours, not including navigating the congested London roads. If he's still here by half-past, he'll call it quits. Crane seems like a man who will understand.

He relaxes back against the headrest and has a staring contest with his own reflection in the windscreen. He wishes he brought something to read, understanding why Apollo had taken to it. You have to be willing to do nothing to work for Crane, it seems.

The Mercedes is lit up as a car swings into view under the bridge. Nick's shadow wipes across the car's interior. He sits up, turns off the interior light. Shifting his weight alone is a blessing to his ribs. The new car is a false alarm, someone turning, or maybe a lost drunk.

Nick sits back again, huffs, which makes him wince. Fucking ribs. Couple more days and it'll be like it never happened.

Frank still hasn't got back to him, and that makes it longer than what's comfortable, now. Out of all the people who have walked in and out of his life, Nick considers Frank as someone who he can call a friend. Perhaps the only one. He hopes Frank is okay and hasn't gotten himself into any serious trouble.

Nick steps outside. It echoes when he closes the door and something unseen splashes into the inky black canal. He walks, blowing warm breath into his cupped hands, to the front of the car and parks his arse on the silver bonnet next to the Mercedes emblem, shoving his hands deep into his pockets.

He shudders. The concrete around him might as well be made of ice. All he wants is some fresh air, but Nick is pretty sure that the toxic fumes outside are worse than what's inside the Merc.

He looks up at the bridge. Cracks in the concrete show a partial skeleton of rebars and girders. He is able to make out the blob-like shapes of pigeon roosts. Something else splashes into the canal, which by the light of the sickle moon is an unmoving obsidian slab. *You should be in a nice bed in a nice house with a nice wife*, the moon whispers. *Not under here with me*. But there're worse places to end up. A cell, for example, which had once been a possibility too close for comfort.

Nick uses his foot to play with the rainbow swirls of spilled petrol in a puddle when another car enters under the bridge. It spotlights Nick. Unlike the car earlier, this one keeps coming. The fan belt is knackered.

It comes to a stop next to the Mercedes. This car isn't the same pedigree as Nick's loaner, it doesn't even have a badge. The driver keeps the car running, fumes spurt from the rattling exhaust.

Nick goes to the driver's side window and waits. Whoever's inside is looking dead ahead. Not wanting to wait any longer than he already has,

Nick knocks on the window.

The driver turns off their car. The fan belt gives one more wail. The engine ticks as it cools. The driver winds down the window.

Nick speaks first. "Alright, mate. I've been waiting a while."

From under the brim of a trucker hat too big for their head, the driver mumbles, "Run, run, as fast as you can."

"Eh?" Nick asks. In the car he can see fast food litter all over the passenger seat and crammed in the footwell.

"You can't catch me…" The driver trails off, distracted by something Nick can't see.

This person is unhinged. He leans in closer. "Are you okay?"

The driver snaps their head up. It's a woman. She has sunken eyes that blink out of sync, herpes is wet in the corner of her mouth. Tufts of gangly hair spring from the sides of the hat, much like the scrub on the edges of Tutt's.

"I'm fine," she spits.

Nick steps back, "I didn't mean to- "

"You pickin' up the thing?"

"Yeah, that's me." He tries on a smile, though she's unresponsive to it.

She reels off her words like an auctioneer. "Fuckin' mistake, that. Just you? Just you?"

A junkie. Nick has dealt with them before. They tend to carry knives, or will use a syringe on you if they're particularly jacked up. If she showed him her arms they'd look like the surface of a crumpet, he reckons. Nick is wary now, mentally thanks Crane in advance for warning him he'd be meeting up with a headcase.

He looks over his shoulder without making a big thing of it, more for her than himself. "Just me. Are you sure you're- "

"Hey diddle diddle, the cat and fiddle," she twitches, looks down at her legs. "I'm fine. Thing's in the boot."

Nick shrugs. "Okay. Shall I- "

"The cow jumped over the moon," the junkie finishes. She's looking at Nick again. Her left eye is milky white, piercing him with as much scorn as the good one, as if it's forgotten it doesn't work.

Nick mutters, "I'll get it myself."

The junkie grunts.

As Nick is making his way to the back of the car he can hear her muttering another nursery rhyme.

The boot springs open on squeaky hinges. Inside, amongst a collection of dirty clothing and crushed toilet rolls, is a large box wrapped in clean linen. Nick doesn't want to touch it. There's something revolting about it.

"I didn't wanna touch it either," the junkie calls from the front, flicking on the inside light. "Don't bother opening forra peak."

After staring at it a while longer, Nick says, "Don't want to," and picks up the package. He closes the boot, a broken slam that knocks off a brake light cover. "Sorry."

"Just leave it. Come 'ere a mo, will ya? Will ya?" The junkie ends again with another double-barrel.

The package is heavy. When he reaches the window, the junkie looks up at him with a crooked smile, teeth too large, dirty. Her red long-sleeve top clings to her underfed frame.

"You're too nice lookin' to be doin' this," she says.

"And what's this?" Nick humours her.

"Collecting unsolicited parcels for strange men."

On the outside she's a ruin. Inside there's intelligence, as if a functioning woman had been or is still there, somewhere. Many secrets have been locked inside this junkie's dry, flaking lips. They all have them, those lips. Secrets, too.

She purred, "Could be anything, as far as you know."

"Could be," Nick replies.

"But you don't care, do you?"

He considers the revulsion it stirs in him, the sickly weight of it in his arm, how even now he wants to toss it away as if it were a cockroach.

"No," he says. "Long as I get paid."

She shakes her head, tuts, then in a burst of Tourette's speech, "Itsy bitsy fuckin' *spider*!"

She slaps the rear-view mirror, knocking the scentless tree to the floor. She scrambles to pick up the tree and readjust the mirror.

Nick takes some pity on her. This woman is wretched. More than himself? In a different way, yes. "Listen, maybe you want to lay off whatever it is you're- "

She glares at him, crushes the tree in her grip. "I ain't a fuckin' addict."

It's a lie.

Has to be.

He can't help but look into her fogged up eye. It watches him fiercer than the other, more bloodshot.

"Sorry," he says.

The lying junkie snaps, "Don't give me ya sorry I don't want ya bloody sorry."

Nick takes a breath. This is going nowhere. "Are we done here?"

"Listen." She leans her head out the window. "What you're getting involved in," she cracks her neck, "itsy...itsy bitsy climbed...*fuck*...whatever it is, let this be as far as it goes. Drop that thing and get the fuck out."

"Yeah. I think we're done," Nick replies.

"Crane isn't who you think he is." She grabs his arm when Nick takes a step away. Her fingers are arthritic, covered in filth. He pulls free, ready to knock her mangled teeth out if he spies a blade.

The junkie is close to tears, most likely can't spare the fluid. "When I woke up this morning, both my eyes worked."

Nick walks away. Nothing she says can be taken seriously. She screams about the itsy bitsy spider. He is almost to the Merc when she stretches over her junk food litter and winds down the passenger window. The glass inches down, sticking every so often.

She scowls at him. "Up the fuckin' water spout!"

Nick opens and reaches into the Merc, picks out the package Apollo gave him. He throws it into the junkie's car, intent on hitting her in the face. She may be a freak, but a quick one, dodging the package and laughing at the same time.

"Nice try," she croaks.

The engine splutters to life, the fan belt's torture starts again. Giving Nick the finger, she pulls away, tires squealing. The bridge becomes an echo chamber. She skids to the left outside and is gone.

"Damn nutcase," Nick sighs.

Opening the Merc's boot, he goes to toss the package in, but stops. The package…the *thing*, it has to be a *thing*, shouldn't be tossed. He places it down, revilement curdling his lips. Nick closes the boot and the package in darkness. The sickness abates somewhat.

Nick strides to the driver's side. He pauses when he sees it standing under a streetlamp outside this rat den.

The Figure.

A black shape even under the cone of yellow light. It has no eyes, but is watching him. The shape of a man, nothing but darkness. Its wispy hair is illuminated by the light.

Nick has never spoken to it, and he doesn't now. There's no fear seizing him, only regret, guilt.

He gets into the Merc. When he switches on the headlights, the Figure is gone. It never stays long, doesn't appear much, only enough. The last two times have, admittedly, been closer together, but that doesn't have to mean anything. The Figure comes and goes as it wishes. Nick regards the empty space under the streetlamp for a few seconds more, then turns on the Merc.

He flicks on the radio, pressing glowing buttons until he gets something he can put on low and not really listen to. He settles for something that sounds like lazy rock music. It'll take forty-five minutes to get back to Crane. The geezer will be fast asleep by now. He leaves the bridge behind, allowing the rats to quietly reclaim it.

When he pulls up to Crane's building, there are still lights on inside. He enters with the package, ignoring his discomfort at having to handle it again. It's log fire warm, though he can't see one. He moves between the bookshelves to the front desk, places the package on top, wipes his hands down his coat.

On the desk, near an old-school cash register, he sees a button, or pin. He picks it up. It's metal. Copper, maybe. It looks like a symbol. A circle with a diagonal line slashing through it, a small V dangling at the top of the circle. Or the bottom, if he's holding it wrong.

"Nicholas?"

Crane, calling from somewhere.

"Hello?" Nick answers, returning the...brooch! That was the word.

"Up here, young man. In The Orphanage."

Nick ascends the spiral staircase. At the top, there are leaning stacks of books rising up like towers of Babel, becoming increasingly insecure the higher they get. Books that aren't stacked are strewn on the floor, or pushed up against the walls.

"Over here."

Crane's bony hand appears over the top of a large bundle. He tinkles his fingers playfully.

Nick finds Crane on his knees under another chandelier, though this one has modern bulbs. Crane catches him looking at it.

"I need to see better up here."

"What are you doing?" Nick asks.

"Well," Crane gestures with a sweeping hand to the copious books around them, "they need homing, hence The Orphanage. I spend hours up here sorting through them, creating new stacks, each one a different category."

Nick picks up a thick tome, turns it over, "There can't be *that* many kinds of book, can there?"

Crane politely takes the book from Nick's untrained hands and places it back down. "That many and more, young man."

"Your knees must hurt. Can't your man Apollo give you a hand?"

"And why would I do that? This is one of my most treasured places to be, a place I can learn, a place I can come to give books a new home, a place downstairs perhaps, where they will join their long lost brothers and sisters." Crane gazes with love around The Orphanage. "There are many gems up here, just waiting to be discovered."

Once again, Nick feels implored to carry on with the line of discussion. What he really wants to tell Crane is that the package is on the front desk, receive his pay and go the fuck home. He'll have to walk too, and tonight he'd rather not.

He asks, "What if your idea of a good book is different than mine? It's all subjective to a point, isn't it?"

Crane chuckles. "No, Nicholas. Not really. But I understand your meaning."

Using his cane, Crane pushes himself up. Nick doesn't help. Germaphobe.

"What do you mean?" Nick continues, finding that he actually *wants* to hear Crane's answer.

Crane checks his pocket watch, rubbing his thumb over the glass. He tucks it back and gives the lump in his waistcoat a pat. Smiling, he answers, "Think of it this way. You can read a book…do you read?"

"Not really."

"Ah. Well, anyway. You *could* read a book, you could *enjoy* that book, but that does not make it a good book. Same as a painting, or a poem, or a piece of music. You can enjoy these things, but that does not grant the thing the title of good. Good is," Crane holds on to the s, drags it out, twirling his hand. "Good is a technique. Good is *real* technique. Some books are fun, engrossing, funny, scary. Everything. Yet the technique might not be there. Other books might be a chore, have no real plot or rhyme or reason, but the technique used in crafting them is sublime. I have indulged in books that I have found completely without spirit, no soul, and yet I recognised that they were still good works. Every so often, after moiling through all of these lost children, I shall find the diamonds in the rough that embody all of these things."

Nick looks over the piles, then says, "Good technique might be bad technique to someone else."

Crane titters.

"So it seems to me," Nick goes on, "that subjectivity is as liquid as reliability."

"I can see we are going to get along just fine." Crane smiles warmly.

Nick smiles back, amazed he is enjoying the discussion when a couple of minutes ago he just wanted to be gone. He pulls himself back, drops the smile.

"Is it downstairs?" asks Crane.

"On the front desk."

Both of them go down the staircase, Crane leading the descent.

At the desk, Crane strokes the linen package but doesn't untie the yarn. He notices the brooch and, Nick sees, quickly bundles it into his trouser pocket. Crane's breathing has gotten heavier.

"I wish you'd've told me about the junkie I collected it from," says Nick, folding his arms.

Crane waves a hand, "Ah, do not worry about her."

"She could've been dangerous. Next time, I'd like to know beforehand is all."

"Are you telling me off, young man?"

"A little, I s'pose."

A small laugh. "Then it shall not happen again. I should have told you, Nicholas. In your profession, I assumed you had seen it all."

"Not all. But thanks," Nick answers, noting that there was no real apology there. Men like Ulysses Crane don't apologise.

Crane turns from the package, asks, "But no trouble, I do hope?"

"No."

"Excellent," Crane smiles. "Did you look at it?"

"Nope, none of my business," says Nick.

"You could have, you know?"

Didn't fucking want to, Nick thinks. "You told me not to."

"I did, yet at the same time I cannot abide the suppression of curiosity. I am a walking paradox of myself."

"Even so," says Nick. "Curiosity isn't in me."

"You were curious enough to come *here*."

Nick doesn't respond.

"Is everything alright, Nicholas?" Crane asks.

The old boy tips his head forward, the wrinkles around his eyes intensify. His eyes twinkle in the firelight of the chandelier. Crane is daring him to say something. *Daring* him to say that the package disgusted him even though he doesn't know why. *Daring* him to say that it felt like a corpse in his arms. Nick hears the flickering of the candles, each flick is a whipcrack. The room is sinking, darkening. There is an atonal drone, the ticking of the grandfather clocks falls into it, the gears crashing as it smashes. His stomach twists and Nick wants to throw up.

"Young man?" Crane persists. Everything normal again.

Nick holds his composure. "Yeah. Everything's fine. How was your luncheon?"

"Which one?" Crane stands straight. "I have many luncheons in a day."

"All of them, I s'pose."

"Fine. Just fine. Now, the hour is late, you shall be wanting your payment."

Crane tucks his hand inside his waistcoat and pulls out a plain white envelope. He hands it over. Nick takes it. Counting money on payment is a habit spanning years. If you're someone who doesn't, word soon gets around and people try to fuck with you, because most people are shit, and as yet Nick won't put it beyond even kindly Mr Crane.

Crane gently places his hand on the envelope before Nick tears it open. "If it suits you, as it would me, could you wait to do that?"

"Why?" Nick asks.

"I am not trying to pull the wool over your eyes, Nicholas. I would just prefer you to look outside. If you are not wholly satisfied, you can come back in and we can discuss future payment."

Nick is suspicious but agrees. How far can Crane run if he's been a bastard, anyway?

"Wonderful," from Crane. "Now, you will probably want to be off, and I would like to inspect my package. Will I see you tomorrow?"

Nick pockets the envelope. "Tomorrow?"

"I have need of assistance. Chauffeuring, that sort of thing."

"Yeah. I can do tomorrow. What time?"

"Whenever suits you, but please, if you will, before ten of the clock."

"Not a problem," Nick says.

"Take the Mercedes. Treat it as a company car."

Nick nods. "Cheers. I'll park it round the corner from my flat. Area's a bit dodgy."

"I would not worry about that. That car has been through many a corner of the city where it should not. I shall see you then," Crane says, inviting Nick to see himself out.

Nick takes one more look at the package before leaving. Nausea places its hand on his shoulder and turns him from the site of it. He wonders if Crane feels the same sensations he does.

Outside, at the Merc, he pulls out the envelope. He half expects it to be sealed with stamped wax. Nick opens it up, looks inside, flicks through the notes. His eyes widen.

"Fuck off."

This shit's going to be lucrative.

CHAPTER 8

Nick doesn't go home straight away. Before that. He goes to Murray's 24-Hour Groceries, a decent shop which manages quite well in spite of its low quality.

Nick, treating himself, has picked up a microwave meal that promises a gourmet experience, and a new kettle, one that isn't made of plastic. The lights in Murray's are too bright. A strange blue tint in them makes shopping at this time of night abstract, much in the same way the light is strange in all-night public toilets. Nick is perusing the magazine section when he spots the man studying him from the end of the aisle.

The man is holding a bottle of ketchup as if he had been reading the back of it. The shelves around him are festooned in pink, yellow and orange stars cut out of card that display bonkers prices at Murray's.

Placing the bottle back on the shelf, the man makes his way towards Nick. The mullet he sports has been poorly styled.

Nick takes the first magazine his hand reaches (something about fishing) and pops it in the basket stolen from a supermarket, then starts to leave.

"You've been followed," the mullet man says.

Nick stops and faces him. "'Scuse me?"

The mullet man browses the magazines, his eyes naturally going to the top shelf. "You're always being followed, but you know that."

"Listen mate, I've had just about enough of people like you tonight, so if you don't mind I think I'm gonna- "

"Who is he?"

"What?" Nick's hand tightens around the basket handle.

"Who follows you. Who is he?"

Could he be talking about…the Figure? Surely not. This man in his faded U2 tee-shirt can't have any idea about that. He's just another nut, probably talks to everyone he forces himself onto like this.

Nick keeps calm, but he can feel his fuse burning. It's been a long night. A long fucking week. The tasty pay packet he received can't erase that.

He says, "I haven't been followed, and I'll be off now. Goodnight."

The mullet man tip-toes, snags a magazine from the top shelf. The front cover has been partially hidden, but Nick can see that it caters to the man or woman who enjoys MILFs.

"That can be fixed, you know? Made better," says the mullet man, turning to Nick again.

"Right. Enough." Nick steps forward, patience and fake smiles out of stock. "Yes, I *have* been followed. I've been followed by arseholes like you all night, so do yourself a solid and leave me the fuck alone."

He stares at Nick for a while. His nostrils flaring. The too-bright light strip above them hums quietly.

"My therapist…" The man starts. "My therapist says…it's good for me to…to talk to new people."

A portly man appears in the aisle. His brown apron doesn't quite cover his whole stomach, and his Friar Tuck hair is peppered grey.

"Everything alright here?" he asks.

"No," snaps Nick. "No it bloody isn't."

The portly fellow, who must be Murray, glares at the mullet man. "Stop bothering people, Simon. Get what you need or get out."

Simon grumbles at Murray, curses him under his breath, turns to go back to the star-spangled shelves.

Murray apologises to Nick before returning to the counter. Nick is ready to pay. He takes one last look at Simon, who has the ketchup back in his hand.

Through a tensed jaw Simon says, "It can also be made worse."

Shaking his head, Nick leaves him to his condiments.

Nick pops his basket on the counter. Murray apologises a second time, takes Nick's items to scan. His top lip is covered by a thick grey bush.

"Simon doesn't mean any harm," Murray explains as he beeps the kettle through, "but he creeps people out, makes them uncomfortable, and that isn't good for business."

"I can imagine," Nick answers, pretending to care.

Now the gourmet meal. Nick thinks he should have picked up another, one without carrots.

Murray scans another item. "I think he might have something wrong in the head. Maybe autism, or OCD. He'll be here for another thirty minutes."

The rest of the items are totalled up, ibuprofen and paracetamol amongst them. Murray tells Nick the total to pay please, then asks, "Is there anything else you need tonight?"

"Don't think so." Nick looks around for the hell of it, but does see something. He almost doesn't buy it.

The cat is waiting for Nick outside the flat. He doesn't tell it to play with the traffic or to fuck off tonight, but offers it a reserved hello. He's quickly gotten used to it being around. It was there this morning when he left, in the same place it is now. Where the welcome mat won't go.

As Nick unlocks the front door, the cat prances around his feet, rubbing itself on his legs. He nudges it away, trying to put it off getting too friendly. It persists, purring with delight. When he gets inside and looks back, the cat sits again, watching him. "You're relentless," Nick tells it.

It's a joy to unplug the old kettle and push it to one side. The new one isn't cheap plastic, but is instead cheap metal. He plugs it in (even that slots into the wall nicer), fills it up and flicks it on. There is no screeching as it begins to heat the water, only the sound of gentle boiling. Nick has never been so excited over something so trivial. When did silent hot water become so enjoyable? He can't help but smile. Boiling the water had at first been a pilot run, and Nick thinks now he'll actually have a coffee.

Nick makes his coffee, sits down at the table, retrieves the envelope from his pocket and pulls the money out.

The wad is thick. About a month's worth of thickness. There are tens, twenties and some fifties, all this for picking up one thing. One weird, messed up thing. It won't be long before he can kiss all of his debts goodbye if Crane keeps paying him like this. It won't make things perfect, not by any stretch, but it will make things a lot easier. Whoever said that money doesn't buy happiness is a tosser.

He counts through the cash, separating the different notes, already doing the sums in his head of what can be paid off first. The eviction letter pops into mind.

The last-second purchase in the Murray's bag is half-out on the table. The feline face on its side licks its cartoon chops. Nick sighs, questioning his impulsive buy.

The cat hoists its tail the second the door is opened, bathing in a rectangle of light. Nick leans out and places a chipped saucer on the ground. On the saucer is some cat food.

The cat stops, its front legs criss-crossed.

"Go on," Nick says.

The cat takes to the food in an instant. Nick watches it eat, which takes less than a minute. Fucking thing better not get used to this, he thinks, knowing damn well what he's just started.

Finished, it stares up at him with its moon-yellow eyes. It takes a few furtive steps forwards before Nick blocks the doorway with his foot.

"Don't push your luck," he says, and shuts the door.

After the rest of the shopping has been put away and the last quarter of the coffee tipped down the drain, Nick heads to bed.

He lies there for some time, unable to sleep, yet feeling better than he has done in a while. There's an air of promise he hasn't experienced since he was making a name for himself in the boxing circuit. He switches between gazing up at the knackered ceiling fan – one blade has been missing since he moved in – and closing his eyes, drifting in and out of dreams, never entering sleep.

Nick sinks deeper into the pillow, deeper into the mattress, on the precipice of finally falling asleep when he is drawn out by a familiar presence in the bedroom.

The Figure has followed him home.

Simon the Mullet Man had, somehow, been correct. Crazy people, scarily enough, end up being right more times than they should.

Nick doesn't need to open his eyes to know where it is. Whenever it comes into his flat, it always sits in the same place. A chair in the corner of Nick's bedroom. On it are unwashed clothes. The Figure is just an outline, its eyeless glare a night-long harassment. It doesn't move much, only its chest as it breathes. Its knees point a little too high, fingers curled over the ends of the arm rests. Nick can hear its nails scratching on the fabric.

In the morning, it shall vanish, and the hours of sleeplessness will be as if a dream. Nothing left but an indent in the dirty jeans and creased shirts.

He could have guessed it would be here tonight after seeing it at the bridge. It's here to remind him that money doesn't mean shit. You can't buy redemption.

Its breath frosts with each exhale. The bedroom isn't cold.

Nick swallows, and for the first time since the Figure started showing up, he speaks to it.

"You're never going to leave me alone. Are you?"

It doesn't move, only sits.

Eventually, after a few minutes – maybe hours – it leans forward and the clouds of breath stop puffing from its black mask of a face. In a voice that is painful to Nick, it answers him.

"No."

Nick sits up in a flash, turns on the bedside lamp. The chair is empty.

Already, it's as if the night has been a dream. The only thing that reaffirms otherwise is the dent in the clothes where it had been sitting.

§

It's gone midnight.

Ulysses Crane is in the Secret Room, a snug cube lit by trios of candles. He is naked. His back is striped by the scars of flagellation, each smooth line a reward. He kneels on callused knees that he has grown bored of.

On a podium sits the package, still wrapped in its linen. He gazes upon it with adoration, savours the bile it brings up into his throat. Such an artifact has the potential to turn lesser people into lunatics. *Has* done. Each one of them silenced inside tiled asylums.

He raises his arms. Wobbly, stretched skin hangs where biceps had once been. Crane smiles, closes his eyes, bunching every wrinkle on his face. He does not desire to use the artifact yet, only to get acquainted. To show himself to it.

On the black walls of the Secret Room, shadows shift, darken. One by one, the scars on his back open up, little red razor slits. It stings. It is delightful.

The scars continue to open and close, sipping from the air. Blood runs to the floor, pooling beneath Crane's sagged buttocks.

"Thank you," he exhales. "Thank you."

CHAPTER 9

Not all days working for Crane offer the same level of weird and wonderful as his first, but Nick soon settles into the way things are run.

His second day – he arrived at nine sharp – saw him running Crane around to different clients. Then he helped in The Orphanage.

Picking out books the likes of which Crane covets is something Nick doesn't ever think he'll get the hang of. How is value measured if it isn't by cash? There is sentimental value to things of course, but when it comes to running a business (even one that works in denial of itself) sentiment is as welcome as an I-owe-you. It goes without saying, helping in The Orphanage is Nick's least favourite job with the Crane.

On the third day Nick's premonition had come true. Crane sent him out to collect meat and veg from the markets. That day was a short one, but the pay didn't suffer. Crane dishes out a daily wage as opposed to an hourly one, which suits Nick just fine.

The fourth day was more interesting. An upgraded version of the night under the bridge. Rather than pick up a package, it was Nick's job to deliver one. Crane handed him a book tightly sealed in bubble wrap inside a brown paper bag with that circular emblem stamped on it.

"The customer is a client I have had dealings with before, Nicholas, and he will not be any trouble. A simple case of you hand him yours and he shall hand you his, then back to the homestead."

The customer had been waiting for Nick at the Shard. A pallid man trying to cover it up with a blue suit and fedora. He might not've been like the junkie, but still clearly wired. Book and money exchanged hands with only the basest of formalities spoken, which also suited Nick just fine.

It's on the fifth day, a Friday, that things change up.

Nick is in the building, once again charged with spending another morning in The Orphanage. Crane calls to him from downstairs. He's taught Nick enough to trust him to dig up uncommon books.

"Nicholas. Would you mind popping down here for a few minutes?"

A few minutes. In the world of Ulysses Crane, a few minutes could be anything from an actual few minutes to an hour. All complaints aside, anything is better than rifling through these books so heavily worded they are close to unreadable.

Crane has retreated back into his office. Nick goes inside.

"Close the door, would you Nicholas? And rest yourself," says Crane, indicating the chair opposite himself.

Nick does both.

"How are things in The Orphanage?" asks Crane. He knits his fingers together. "Is it wise of me to leave you alone up there as early as I have?"

The question is asked in good humour.

Nick scratches the back of his head. "Maybe not," he replies, "but anything I suspect of being a good one has been set aside."

Crane doesn't answer. He instead looks at Nick with disappointment mixed with an apologetic smile.

Nick takes his hand away from his head. "What?"

Crane opens a draw, pulls out a wet wipe. He hands it to Nick. "Scratching your scalp. You may have flaked the back of your chair. Please, would you give it a wipe?"

"Sorry," says Nick. It hasn't taken long to get used to Crane's germophobic behaviour, though from time to time he forgets.

"Thank you," Crane says. "Now. Nicholas. I shall cut straight to the chase. Are you available to assist me this evening?"

Nick replies, "Sure, I'm not doing anything else."

"Excellent. Wonderful. I need you to drive me to a club and then be by my side for the duration of our time there. Think of it as chauffeuring with a little extra. If we go beyond midnight there shall be a bonus in your envelope."

"What's the club?" asks Nick, thinking he might know it.

"An establishment named The Cross. Are you familiar?"

Nick has never heard of it. "No."

"Not to worry, I shall direct you there. Actually, it is a rather pleasant drive through some of the city's forgotten streets. I shall be able to give you a history lesson on the way, if you wish?" Crane offers.

"Maybe you can," Nick smiles.

"I shall warn you now," Crane leans in his chair. "You will see a charming array of characters, many of them will come to me. At first they will think you an outsider, which I suppose you are for now, but do not fret, hold your steel and they shall forget you are there before long. Apollo once had to go through the same rite of passage."

"Why isn't Apollo going with you tonight?" asks Nick.

"Busy. I already have the poor man doing so much as it is, I did not have the heart to ask him to come along on this jaunt."

"Aren't you worried? I thought that bloke was your bodyguard or something?"

Crane laughs, slaps the desk. Nick can see the cracks in his skin. It must hurt him to touch things, let alone slap them.

"How amusing. Think you are up to the challenge?" says Crane.

Nick answers, "Challenge?"

"Like I said, the poor man Apollo is a busy soul. He will soon not have the time to follow me around like he used to. I shall be needing a new…let us say, *l'homme de droite*."

"I'm afraid you'll have to translate."

"Right hand man. Or…what was it you called him?"

"Bodyguard?"

"Yes," Crane claps. "I shall be needing someone to accompany me most places. I know you are more than qualified, Nicholas. You have already apprehended one assailant before they could do me harm."

"I was only doing my job- "

"And that is what I need. Someone to do their job. Think of tonight as a trial run, though I doubt you shall have any trouble."

"So this is what? Like a promotion?"

"Perhaps," Crane smiles, then checks his pocket watch. "You had best be done here for the day. You can come pick me up at say…seven?"

"Yeah, no problem. Do I, uh…have to dress in a particular way?"

Crane enquires, "Do you own a suit?"

Oh, shit. He'll have to dig it out, give it a wash and an iron. "I have one," he replies.

"Good. Nothing quite speaks like a suit does. And Nicholas?"

"Mm-hm?"

Crane raises an eyebrow. "Have you ever driven a Rolls-Royce before? *They* are reliable."

§

The journey to the nightclub takes little less than half an hour, and on the way Crane regales Nick with some of those history lessons he hinted at. Nick couldn't care less about the history of the places he passes. Though Crane has a way with words that can make you second-guess your opinions.

The club, on the outside, is a black-fronted newish build with twin spotlights that burn an X above the roof. There's no queue, instead people file in from all angles, dancing already. The inside isn't much better. Laser lights cut up the ceiling to the beat of electronic music. The Cross is different from any of the nightclubs Nick has worked at. It's an alter-ego to Tutt's. The patrons are colourful, most of them wacky, looking like they've just moved on from a rock star's party. At its core, however, it's still the same as anywhere else. A thumping pit of perfume and testosterone. It's hard to not bump into nearly everybody.

Crane leads the way across the sunken dancefloor. Dancers part naturally, as if sensing his approach. Above, a disco ball that cheapens the aesthetic boasts that this gaff is so retro, *man*. Well, so is snorting coke in toilets, yet Nick doesn't see them hanging *that* up to sparkle.

"You don't really like this music, do you?" Nick shouts over the heavy synth and drums.

"The music is dreadful," Crane shouts back over his shoulder, his voice carrying clearly, "but it is also an effective cloak."

"What does that mean?" Nick shoulders past a dancer in a glittered neck brace.

"Well, Nicholas. Would *you* expect to find *me* here?"

Crane turns to smile. Dark blue and purple lights wash over his face. A black light brings out his teeth.

From the dancefloor they enter into an area with plush VIP booths. None of them are occupied. The music is quieter, meaning they can talk at more acceptable levels. Plenty of shadows, too, Nick notices. Enough for him to slip into for a few minutes if the *cirque* gets too much, as Crane might say.

Crane sits in the middle of a horseshoe-shaped booth. Behind him are strings of blue fairy lights woven around empty bottles. He sits his cane next to himself on the seat, pats it gently.

"Would you mind fetching my tired legs a neat brandy, Nicholas?" he asks. "And whatever you would like for yourself, of course."

"Sure," Nick answers.

Back into the noise he goes.

The Cross's bar is its own red light district. Men, women and couples are lined up, viewing the pickings or waiting to be picked, peacocking themselves in clothes that leave little to the imagination, or too much. Either is a tease to the prowlers. Nick squeezes into a gap, orders the brandy.

"For Mr Crane?" the bartender asks, a bowtie tight around his neck.

"Yeah," Nick replies, plugging his cauliflower ear to hear better.

"On the house." The bartender leaves to prepare the drink.

A woman with short brown hair and a monocle sidles up to Nick, gives him the eyes. Nick knows they're the eyes because it's painfully obvious. He's seen them in the sockets of the drunk and suggestible many times. Love me or fuck me, those eyes say. *Anything* me. She bops her body to the beat of the music. Nick averts his attention.

Behind the bar is a sculpture of a white cross backlit by pink lights. A water feature trickles behind. It may be an unspoken joke here that saints and sinners alike meet in front of the religious symbol. There is a strong sexual vibe in The Cross, a perverse church of eroticism, making Crane's presence here all the more confusing.

The woman taps Nick's shoulder. Her makeup is generous, like a singer from an eighties music video. Using her index finger, she caresses Nick's forearm. He softly removes her hand and declines with a smile.

Not a moment too soon the brandy arrives.

When he reaches the booth, he sees that Crane has a visitor in a velvet dress and heels. Crane is holding the slender woman's hand, she his, nodding at every word she says. Nick sets the brandy on the table. The woman kisses Crane's hand and stands straight, the curve in her lower back advertises her worth like the punt of a wine bottle. She flicks her photoshoot-ready hair as she passes Nick, giving him just enough of her time to let him know he isn't worthy of it.

Crane winks. "What a dish."

"If you say so," says Nick.

"Please take a seat."

"I'd rather stand, if you don't mind? I don't like to get too comfortable in these places."

"Hence your lack of liquor." Crane salutes Nick with his brandy and takes a nip.

How does the geezer do it? Nick wonders. Crane has to be pushing ninety if he's in each of the photographs on the office wall, yet he has so much vigour. His hair seems shinier than yesterday, the cracks in his face not so deep, the wattled neck looks like it's had a lift. Maybe that's why

Crane comes to these places. They supply the placebo of youth. And maybe he likes to keep it under wraps because, somewhere deep down, he's embarrassed by it. Nick realises that he is pondering the inner workings of Ulysses Crane in much the same way that Crane cross-examined him. He's also realising he quite likes the geezer.

The night continues. Nick stands sentinel.

After a woman who resembles Betty Boop finishes a short chat with Crane, Nick asks, "So what's with the cloak and dagger, anyway?"

"Meaning?" Crane sips his drink.

"You said yourself that this place and it's awful music- "

"Here, here."

"-is like a cloak. Why the need to remain hidden? For a bodyguard?"

Crane mulls the question over, rubs his chin. "I have made many people happy, Nicholas, but I suppose I have also made an enemy or two in my time. I cannot be too careful about when they may or may not spring from the rafters."

Squares of light twirl over them as the disco ball spins.

"Didn't work at Tutt's, though, did it?" says Nick.

Crane rolls his eyes, red veins hug his whites. "That dishevelled being has been a boil on my behind for a long time. It was only a matter of time before he found me. When you popped him, you popped him good. He shall bother us no longer, you can forget about him."

"Is the world of trading really that unforgiving?"

"I would not say trading, but knowledge, for definite."

"Knowledge?"

"Much have I discovered, learned and practised from my books, Nicholas. Trading, I suppose you could say, is my business. Knowledge, you could counter, as I would, is my ordnance. The two co-exist. Not every person who is exposed to that knowledge, or the trading of it, leaves a better human being."

"But most do?" Nick asks.

"Most do. Others find it difficult to process, or are unhappy with results, and so their lack of intelligence mutates into madness, or violent jealousy. They have enabled that violence before, and so I have become as cautious as you have cynical, hence my desire to keep myself hidden."

Nick recoils at the sudden accusation.

"I'm not cynical," he protests.

Crane waves his hand dismissively as he sips more brandy. Setting the glass down, he says, "But you *are*. You are a nice man, yet a cynic all the same. There is nothing wrong in that. Cynicism can save lives. Whatever life has thrown your way, you have survived to this point, but you have also become wary of the world, distrustful. That is a good thing, in my old eyes. The world is not a perfect place, it is not sunshine and rainbows and chocolate drops in a sugar fountain. For that matter, being a cynic helps you to *really*" – the word comes out as a growl – "grasp what is beneath the patina of life, because when it finally reveals itself to you, you cannot help but believe it. It is in front of your eyes and cynicism cannot deny it. It dictates that you have no choice but to accept it, because it is there, happening."

This is obviously a topic that Crane is hot on.

Nick replies, "I s'pose you could say things didn't go the way I planned." *Don't ask me*, he thinks. "And maybe I have become…resentful."

"Of course your life derailed," Crane snaps. "What desperate man ever claims that life went the way he planned it out?"

"What about you?" Nick asks. "Are you a cynic, Ulysses?"

It's the first time Nick has used the name and it causes Crane to tighten his lips as he stifles a laugh.

Crane answers, "Me? Not anymore. I was cynical once, when I was young, but was able to quash it when my path was revealed to me. I already know what is and what is not. Where you expect the worst, I expect the best. I am now only cynical that before too long my brandy will reach the bottom of the tumbler."

Nick takes the glass. "So you *are* a cynic?"

"Young man, we have touched upon reliability and subjectivity, debates which I do not consider tackled. Let us not add cynicism to the list just yet."

"Refill?" Nick shakes the tumbler.

"I thought you would never ask," Crane grins.

As he leaves for the bar, a man wearing a scrapyard of jewellery passes Nick on a beeline for Crane.

The crowd on the dancefloor whoops as an apparently popular hit blasts out to the visuals of LSD bubbles on big screens. To Nick, it sounds exactly like the last song. Cynical. He laughs in his throat.

The woman at the bar spies him again, only this time she leaves him alone, deciding that he is boring news as opposed to bad, which is what Nick reckons she's after. He can pick out at least ten people at the bar who could show her a bad time.

The jewellery man has been swapped for a buxom madam when Nick returns to the booth. He has bought two tumblers of brandy – both on the house – to supplement Crane's wants. Plus, it means less trips through the throng of dancing crazies. The chesty woman doesn't leave immediately, inspects Nick like a piece of so-so art. Her ample cleavage is packed tight, breasts almost spilling over the top of her ridiculous corset. Before long, she leaves, satisfied that she's had her time with Crane.

Nick asks, "What is it you've done, then, to make these people come to you? Even the drinks are free."

"That lad at the bar? Before me, he could not speak, or barely move." Crane takes his cane, uses it to prop up his hand. Nick hasn't noticed until now that the silver ball at its top is a face of some kind. "These people. I have helped them."

"Through trading?" Nick raises and eyebrow.

"And knowledge," answers Crane.

"In what way?"

"In what *way*? In ways I am able. Do they not seem happy to you?

Full of life in a society that wants to rob them of it? Take the people in here, for example, those who are indebted to me. Look how they dance to this inane music, how they confidently display themselves. They have no inhibitions, they are celebrating themselves, unafraid of judgement or ridicule. That comes only with true happiness. Chances are they hate all this too, some of them, but they are savouring it simply because they can, because the things that used to hold them back have been erased."

Nick stares out at the night's castaways. Each person here is as they are because there is no niche that will accept them. "Could be a front. People lie to themselves as well as others," he suggests.

"Not those *I* have helped," Crane holds his head high. "They sought better understanding of themselves, were too afraid to *be* themselves, there were obstacles in their way, difficult to move. They may have been nobodies. Their lives are better now."

Nick jokes, "What's the price of a better life, then? Surely you don't hand out life coaching for nothing?"

Crane laughs. "No price, as such. Loyalty is all I ask."

"So, everyone in here, you've helped?" Nick can't hold back his apparent cynicism. He feels Crane is making it sound grander than it is with lots of words.

Crane frowns, "Good heavens, no. I am not as yet a miracle machine. The ones I have helped are those you see coming to say hello. As well as keeping me away from any wrongdoers, I like to drop into the places where the people I have aided go. Could be nightclubs like this or Tutt's, could be dive bars, or a restaurant, gambling establishments. My frequents have become somewhat known to them. In spite of my age, I hold no prejudices as to what people are *into*."

"Not much cloaking in a restaurant," Nick says.

"You would be surprised. Plenty of cloak*rooms*. A quieter establishment is where a bodyguard really proves his or her worth."

"Why the need to see these people, and why their need to see you?"

"Because they are grateful, of course. They may never step foot in my residence again, but that does not mean they have forgotten what has been done for them. It would be hard for them to forget. As for me, think of it like a doctor checking up on their patients."

"Ha," Nick scoffs. "I guessed it from the start."

Crane lifts his chin. "Do tell."

"You're a psychiatrist." He has to be. How else could Crane afford to pay what he's been paying Nick unless he's been overcharging the vulnerable by the hour? There's more to him than the book trade, that's for certain. "All this deconstructing of words and character, only a head doctor talks like that."

Crane chuckles. "Still wrong on that count, young man. I am by no means a doctor."

"And you don't just come to these places to feel young again?"

Seeming almost offended by the suggestion, Crane answers, "There are ways to feel young again, and this is not how."

Nick's analysis of Crane had been wrong then, if the geezer was to be believed.

"I don't get it, then," Nick says. "If you're some sort of *guru-* "

"I reject the word," Crane interrupts.

"-and not a professional with a certificate, couldn't these people get the same result from a self-help book?"

"Are you doubting me?" Crane narrows his eyes.

"Wouldn't dream of it."

Crane takes a sip of brandy, holds it in his mouth to let his tongue baste in the flavour. After he swallows, he says, "Cheap, throw-away books help nobody."

"Okay, so how'd you do it? You still haven't told me *how*."

Crane audits Nick, taps his temple where there was definitely a mole a couple of days ago. "I have already told you, Nicholas. Knowledge."

Happiness and help through the power of knowing things. "What knowledge do you have that's so effective? They love you for it."

Now it's Crane's turn to think. He gazes into the crowd beyond the booths. He answers the question without providing a real answer. Crane is a fan of ambiguity.

"Everyone has wishes, Nicholas. For better. For things they believe will bring them fulfilment. To me, they bring those wishes."

"Like money?"

"Hardly ever." Crane straightens his back.

"So all this makes you…what?" Nick asks.

Crane's eyebrow twitches. He smiles softly, proud of his coming response.

"The Wishmaster," he says.

A tall woman in a trench coat steps up to the booth. She doesn't look twice at Nick. She looks nervous to be in front of Crane.

"Ah!" Crane raises his arms. "Our very own Poirot! It is so wonderful to see you Detective Inspector Vance."

She half-smiles, brushes loose strands of her bob out her face. "I heard you would be here tonight," she says, forcing the cool. "Thought I'd drop by, say hi."

"So nice of you to do so, my dear," replies Crane.

Vance takes her hands out her pockets, letting her coat open. Suit trousers and a white shirt, nothing fancy. A badge attached to her belt. "Will, uh, will everything be going ahead as planned?"

"Yes, yes, of course my dear, of course."

Something about her tells Nick that policing wasn't her first career choice. Maybe it's the lack of laughter lines, or the constant frown on her forehead. The policing life, regardless of the impressive ladder she's climbed, looks to have done her few favours.

Crane touches Nick's arm. "So spellbound by the taste of brandy am I, that I seem to have run dry again. Would you mind, Nicholas?"

Their chat about knowledge and wishes, for now, is at an end. Nick still has no idea how Crane helps these people. Obliging, he takes both glasses with him. The Detective Inspector watches him leave with the suspicious eye the law is trained to have. As he enters back into the club proper – the dancers more sweaty but no less energised – the woman Vance takes a seat with Crane. Whatever help Crane provides these people, like liquorice he attracts all sorts.

Shortly after Nick's return, the Detective Inspector dissolves back into the crowd and out of sight.

"Coppers, eh? In with the big leagues," says Nick.

Crane shakes his head. "Detective Inspector Vance is no more than a woman who desires my unique help. Call her an initiate, if you like."

"Help by way of knowledge that you won't yet reveal," Nick smirks.

Crane laughs. "No, young man. Not just yet."

They stay for another hour before Crane tells Nick that it's time to go. The people who came to see him have done so, and there is no use in waiting around for visitors who will not come.

"Take the day off tomorrow, Nicholas," says Crane as Nick closes the door of the Rolls-Royce. "But please do come back on Sunday. I would like to speak to you about something important."

Nick starts the engine. "Nothing bad I hope?" he asks.

"Nicholas, my boy," Crane beams, "what could there possibly be that I would need to talk to you about that could be bad?"

CHAPTER 10

It's Nick's day off. Rain falls heavily, washes away the colour of the day. The street is a grey line with grey shops and grey people. The only colour is from the umbrellas, which from a bird's eye view must look like sweets floating down a stream, colliding with one another.

Nick doesn't have an umbrella. He's never used one.

He jogs across the road. The rain has plastered his hair to his head, is dripping from the tip of his nose.

Steam drifts through vents in the shopfronts. In doorways a few people have taken shelter. Nick has ventured out today for a few reasons. One is to stop by Estelle's to see if Frank has returned. Another is to stock up on some things for the flat – including more cat food – and the last is to have a peak through the windows of various estate agents.

The quality of life has been steadily improving for Nick in the short time he's been working for Crane. He can pay bills, catching up with any that've backed up. The goblins at the bank are no longer calling him outstanding. Now that he's satiating them with gold, they're leaving him alone. He has bought some paint for the patchy areas in the flat, still yet to muster the get-up-and-go to get it done. Food is better, too. No longer is he surviving on cheap frozen food alone. He's liking the gourmet microwave meals, they're hard to fuck up, but has decided that he could do with some *real* food, which also means he'll be needing some proper pots and pans. It'll be a busy shop today. Above all this, Nick thinks it's time to find somewhere better, somewhere owned by a real landlord and not a slum kingpin who does fuck all for the wellbeing of his tenants. Nick can't wait to tell the cannonball-shaped slob he's moving out.

He has Crane to thank. Not in his stupidest dreams did he imagine working for an eccentric old geezer would bring in this much cash.

Already he has much to spare, happy to take it easy for the time being. Nick hates the fact he has someone to thank for anything, but if it has to be anyone, Crane isn't so bad. There may even be a friendship on the cards here, and for once that doesn't repel him.

Weaving in and out of the umbrellas, Nick arrives at Cobble Road. Estelle's looks no different, except that the windows have become translucent with unchecked grime. Nick knocks, calls Frank, knocks again. He isn't optimistic.

Nothing.

Again.

Maybe Frank had a change of heart overnight, took all of his money from the unlicensed boxing game and any other deals he was involved in and ran away. Frank used to talk about Marbella, how it would be nice to retire there, where the only familiar face belongs to the sun.

It makes Nick smile just to speculate. If that is what's happened, then all the best to him.

Nick cuts through an alleyway. Bin bags stretched to breaking point are piled up next to wheelie bins. Empty polystyrene food containers have been flattened, vomit is being diluted by the rain. Water plops from clogged guttering and a dog barks from inside one of the buildings.

At the other end of the alleyway, a man holding a dripping black umbrella turns in and strolls towards Nick, his face hidden beneath his brolly.

Nick stops. Instinct sets off the alarm bells in his muscles. The umbrella man keeps coming. Nick looks behind himself and sees three other men without umbrellas advancing on him.

The man with the umbrella relaxes it against his shoulder, revealing himself. "Nick, Nick, Nick. What a total and utter surprise."

Close behind, the three men come to a halt. Each one of them has a pinched, ugly face suited for pool hall hustles and crowbar negotiations. They all wear suits with thick raincoats.

Fuck sake, Nick thinks.

"Walter," he says. "This *is* a surprise."

Walter George spins the umbrella in his grip. Drops of rain fling from it like sparks from a Catherine wheel.

"Oh, but it isn't, is it? Always expect the unexpected, Nick. My brother has already spoken to you."

"Yeah, he has, and I told him the same thing I'll tell you." Nick's hands are in his pockets. He clenches his fists. This situation is about as volatile as it gets. "Does he know you're here?"

"He knows I'm about," Walter grins.

"That's a no, then."

"You think my brother controls me?"

Nick replies, "Anyone who knows you does."

Walter bites, "He isn't as in control as he thinks."

Walter takes a few more steps forward, toying with each one, like he's at the start of a musical number just getting off the ground. He has a square jaw, a moustache that's been waxed into two curled points. He's much thinner than Harvey. His suit fits perfectly over a wiry, lightweight frame.

"Harvey expressed that you owe us our favour, right, Nick?" asks Walter.

"And I expressed I'm not interested." Nick's body is tight, spring-loaded.

"So I heard. You know- "

"It's rude to not return a favour. Yeah, I know," Nick says. "Paint me rude, then."

Walter George is the younger brother by a year. Tenfold more fiery than Harvey, doesn't have the same patience. He often, in Nick's experience, mirrors things his brother says.

Walter chuckles, "I'm afraid it doesn't quite work that way." He brings the umbrella down, shakes it before closing it up. It takes that amount of time for the rain to soak his head, though his excessively gelled back hair is unaffected. "And I'm all out of paint."

Nick shrugs, "You here to teach me a lesson, Walt?"

Anger flashes in Walter George's eyes. Nobody calls him Walt. He hates the name and hates whoever uses it. Neither of the Georges like their names shortened, a fact that many poor sods have learnt the hard way.

Walter replies, "You might've been old school pals with my brother once, but don't for one second think you can pull the same bollocks with me. I can't see why you won't help us after what we did. You were so promising, such a bright prospect. Coulda won titles, you coulda. Worried about your future- "

Nick interrupts, "I don't need the backstory."

"-came to us, your friends, and we solved that little problem for you, didn't we? Solved it good." He finished by cracking his knuckles.

"I don't remember coming to you," Nick says.

"You did, though. In the end."

"You ruined my life," Nick snaps. "I didn't want anybody *killed.*"

Walter snorts laughter. "Yeah you did."

"Fuck you, Walt."

"Look, Nick. I'm not here to try and convince you to see our way of things. We're past that."

"You and Harvey? Or just you?"

He can't see Harvey ordering a beating on him. Not yet.

Nick removes his hands from his pockets. His fists are tightly balled into fists. He won't bow to the Georges so they'll fuck him up for it. Harvey definitely doesn't know, and will more than likely give his younger brother a beasting for it, but by then Walter will have filled his boots and have a wet flannel over his bloody knuckles.

Walter is definitely going to be Harvey's undoing.

Tutting when he sees Nick's fists, Walter says, "Oh Nick. You didn't think I'd fight fair, did ya? You and I, we're a little too evenly matched. If we were to go toe-to-toe, I'd have my boys lay down bets. It could go either way…if I had only one arm." The fuckers laugh at that.

Nick growls, "So take a chance."

Walter laughs. "I don't take chances."

The umbrella comes up and whacks Nick in the knee. He stumbles, is grabbed by the three behind. Kicking up water, they drag him to the side and hold him against the wall. One of them gets a gut punch in, winding Nick. Water running down the bricks trickles into his collar, wetting his neck. Walter checks the coast is clear. He gets face to face with Nick and holds him by the chin. Abstract, quietly lunatic eyes burn in Walter's sockets.

"Now, Nick," says Walter, "I'm going to give you a thrashing."

Nick throws his head forward. It connects with a white flash against the bridge of Walter's nose, making the gangster cry out. Blood runs from his nostrils in an instant. Another henchman puts a sledgehammer of an elbow to Nick's jaw.

After Walter has recovered, grinning furiously, he says, "I should fuckin' kill you for that! I should! You know I can, Nick!"

Nick spits, "Just fucking do it then, Walt!"

Walter chuckles, "You're mad." He spits blood, rain washes it away. "My nose'll never look the same again. You know, Nick, one of my little birdies has informed me that your ribs have been giving you a bitta jip recently. Is it...here?"

Walter presses Nick's side. At first it doesn't hurt, then, as Walter increases pressure the pain ignites. Nick cries out, gritting his teeth against the agony. Walter smiles.

"Sorry Nick," Walter says. "I'll try to leave out that area. I can't make any promises though."

Nick tries to struggle free. Walter's boys have got him well and truly pinned to the bricks.

Grabbing Nick again by the chin, Walter whispers with mock emotion, "D'you still think about it, Nick? Do you still think about what you made happen? He was only young, Nick, just a *boy*."

Nick hangs his head, out of breath. Water drips from his hair. "Just gimme the fucking thrashing" – he looks up – "*Walt*."

So, Walter gives Nick the thrashing. It goes on for minutes, each one feels close to an hour. Just when he believes he can't be winded anymore, Walter proves that belief wrong with another hard punch to the stomach. Just when he thinks he'll pass out, Walter slaps him conscious. When it's over, Nick is a crumpled pile in a puddle, has his knees pulled close to his stomach, one hand over his head, the other on his chest. Rivulets of blood drain away from him, running into a manhole.

"I'll be seeing you again, Nick. Maybe you'll give our proposal some more thought?" Walter reopens his umbrella, crooked nose leaking blood. "In the meantime, keep an eye on that rib. You can't be too careful."

Nick attempts to tell Walter to go fuck himself, but the words fail to rise. His bottom lip is swollen, right eye blackened. Walter and his henchmen walk away, becoming a hazy image behind the curtain of rainfall.

Every inch of Nick's body hurts. There'll be no one along to see if he's all right, that sort of thing doesn't happen here, and thank God. Nick doesn't want to deal with a good Samaritan and their worries, he just wants to regain himself and go home.

He gets himself against the wall, only to find that he has sat in the watered down puddle of vomit.

"Fuck you," he is finally able to say.

CHAPTER 11

The damage isn't as bad as Nick had expected it to be. Looking in the mirror, he can see throbbing knots beneath his skin, scratches that will probably become scars. The cut in his lip has allowed blood to spill overnight – there's a sticky red stain on his pillow – and deflate the swelling. His eyes are the worst, still puffy and bruised. Panda eyes. His body aches, especially his ribs. At least it doesn't feel like anything is broken.

Nick gets dressed, swallows a few painkillers with water, leaves a dish of cat food outside and heads to Crane's. The black cat has gotten used to food being left for it. Nick has found himself – annoyingly – softening to the feline.

On the walk, Nick looks over his shoulder more than once. It's highly unlikely Walter will make another move against him so soon as the day after, but Walter is not as predictable as his brother. Next time, Nick will make sure he's better prepared. If Walter George wants to play it dodgy, then there are ways to level the playing field.

When Nick enters the warm building, Apollo is wrapping packages at the front desk. Whatever pulp novel he's reading right now is open and turned face down on the counter. Nick says good morning, gets nothing in return except for a sly smile when Apollo sees his face.

Funny, really. Nick didn't know Apollo knew how to smile.

Crane stands as soon as Nick enters the office, whips off his reading glasses.

"My goodness! What on earth happened to *you*?"

"It's nothing." Nick takes off his coat with some difficulty and hangs it on a standing hanger that looks like a little bit of magic would bring it to life.

"*Nothing* is nothing, Nicholas. Let me take a look at you." Crane tosses his spectacles on the desk.

"Really, it's nothing I can't handle, I'd just like to forget about it, okay?" Nick sits, holding his side again.

"It might be easy for you to forget it, but *you* do not have to *look* at you." Crane stares with concern.

Nick smiles humourlessly, "Well, I'm afraid you'll have to try your best."

"You are upset, any fool can see that. Can I offer you a nip of something strong? Works better than any painkiller you are likely to have already ingested."

"I'm fine," Nick sighs. "Thanks."

Crane tightens his lips, rubs his cracked hands together. He examines Nick. The grandfather clock ticks metronomically.

"We can do this another day, if you would prefer?" Crane offers.

Nick says, "No. Today is fine."

Carefully, contemplating whether to bring it up or not, Crane says, "Does this have anything to do with your connection to the George brothers?"

Nick's eyes widen. He gawks at Crane. "How d'you know about the Georges?"

"An old man I may be, *young* man, but I am not naïve to the world of crime, and I may know a little more than you think I do. You should expect it by now, I make a point of knowing the world around me."

Nick replies, "I'm not moonlighting as a crook, if that's what you're worried about."

"It concerns me not. One look at your face tells me there is no ongoing love. I quite believe you. However, I do not believe that is the way the brothers George see it."

"You'd be right there." Nick grimaces as a shot of pain charges across his eye. "How much do you know?"

"I know dribs and drabs. I do not know what you did for them or vice versa, I only know that you had dealings with them and they are eager to see those dealings repaid."

"That all you know?"

"I never was a scout, but I shall swear on their honour."

"And how did you find out?" asks Nick, knowing that any layman could do minimal digging and find a clump of the shit he has tried to bury.

Crane answers, "I told you I was interested in everything, Nicholas. There are a few who are close to me that act as extra eyes and ears, the pickers of the grapes from the vine, if you will."

"People you've helped?"

Crane nods. "People I have helped. It is strictly so that I might know who is around me better. I hope I have not offended you, or that you feel intruded upon?"

"Nah," Nick rubs his swollen eyes lightly, "don't worry yourself. Just caught me off guard is all." Does Crane know more? Dig up one turd, you're likely to find another.

Crane smiles. "I never worry myself."

Nick smiles, too. It hurts.

"You do look awful, Nicholas. Are you sure I cannot do anything? Perhaps I could ask Apollo to seek an audience with the George brothers and I could have a word?"

"No," Nick barks, then looks away. "I'm sorry. But no. Thank you. I'll deal with this myself. I don't want anyone else getting mixed up with them."

"You flatter me, but I really think that- "

"Ulysses," Nick stresses.

He can't let Crane involve himself. The Georges will take the old geezer to the cleaners.

"I might have some sway," Crane suggests, adjusting one of his desk trinkets.

Nick clears his throat, repositioning himself in the chair, wincing. "I *do* have some sway. Me and the older brother, we used to be friends. Please, leave it with me."

Crane exhales helplessly. "As you wish," he says. "But on one condition."

"Yeah?"

"Let me pour you something. Trust me, the edge will be blunted."

"I don't drink."

"This is not drinking," Crane wobbles up, goes to a small cabinet to the left of the desk. He gets down on one knee that cracks as he bends it, though he refuses to acknowledge it. Nick feels that he should offer to do it himself, yet his aches and pains dissuade him from the task. Crane goes on, "It does not count as drinking if it is being applied for medicinal purposes. Not in my book anyway, and of those I have many, medicinal or otherwise."

Nick can hear bottles being clinked around in the cabinet. Before long Crane pops two crystal tumblers on top of the cabinet along with a bizarre shaped bottle, a sort of stretched teardrop, of amber liquid. At the tip is crumbling purple wax.

As Crane pours the drinks, Nick says, "You having one, too?"

"You know, Nicholas, I feel a little woozy myself this morning."

Although Nick can only see the back of Crane's head – moles beneath the wisps of hair seen as if through tracing paper – he can imagine the grin on his face being coaxed out by the glugging of the bottle.

Crane hands Nick the glass. "Only sip, and space them out."

Nick swishes it around before taking the tiniest of tastes. It burns instantly, stings his cut, sets his tongue on fire and posts a hot stream down his throat where it sits in his belly, releasing a bomb of warmth. At first it's unpleasant, then after a few seconds it isn't. Crane watches him with great interest.

Nick coughs. "It's good."

Crane lifts his glass, "I know it is," and takes a sip of his own. He smacks his lips after he swallows.

Nick goes to take another swig.

"Ah, ah, ah." Crane stops him. "Not so soon. Let it do its job for a while."

Nick sets the glass down on Crane's desk. With a pained smile, Crane grabs a placemat from a drawer. slides it under Nick's tumbler.

Motioning at the desk, Nick asks, "What *is* all this stuff?"

"Just bits and bobs that have found their way into my possession over the years. Gifts, some of them. I have a penchant for these things." Crane picks up a glass ball with a praying mantis sealed inside, cradling it in his fingertips. Through the curved glass Nick can see Crane's distorted face. "They all have or had significant meanings to peoples or a person. Most of them are religious. I like to have them around to remind me that our beliefs are only true so far as we believe in them."

"Doesn't that mean that nothing's true? That everything is in some way a lie?" from Nick.

Crane is amused by the observation. "You are getting the hang on these debates."

"That bug ball religious?"

Crane rotates the glass sphere. "Paperweight."

"What do *you* believe?" Nick continues, looking around the mantis.

"I believe in a bit of everything. I have to." Crane puts down the ball, it rolls to its spot, landing the mantis upright. "We can learn more of everything if we *accept* everything."

"Knowledge?" Nick taps his head.

"Knowledge," agrees Crane. "Take another sip."

Nick does so without question. This time the alcohol doesn't hit like acid.

Crane indicates with a nod behind Nick. "Do you see that, Nicholas?"

Nick turns. All he sees is a wall plastered with photographs with one gap in the middle.

"See what?"

"Precisely," Crane winks. "There is an empty space there for the next picture. That is why I wanted to see you. Soon, I shall be having my next annual meeting, and I think you may be ready to accompany me. Should you be interested."

"I see," says Nick. "Look, I don't wanna sign up for anything- "

"You are not expected to. You would be there strictly as an attendee. My guest."

"Can you tell me more about it?" The last thing Nick wants to do is attend an antiquity swap meet full of boring chatter and orange squash.

"We like to remain covert."

"You're like a...what? Secret society?" Nick smirks.

"I would not use that term myself," Crane answers. "Sounds awfully dramatic, do you not think?"

"I s'pose. You have a name or anything?"

"We do not. A name betrays secrecy. We do, however, have a symbol that represents us. I believe you may have already espied it once already."

Crane slides his hand across the desk towards Nick. When he removes it, Nick sees the bronze circle brooch slashed with a diagonal line with a small triangle pointing down above it. The tip of the triangle glints in the lamplight. Crane swills a sip of alcohol in his mouth, stands and shuffles around the desk, his cane knocking rhythmically. His waistcoat hangs loose, the pocket watch absent.

Nick can't make sense of the bad logo in front of him. "What does it mean?"

"It is a representation of the world," Crane begins, sitting on the edge of the desk, switching to storyteller mode, "and the divide in it. The divide between those who seek better and those who do not. The top piece, the triangle, is us. Those who – above the rest of the world whilst still being a part of it – search out enlightenment. A tiny slither of life."

Enlightenment? Sounds churchy. Having their own symbol...maybe it'll be more than an antiques deal day.

"I don't get that right away," Nick says.

Crane waves his hand dismissively, jests, "It is an old design. We stuck with it."

"If it ain't broke don't fix it."

"It is to be an extra special meeting for our group. If all goes as planned, it should be rather spectacular. Something not to be missed."

Nick leans away from the brooch. "This thing you do, I've got no idea what it is. I'd be a stranger. Surely you don't need a bodyguard at your own event?"

Nick wants Crane to rescind the invitation. He likes the geezer fine, but taking part in poncy masquerade parties or whatever it is the eccentrics do is not his idea of a good evening, or a worthwhile money maker.

Crane says, "The truth is, Nicholas, that in the short time you have been working for me I have become rather fond of you. You may feel differently, but I consider you a friend. Maybe the only friend I have had in a while. You talk to me, you ask questions and answer them. I thrive on the asking of questions, they show a person's character. You have become someone I highly anticipate sharing a discussion with. Even now, you get my words flowing."

And there it is. The *other* f-word. Used *twice*. Nick has been enjoying his time with Crane, that can't be disputed, and on occasion he has looked forward to it, but he has made a point of distancing himself from that bloody f-word. Having friends just leaves you vulnerable, and in turn it leaves *them* vulnerable, in turn opening the door wide open for betrayals. It's too much responsibility, a responsibility Nick would rather not endure. *Fuck sake*, he thinks.

Crane moves in front of Nick. Behind him, surrounding the drinks cabinet, are hanging tribal masks, all different lengths and widths. A few sport straw hairdos.

"Do you want me there?" asks Nick. It's hopeless to expect a no.

"I do Nicholas, I do. Only, I ask you with some trepidation. An outsider, someone who is not even an initiate, has never witnessed what we do. Our customs could be considered preternatural."

"Which means?"

"Strange, for lack of a better word. I just want you to be prepared for that. Keep your mind open, as I know you can, and see what you see. You may have something to gain from it."

"If I come," Nick asserts.

"Yes," Crane nods. "If you come. I may as well tell you now that there is a price for admittance."

Nick cocks an eyebrow. "A fee?"

"It is not a monetary price."

"Then what kind?"

Crane crosses his legs, laces his hands together over his knee. "If I tell you the price, I will have to take that as your acceptance."

Nick picks up his tumbler. "Another sip?"

Crane says he can. Now the alcohol is nothing but pleasant. The warmth spreads over his body immediately and Nicks thinks that, if it's just this stuff, maybe he can allow a drink from time to time.

"What's the price?" he asks.

"I want you to tell me one of your wishes," Crane replies, deadpan.

Nick laughs. "I don't believe in wishes."

"Ever the cynic," Crane laughs with him. "But I have told you now, Nicholas. Believe in what you do or do not believe, but I would like my payment of one wish."

There are many things that Nick would like to change in his life. He wouldn't ever refer to his wants as wishes. Wishing was for upon a star. The stars had gone out for Nick years ago. He thinks, trying to produce an answer that Crane will be satisfied with. If the answer isn't up to snuff, Crane will demand another.

"I'd like to go back," he says.

"You would like to be young again?"

Nick shakes his head. "No. I would like to do things differently."

"Ah. You would like to rewrite some wrongs?" says Crane.

Nick nods. "Yeah. I think that's the best way to put it."

"In other words, you seek redemption."

"Redemption?"

"To clear yourself of sin. To retake possession of what we hold most dear. Your soul."

Nick scoffs, "I know what redemption means."

"Then…if it is true…" Crane leans forward. His face blurs between the ages he has been and will be. It is sudden, not long enough to truly register. "*Wish it.*"

"I'm sorry?" Nick says with derision.

"*Wish it*, Nicholas."

The office begins to change. Stretching walls creak. Floorboards warp, knots sprout from the grain. The ticking of the grandfather clock becomes a drip at the end of a tunnel, sound morphing as if a record is slowing down. A crystal windchime. The masks are alive. Each socket is filled now with flesh, human eyes peering out, watching, listening for the answer. No longer masks but shrunken heads, enlarged heads, alien heads. They are crying.

The words begin to climb from Nick's throat, against his will, the alcohol throwing them out.

"I…I…w…wish."

It all stops. The office back to normal. Crane perched on the desk with a smile on his face.

"Perfect," says Crane and drops his legs to the floor.

Nick gawks around the office, looking for any other abnormalities. There are none. He looks at the empty tumbler and sets it down on the table, not remembering finishing it. He blames the hallucination on the alcohol.

Crane hobbles back to his seat. "Is everything okay, Nicholas?"

"Yeah," says Nick. "Just, uh, that stuff is a little strong, I think."

"It is a touch too much, perhaps," Crane chortles. "I apologise for that." He sits, the leather suspires. "My own blend. Gets in your head if you are new to it."

Understatement. "So what now?" from Nick. "You planning on granting my wish?"

Crane replaces his reading glasses. "In time," he answers, "I just might. *Or.* I might not. But you have paid, and that is enough."

Nick is still shaken by the way the office changed and seemed to almost come alive. He feels a trickle of cold sweat run from his armpit.

"Bit of an odd way to bring someone into the fold," he says.

"Oh, Nicholas," Crane replies. "You are not in the fold. To you the fold does not exist, and mayhap is not even a thing. But did I not warn you? Our customs may come across to you as strange. That was just the first."

Nick breaths deep, exhales, "So when's the gig?"

"The gig?" Crane tips his chin, looks at Nick through the squashed lenses of his glasses.

"Your meeting."

"Ah, yes. Not until this weekend. And young man? Please leave that suit of yours in the wash basket. Dress comfortably. That suit did not become you and is not practical for your position."

"Couldn't agree more." Nick manages a smile.

Crane smiles back. "Now. I believe Apollo has some packages wrapped up that need delivering. I am sorry to usher you out, but I am rather busy today and need to catch up on my letters."

Nick gets up. He expects to feel wobbly on his feet but experiences no such sensation. He gives the masks one last glance. Their faces are nothing but empty holes in carved wood. As he opens the door, he turns back to Crane.

"Ulysses?"

Crane mumbles, his attentions fixed on his parchment paper.

Nick asks, "What do *you* wish for?"

The paper ruffles as Crane lets it roll itself up. He looks up, setting his sight on nothing in particular.

"Acceptance," he says.

"Acceptance from who?" Nick responds.

Now Crane focuses on Nick. "From the *better*. Through acceptance, I may finally begin to repent for my past yet necessary transgressions. Through acceptance, my scars will not only mean something, but start the process of healing. Through acceptance, I shall finally rise to the status destined for me ever since I was a young boy. Through acceptance...I shall be just."

Dramatic, Nick thinks. "What do you need to repent for?"

Crane ponders. "We have all had a spot of blood on our hands." He adds with a wink. "In some fashion."

Nick laughs inwardly. It's exactly the kind of answer he expected from Crane's thin lips. "And what is this...*better?*"

Crane taps his desk with four fingers. "Something yet beyond your understanding. Stay cynical, and then see." After a pause, he changes the subject. "I must say, you are already looking healthier."

Nick catches his reflection in the grandfather clock's face. Crane is right, the bruising has retreated.

"Did I not tell you a nip of something strong would be good for you?" Crane asks with delight.

Nick thinks he'll ask to take some home, then remembers all too vividly the masks and their accusing gazes.

The package's delivery is uneventful. It isn't until the following Saturday that Nick attends the meeting of Crane's secret society.

CHAPTER 12

Overlapping sketches adorn the cell walls, the sickly green now a black and white mosaic. Those that couldn't hold their position have slipped to the floor.

A crisp pile of pencil shavings is blown under the bed like autumn leaves as a new sketch floats to the ground. Katy is on the mattress, hunched over her fifth notepad. She knows it's her fifth because she has kept the ring bindings from each one. In an attempt to make things more comfortable, she has rucked up the covers of the bed, just like at home, a teenage habit that Mum goes mad over. "Are you a hamster?" she would've said. It's a poor substitute for home, but when life gives you lemons, mess up your bed.

Her hand keeps cramping. She's been drawing for what has to be forever. Between her thumb and index is a coarse heap of yellowed blisters. They have become a project, something to focus on, to see how bad they can get before they erupt.

Drawing is one of three things Katy has in the cell. The second thing is songs. For a while she talked to herself, stopping when she remembered a story she'd read about a man in a mental institution who talked to himself to hold off the crazies. The only problem being that the only reason the man was crazy was *because* he talked to himself. But songs? There is nothing crazy about them. Songs are treasure chests of times and places.

The third thing she has is the woman.

The woman is the only person who speaks to her. She's the one who has supplied the notepads, each time making it sound like their own little secret. So, too, did the woman supply Katy with a pencil sharpener. That almost didn't happen. The woman was scared that Katy might try something with the razor. What could she do with a little razor like that?

Katy knows if it's the woman on the other side of the door because, if it isn't her, the slat is pulled open, the tray of food slid in and the slat yanked closed. The woman always begins by saying hello. They have built a trust, in a sense, though the woman still refuses to tell Katy where she is or why.

Katy hums a song she knows Mum likes. A knock at the door scares her into standing off the mattress. The pencil sharpener shatters under her shoe.

No one has ever knocked before.

"Y…Yes?" she says. Her hands go straight to her unravelled ponytail, kneading it.

The clunk of a bolt being opened, then the door moans open, sounds like a tuba. The drawings on the wall flutter in the breeze, one of them swishes to the floor. Katy tells herself to be brave, wishing that someone could do it instead. Her stomach has turned into a helium balloon.

A woman stands with her hands behind her back in the doorway. Behind her are varnished dark wood panels.

Katy can feel her bladder tremble. There is something terrifying about this woman, a headmistress gone bad. "Is…it time to…eat?"

The woman takes a step forward. Her face is powdered, severe, black hair scraped back into a tight bun that gives her a homemade facelift. She isn't the prettier for it. Only when she speaks does Katy realise who she is.

"No, my dear. It isn't."

The woman guides Katy down a long corridor. Her shoes are hard, pounding on the floor. Under her own foot, Katy feels something lodged in her rubber sole. A stone?

"Where're we going?" she asks.

"Not now," the woman says.

Her voice is more rough than it was when the door was between them. Not at all what Katy had imagined. She had drawn a few sketches of what she guessed the woman looked like (most of them grandmotherly) and not a single one of them resembled the woman marching her up the corridor now.

They go into a room that could be a stripped back school locker room, without all the stickers and amateur art. Against one of the walls is a wooden gym bench with a towel and some folded clothes. The sound of running water comes from a nearby closed door.

"You have to clean yourself up," the woman says.

Katy turns. The woman's hands are now clasped at her front, holding an invisible birch cane. "What about my drawings?" Katy feels stupid bringing them up.

Moments ago she would have bargained anything to be free from the cell, now she's acutely aware that she has left her safe zone. It's where Mum and Dad are, her animals and the things she loves, and where the version of the woman was a better one than the arched eyebrows madam she has here.

The woman attempts a smile. Cracks appear in the powder around her mouth. "I wouldn't worry about those, Katy Robbins. You won't be needing them anymore. Now please, clean yourself up." She gestures to the closed door.

Knees knocking, Katy sits down on the bench, gazes around the locker room.

"It's important that you make yourself presentable," says the woman. "The shower is hot, we have supplied you soap and shampoo and any other items that a young woman needs. You have thirty minutes, so I suggest that you enjoy your time and make a good job of yourself. I'll be checking behind those ears, my dear."

Realising she'll be alone for a whole half hour, Katy can't help but look in all corners of the room for some opportunity of escape. All she'll have to do is get on the street and scream and scream. Someone is sure to notice her, then the police could come and take her home. Thinking about Mum and Dad and how they must be handling her kidnap is…

Her kidnap.

Only Katy knows it's kidnap. As far as her parents and teachers could tell, she's just gone missing, or…or is dead. How long will they search before believing the worst? Kidnap might never have come into their minds. What if they were looking in all the wrong places? What if…

No. Mum and Dad know her. They know something must be wrong. Their daughter is smart, wouldn't get herself lost, would never slip in the stream or go to see puppies in a stranger's van. She has to trust they're doing all they can.

"It's no use, my dear," the woman interrupts her thoughts. "There is nowhere you can go. I would take this privacy and use it well rather than hoping hopeless hopes."

"Can you…tell me anything?" Katy asks.

With prim steps the woman goes to the shower room door and opens it. Steam billows around her feet.

Adapting an almost musical tone, the woman replies, "Too many questions Katy Robbins," then walks away from the shower.

As the woman crosses in front of her, Katy mumbles, "You seemed nicer when I didn't know what you looked like."

The woman swivels around as if hurt. "My dear, I *am* nice. I am your friend. I just want you to look your best, and I aim to see it done. When you finish washing you can slip on the dress I've folded for you."

Underneath the towel next to Katy is the dress. It's grey.

Katy says, "Can you at least tell me what day it is? Please?"

The woman turns the question over in her head. It's hard to work out what she's feeling because her tugged-tight face struggles to form expressions. Finally she relents.

"It is Saturday, my dear. Now I won't ask you again. Into the shower with you."

The woman exits the room, closes the door behind her. Before the lock turns Katy is up on her feet. She is looking for anything to take advantage of. A narrow window, drainage system, *anything*. But there's nothing.

She hasn't really left her cell, it seems, only been brought to an extension of it.

She gives up, sits back down. She gives the bench a punch that bursts one of her blisters. The clear fluid drips down her hand, more relief than pain. With at least a hot shower on the cards, she resigns to do as she's told. Katy brings up her right foot, sees something glint in the sole of her shoe as she starts to untie the laces.

This could be useful, she thinks.

CHAPTER 13

Saturday night.

The last of the day sinks behind a pointed horizon, the city impatiently lights up for another evening, a manmade mirror of the sky it can't see.

Nick walks on a street forgotten by the bin men. Black refuse sacks fat with waste line the pavement. In his boot Nick has sheathed a hunting knife, purchased from an army surplus store run by a bloke who was big in the belly but not on questions. The knife is insurance should Walter bump into him again, accidentally on purpose. Using it would be a last resort, having it is a comfort.

In minutes, he rounds the corner onto Crane's street. Gleaming cars are parked along the roadside, as well as a few rustier ones with not quite enough air in the tyres. Apollo fills the doorway, wearing a suit struggling to keep his bulk contained.

"Not too late I hope," says Nick.

He rubs his hands together because that's what you do when you want the big fuck to move so you can get out of the cold.

Apollo says, "Hasn't started yet."

His vocal cords have been detuned to a deep bass.

Reacting with a smile, Nick says, "He speaks again."

Apollo turns his back on Nick and clomps into the building.

"No he doesn't," Nick shakes his head, follows Apollo inside.

Apollo hauls open a trapdoor that was hidden under the Afghan rug. It must be heavy given the way the big fuck grunts. Big Fuck, that's a name that might stick. Nick peers down, concrete stairs descend into a brick tunnel, around a bend into what must be a cellar. Add some candelabras and you'd have a dungeon. Apollo gives Nick a nudge too close to a push, pressuring him to go down. Clearing the pique from his throat, Nick enters. Apollo shadows, letting the trapdoor slam itself shut. It's total darkness. Nick ducks to avoid scuffing his head on the low ceiling.

"Keep going," Apollo's deep voice bounces.

"Like there's anywhere else to go." Nick presses his hand against the rough bricks, feeling his way down.

At the bottom is a devil's door, its pope's hat shape defined by a border of light bleeding through from the other side.

Apollo grunts, "Open it."

Nick strokes the wood until he touches a circular handle. It's stiff, he has to twist the wrought iron a handful of times before he hears the latch clink. The door judders open an inch, the gap letting through warm air. He helps it, on groaning hinges, the rest of the way.

After being in the gloom of the stairwell, the light that meets his eyes makes him squint. Nick blinks away the sudden change and can scarcely believe what he sees.

What he thought would be a dungeon turns out to be a chapel. That it's possible underground doesn't make sense. Orchestral music serenades from mounted speakers at all four corners. Hanging along the walls are red drapes, bunching on the floor in uniform rolls. On every one is a gold print of Crane's society logo, that peculiar symbol. A carved lectern stands front and centre on a stage at the back of the chapel. To either side of the room are five pews, leaving an aisle in the middle. Everything is lit by both electric and candlelight. There's a buffet table at the back, all the generic finger foods are present, still wrapped in cling film.

Many guests are gathered in chatty knots that follow the same rules as high school cliques: If you ain't in, you're out. Nick is happy to remain out.

Apollo latches the devil's door shut. "Shoe's off."

Pushed up to the cream coloured walls are ranks of shoes. Highly polished Oxfords, short heels, high heels, muddy boots, plimsols. He isn't too keen to join his trainers with them. Apollo has already stridden away to the back of the chapel, disappearing behind the stage, so isn't around to enforce the rule.

Nick sees a couple of faces he recognises from The Cross, including the detective. She's on her own, clutching an untouched drink close to her chest, sauntering between the pews and occasionally admiring the beams above. Nick remembers her name. Vance. Detective Inspector Vance. Apparently, she only has the one outfit.

Nick makes no attempts to mingle with the different sects. He blends into the cracks between them, taking stock and hearing plenty. They are so enthralled in their own bullshit conversations that they don't notice him. They have each other tricked well, these cliques, believing that they all care about what each other has to say and that it isn't just a pissing contest about who has what, who donated how much, who went on a holiday to this place, who's hit big in the stock market. Even the dropout cliques with their staged liberal views are only trying to one up each other, only truly joining forces when they talk shit about their obviously richer counterparts. It hasn't been five minutes, and Nick is sick of the façade already. People are all the same. However he's helped these individuals, Crane hasn't managed to unite them.

But that's the thing with people. Wherever you go, they herd into their groups. They sniff each other out like bloodhounds and tear up the rabbit if it gets too close.

Nick judges that it's going to be a long night.

Next to the buffet are hot drinks facilities. He pours himself a cup of coffee from the dispenser. It looks like a silo, not one water spot to be found. He takes the coffee – black with one – and himself away from the food. Buffet tables turn into a hub when the food is available, Nick doesn't want to be forced into pointless conversation he isn't in the mood for. The devil's door becomes his refuge spot, not too close to the shoe display, which now that he looks at it, is also an exhibit of social groups.

The orchestral music fades, a new track starts. A solemn piece.

A person leans against the wall next to Nick. "Too good to take your shoes off, huh?"

Nick didn't see the guy when he came in. It's the mullet man from Murray's. Simon, Master of Nerve Annoyance. Nick glances down at Simon's feet, a big toe with a nail that's too thick says hello through a hole in his sock. Nick tries to ignore him but Simon makes it impossible.

"Gotta take 'em off so you don't drag in dirt or fag ends or gum or shit."

Nick gives a non-committal nod.

"Not gonna talk to me? That's fine. I can talk. I had no idea you were in with the Master."

Nick asks with some puzzlement, "Crane?"

"That's what I said," Simon responds. "The Master."

"Not like you are," Nick says.

"There's only one way you can be in," Simon laughs.

Nick avoids eye contact. "Would you mind leaving me alone?"

"A little. No one else'll talk to me. Oo!"

Simon dashes to the buffet table, starts fumbling with a tray covered with foil.

"Christ," Nick sighs. This is all he needs.

"You say someth'n?" Simon drops back against the wall, flakes from the sausage rolls he's brought back are spilling to the cream carpet.

"Not a word."

Simon tosses a whole roll into his mouth. "Your stalker with us tonight?"

Nick looks at Simon but wishes he didn't. Simon is managing a smile as he churns the pastry around in his mouth, debris dropping out that he is either oblivious to or never learned to care about. He's wearing a sleeveless denim jacket that almost takes the focus away from his ill-considered hairstyle.

Nick clenches his jaw. "You tell me."

Simon shrugs, "Can't see." In goes the second sausage roll.

"Crane's helping *you* is he?" Nick asks with some malice. He can usually get on with most fools, but something about Simon rubs him the wrong way. In his unlicensed career, Nick has managed to stay civil with Scottish bull Cannonball Aron, denied many pints offered to him by Ricky Sticky McVitty, and actually shared a laugh or two with the comically named Punch 'Em Bob after a bare knuckle fight in an unheated barn which the cows were still using. All of these crazy men he could fake a friendship with, but not Simon and his moronic mullet. "What's he helping you with?" Nick continues. "Stopping you from seeing things that aren't there?"

But the Figure *had* been there that night, and this nutcase *had* seen it. Simon could've been bullshitting, gotten lucky, which is what Nick has put it down to. What would it mean if the Figure existed beyond the boundaries of his own head?

Simon stops chewing. With a lump packed in his cheeks he says, "Oh, no. Master *gave* me the sight."

The music stops abruptly, heads turn like meerkats. New music plays louder, a fanfare of sorts.

"He's here," Simon wipes his mouth and leaves the wall.

All of the meerkats put aside their social differences and scrabble to the pews. Those more eager race to the front, where Vance has already taken a seat. Maybe that's how Crane unites these people, just by being present. Well-groomed next to dishevelled, month's-wage trousers brushing on patched-up jeans, white grins alongside gummy smiles. They natter in hushed, excited voices. Nick stays where he is. He takes a sip of coffee.

Electric bulbs dim until it's only by candlelight that the chapel is lit, the lectern brightened by extra candles. To the cheers and claps of the congregation, Crane enters through a stage door holding his hands as high as his elbows will allow him, dressed in a chequered grey suit that far outclasses any others present. A big smile smooths his cheeks and brightens his eyes, his hair expertly combed back into a wispy ponytail.

He looks older. Nick can't help thinking of those insane revival evangelists in America, with a prayer for the Lor-DA and a repent for your sin-SA!

To the swelling of his orchestral soundtrack, Crane reaches his lectern. He allows his loyal followers to express themselves a while longer before he holds up a hand, silencing the music. The clappers and cheerers shush themselves. Crane basks in the silence for a few seconds, then begins.

"Welcome, welcome, welcome. My wonderful people, welcome. It is extraordinary to see so many of you here again. You all look beautiful. I am delighted, and am unable to transcribe into words how important this meeting is. How many years has it been now? How many of us are there? And how did so many of you find your way here? A mystery I would rather not have solved for fear of destroying the magic that directs the universe's highways, bridges, tunnels, canals, rivers and all other mediums of getting to and from our fates. Though who wants to get away from it these days?"

Applause from the audience. Like children at a school assembly they compete for who gets the last clap. Nick finds the sermon – or mass, whatever these people want to call it – quite humorous, smiling as he sips his coffee.

Scanning his followers, Crane asks, "Have I ever let any of you, my people, down?"

They answer no in unison.

"Who has had a wish come true?"

More excited affirmations.

"Whose life is all the better after trusting in me?" Crane's voice rises.

Yet more acclaim. The congregation struggles to contain their buzz.

He knows how to warm up a crowd, Nick thinks. Crane should have been a public speaker.

"And who here…" Crane points to no one, lowers his voice, "has come here this evening with a wish?"

Only the first-timers whoop. Vance is one of them.

"I ask, are you prepared? Are you willing to trust me with your destinies which never would have been but will soon be?"

Cheering first-timers receive claps on the shoulders from the already blessed.

Crane leans on the lectern, making it creak. "Then you shall have what you desire. And those of you that already have it, I tell you, you shall have *more* of it."

His people voice their praise. Nick can't deny being roped into it. Whilst he doesn't believe in all this mumbo jumbo, it sure is cracking entertainment.

"Excellent. Just excellent. But first, I need to tell all of you something." Crane softens his tone but is no less quiet for it. Without a microphone his voice travels all the way across the chapel. "I have not told any of you what I am about to tell you, nor have I sent out messages to those who could not attend. I have news which may be both a sadness and a miracle the likes of which I have been waiting on for decades."

There are mumbles of confusion from the crowd. Crane's words flow from his mouth like butter and he knows how to spread them.

"Firstly," a pause, "this is to be our final gathering. Of this variety, anyway."

The audience, upset at the news, fire incoherent questions at each other and to Crane, who closes his eyes and nods appreciatively. Nick takes this opportunity to go to the coffee silo and pour himself a second.

"I know, my beautiful people, I know," Crane comforts them, "but here is the greener grass." The audience falls into silence again, there is an anticipation that Crane dines on. "I have a book."

The crowd doesn't understand, chatter rises.

"Over the decades," Crane talks over them, their cue to listen, "the things I have done for you and many more alike have been mere snippets of what is truly possible. Through the accruing of artifacts, letters, books and other such gateways to knowledge, I have only learned so much, and though it has proven powerful indeed, it has never been complete. For long years I have searched for that complete documentation, and now I have that knowledge in its entirety. After tonight, offerings shall no longer be necessary." Crane spreads his arms. "I shall finally be elevated."

The congregation stands and claps wildly, ecstatic on behalf of their leader. Candle flames flicker in response to the racket. Crane accepts his ovation, pleased that his audience has accepted his news without knowing anything about it. Nick wonders what the offerings are. Perhaps they all have to stand in a circle and write their wants on a piece of paper and send it up the chimney to Father Christmas and the Easter Bunny. Or, seeing as they're in a chapel, could be money. People worship with money.

Crane signals for his followers to sit. They oblige with smiling faces. He goes on, "I have had time with this book. It is most impressive. I can vouch," he clenches a fist, "for its capabilities. All it needs is one final offering and it shall be mine. Ours. All of its teachings, its brilliances, its talents. You too shall witness this tome and be humbled as I was by it."

Nick returns to his place at the devil's door, fresh coffee in hand. All these people, so easily manipulated. He doesn't dislike Crane for it. It's obvious Crane believes whole-heartedly in what he's spouting as well.

"But before *that*," Crane raises a bony finger, "I would like to begin the way we always do. Tonight is a night for traditions to be broken, yet we may still adhere to one."

Without further prompting the audience bow their heads. Crane begins to recite words that Nick doesn't understand. The crowd chants the words back to Crane (is it Latin?) in flat, monotone fashion.

All the candle flames flicker, just once, momentarily shifting the shadows.

When the prayer ends Crane claps his hands together. "Now," he begins, "I shall not drag this out any longer."

Anticipatory shuffling from the audience. Simon looks over his shoulder and grins at Nick as if they are friends, holds up his thumb. Nick looks away, embarrassed on behalf of all of them. *Just tell Crane it was fun when it's over*, he thinks.

Crane gazes upon his congregation, his *lambs*. No longer smiling, his cheeks sink into his mouth, making him appear older than ever. "I give to you," he near whispers, "the book."

Apollo enters onto the stage. He's holding something respectfully in both hands, his fingertips doing the work. There's a group gasp from the audience.

Nick recognises the package Apollo is holding, it's the one he collected from the rhyming junkie, still in the linen. Immediately, his stomach turns over. The sensation of sickness floods his gut, stronger than the first time.

Apollo rests the package on the lectern, to which Crane thanks him with a courteous nod. Unprompted, Apollo exits.

Crane grabs either side of the lectern, mantling the package. "Can you *feel* it?" he asks his flock. "Can you *feel* it in the pit of your stomach? Can you feel your legs shudder, your insides squirm and your bile bubble?"

They groan, some of them gag. Instead of disgust, there is joy in their mannerisms. Nick can feel it, alright. He downs his coffee, hoping it'll cancel out the queasiness. It fails. Crane unwraps the package, an excited glint in his eye. When the linen flops open, a book bound in thick leather is revealed. Nick's nausea rises, he swallows it down.

Stroking the hefty spine, Crane speaks as if to the book itself. "I have been patient. Let us not wait any longer. Let us begin with the proceedings." He looks up. "Those of you who are here for the first time, you know what is expected of you. Very soon you shall repeat the wishes you spoke to me. You shall be the last of an old tradition before all of us here, and those who are not, become much greater than what we ever thought possible."

Vance stands first, steps onto the stage. Her badge is attached to her hip for everyone to see, though they do not appear to be alarmed by a police officer in their midst. Three more accompany her. A fat man in a two-piece whose chins look ready to burst, a woman who has forgotten at some crossroads in her life that toothbrushes exist, and another woman whose only wish *has* to be for men and women alike to quit finding her attractive.

Crane holds out his hand for them to kiss. A ring with the society emblem gives them something to aim for. They kiss it one after the other without debate.

"Now," Crane slaps the lectern, his lambs twitch playfully. "Let us meet our final offering."

Meet? Nick thinks.

The chapel falls into a suspenseful silence.

The stage door clicks open. A girl, can't be older than thirteen, is led onto the stage by a lanky woman. The girl is wearing a grey tunic buttoned to the top, damp hair clings to the back of her neck. She is frightened, that much is easy to see. Crane, the initiates and those in the pews all look at the girl with a creepy adoration that makes Nick nervous. The appearance of the girl has made him uncomfortable, his heart rate increases in the same way it does when trouble is about to kick off at one of the nightclubs. He doesn't jump to conclusions, though. Not yet. He isn't a jumper.

With glistening, caught-in-headlight eyes, the girl gawps at her admirers, her steps uncertain. She turns to face the woman, whispers something that goes unanswered. Tears begin to spill down her face, bottom lip quivering. She takes some of her hair in her hands and begins to stroke it. Nick isn't sure what to do, thinks he should say something. This is a turn he wasn't expecting.

Crane turns to his people. "Is she not perfection?"

Silence is maintained.

Shoulders grabbed by the tall woman, the girl starts to scream, kicking her legs, struggling to get away. Her protests are deadened in the chapel, the walls and drapes killing the noise. Nick takes a step away from the wall, knowing he can't allow this to continue, whether he knows these people's customs or not. Whatever ceremonies Crane puts his followers through, this isn't right.

Vance watches the girl. Crane takes the officer's hand in his. "You shall be first. I need you to first repeat the wish that you entrusted to me to everyone here. Declare it, own it, *believe* it."

Vance takes a shaky breath. The girl continues to kick and scream, stifled when the tall woman covers her mouth with talon fingers. The girl's knees go limp, the woman holds her up.

Vance begins, "I want- "

"You *wish*," from Crane, shaking her hand. "You *wish*."

She smiles back. "I wish…" Her other hand moves to her belt. "I wish…"

Nick opens his mouth to speak up. Before he can, Vance pulls away from Crane, draws a handgun from beneath her coat and aims it at him. "I wish you would put your hands where I can see them. You're under arrest. All of you."

Nick freezes. The line here tonight has just been crossed and snorted. Crane puts his hands up, a look of mock surprise on his face. From the congregation there is no reaction, they simply watch as if a soap opera is nearing its cliff-hanger. The girl continues to struggle, the tall woman holds on, glaring at the officer.

"Detective Inspector Vance," Crane smiles, "whatever are you doing?"

"Ulysses Crane," she begins, "I am placing you and your followers under arrest for multiple homicides committed over a number of decades, as well as a string of charges against you including kidnap and trafficking. You do not have to say anything, but it may harm your defence if you do not mention when questioned something which you later rely on in court. Anything- "

Crane throws his head back, laughs, is joined by the rest of the chapel. Nick cannot move. *Multiple homicides?*

Vance speaks louder, "Anything you do say may be given in evidence." She sidesteps closer to the girl. "Let the girl go. Give her to me."

The tall woman looks at Crane for further direction. Crane, who is drying his eyes with his pocket square, nods for her to comply. Manoeuvring to the back of the stage where she can view the whole chapel, Vance shields the sobbing girl, flicks the handgun at the tall woman, telling her to move away, which she does with calm, measured steps.

Nick doesn't understand why everyone is so nonchalant. They seem to be taking pleasure from the situation. What kind of pantomime *is* this?

Crane frowns. "Detective Inspector. What *took* you so long?"

Vance keeps her handgun on Crane, eyes on the congregation, impatience crumpling her face. "'Scuse me?"

"Excuse you, indeed. I am shocked that you lasted this long, but then I suppose you needed to see the girl before you could make your move. Those were your orders, were they not?"

Nick has inched his way to the devil's door. He tries to unlatch it, finds that it's stuck. His heart pounds. Whatever Crane is into is big enough for a police investigation and he wants no part in it. He may as well have gone with the Georges.

Keeping her composure, Vance ignores Crane's baiting. "Outside at this moment is a team of officers. Any second now they'll storm this place- "

"There is no one outside, Ms Vance," Crane interrupts.

"Wishing won't get you anywhere, Crane. I've been building a case against you for a year now. Everyone involved is ready and willing to raid this place and bring the lot of you down. There's no getting out of it." Vance reaches for her radio, holds it to her mouth.

"Go ahead," Crane encourages, "call for the stormtroopers, the quicker you do the quicker you will find yourself alone. May I ask, though…are you not wondering why they have not ran in yet?"

"There'll be plenty of questions soon enough." Pressing the button, Vance says, "Where are you? All units to follow procedure, now!" A troubled silence ekes out. She tries a second time, only to be answered by static and the grim giggling of the audience. Nick can see her face drop as she realises that no one is coming.

Crane meanders from the lectern, hands behind his back. "Ms Vance, I have known since the day you first approached me what you were up to. I have to commend you, your idea to play yourself in this ruse was rather brilliant, a hide in plain sight mentality that I sincerely hope you are awarded for. You were almost *believable* at times."

"How?" Vance says.

"It is quite simple, really. Your superior is an acquaintance of mine. I helped him get to where he is today, and he returns the favour by telling me anything and everything being plotted against me. It was he who this evening took apart the sting against me that you orchestrated. Not surprising, he owes me rather a lot."

"Fuck," Vance spits under her breath. Reasserting her aim, she asks through gritted teeth, "So what happens now? I won't let you harm this girl."

Spreading his arms, Crane turns to his flock and bellows, "What happens *now*?"

They rally together, cheering, clapping and laughing. Bewildered, Nick remains frozen.

When the audience settles, Crane says, "Now, Ms Vance, we continue with the offering. You see, it is good that you are here, I always like to make sure that we have a little extra. Just in case."

"Extra?" Vance narrows her eyes.

"Oh yes," Crane nods. "Unfortunately for you, there can never be enough blood."

A knife lances through Vance's chest from behind, spurting blood over the stage to the audience's celebration. Crane hops back so it can't touch him. The girl is snatched by the tall woman, dragged away from the bloodshed. Nick recoils as if punched, tumbling over the shoes, his coffee thrown up the wall. He watches on in horror, head ringing.

Vance's mouth overflows with blood, trickles down her tensed neck. Body trembling, she gapes down at the wound, the tip of a blade jutting out between her breasts with a lump of flesh dangling from its tip. She coughs, spraying the stage with red spume. She makes an effort to bring the handgun up, gets halfway before her arm drops.

Amused, Crane flicks his fingers. "Let her drop."

The retraction of the knife from her chest makes a sucking sound, like a foot caught in mud. Vance wheezes, her deflating lungs hiss. She lurches towards Crane, who watches her stagger with a hobbyist's enjoyment. The congregation is rapturous, applauding like a gameshow audience when they see Vance finally collapse to the floor. Her handgun bounces into the aisle. As her body lies spasming, the dead detective's blood drains from her wound, spilling off the stage and into the pews. There shouldn't be this much blood.

Apollo emerges from the shadows, brandishing a decorative dagger, intricate inscribed details swirl up the length of the blade from the hilt, catching the blood of the detective in the pattern.

Crane whirls to face his people, raises his arms, arthritic elbows no longer a problem. "Let the blood spread! Feel it between your toes! As always, friends, show the magic your servitude! Show the book that has given us so much!"

Zombie moans root through the gameshow audience as blood flows around their feet. They wriggle their toes, tittering, empowered by the murder. It oozes beyond the pews with the menace of lava, erupting in a constant stream from Vance's body. Nick kicks away from it, picking himself up from the tangled shoes before it can touch him. Simon is shirtless, on his knees in the aisle, running his fingers through the blood, making nonsense shapes that erase themselves seconds after they have been drawn. Another lamb of Crane's society has taken another one's dick in their mouth.

Crane puts on a latex glove, lets it snap at the wrist. Whilst the congregation wallows in its depravities, he holds his hand out to the girl, his skeletal fingers unfurling one after the other. "Give her to me," he says.

Nick's eyes peel wide open, the sickness is so potent now, he has to cover his mouth to keep from throwing up. The world transitions in and out of focus. Fuck. He *has* to do something. Doesn't he? The detective was doing her job, the risk was always there, but the *girl*? She's an innocent. An innocent Nick has no connection to whatsoever. *Does* he have to do something? He could run, kick the door open and run. There's already one ghost on his conscience, he can handle another…he thinks. He tries the latch again, this time is clacks open, the opportunity to get the fuck out of here is there for the taking. He looks over his shoulder, sees the frightened girl. He opens the door, gawks up at freedom, freedom that the girl won't get if…

Cursing himself, Nick takes the hunting knife from his boot, strides towards the madness.

Grinning, the tall woman shoves the girl into Crane's grasp. The teenager almost slips in Vance's blood before he hoists her up, stronger than he should be. Apollo hands him the dagger, joins the tall woman. Crane casually opens the book with the blade, holds the girl by the back of the head, her neck looms over the pages which flap on their own. She tries to wrestle free but has exhausted herself, resigned now to weeping. One hand finds its way into the tunic pocket.

Nick advances towards the stage up the aisle, thankful as he walks through the blood that he broke the shoe rule. Vigilant members of the society scramble from the pews to accost him. He doesn't strike at them with the knife, isn't sure he even has what it takes to cut someone open. He uses his fists instead, landing combos of hooks against anyone who tries to stop him. Simon dives for Nick's leg, sinks his teeth into the thigh. Nick cries out, reacts by slicing Simon across the face. In that moment the congregation becomes too many, the knife is wrenched away and with a kick to the back of his legs, Nick is brought to the floor. On his knees, in Vance's blood, they hold out his arms in crucifixion pose. Simon, a mask of blood covering his face, holds the hunting knife. He bends down so that he and Nick are face to face, toxic breath wafts from his mouth. The gash Nick has put on Simon's face is a clean laceration that goes right to the muscle, running from the bridge of his nose to his left cheek. Nick sees teeth that he shouldn't be able to. Simon holds the knife to Nick's throat.

Nick cries out, "CRANE!"

Crane looks up from the lectern, his ponytail has come loose. "STOP!"

The frenzy comes to a standstill. Those that have taken sexual joy from the ceremony let limp body parts slop from their mouths. Their expressions are those of the dumb. Nick is held in place, challenges Simon's snarling glare by spitting. Simon presses the knife harder against Nick's throat, growls before he backs off, taking the knife with him, retreating to the pews. A thin red line is left across Nick's neck.

The chapel is quiet, the girl has stopped sobbing, her face sore with the exertion. From the stage, Nick is watched by the initiates, Apollo, and the tall woman. He can't shake the notion he knows her.

Crane says, "What are you doing, Nicholas?"

"Being a fucking idiot," Nick replies.

"Maybe." Still, Crane has the girl positioned over the licking pages. Vapour spills from the book. "What is this all about? And I must say, I am deeply saddened that you have not removed your shoes. Think of the muck you might have brought in."

He's insane. "What the fuck is this, Crane? What the fuck *is* this?"

Crane waves the dagger in his hand, answers as if it's obvious. "Well, this is what must be done."

Nick shouts, "Killing people?! What the fuck *for*?"

"We *offer* them. Think of it as a sacrifice," Crane corrects him. "Without them, I am unable to connect with the- "

"You're a murderer!" Nick throws himself forward but is held fast, pulling a muscle in his shoulder. "You're crazy!"

Angry whispers float up from the congregation. Crane holds up a hand to silence them.

"No I am not. It is *real*," Crane begins, sounding joyful. "You will see for yourself, the cynic in you shall see! I invited you here because I saw a piece of myself in you, a man striving for better. I thought you would be willing to witness this momentous night. Please, Nicholas, do not embarrass me."

"Seems we have different definitions of *better*. You call killing kids momentous?"

Crane's countenance changes, becomes a sinister visage in the candlelight, deep shadows in the place of eyes.

"So what is it that you intend for us this evening, Nicholas?" Crane asks. "Clearly, you have no grasp of my ambition."

"Clearly," Nick spits. "Just let the girl go."

From the lectern the girl looks up, mouth hanging open with snot drizzling from her nostrils. In response to Nick's demand, the chapel falls into uproarious laughter. To them, Nick is now stand-up entertainment. When they have emptied themselves of mirth, Crane speaks up.

"I am afraid that such a request is not possible, Nicholas. I need her blood for this final offering if the book is to accept me, to elevate me into the annals of wish granters."

Acceptance. Nick recalls Crane's wish.

"The fucking *book*? The hell does that mean?" Nick cries, "She's a *child*!"

"Yes, I know, a rather splendid specimen at that. Unspoiled blood, untainted by adulthood. You saw the photographs in my office, did you not? You saw the children in them, yes? I regret each one of them lost, yet it has all been leading to this. They are martyrs, all of them. We would usually have taken the photograph before all this, but unfortunately our photographer could not be here this evening."

One of the congregation calls out, "Laid up in hospital."

Crane affirms, "Yes, so he is. So whilst we are breaking some traditions, we did not want to use a different photographer for fear of upsetting- "

Nick cuts Crane off, "You're all fuckin' mad!"

"Nicholas?"

"Look at yourselves! Look at what you're doing! You should all be locked up!" Nick struggles against the hands holding him in place, a kick to the bottom of his spine stops him.

Crane smirks. "Perhaps so, Nicholas, but then we are not the only ones with blood on our hands, are we? You have an interesting backstory."

Tittering from the congregation. Nick growls, "Go fuck yourself."

Crane chuckles, "Some of us have *tried* to fuck ourselves before, but to no avail." The swear word coming from Crane's lips is out of place, a squatter living in a mansion. "Now, I am afraid we have no more time for nuisances. As you can see, the book is hungry, and I aim to feed it."

The pages restlessly turn themselves. Crane takes the dagger, holds it under the girl's throat. Except for her eyes opening a touch wider, she doesn't react, her hand still inside the tunic's pocket.

"Don't do it Crane!" Nick tries.

Crane ignores him. "I offer this child's lifeblood…" he starts. The congregation picks up where it left off with their chanting and sexual appetites, moaning along with Crane's arcane words. Apollo and the tall woman have joined in, the initiates are on their knees, arms raised, praying to gods unknown outside this place. Nick looks at the girl, who has chosen to close her eyes as she waits for the cut of the blade. Nick thinks he'll do the same. He's certain the same fate awaits him when they are through with her, now that he's exposed himself as definitely not one of them. He hangs his head, defeated. Before he closes his eyes, he spots Vance's handgun in her blood, which is now a gloopy ichor.

Crane babbles on. "I give myself to you as you give yourself to me. Allow the powers of your arts to flow through me and I shall be your eternal servant. Erase from me age, eradicate weakness, give me permission to alter the lives of those who seek it, give me strength- "

With a piercing scream the girl pulls her hand out of her pocket, whips her arm at Crane's face. Whatever she's holding glints. The knife clatters on the stage along with what she attacked him with. He staggers away with his wrinkled hands covering his face, but not before a single drop of blood from the girl's neck has dripped to the book's quivering pages.

The audience panics, the girl runs around Crane trying to find a way to escape the stage. Apollo, in tow with the tall woman, is already making his move to capture her. In their hysteria, Nick's own captors momentarily loosen their grip, giving him the split second he needs to break free. He lunges for the handgun, clutching tight to prevent it from slipping from his hand. Getting to his feet, he fires a round into the chapel's ceiling.

Everything freezes. The girl cowers on stage from Apollo, who has ceased in the pose of a stalking monster.

"I'll shoot anyone who moves," Nick announces. Adrenaline is his fuel now, a puppet to his heroics, a word that means nothing to him. He has never held a firearm before, hopes (wishes, ironically) that no one can see it trembling in his hand. Does he really have the stones to shoot one of these bastards? He believes that he just might.

"Nicholas," Crane groans. He takes his hands from his face and steps to the front of the stage. A ragged line is slashed across his forehead, watered down blood pumps from it. A fire cooks in his eyes. "Is this *really* necessary? You have no idea what you are preventing. I can give you everything, if you just- "

"Quiet!" Nick moves the handgun around, pointing it at all movement. He catches sight of Simon and his lunatic grin, enthralled by the drama.

"I'm going to take the girl away from here. None of you are going to stop me." Nick holds out a hand, beckoning the teenager. Without hesitation, she invests her trust in him, hopping over the detective's body and off the stage, grabbing onto Nick for safety. In any other circumstance, Nick might be warmed – though he'd never admit it – by her gesture of good faith, but right now he just wants to get the hell out of this fucking chapel.

The tall woman mutters, "I knew he'd be trouble."

"Silence, Juniper," Crane commands.

She grimaces, holds her tongue.

"I expect that what she cut me with has not been properly sanitised. I shall need anti-bacterial wipes to kill the germs." Crane says to Nick, "What makes you think- "

"What makes me think," Nick speaks over him, "that I can get away with this?" He aims the handgun at Crane's face, the congregation mumbles their concern. "There's one way. Your loyal subjects won't risk you coming to harm. I'm holding a gun, Crane. I've never handled one of these before. I'm fucking nervous, liable to pull the trigger at any moment. If anyone makes a move, even if it's just a fucking fart, I'll blow your head off. And what's more? You don't have the balls to risk death yourself. Happy to dish it out, though."

Crane dwells on Nick's statement for a few seconds. His lips tremble. He licks at his blood, then finally, after he takes a deep breath he says, "Let them go."

With the girl wrapping her arms around his waist, Nick takes the first steps backwards.

"Clear the aisle," orders Crane.

Backing into the pews, the congregation makes way. They observe in silence, emotional black holes biding their time. Nick and the girl make their way to the devil's door.

Crane places a hand on the lectern, shuts the book. It whispers when it closes, the vapour dissipates. Some of the sickness that plagues the chapel disperses. Crane warns, "This has to be finished, Nicholas. Her blood has already touched the book, only hers will do now. Your conscience won you over tonight, you have played your hand well. But after this evening the ball is in our court. We *will* find the girl, Nicholas.

We *have* to."

"Not if I can help it," Nick says. He's pointing the handgun, isn't sure he's doing it correctly.

"Whatever will you do?" Crane goes on, pocket square dabbing his forehead. "There are many of us in the city, Nicholas. Believe that. We shall be watching, waiting. The city is not as large as you would believe, nor shall I be bound by physical barriers. And I do hope you do not seek to call the police. As you can see by Detective Inspector Vance's folly, the police will not help you, should you choose to test my bluff."

"Go fuck yourself, Ulysses."

Crane laughs. For one instant his body cannot decide what age it is.

Nick and the girl reach the devil's door. Kicking shoes out of the way, he pulls it open. Stale air rushes out of the stairwell. He urges the girl to go up first, but she is oblivious, clinging to him. Careful not to trip the both of them up, Nick leads, keeping the handgun as steady as he can. A member of the society dashes forward, slips in the detective's blood. Nick pulls the trigger, a deafening blast flashes from the handgun's muzzle. The congregation cries and the girl screams into his back.

The discharged round leaves a smoking hole in the lectern. Crane has not moved, watches Nick with a mixture of hate and admiration.

As Nick pulls closed the devil's door Crane says, "We shall be seeing you, Nicholas, before the passing of seven days."

Nick latches the door closed, expects to hear commotion on the other side. There isn't. Somehow the silence is worse.

He and the girl make their way to the trapdoor. Nick heaves it open. It rams against one of Crane's bookshelves, denting the pristine spines that the crazy old fuck takes pleasure in. Nick slams it shut, tips the bookshelf on top for good measure.

He asks the girl a stupid question. "You okay?"

She's gazing at the floorboards, eyes wide, her hair a frayed mess, shivering. She hasn't said a word and no one can blame her. If she will ever talk remains to be seen. Lot of shit for a kid to see down there. Lot of shit for an adult to see. Nick throws the handgun up into The Orphanage, hears a column of books topple over.

At the front door, the girl stays close, her nails digging in. For the first time he notices both of them are spattered in blood, his knees are saturated with it. Hopefully, they won't bump into anyone when he takes her…

He supposes the only place he can take her for now is the flat. No one from Crane's society has been there. It's a safe house. For how long, Nick isn't sure. He isn't going to take her to the police. He has no idea what he's going to do, decides that for tonight it doesn't matter. Those problems can be addressed in the morning.

They walk into the freezing street. Frost glistens on the steps. The girl huddles closer for warmth, Nick knows he should help by putting his arms around her, but doesn't. Affection is one of life's big conundrums that he definitely isn't ready to tackle yet. He contemplates stealing one of the lined up cars, quickly comes to the conclusion that would be a mistake. Besides, walking will be better. There are more places to hide, if needs be, on foot.

"Come on," he says to no reply.

As they make their way down the road, Nick can't help but glance at the drains, anxious that he'll see faces from underground staring up at them.

PART II

'*Bad Places*'

CHAPTER 14

Thoughts come racing in at the same time, tumbling under and over each other so that they make scrambled codes instead of sentences, nonsense that means something underneath all the mess. Snapshots of blood, death, lunacy, spinning in a crazy kaleidoscope.

It's just before seven o'clock the following morning. Nick is in the shower, standing still until the hot water becomes cold. It doesn't matter. He needs the hot water to wash away the crusted blood and the cold water to keep him awake. Diluted blood gurgles down the plug hole, he tries not to be hypnotised by the swirling but it's hard to not let himself shutdown and pretend that what happened at Crane's was just a vivid dream. A nightmare.

The girl is in his bed, asleep.

When they got back to the flat she didn't say anything, only looked around his home with the same detached expression that she'd been wearing since the escape. Nick tried to make small talk, though in the end the only semblance of a response he got was when he asked her if she was tired, to which she nodded. He took her to his bedroom and without a word she crawled under the covers of the bed and was gone. He himself had slept a restive sleep on his settee.

He shuts the water off, the sound of the pipes lumping off resonant in the bathroom. For a few more seconds he stands, letting drops of water drip from his nose as the last of the blood – just a pink hue now – spirals away.

The question now is what to do next. It *should* be an easy answer: Get the girl home. But there's more to think about than just that. He could get in contact with the girl's parents, the only problem is Nick doesn't know how deep the roots of Crane's society run. Certainly he has people within the police, so who's to say that he doesn't have connections elsewhere and they all interconnect into one big hivemind? If he has a portion of the police on his side then Nick has to assume that Crane will have access to communications networks. Bringing the parents in might be putting them in danger. Will it be difficult to catch a train, a bus, a taxi, an Uber? The word'll be out now to find the girl, eyes will be on the lookout. Crane said it himself, they *need* the girl, though Nick isn't exactly sure why. Are the powers, the magic, that Crane spoke of all true? All that hoodoo about wishes? One thing's for sure, Crane believes it enough to kill a child. Many children. Whatever that book is, it was definitely floating on that lectern.

He realises it might be up to him to see the girl to safety. Why'd he go and get himself into this shit anyway?

Dressed, Nick walks into the kitchen drying his hair. When he takes the towel away he finds the girl sitting at the table in her grey tunic, stroking the black cat. It purrs with enthusiasm, pushing its head into the girl's hand. On the girl's face are smatterings of blood.

"Uh, morning," Nick says.

The cat looks up, the girl doesn't.

How the hell do you even start a conversation in this scenario?

"You…" Nick starts, "…you okay?"

The girl shrugs, petting the cat, a talisman that will keep her safe.

"You want something to drink?" Nick, barefoot and with his tee-shirt sticking to his back, goes to the sink. "Water? Or…" He opens a cupboard. No juice. He doesn't drink squash. He closes the cupboard, holding the handle. "Tea or…coffee?" he suggests.

The girl acts as if he isn't there. This is getting awkward, perhaps it's time to cut the shit.

He asks her, "Are you hurt?"

"This isn't your cat," she blurts. Her voice is hoarse.

"No, it's not," Nick crosses his arms. "How can you tell?"

She shrugs.

136

Unsure of what else to do, Nick chases the conversation. "We started off hating each other, but've come to an understanding. I've only just starting letting it in for a couple- "

"He."

"Sorry?"

"He's a he," says the girl, stroking between *his* ears.

A coy smile is all Nick can manage. "Right."

"Where are we?"

"My flat."

"No. I mean...*where* are we?"

Though the girl is engaging with him, she makes no eye contact. Nick doesn't hold it against her, maybe neither of them is a people person.

"Uh, the city. London," says Nick.

The girl takes her hand away from the cat.

Nick picks up the kettle, and fills it up. He goes on, "Where're you from?"

"Not from here." She's reluctant to give anything away.

"I can see that" – he flicks the kettle on – "but where?"

"Will you get me home?" The question comes suddenly with shreds of anger. She finally looks at him, her eyes welling up.

Nick crosses the kitchen and sits at the table. The girl scrapes her chair away from him, the cat hops down and jumps back up onto the kitchen counter in one slick movement.

Taking a few seconds first, Nick says, "I dunno. You know it's too dangerous to call the police, right? You heard- "

"I heard what the man said," she cuts in.

Smart girl, if not abrasive.

"Yeah," Nick glances away. "So I think it's up to...to me, to get you back to your parents. I'm not sure how easy that's going to be. Those people, back there...they're serious."

More serious than he'd ever have believed.

"I don't know you," she mumbles.

"Right, and I don't know you, but here we are."

She argues, "I didn't ask for this."

"Me neither," Nick snaps.

The two of them maintain a silent standoff until the girl gives in. "Do you have a phone?"

"Yeah."

"I could call my mum and dad."

"I thought of that," says Nick, "but I think it might put them in danger. I don't think Crane will hesitate to ki...to hurt anyone who gets in his way." Guilt pangs his body, it feels as if he's trying to scare the girl out of reuniting with her parents. "I think they're trying to do more than scare us. They've been doing this for a long time now. They follow Crane like he's a messiah. I think the best option is get you away without leaving trails for them to follow. If...when I get you home, your parents can handle this how they want."

"They need to know I'm safe."

"They will, it's just too risky right now."

The girl's eyebrows ruffle as she contemplates what Nick has said. She takes a clumpy length of hair in her hands and starts to run her fingers through it. The kettle comes to a boil and Nick stands.

"Who's Crane?" the girl asks.

Turning, Nick answers, "The old man who" – *tried to murder you for the sake of a book* – "who you saw last night."

"What was...he trying to do?"

"I'm not sure. He believes you're the key to...something."

"That book," she says, "was trying to eat me." A tear falls down her cheek. "I don't want him to hurt my mum and dad, too."

Nick has never had to deal with tears from anyone other than a hysteric man or woman who'd had three too many and decided to declare their love for someone by being a factory line pisshead, and in those situations you only had to turf them out.

"We won't give them the opportunity," he says. "I'm, uh...I'm sorry you can't call them. I'm sure they're worried sick about you."

The girl sniffs. The bags under her eyes look heavy, Nick wonders if she slept at all.

"How long've you been missing?" asks Nick.

"I…I'm not sure."

"A few days? Weeks?"

"It feels like forever," she says.

Nick puts his hands in his pockets. "Did they…uh…did they hurt you?"

She shakes her head. The girl understands what he was really asking.

Nick spoons a heap of coffee into his mug when the girl asks, "May I have a tea, please?"

Well-mannered. Nick doesn't know her, but she's handling this like a champ, all things considered. She should be scarred, frightened of her own shadow, suffering severe PTSD, but she isn't, at least not on the surface.

He makes his coffee and brews her tea. She wraps her hands around the mug, draws it close to her chest, breathing in the scent.

"What's your name?" Nick asks.

She doesn't answer straight away. Handling this well she might be, but Nick is still a stranger and strangers haven't been good to her. It'll take more than a cup of tea to forge a trust between them.

She flips it around. "What's *yours*?"

Nick laughs through his nose. "Nick."

She blows on her tea, flinches when the steam touches her lips.

"Careful," says Nick.

"I know," she snaps quietly.

"You going to tell me your name?"

"My name's…Katy."

Nick smiles. "It's nice to meet you Katy."

She smiles back, pulls it away, not quite ready to make herself vulnerable again.

The cat leaps back onto the table, prancing in circles. Katy strokes the cat and the cat stares at Nick, asking where its breakfast is.

"I like your cat," Katy says.

"Someone has to," says Nick, then gives the cat a heavy-handed pat where its tail begins.

"Are we…" Katy begins, "…are we safe here?"

"For now. I haven't seen anything out of the ordinary, 'cept for this bloody cat taking a shine to me."

"I love animals," says Katy.

"I hate cats," Nick counters.

"But not this one."

"I didn't have a choice."

Katy pops her tea on the table. Pipes groan around the flat for a while, then stop. "What, um, what next?"

"Well," Nick leans back in his chair, scratches at the table with his index finger, "the best thing I can think of off the top of my head is to go to a bus terminal. Victoria, I 'spose. There'll be lots of people there, so it'll be easy to keep a low profile."

"Will you come with me?"

It's the first impression that she doesn't entirely distrust him.

"Yeah," replies Nick. "I'll come with you. Just need to know where we're going."

Stroking the cat, the girls says, "East Anglia."

"That's quite a way." And inconvenient.

Nick hadn't expected for the society to be working as far away as that. Did they purposefully travel afield to cover their tracks? Don't shit where you eat? Then again, Vance had apparently been building a case against them for the past year, which meant that Crane's society wasn't as clandestine as he'd boasted.

Katy asks, "Are we going soon?"

"As soon as."

"I want to go *now*."

"Look. I *get* it. I want this over too, but we have to be careful. I think you should eat something first, clean yourself up a bit so you don't draw attention. I don't have any clothes that'll fit you but we can nip into a shop and pick some stuff up, okay?"

"You want to go shopping?" she says. Her whole face is a scrunched question mark.

"No, I don't..." Nick closes his eyes, rubs his temples.

Katy frowns. "Why did you even rescue me?"

"Why'd I rescue you?" repeats Nick, caught off-guard by the question.

"You said you didn't ask for this, so why?" she persists.

Standing, taking both their half-finished drinks to the sink, Nick answers, "I just...did. I shouldn't have been there. Didn't want to be. It was a mistake. Leave it at that." He adds, "Be grateful."

Now Katy stands. "You know, you can be pretty mean."

"Yep." Nick turns on the sarcasm. "I'm only gonna help you get home. Now," he turns it back off, "what do you eat?"

Katy leaves the kitchen.

This is going to be difficult, he thinks, annoyed at her as well as his own impatience.

He leans over the sink, taps his thumb. Nick looks out the window. Outside is foggy, he can hardly see the opposing brick wall. He hadn't noticed the fog earlier, it's drifted in like a ghostly insurgent.

The cat meows from the table, its tail whisking around. Nick takes a pouch of cat food and empties it into a saucer crusty with the last pouch's remains. The cat waits until he has stepped away before it leaps to its feast.

After getting dressed properly, Nick finds Katy, now clean faced, fussing the cat on the floor. It willingly stretches its neck so Katy can get access to better scratching areas, then rolls on its back to expose its stomach. Katy wastes no time in running her fingers through the dark fur. Nick contemplates saying sorry, instead he moves the toaster on the kitchen counter. Marking where it had sat is a horde of crumbs, which he sweeps to the floor. Out of sight, out of mind.

He asks, "Toast?"

"Does he have a name?" she replies.

"Who?"

"Your cat. Have you named him?"

"Oh. Uh, no. No," Nick fumbles with his words, takes the bread out of the cupboard.

Katy says nothing for a while, then adds, "You have to name him."

So far the cat is the only thing the two of them can talk about without clashing. They are clearly two different people, both struggling to come to terms with the position they're in. The cat though, that was the key to normalcy. Anything could be bridged if it somehow involved the cat.

Pressing the toaster down, Nick says, "I've never named a cat before."

"It's easy," Katy keeps her focus on the cat. "I've had three cats before, I named them after things I like." She shrugs. "River. Petal. Larry."

"Larry?"

"A character from a cartoon I watched when I was a kid."

"I see," says Nick.

The menu for things on toast is two items. A jar of Marmite which has glued itself down, or butter from the fridge. The only other item in the fridge is the bulb, and a tuft of mould.

Butter it is.

Katy persists, "What do you like?"

"I like toast," says Nick, opening the butter.

"You can't name a cat Toast, that's stupid."

Scraping the slightly burnt toast, Nick replies, "Why not. I like toast. You said to pick things I like."

"Toast isn't a name," she argues. "What else do you like?"

Nick can't think of an answer. There's only so much they can talk about the cat before the conversation will run dry. He tries to come up with something that the girl will accept. The smell of the burnt toast brings a wave of nostalgia to him that is so distant a memory he isn't sure that he isn't making it up, but when the name that comes out of it flashes in his head like a neon sign, he finds that, actually, he quite likes it.

"How about Pop Tart?" he suggests.

Katy pauses with her hand hidden in the cat's fur. "Pop Tart?"

Putting the two pieces of buttered toast on a plate, Nick asks, "Any good?"

"Why?"

"Well, when I was little, I'd go riding my bike around the neighbourhood. At a certain time of day from one of the houses, I'd always smell something burning. That smell always made me think of Pop Tarts." Nick brings the plate to the table, Katy gets up and grabs a slice.

She swallows a bite, then says, "Okay. Pop Tart is a name."

"Cheers," Nick replies, picking up the smaller slice of toast. "A good one?"

"A name," she says.

Sitting, he watches her eat. She takes tiny mouse bites and chews each one thoroughly. She isn't malnourished, which means that for however long Crane's people had her, they had at least fed her properly.

Katy jerks her head up, "Did you hear that?"

Nick listens, mouth stopped mid-chew. A faint creaking, then more. He knows how this building sounds, sometimes it creaks for no reason, still settling into itself, but this creak was different. Too careful to belong to the building. Too unintentional. He drops his toast, splashing crumbs onto the tabletop, pushes his chair out. He keeps his footsteps as light as he can without actually sneaking. Katy looks over the back of her chair, nose poking over the top. Another creak, closer now. Nick looks through the peep hole, only to see the fish-eyed top of the stairs on the other side.

Maybe it was nothing. Both of them are one edge, making mountains out of molehills.

Nick says, "It's nothing."

An explosion of splinters put Nick and Katy on a knife thrower's board as the door is rammed open. Nick is shoved to the floor, winded. Katy screams, hides under the table. Hands grab Nick by the shoulders whilst he is still trying to catch his breath, drag him up and slam him into the wall, cracking the plaster. When he opens his eyes he sees Apollo's face in the eddying dust. The big fuck's face is contorted into a happy sneer, his five o'clock shadow at an advanced stage.

Nick grabs Apollo's wrists, rams his knee into the bastard's stomach. It's like trying to fight off concrete. He knees again, hurting himself more, then throws a right hook that lands where the sweet spot should be on Apollo's jaw. It does nothing except up the entertainment for the South African machine. Nick should've known Apollo didn't have a sweet spot.

Apollo throws Nick from the cratered wall into the kitchen. Splinters jab into his arm as he slides across the floor and hits his head against a cupboard.

Katy hasn't moved from under the table. She's covering her ears, rocking back and forth. The cupboard door breaks off its hinges and knocks Nick – corner-first – on the head. Apollo strides over to the table where he reaches under and grabs Katy by the leg. She kicks out, every time hitting him dead centre in the face, leaving shoe prints. It's only an inconvenience for Apollo, who hoists himself up and flips over the table instead, sending toast flying across the kitchen. Katy scrambles away but a swift kick to the back of the ankles from Apollo sends her sprawling.

Nick bulldozes into Apollo's side as hard as he can, using his shoulders to try and bring the big fuck down. Apollo grunts, which is something. That simple grunt is an indication to the freakishly big man's mortality. They collide into another wall, an empty picture frame falls down along with clods of plaster. Nick pulls away from Apollo, starts throwing combos into his abdomen. Left, right, left to ribs, right, right to the ribs, left, right. Apollo swings a right that Nick ducks under, hearing the whoosh as the punch breaks air. Coming back up, Nick launches an uppercut into the big fuck's chin that not only lifts Apollo's head, but feels like striking marble. When Apollo brings his head back down he's lost his sneer, a cut turns his square chin into a cleft one. Nick shakes his hand, retightens it into a fist. He's light on his feet, dancing on his toes. With a roar, Apollo starts unloading unskilful, merciless punches, driving Nick backwards. Not one manages to hit, though Nick has to utilize muscles he forgot he had in order to keep himself from catching one of those hurt bombs.

Eventually, room runs out and he is driven back against the kitchen counter. Apollo laughs. Stupid move. Nick snatches the brief window and delivers more strikes to the big fuck's torso. Apollo lunges forward and picks Nick up in a bear hug, squeezing the oxygen from his lungs. Nick struggles, working hard to keep his spine from snapping under Apollo's inhuman embrace. Veins stand out on his neck, skin turns purple, red mist starts to creep into his vision. He glances to his right and sees the new kettle, a ribbon of steam trailing from its spout. He reaches for it, fingers twitching inches away from the handle. Apollo dials up his bear hug, growling through it, using his right arm to pull his left tighter. Nick grits his teeth, tastes blood in his mouth. He drives an elbow into Apollo's head. Darkness blurs his peripheral now, it'll only be a few seconds until he passes out.

The girl races to the kettle, pushes it closer so Nick can grab it. After she does she drops down and crawls away.

With his last ounce of strength, Nick picks up the kettle and with both hands beats it down on Apollo's head. The big fuck drops Nick and cries out, trying to swipe away the scolding water, burning his hands.

Nick falls to his knees, draws in raspy breaths, hacking up phlegm. It hurts all over. Some of the water splashed onto his forearms but not enough to render him a boiling mess like Apollo. Looking over at his lurching attacker, who has blood dripping down his face, Nick forces himself up. It's now or never. He charges at Apollo, and jumping for extra power, hammers the dented kettle into the big fuck's face.

Apollo goes down, the lump shakes the flat. He isn't out cold though, still mumbles as he rolls on the floor with a steaming head, leaving imprints of his blooded grimace on the floorboards.

Nick stands over Apollo, sickened by his readiness to cave the big fuck's head in. He kicks away Apollo's grabbing hand, moving of its own volition like a severed limb. Nick glances at Katy, bunched up on the floor near the ruined doorway, shards of wood littered around her. She's crying, watching him through waterlogged eyes. He wonders if she'll ever trust him if she witnesses him beat a man to death. Apollo had meant her harm, had come to take her back, but killing was for the guys in black hats. Looking down at Apollo again, a snarling crimson impression staring back up at him, Nick isn't sure what colour hat he wears.

Time to decide is cut short. Police sirens approach. The neighbours in this building have been nosy before, and one of them might've called the Old Bill after listening – with a glass to the wall – to the warzone now taking a halftime in the flat. Nick drops the kettle.

He turns to Katy. "We have to go."

She nods, wiping her eyes.

Stepping over Apollo, Nick grabs his leather jacket and another coat that has gone unused for years. He helps Katy to her feet, she clutches to him just like the previous night.

"Wait." She sniffs.

"What?"

"We can't leave Pop Tart."

Nick sees the cat washing itself on the kitchen counter as if nothing has happened. Has it been spectating the whole time?

"We can," says Nick.

"No!" Katy twists away.

"Wait!"

"We can't just let him die."

"Yes we can," Nick argues. He likes the cat, but not *that* much.

She skirts around Apollo's squirming body. The cat makes no protest when she picks it up and holds it close, tail dangling. She doesn't return right away, instead glares at Nick. The sirens get closer, they don't have time for another argument. Let the girl have her damn talisman.

"I'm not going without him," she says with defiance.

"You only just met him!"

"You only just met me!"

Apollo grumbles, Nick punts a foot in his gut, winding the big fuck.

"Fine," Nick snaps, "but we have to go right now!"

Nick opens the front door. No need to turn the handle, the lock is useless. "Try to do as I say," he tells her.

The fog is dense. Nick can barely see more than a few feet in front of himself, let alone the end of his street. It's the kind of fog that squeezes cities into villages, disconnecting them with the wider world. The sirens have stopped.

Nick wraps the spare coat around Katy's shoulders, it's large enough to cover the cat and touch the tarmac. She makes no reaction. She's descended back into the girl without a voice, except now she has a cat to cling to instead of Nick. He slips his own jacket on, feeling the material pull on the pin missiles embedded in his arms from when Apollo had savaged the door.

Nick leads them left, looking over his shoulder for the big fuck. No sign of him, and surely, Nick thinks, they'd hear if he was coming.

The street is empty. Either no one has braved the fog today, or it's thick enough to keep them hidden. Katy hums a tune.

He knows it's dangerous, but Nick plans on taking the Merc. Crane will easily find them once it's back on the road, but for now, whilst the fog is at its murkiest, it'll get them somewhere. After that, there are plenty of forgotten harbours that will gladly keep the car a submerged secret. The flashing sidelights of the unlocking Mercedes barely pierce the fog.

They get in, Katy refuses to let go of the cat. Pop Tart seems happy enough to be coddled. Actually, the cat doesn't seem bothered at all.

Nick turns the key in the ignition, the Merc splutters. He turns it again, holding for longer, risking a flooded engine, shaking the fob because shaking things has *always* helped, hasn't it Nick? The engine ticks over, doesn't catch.

Katy speaks quietly. "How'd they find us?"

"I don't know," says Nick, trying again, stamping on the accelerator.

"You said we were safe."

Nick smacks the wheel. "I know."

Katy jumps, Pop Tart doesn't.

"Ah, *fuck*. Sorry," says Nick. "Just…let me think."

The fog has closed in around the car, drifts over the bonnet with indifference. With a sudden and cruel realisation, they both see it.

Around the car are human shapes, staying to where the fog can hide any features they might possess. They stand still, watching. Some are further back into the veil than others, just how far back the phantoms go into the murk cannot be seen. They are inventions of the smog, neither solid or air. Their eyes are pinpricks of light, shining through the fog as if it isn't there.

Katy's lips have lost control of her words, they leave her mouth before she can shape them. "T-T-There's s-so m-m-many of th-them."

The cat remains unmoved. It returns to washing itself.

Nick turns the ignition. The phantoms take a step forward, rippling the fog, moving as one. He tries again, fumbling with the key. The phantoms take another step. They move not with the gait of people but of puppets who have had their strings amputated, and they only move when Nick attempts to flee. Voices whisper inside the car. If these are the voices of the shadow people, he doesn't want to understand them.

His blood runs cold when he sees they have a passenger in the rear-view mirror. He doesn't turn, knowing that if he does the Figure, *his* Figure, will disappear. Its chest heaves as it breaths wasted oxygen. It…the Figure…*he*…certainly picks his moments to show up, and this time has apparently brought along his friends, the spirits of the wronged, of the unfortunates.

Of the Murdered.

It can be made worse. Simon's words play themselves back in Nick's head. *It can be made worse.*

The Merc coughs, revs itself to life. The phantoms outside dart away, fog swirls in the spaces they occupied. *Cowards*, Nick thinks without wanting them to prove him wrong. In the back, the Figure holds on for a while longer before slipping through the upholstery with a final, unintelligible whisper. Why'd it not speak this time? Nick grabs the gearstick and jams it into first, making the gears grind.

"Go-go-go!" Katy says. "Before they come back."

"What d'you think I'm trying to do?" Nick wrestles with the gearstick.

The passenger window detonates into particles. Katy screams as Apollo clutches her chest. Pop Tart hops into the chilled seats where the Figure had sat. Ramming his foot on the accelerator pedal, Nick tries to pry Apollo's meaty hand away from the girl. The Merc skids in place before the rubber gets a grip on the road.

Apollo hangs on, shoves his glowering face into the car, a golf-ball-sized lump parting his hair. Katy slaps the big fuck and Nick jabs the big fuck, but the big fuck doesn't let go.

Nick gets on the road. It's a matter of seconds before the fog quits delivering tarmac and gives them a brick wall instead. He squints, sees double-yellows that take a sharp turn to the right and, although it's not the way they need to go, Nick follows the paint. The Merc screeches, leaves two black snakes on the road behind it. Apollo holds on, and would have continued to hold on until death do they part if it wasn't for the bus shelter the car smashes into. Katy covers herself as the glass shatters into the Mercedes. The metal railing that bends around Apollo's body drives blood into his mouth, is filtered through his teeth, then the big fuck's hand unfastens itself and he wilts out of the car.

A bulldog clip pinches Nick's leg. He sees Katy's hand when he looks down. She has turned herself towards him, buried her face in the car seat. Her grey tunic has ripped at the shoulder, skin embossed by two of

Apollo's fingers.

The Merc judders away, lumping over what Nick assumes (and hopes) is the big fuck's legs. If Apollo isn't dead, which he bloody well should be, then two busted legs will slow him down.

The car is fucked, won't take much for Crane's acolytes to find them, though he can't imagine Crane declaring, "Look for the fucked Merc, chaps." It might be wise to dispose of the car before they do anything else. It's a billboard on wheels. It'll be a long walk from the harbour, but a long walk is better than the alternative.

Street names are hard to solve through the fog, though it's starting to clear up. Ordinary human forms can be seen now, trudging along the pavements with hanging heads and shopping bags in both hands. Other cars begin to appear, early morning honkers who seem to only be on the road for rage.

Katy's hand still clutches Nick's leg when she asks, "Where are we going?"

Nick indicates, takes a left through a traffic light that has just turned red. The driver behind honks their annoyance.

"We have to get rid of the car," he says, "then I want to see…"

A friend. But it's not a friend, because friendship is dangerous. Crane has proven that.

"…someone I know," he finishes. *If they're in.*

Katy doesn't reply, but she does let go of his leg. She looks in the back, smiles when she sees the cat curled into an ornamental ball.

A police car screams past them on the other side of the road, blues-and-twos flashing. Suddenly the fog is a gift. The damage to the car goes unnoticed. Crane can cloak himself in the nightclubs if he wants, Nick will take the weather forecast.

The harbour, formerly called Shitetown in the good ol' days of drinking cheap lager made from washing up liquid and arsenic, whittling away the hours by finding unbroken windows to pelt bricks through, hasn't changed much throughout the years. Any and all metal is rusted, anywhere with windows has had them smashed in. A few businesses still operating have protected themselves with spiked steel fences with numerous warning signs. Nick drives the squeaking Merc to an area they never went because older kids had claimed it and marked it permanently with piss and broken bottles and – if tall tales where to be taken seriously, which they so often were – the juices of pleasured girlfriends. On the concrete platform by the water's edge is a burnt black mass of furniture, household appliances, charred bottles and any other shit that people dump. The other side of Shitetown is non-existent in the fog. They are utterly alone, barring the dopey droning of foghorns.

Katy takes Pop Tart from the back seat and bundles him into her oversized coat. She wraps it close around herself. Without words Nick, pushes the Merc into the brown water that sploshes against the platform. It doesn't make much of a splash. Nick wonders how many other corpses are buried here, car or otherwise.

"I've never done anything like this," Katy says.

"Just do as you're told," Nick snaps. "Keep quiet."

"How often do you break the law?"

"I said *quiet*."

Katy dips her nose in the coat, sniffs the cat. Nick wonders if he had to be so hard on her. After all, he's never done anything like this, either.

Both of them watch it go down. As it sinks from sight, Nick is sure he sees the Figure in the back turn its head to watch him. It sends a wave of chills up his spine the likes of which are, though common when it first started, alien to him these days. It's not pleasant. He half expects to turn around and see the other twinkly-eyed spirits of the Murdered surrounding them, but when he does they are still alone.

They begin the long walk. Nick kicks a bottle into the water, Katy keeps her eyes just ahead of her feet. She has tiny scratches on her face from the broken window, nothing that will scar.

"How long will we be walking?" she asks.

"'Bout a couple of hours," Nick says.

"My feet hurt."

"Mine, too."

"Did you have to get rid of the- "

"Yes."

They pass by a brick wall with its bottom half covered in graffiti. Each area of the city has its own artistic language, not all of it good. Maybe it's how the urban rabble tell if they've crossed into enemy territory.

Walking towards a wire fence with coils of barbed wire along its top which, if Nick remembers rightly, has a corner they can pull up to get through, Pop Tart starts purring hard enough for the coat to vibrate.

Katy strokes over the coat. "Why're *you* so happy?" she says with some jealousy.

Nick answers, "I know."

"Why?"

"He's always happy at this time," Nick says, remembering to call the cat a *he* this time, a sort of apology for the snapping. He grabs the corner of the fence and rolls up the wire, just like old, supposedly better times. As Katy steps through he says, "It's time for second breakfast."

Again, it's the cat that makes them amicable.

CHAPTER 15

In the kitchen, the radio dishes out the headlines. Frank is into his second mint tea and fourth cigarette of the morning. Hunched over the paper at the breakfast table and wearing oversized slippers that used to look like Garfield, Frank had always been a red-blooded English tea drinker before, by chance, a friend recommended drinking peppermint tea to settle his ever increasing stomach pains. The rest, as they say, is history. Mint tea is the only hot drink that will pass his lips. Pity that not one friend has suggested cutting back on the cancer sticks.

Though wearing his grots – a black, bleached-blotted vest tucked into blue tracksuit bottoms *avec* pinstripes – Frank has already decked himself out with gold. His fingers are heavy with rings, wrists jangle as he stirs the tea bag in his mug, and the sparkling chain around his neck is as comfy as a collar. His glasses, which are still the same style as the previous pair, are new, now with gold frames. Frank likes gold. No, Frank *loves* gold, and should any man, woman or child call it tacky or, paradoxically, cheap, then they could go fuck themselves. Yes, the kiddies, too.

The business deal has paid off in a big way. There are things he still has to work out, and for a while things might be a bit dodgy, especially when it comes to law involvement, but he's been assured, reassured and re-reassured that any possible trouble that might come his way won't fall on him, he's simply the man who runs the gaff. He suspects that isn't entirely true, but the money makes the risk worthwhile.

Frank stubs his cigarette out in his crystal ashtray and reaches for the packet to spark up another. He moves aside the paper and slides another in front of himself. A pen bookmarks the pages he wants and he flips to them immediately.

Making extra cash on the horses is Frank's only vice besides gold. He starts circling prospects, mumbling to himself, the full cigarette springing up and down between his lips like a smouldering diving board. A van outside takes his focus off the pages. Though he is on the upper floor, he looks out the window. He's awaiting a delivery of...something. He doesn't know what, nor does he know how his new business associates work. Today is the first of what will become a regular drop-off and the less he knows the better. But it's not this van, which sputters away with a backfire.

Circling the bookie's favourite, Mallet Toes, he's interrupted by a banging on the front door. Frank looks up from his paper, listens again for the banging, which comes suddenly after the first round of knocks. Maybe it *is* the drop-off. He pushes himself up with a wheeze. Years of tar and smoke inhalation has turned his throat into a grimy tunnel. He makes his way out of the kitchen, the pendant on his gold necklace entwined in a cloud of grey chest hair. The banging continues as Frank descends the narrow stairwell into the bar.

For a second the sight of the place stuns him. After so many years of having it a certain way, he can't help but be shocked again. The sticky carpets have been replaced with navy blue ones, all the tables and chairs now matched, gutted upholstery is plush once again. A couple of brand spanking pool tables sit where the boxing ring had been, complete with new hanging light fixtures and a nearby jukebox for the punters to feed quids into. The bar still looks the same, and his request to leave the screws where the Kray bar had been has been honoured. "You can't tamper with history," he'd told his new associates, and they'd listened. Well, one of them had.

The banging on the front door has stopped. Frank can see the indistinct figure of a bloke in the fog taking a gander through the windows. Fucking hell, isn't anyone patient these days? Frank begins opening the many locks, top to bottom.

"Alright, alright, keep yer head on."

When he pulls the door open he is met by the spirit of a workhouse child holding a cat. She stares at him doe-eyed, and he stares back.

"Jesus, girl, whatever's 'appened to you?"

She stumbled over her words. "I…uh, we…"

Frank screws his face up. "Eh?"

"Frank!"

Nick steps in front of her. He looks like shit, his clothes are torn and what looks like relatively fresh blood is spattered over his face. Some on the child, too.

"Nicky? What the hell- "

"Where the fuck've you been?" Nick interrupts, then pushes his way into Estelle's, the girl, and her cat, following close behind.

Frank, muscle memory ingrained in his neck, takes a look out the door before closing it. Re-engaging the locks, he says, "Nicky, I was gonna get in touch with yer, it's just that- "

"Yeah, don't worry about that now," Nick has his hands on his hips, pacing.

One last clunk as the vertical bolt at the top of the door is slid into place. "Nicky," Frank switches his focus between Nick and the workhouse girl, "what's this all about? Who's this?"

The girl sits herself on a stool, the cat strolls onto the table. It dances around her hand, stroking itself. This girl's been through the trenches by the looks of it. She notices his Garfield slippers, then when she catches him looking she turns away.

Nick slides a hand through his hair. "This is…this is Katy. She's an..." Nick concentrates on her. "An acquaintance."

Frank takes a second, then says, "Well listen Nicky, I don't know what kinda- "

Nick snaps, "Oh, leave it out, Frank."

Frank crosses to the bar, behind it he says, "Sorry. You've sorta caught me off guard a bit 'ere. It's what? Not even half eight yet and you're paradin' in with this girl. You look like you've been dragged around by a horse and- "

The girl replies before Nick can.

"We're in trouble," she says.

Nick stops her. "Let me- "

"I'm just trying to help!"

"Well," Nick clenches his fist, closes his eyes. "Don't."

The girl sulks.

"She's right," Nick continues, calmer. "We need help."

Pouring a nip of good whisky which is only served to punters who ask for it by name, Frank asks, "What kinda help? What kinda trouble, Nicky? Come over 'ere for Chrissake, you're givin' me an 'eadache."

Approaching the bar, Nick answers, "The deep shit kind."

Lowering his voice so the girl, Katy, can't hear, Frank says, "How deep're we talkin'?"

Nick exhales laughter, cocks his head like the joke is a real knee-slapper. "The Georges are a puddle now, mate."

Frank tackles the whisky in one gulp, pours himself another, the rim of the bottle tinging musically against the tumbler. The alcohol, a treat at this time of morning, quickly gets to work calming his unwanted excitement. He shakes the bottle in his hand, asking Nick if he would like to partake, whilst knowing, and pleased by it too, that Nick will reject the offer. Nick dismisses the good whisky with a wave of the hand.

"May I have something to drink?"

They both turn to the girl. She's still on the stool, her cat has jumped down and is washing its bits.

"I'm thirsty," she finishes.

Nick nods, doing his best not to bark at her again, Frank can tell. "Yeah, sure. Not hungry are you?"

She shakes her head.

"You got any orange juice or something, Frank?" asks Nick.

Frank puffs out his cheeks. "Uh, I have," each word is elongated until he realises he could offer the girl some, "lime cordial. Blackcurrant?"

"Blackcurrant, please," she answers.

Frank's lips turn up into a smile. It's been a while since anyone in this gaff used the word *please*. He fixes the drink, Nick takes it to her. Frank doesn't pretend that he can't hear the two of them talk. They're an argumentative pair.

"I don't like this place," she tells him.

"I don't know what to tell you."

"How long do we have to stay?"

"Long's it takes."

She says, "Can I ring home yet?"

"Not yet," Nick leaves her.

He returns to the bar. Frank straightens himself out, his back clicking in several key places…and a new one.

"She okay?" Frank asks.

Nick plops himself on a barstool, rests his head in his palms. "She's been through a lot."

"Looks it."

"Believe it."

"Polite enough," Frank puts in.

"A pain," Nick says.

"Why involve yerself, then?"

"Because."

"Nicky," Frank slurps the good whisky, a gentlemen's mouthwash. "I'm sorry I didn't get in touch or anything. I've been busy lately and, well, I didn't think much of it."

Nick takes a gander around the new and improved Estelle's. "I can see you've been busy." His face drops. "Where's the ring?"

That knackered old boxing ring had been one of the first things to go into the skips. It hadn't taken much for his new associates to dismantle it. A long enough piss in the right corner would have caused it to domino to pieces. They've promised him that, in time, a new ring will be provided, that first they just need to let the new way of things settle before branching back into familiar territory. Still, he misses that old ring. Every patch-up it'd been through had its own story, each story now in a scrapyard somewhere.

"Yeah. About that," says Frank, placing the whisky back on its shelf.

"I preferred how it was," says Nick.

"Crusty an' fucked?" Frank snorts.

"Yeah, crusty and fucked."

Frank leans on the bar with his arms spread like he has countless times over the years, ready, though not always willing, to listen to the troubles of the East End's sad cases. Nick has never been one of those sad cases, though he does have a story of which he has never gone into detail about.

"Nicky," he asks, "what's this trouble with you and uh…" He looks over to the girl. "What'd you say your name was sweet'eart?"

She swallows some blackcurrant squash, wipes her mouth with her forearm. "Katy."

"Thank you, Katy," Frank smiles.

"Nick says you'll help?" she says.

"I'm not sure yet sweet'eart, just gonna find out about this mess yer in and see what I can do."

The cat hops back up onto the table for another pampering session. Frank reckons it could be one of those show cats, bred for looking good and accepting awards.

Speaking to Nick again, he becomes more serious. "Why don't you start from the start, Nicky."

"It's fucked up, Frank," warns Nick.

"Not much I ain't seen or heard."

Nick tells what Frank believes is the abridged version of the whole story, condensing it into less than ten minutes, and Nicky boy wasn't lying. It's a fucked up story. Murder of a cop, child sacrifice and a blood orgy isn't exactly Sunday paper standard.

Frank stubs out his cigarette, reaches for the packet in his pocket, forgetting that he's left them upstairs in the kitchen. As a substitute, he drains the golden-amber button of whisky left in the tumbler.

"Jesus. You're not having me on, are yer?"

"It's all true." Nick drums his fingers on the bar, pokes his nail into the new varnish.

In all the years he's known Nick, Frank has never heard the lad tell a bullshit story.

Frank says, "You get yourself mixed up in some shit, don't you?"

"Maybe it's a talent."

"I can't believe I'm saying this Nicky, but you really can't call the Old Bill?" *There's a first time for everything*, Frank thinks.

"If I do that, they'll come for her."

"You know that for sure?"

"I don't know what I'm sure about anymore," Nick rubs his eyelids.

Letting the dust grind itself away from the cogs in his brain, Frank says, "I don't want to jump to any conclusions here, but, this guy you said about, Ulywhatsit Crane?"

"Ulysses."

"Whatever it is, it sounds like he's into some cult lark, the way you're tellin' it."

"He's adamant about the power of" – Nick air-quotes – "wishes."

Fiddling with the gold pendant in his chest hair, Frank shrugs, "Sounds cult-ish."

Nick scoffs, "What d'*you* know about all that bollocks?"

"Nothing much, but I know the sixties and seventies, back when there was a real boom in all that black magic nonsense. Satanic rituals and all that malarky. You ever heard of the Process Church?"

Nick shakes his head. Behind him, the girl Katy seems happy enough attending to the needs of her cat. The cat appears interested in their conversation, blinking slowly.

"Didn't think so," says Frank, looking away. "They were quite a big thing back in the day, influential in places you wouldn't expect. Sorta came across as a bit of a laugh until the accusations of ritual rape and murder started poppin' up. 'Course before all that was the Crowley fella."

The lines on Nick's face deepen. "Sounds like you know quite a lot about it."

"Might sound that way," Frank manages a half-smile, "but I was young once, y'know. The new stuff going into my head is starting to come loose, maybe, but the old clobber makes a strong foundation. Anyway, all I'm saying is, everything you've told me points to the same sorta culty nonsense."

"This ain't nonsense." The outside world is a noiseless white drape hanging over the windows, Nick looks over his shoulder, checking all of them. As he does he says, "I had no idea it was an interest of yours."

Franks grumbles, "It isn't, Nicky. Some things make an impact when they're happening and just stamp themselves in yer grey matter for later days."

Nick asks, "You reckon Crane belongs to this Process Church?"

"God, no," Franks says. "They're long gone. Just pointing out what you might be dealing with."

"I don't know about that, but I do know that the girl has been through hell and now I'm along for the ride. My fault, I guess," says Nick.

"Not a fault, what you did. She holding up?"

"For a kid, she's- "

"I can speak for myself." The girl's voice isn't loud but reaches them easily. She's finished the blackcurrant squash. "And I'm not a kid."

Frank addresses her. "I can see that. Would you like a kip, or a lay down somewhere? This ain't a hotel, but there're a few spare beds, it might be just what you need. Or I can stick a radio on for you? We'll be right here if you need anything."

"I don't need anything," she answers, running her index finger through the ring left by the blackcurrant squash. "I just want to go home. They've come for me this morning and they'll come for me again."

She has bags under her eyes the likes of which Frank has only seen on terminally ill patients. "You'll be alright here for a while."

"I don't think so," she says, looking around the pub as if the walls might close in around her at any moment.

"I'll get it sorted," from Nick.

Jesus, the kid's seen too much of the world's crap already.

Frank and Nick return to a more huddled conversation. Frank didn't realise it existed, but Nick has the smell of struggle on him. It's like sweat, but not quite. Blood and broken glass and salt. Maybe it's the same kind of thing animals smell when they sense a person's mood, or if they're afraid. Frank has never, ever seen Nick afraid of anyone or anything, though he supposes that after all he's been through in the last ten hours, perhaps a bloke is permitted to be a touch off his usual manner.

"I like her," says Frank.

"She's growing on me," Nick replies.

Frowning, Frank asks, "That true?"

"Dunno."

"Why'd you do it?"

"Eh?" from Nick.

"Get 'er outta there?" Frank says.

Nick folds his arms, his decaying jacket tightens around his solid biceps. Unless he's in the ring, Nicky is the kind of unassuming bloke you'd think wouldn't hurt a fly, and maybe he wouldn't, because a fly hasn't done anything to him, but every now and then you're reminded that this unassuming bloke is a trained, perhaps a bit rusty, fighter. The girl has a good protector at her side, though the big chap he'd told Frank about, Apollo, sounds like a hard man. Could he have more of an arsehole name, though?

"Wouldn't you?" asks Nick.

How has the morning gone so swiftly from circling prospects on the horses to Nicky and a girl on the run from what sounds like a damn cult?

"I'd've never gotten myself involved in the first place." Frank checks under the bar, sure that he's still got a carton of…there they are! He slips a cigarette between his lips, sparks it up. He closes his eyes to get the full effect of tobacco, tar and nicotine rolled into one. The tobacco is stale, but that just means a different flavour.

Nick sighs. "Maybe you wouldn't have. I told you, it happened out of the blue. Until last night I was just helping an old geezer collect and deliver packages. And," Nick gestures to the girl, "I couldn't just let them kill her."

"You're a good bloke, Nicky." Frank feels the need to remind Nick.

"Yeah, well. What if I'm doing this for the wrong reasons?"

"What the hell could a wrong reason be?"

Nick shakes his head. "Righting wrongs?"

"Sounds like you're sabotaging yerself. Took bollocks to do what you did. Try an' find some common ground with her."

"A grown bloke and a teenage girl? Yeah, *that's* happening," Nick rolls his eyes.

A car that sounds like it needed an M.O.T. yesterday slows down outside Estelle's. Please don't let it be the drop-off now, let that happen another day, or at least in a couple of hours when, hopefully, Nick and the girl have moved on. Quite how the subject of a murdered cop and the aging bigwig of what has to be a cult can just be moved on is beyond Frank. Whatever happens for the rest of the week, he knows it'll be lodged in his brain like beef in teeth. As luck would have it, the write-off on wheels outside moves on, but how long that luck'll last is its own mystery.

"Nick," Frank starts, "not that I don't appreciate you feel you can come 'ere in a time of need, especially concerning something so nuthouse mad as what you've told me, but if you've come for my help, I really don't know what to tell yer. I can give you a bed, much more'n that I'm afraid my hands're tied."

"Oh, come on Frank. Don't think I don't know your past, what you used to get up to. You must still have contacts. People who know how to move people without being seen. All we have to do is get the girl outta the city. From there, I reckon it'll be fine." Nick has a desperate look in his face unfamiliar to Frank.

Frank leans in closer, lowering his voice. "It ain't that easy anymore, Nicky."

"Just make a call. I'll pay whatever the price is. What about some old bank job guys? They know how to get about unseen. Get us past any interference – and there'll be some – and that's it."

"You're not listenin'. I still have the contacts Nicky, but…I can't help you. I'm sorry."

"Why *not*?" A vein bulges on Nicky's neck.

"I don't strictly *own* this gaff anymore. I'm working with…new associates. That's why I've been outta the picture for a while, gettin' things sorted. Things're being run differently, and I can't make decisions that concern this place in any way. Everything I do, even on the side, has to be run past the new owners. I don't wanna fuck this up by pissing them off before it's started, there's a lotta money in this for me if I play my cards right."

Nick doesn't say anything for a few seconds. The girl Katy is humming to herself, though she doesn't have the look of someone enjoying a song.

"This's bigger than money, Frank." Nick slams his fist on the bar, quickly turns to see the girl's reaction. Apparently, she doesn't have one.

"Nicky, I appreciate your situation, but I still have to think of myself. A favour under the radar might be just that to you, but to me it could mean the end of my business. And believe me, my associates *will* find out." Unable to find an ashtray on the bar, Frank flicks the ash onto the floor.

Nick narrows his eyes. "Who're you're new associates, Frank?"

Frank knew this would come sooner or later. He'd hoped for *much* later. This conversation was always going to be difficult, especially considering Nick's own past with the same associates. Frank clears his throat, strokes the loose flop of skin where once a solid Adam's apple had sat in the middle of a powerful neck.

Frank respects Nick, gives the answer straight. Nick'd do the same for him.

"The Georges."

Nick stares at Frank, disbelief hidden under his stony gaze. Finally he asks, "This what your business was about the last time I was here?"

Frank nods. The ash on his cigarette starts to curl under its own weight. "The place wasn't doing too good, Nicky. I have to keep things going. The brothers are being very generous to me."

The girl asks, "What's wrong?"

"Nothing," Nick answers without looking at her. He keeps his eyes on Frank, and Frank can read between the lines. He knows enough about Nick's history with the Georges to know how he must be feeling.

Frank tries, "Look. Nicky, I- "

"Call them," Nick butts in.

The cigarette almost slips from Frank's mouth. "Call 'em?"

Nick stands. "Call the Georges."

At last the ash falls from the cigarette and into Frank's chest hair. He hisses inwards, pats away the heat. He wants to ask Nick if he's sure, but Nick has already gone to sit with the girl, struggling, it seems, to find any lasting conversation with her.

He calls the brothers, has a short conversation with one of them. Fifteen minutes later, the drop-off is made, and two minutes after that, Nicky and the girl, along with the cat, are out of Estelle's.

Nick doesn't say goodbye. The girl does.

CHAPTER 16

Entering Master Crane's private quarters through a creaky door, Simon is struck by not only the warmth but its grandness. A blaze crackles within a stone fireplace big enough to walk into, there's a four poster bed fit for Scrooge, furniture so ornate it must've been designed to be admired as much as sat on, paintings of smudged nightmares and an array of bookshelves that are, unlike the shop, only half full. The room is dim, as per Master Crane's preference, an atmospheric pool of woody browns and burning oranges. It could be a chamber in a haunted castle, though in all the films Simon has seen, not one Hollywood monster mansion came equipped with carpets as plush as these.

At a small round table, Master Crane is a shadow sitting cross-legged with his back to the fire, his hands overlapping at the top of his cane, fingers made to look longer by trick of the light. Eyes bright even in his private gloom, they are fixed on Simon, sending a shiver up his bare, sinewy arms. He rubs his non-existent biceps, feels like a nervous schoolboy due for the cane.

Only when you are personally summoned are you permitted entry into Master Crane's private quarters, located somewhere within the labyrinthine hallways of his building. Only the Master and his closest followers, Mr Apollo and the Black Rose, know how to find their way through all the corridors without getting lost. There might be trapdoors and secret levers, Simon thinks.

"Simon Schaeffer," Master Crane says, though his mouth doesn't appear to move.

Simon tries to stand without the aid of nervous rubbing, but can't find the courage. Great men like the Master demand your servitude, and only the meek serve, so Simon must be meek, an honour in this circumstance.

He squeezes his arm instead, lumpy as chicken gristle.

"Yes, Master Crane?" He bows his head.

What Master says next comes laced with poison. "Stand straight. Leave yourself alone."

Simon does as he's told. His balls shrink up inside him. What awesome power Master Crane emanates, glaring at him now, jaw muscles twitching. A near empty glass is on a coaster in front of Master Crane. He traces his finger around the rim without breaking eye contact with Simon.

The Master queries, "Have you sanitised your hands?"

"Yes, Master."

"Shoes off?"

Simon wiggles his toes. "Yes, Master."

"Good."

Fighting off the stutter, Simon asks, "You wished to see me, Master Crane?"

"You know why."

Simon does. It was stupid of him to think that he could take such a moronic risk and actually come off the winner. He had so wanted to please Master Crane, had so wanted the great man's favour. Simon swallows, a dry click in his throat, trying to wet the words so that they'll slide up and he can explain himself.

WHACK!

The crack of the Master's cane on the table brings a quiver to Simon's bottom lip. The glass spills a blob of dark liquid. Whatever you do, he tells himself, don't cry.

"You know why," Master repeats.

Master Crane is fond of whacking out his exclamation marks ahead of what he's about to say.

"I know why," says Simon.

Master raises an eyebrow as he judges Simon further. This is the longest Simon has ever been in his presence one-to-one. Never before has he felt such terror and pleasure both at the same time. The gaze of Master is too much to handle and his hand finds its way back to his bicep to continue rubbing.

"Step further into the light, please," from Master Crane.

In the middle of the room is a cone of light coming out of the ceiling. Simon prepares himself, obeys Master Crane, the right side of his face glistens as he comes under the spotlight.

Only a hint of disgust bends Master's face out of shape. Simon can see that the great man is repulsed, though unlike most other things, Simon doesn't mind that Master Crane reacts this way. Actually, it's exactly how he hoped people would react to his never-handsome face.

Swapping his crossed legs, Master Crane says, "There are better methods of healing a wound than the vile torture you have committed upon yourself, Mr Schaeffer."

Smiling inside, Simon traces a finger down the right side of his face, pinging each metal rung of the crooked ladder.

It had hurt when he'd stapled his face back together, but that had been good. Being a sadomasochist came with its perks. Each piece of metal he'd punctured into his face came with a joyous shudder, erecting his dick one stinging click at a time. The best one had been the staple he'd saved for last, just under his right eye. The stabbing of the metal caused his eye to go bloodshot, it was also when he finally allowed himself to climax. It was lucky that Simon's biggest kink was making himself his own victim. There was no other power like that, perhaps not even Master Crane's.

Between staples the skin isn't staying together very well. Puss leaks from each opening. He'd washed his face after his demented surgery, though new liquids with their own smells quickly took the place of blood.

Feeling the staples releases some of the pain, though it's already nowhere near as good as what it had been. Maybe later, when he's alone, he'll plier them out so he could do it again.

Simon begins his reply, "I thought that- "

"You did not think at all, Mr Schaeffer," Master Crane snaps. "Just like you failed to think this morning when you unleashed your rabble of ghouls on Nicholas and the girl."

Simon knows it's best to not argue with Master Crane, yet the words fly out of his mouth before he can stop them. "I was trying to help Mr Apollo."

"Mr Apollo," the *O* gets extended, "does not *need* help."

"But- "

"But nothing!" Master Crane shoots to his feet with a litheness that shouldn't belong to a man of his age. His face is pale in the light, his eyes burning with a light that seems to come from within. "It is exactly this kind of nonsense that I do not need from you, Mr Schaeffer. Look at yourself!"

Master points to the right where a gilded mirror is mounted on the wall. Simon beholds his new monstrous appearance. The Master wants him to feel shame which doesn't make itself known. Simon enjoys his new look. Who would've believed that a mullet and a stapled face would look so *amazing* on him.

WHACK! from the cane. Simon jumps, lip quivering all over again.

"We are a society of men and woman, not all of them fine, who are supposed to be secretive," explains Master Crane. "We may have resources and we may have people within our ranks who help us to stay hidden, but what kind of fool are you to draw attention to yourself this way? As if your garish haircut was not bad enough, now you will never be able to show *that* face anywhere without receiving due scrutinization from the rest of civilisation. And your blasted ghouls, the passed-on whom you adore so much. You call upon them in daylight in the *city*? Where anyone might be able to see them?! You have risked our society, Mr Schaeffer. You have disappointed me and damned yourself."

Hearing it is all he can take. He was only trying to do right by Master, to help get the girl back as quickly as possible. But, oh, why didn't he *think*?! Why didn't he take his stupid time and wait for Master to come to *him*? You're such a fuckwit, Simon Schaeffer, you've always been a fuckwit! He pleads with Master Crane, "I'm sorry, Master, I only meant to help! I promise you! I'm sorry!"

"It matters not that you were trying to help." Master Crane turns to face the blaze, the logs still fat with burn time. "Mr Apollo's being there was a gamble on my part, and it should have been the only gamble. A striking of the iron whilst it was still hot, so to speak. I never expected it to work, but it was a chance I was able to take with Mr Apollo because *he* knows what he is doing. He may have come back empty-handed, but it allowed us to get a handle on Nicholas's abilities as a man on the run. Turns out, he is good, as I thought he might be, but now we have the upper hand, and we just need to await the correct moment."

Hopeful, Simon steps forward, his fingers scissoring. "I can make it up to you, Master. I can use the dead to watch them, the man and the girl. The man already has his own ghost that follows him, I can ask it to- "

Master Crane grabs the half full glass and tosses it into the fireplace. It smashes, the blaze grows to lick over the mantlepiece, charring the glass face of a clock. Master turns on Simon, his face furious in a way the Devil would envy. Simon cowers away, however he cannot take his eyes off the magnificent wrath of his Master.

"We already *have* eyes on them, Mr Schaeffer. Make no mistake about it. We have had eyes on Nicholas since the beginning. There is nowhere he can go without us knowing."

"H…H…How?" asks Simon.

"*That*," Master Crane regains his posture, "is not for you to know. Mr Schaeffer, I have pondered on what to do with you as punishment for your lack of brain power today."

The fire gutters to normal size.

"Please, Master Crane, I…" Simon runs out of words.

The Master taps his cane on the floor, from the shadows emerges the Black Rose. Always she is near Master, held in high esteem. Simon hates her. *She* was the one who fucked up with the girl. But has or will *she* receive any punishment? Most likely not, fucking bitch.

She has a name, but Simon is not the only one within the society who calls her Black Rose. It suits the bitch well. In her hands, the Black Rose is holding something wrapped in a green velvet sheet.

"Say hello to Miss Juniper, Mr Schaeffer," from Master Crane.

The Black Rose smirks at Simon, her red lips don't appear to have a parting. Good, stitch them shut and silence her.

"Hello, Miss Juniper," he says.

She doesn't say anything back, only holds onto her smirk whilst Master pulls the velvet off.

It's the book Master Crane had at the gathering. Instantly, Simon's stomach turns into a dishwasher. It's about the only pain he doesn't find pleasurable. Master takes it, places it on the round table, patting it gently. Left over on the green velvet is black goop.

Stroking the book, Master Crane says, "I was good to you, Mr Schaeffer. I granted your wish to commune with the deceased. Now I have this book, it would be all too easy for me to take it away."

The threat is immediately too much for Simon. His lungs deflate and hang in his chest like limp balloons. He drops to his knees and clasps his hands together in prayer to a man that stands above all gods.

Simon begins to beg, secretly enjoying the demeaning action, knowing that it will please his Master to see him squirm. "Please, my Master," he sobs, "you can't do that to me. Anything but that!"

"I may do as I please," Master teases.

Simon's head droops, he weeps. The gaps between his staples are weeping their own fluid. He mumbles sorry after sorry, and his regrets for having acted without leave. He feels again the glacial stare of his Master.

It's the worst thing imaginable to Simon Schaeffer, to be stripped of the ability to speak and laugh and play and frolic with the spirits. Without it, he will be nothing. To be sent back to being plain, unloved Simon 'Pisspants' Schaeffer would be a waking nightmare. He has never known what it means to be loved by anyone, not his mother, not the father he never knew but was told was a piece of shit. Only when he messed around with the tatty-edged Ouija board he found when digging through Mother's 'work clothes' did he hear, or read, those first words of affection, calling to him from a place he would only know in death. He knew this at six years old, and he knew it through the school that branded him Pisspants and through his failed university application (why he had even tried he doesn't know). Those words spelled out by the planchette – *we love you* – was the beginning of his obsession with speaking with the dead. He had never stopped searching for a better way to communicate with them. No so called psychics, mediums or ghost whisperers had helped him. Phonies and fucking fakers the lot of them. It had only been after the burning of his mother's home, leading to her death, that Simon met, perhaps by chance, one of the Master's followers. With Master Crane as his guide, Simon made the wish and sliced the throat of the offering and was shortly after able to see the spirits of the dead all around him. There aren't many places they don't like to stand. He's never been happier.

The police left the case of arson on his mother's home unsolved, but Simon knows better.

As for his sadomasochism, *that* was something which developed after speaking to a particular ghost who channelled itself through Simon. It had its fun with him for several nights, taught him so many wonderful things.

Simon glances up. Master Crane is checking his pocket watch, the Black Rose is shaking her head at Simon, tutting.

He tries again to plead with his Master. "Master, I…please…*the fog!*" He raises his head, eyes wide. "I knew the fog would hide the spirits, so no one would see, I- "

"The fog was dumb luck, Mr Schaeffer." Master Crane pockets his watch. "Much in the same way, I expect, that me doing what I am about to do may be considered dumb by others."

Simon awaits the Master's next words.

"Do not think me such a beast that I would not first give you a warning before I elect to use proper punishment, Mr Schaeffer." Using his cane, Master taps Simon on the shoulders. It's like a knighthood. "Please stand, for your own dignity. Consider your thoughtlessness forgiven."

Relief washes over Simon, he quickly gets to his feet. The Master is a lenient man. He catches a glimpse of himself in the mirror again, the skin around the staples is red. His lungs re-inflate, the tears dry themselves. The relief is wonderful, but it's also a tightrope beneath his feet, a reminder that he has to watch his balance from here on out, something he will do for his Master. A pity, though, that the imaginary tightrope is not razor wire. The feet are such a sensitive area.

"I am so thankful, Master," says Simon. "I thank you so, so much."

The Black Rose scoffs at Simon's weakness, then walks with dolly steps to the fireplace.

Master Crane holds up a hand to stop him. "Enough of that Mr Schaeffer, I beg you."

The Master begs me?

"I do have use of you and your ghouls," continues the good Master Crane. "Or should I say, *one* of your ghouls?"

Simon thinks he knows where Master Crane is going with this. "You want me to send a spirit to grab another offering? Like we did with the girl?"

WHACK!

Simon flinches. Gritting his teeth, one of the staples rubs against them. Eventually, it'll carve the tooth hollow, like a pumpkin.

"Listen…Mr Schaeffer," Master Crane growls. He flips open the book, the blaze flutters. "No, I do not want you to acquire a new offering, as well as we know that works. You may not a have heard at the gathering due to your," Master Crane's features screw up, "injury, but we cannot use a different offering. The book has tasted the girl's blood and will only accept the girl's blood. Look here…"

With hesitation, Simon leans to look at the book. It startles him when the pages turn themselves to a splotch of blood.

"You see? A new offering would be useless. It has her scent, if you can accept the phrase. The girl is vital, Mr Schaeffer, and though you blundered this morning, you *are* going to aid in her recapture," Master Crane finishes, sitting back at the table. He pulls the book closer to him, though it seems to also float.

Simon's pride swells. "How can I help?" he asks.

Smiling, Master Crane says, "You are aware that Nicholas's own spectre follows him. Correct? His own manifestation of choices irreversible."

From her position at the fireplace, the Black Rose hisses, "I knew that man would be trouble the second I saw him on that bus."

Chuckling, the Master says to her, "The past is the past, Juniper. Best we do not dwell on it."

The Master's voice is different when he talks to the Black Rose. It seems to brighten the room for all of a second before he turns his pale eyes back to Simon. "Correct?"

"Yes, Master Crane."

"Good, Mr Schaeffer. Very good. So, here is what I would like from you. Do you think you could run some…interference, for me?"

A grin greases itself on Simon's face. Master tells Simon what he wants, and the plan is, obviously, excellent.

Master Crane adds, "If you do this correctly, the girl shall be ours and the book will have what it wants. You shall be rewarded, Mr Schaeffer. You thought being able to confer with the deceased was everything? You could be the general of the dead."

There is such confidence in the way Master says this that Simon's stomach explodes with hordes of butterflies.

As Simon is leaving, Master Crane stops him. Simon spins around, sees the Master standing, the Black Rose coming to his aid. Silly bitch, doesn't she know Master doesn't *need* any help?

The Master says, "Do not think for one moment that your pleasures through pain are unique. You are not unique. I know such things, have delved deep in my time. Your ways are disgusting, Mr Schaeffer. There is nothing dignified about them. If you do anything more to disfigure yourself for all to see, I will not hesitate to relinquish you of your abilities. Work carefully, and when the time is right…interfere."

With a final bow of his head, Simon exits Master Crane's private quarters. Despite the negative parting words, Simon can only smile as he strides down the dark corridor, staples winking as he passes under each cone of light. The corridor is lined with stone statues of what might have been lions once. Their snouts and manes have eroded, fangs blunted.

Simon is eager to begin his mission.

And he has something good to tell his therapist, now.

CHAPTER 17

And now Katy is in the back of a van.

It's not a smelly van, not a rusty van or a van that you'd see being chased in a crime show. It's still a horrible van though, and the driver is even more horrible. He told them that they couldn't sit in the front because he "doesn't want no kids messin' up" his van. Actually, there'd been an F-bomb in there which he made sound even worse than it already is.

Katy watches the man sitting on the wheel arch opposite her. He's kneading his hands together, rubbing them on his legs when the sweat gets too much. She still hasn't made up her mind if she can trust Nick. The last adult she thought she could trust took her out onto that stage. It was stupid of her to trust that powder-faced woman in the first place.

Nick looks at her from time to time, offering what he probably thinks are reassuring smiles. He can be mean, but he also seems quite sweet. Sometimes, he even asks her how she is, to which she replies that she is fine, thank you. She isn't. Who would be? She's a ball of nerves, the slightest bump shaking all her leaves from the tree. Katy finds it hard to contain her tears, she's unable to think straight or rationalise anything, and it may be this way for a while. She can't even view herself as the girl she once was not so long ago, which wasn't a girl who would cut a man's face open. It'd been a move she didn't know she'd be able to pull off, yet when it came time, it was like there was a voice inside her, prompting her, looking out for her. She doesn't believe she'll be able to do it again, because it hadn't been her, not in one sense but...maybe in the other. *This*...all this that's happening, is what that group who visited her school last term with their loud music and louder clothes called a crisis situation. Speaking of clothes, she looks down at her horrible grey tunic. It's itchy and feels like it was sewn from sandpaper. She hopes she can bin it soon.

Katy knows she has no great reason to not trust Nick. He *did* rescue her, not once but twice, and he's trying his best to get her somewhere safe, though he doesn't seem too happy about it, especially since they were huddled into the back of this van. It couldn't hurt to get to know him better.

There's no light, only what leaks over from the front where the driver periodically mumbles to himself. Katy combats her nerves by watching Pop Tart, who doesn't seem to be minding the journey in spite of the many stops, starts and speed bumps. Finished with washing his silky coat, Pop Tart is content to sit by her, expertly counter-balancing his body whenever they turn a corner. Katy likes that Pop Tart is here, it brings her one of the comforts of home that had only yesterday been a sketch on a cell wall. Pop Tart is nothing like her mangy tabby that treats Mum and Dad's house like a cat hotel. She feels bad for thinking it, because Bales is an otherwise lovely cat who cuddles with the best of them when the nights are cold. But Pop Tart, silly yet loveable name forgiven, is a different breed altogether. Like a big cat – a *panther* – that's gotten stuck in a little cat's body. Then, Pop Tart isn't that little. Pop Tart must have some Bengal in him, somewhere in the bloodline.

The van brakes hard and Katy nearly tumbles over. Nick moves to keep her up but she has already readjusted herself.

"Sorry," the driver cackles, a poor liar.

Nick offers another smile, and this time it prompts Katy to try and strike up a conversation. It's quite clear that at this point Nick isn't going to.

She brushes hair out her face. "Where are we going now?"

Biting his nails, leaning back against the van's hull, Nick replies, "To some people that should be able to help us."

"More friends of yours?"

"No. They're not my friends."

"Then…why would they help us?"

Nick sighs, lets his chewed fingers fall away from his mouth. "They might not, but I don't know anyone else who will. If the answer is no, we're on our own."

She says, "If they're not your friends, and they might not help us, why are we going to them?"

"Like I said, I don't know anyone else."

Katy strokes her hair. "What about that man we were just with?"

"He can't help us."

Nick is full of insights, Katy inwardly huffs. There is something about where they're going that's making Nick very uncomfortable, you didn't have to be clever to see it.

"You must have some more friends?" asks Katy.

Looking towards the front of the van, ignoring Pop Tart who comes for a closer seat, Nick says, "No."

Katy thinks for a while. "You know, I used to have friends who weren't really my friends. They said they liked me, they also teased me all the time. They made me feel like they were the only people I could turn to, but actually, they were just bullies. They used to get me in quite a bit of trouble. That's why I kinda keep to myself, now."

"It's a bit different for me than that," says Nick.

Katy shrugs, "Maybe, I dunno. Bullies are bullies. Know what I did about it?"

"Do tell."

He might not be interested, but Katy is going to tell him anyway, because it's her story for God's sake and he can listen to it.

"I let them go. They treated me badly, used me, so I got rid of them. Life improved after that."

Nick scoffs with a little extra something, might be amusement, not meant in a horrible way.

"That's, uh, great Katy," he says, looking at her again. "I'm glad you were able to make your life better. But it's more complicated for me. I can't just let these people go."

"Why not?" Katy wiggles her fingertips together so Pop Tart can come and get the attention he deserves, which he does without a second thought.

"Because they won't let *me* go."

The van slows and comes to a stop with a faint squeak from the wheels. Nick stands, knowing more than Katy does, apparently.

"We're 'ere," the driver grunts. He slides out of the van.

The driver doesn't come straight away to let them out, instead he stretches, makes a lot of noise doing it. There's another person here too, chatting to the driver, though Katy can't make out what they're saying.

Her private time with Nick is about to run out, they may not get many opportunities to talk just the two of them, so she says the first thing that pops into her mind as she hears the crunching of gravel as the driver makes his way to open the back doors. It might be important, it might not, but it's something they both experienced and that makes it at least a *little* important.

"Nick?" she taps his hand.

"What?" He doesn't look at her

"I've seen one of them before."

A searching look creases his face.

"Those things," she says.

"The things?"

A key twists in the lock of the doors, gets stuck. The driver swears the worst of swear words when he has to force the key to turn. Katy might utter something light when it's just her and a riverbed, but she doesn't ever use the C-nuke. It might be, she ponders, because she uses terms like F-bomb and C-nuke that other teens find her...weird. Well, that's their problem. The good thing about being a voluntary outcast is that you don't care about the stereotypical opinions of your peers, even if, sometimes, you do.

"Those dark shapes," Katy says, standing, "before we got away."

Nick closes his eyes. "Hang on a sec- "

She cuts him off. "I saw one right before I was taken."

The doors swing open, flooding the van's interior with light. The fog has finally cleared. Katy holds her forearm over her eyes, peering at the driver who, with spread arms holding onto the doors, is gawking at the pair of them. Pop Tart, on the other hand, leaps down from the van and trots around the gravel, getting his bearings. Most cats would dart off into a bush, never be seen again, not Pop Tart though, he just likes to get to know where he is.

The driver haphazardly kicks out at Pop Tart, missing by inches.

He's not a handsome man, the driver.

He barks, "Come on, then. Get out."

Nick jumps down first and holds out a hand for Katy. She thinks about taking it, then doesn't. Nick doesn't show any reaction when she gets out on her own. They're in the middle of an industrial area, empty and without any kind of workforce. The driver slams the doors shut and stomps back to the front, gets inside and starts the engine. When he pulls away the rear tyres kick up gravel and it scratches the backs of Katy's legs.

Nick speaks out the side of his mouth.

"Just stay close to me and don't say what doesn't have to be said," he whispers.

Pop Tart parks himself next to Katy. "Huh?"

Nick doesn't say anything else. He's stopped fidgeting, outwardly anyway. Inside, Katy can tell he's a tornado. Unfortunately for emotional closets like Nick, the inside can sweat out. Her attention is snatched when a voice calls over to them.

"Good to see you, Nick!"

A man is walking towards them. Behind him is a wall with an opened gate, and behind that is what has to be an old factory, only this one's had a makeover. It's closer to a fancy hotel. There are statues either side of the gate, sculptures of woman with water jugs or something, and inside Katy sees patches of green grass and tall plants.

Becoming larger as he gets closer, the man is wearing a suit and shoes that stay shiny despite the dusty gravel. There is also another man standing over by the gate, leaning on the wall with one foot up and his arms folded. Katy can't see much of him except for his moustache and dark eyes. Is he smirking? He creeps Katy out.

Nick doesn't look happy about it when the large man lumps a hand on Nick's shoulder. It's the gesture of a friend. Nick said in the van that these people were not his friends.

"Nick. It's a surprise to see you. When Frank called, I told him immediately to send you over." Looking Nick up and down, the large man's smile drops a bit. "You don't look so hot." Then he glances at Katy and she takes a step back, not sure why. "And who is *this*?"

"How much'd Frank tell you on the phone?" asks Nick.

"Just that you might need some sort of service," the large man shrugs, then focusses on Katy again. There's something in his eyes that, in contrast to his body language and his tone of voice, frightens her. Like a wild dog. "Little Cherub, you look like you're in need of a good wash. Why don't I get the two of you inside and we'll see if we can get you in some proper clothes."

Without waiting for a reply, the large man begins to lead them inside. The creepy, smirking man has disappeared. Pop Tart keeps close to Katy, keeping a close eye on all his surroundings, alert to any noise or threat, just as a cat should be.

The gates close solidly behind them when they enter what now feels like less of a refurbished factory and more of a compound. Bushes have been trimmed into animal shapes, including an elephant and tiger. There are smaller statues of mystical creatures, nymphs and elves and stuff. Patrolling the garden are scary looking men in suits. Katy is sure she sees one or two of them with guns.

Nick doesn't say a word, makes sure that Katy is never far from him. He doesn't have to worry, she doesn't feel like exploring this place.

Before they enter the building, Katy overhears the large man whisper in Nick's ear.

"I told you you might need a favour one day."

CHAPTER 18

It's been a long time since Nick was in the company of the Georges in their own manor. It's the last place he wants to be. They've come a long way, and even way back they boasted an impressive budding empire. The converted factory with topiary animals is a bit much, not to mention the armed goons. Each to their own.

The place isn't exactly what he thinks of when imagining the criminal underworld. The whole place is a boast to both the Georges' enemies and friends. It has an air of look-at-me that is maddeningly confident. The brothers have always been good at covering their tracks – legally and literally – so they've never had to keep their domineering presence in the city a secret. They're the kind of blokes who the police can never pin anything solid to, and they love it. That's what this factory conversion is all about, it's a statement that says *look how well we're doing and you ain't got shit on us*. As Harvey George flaps his gums, Nick tries to identify points of entry and exit, a good habit to have in a place where you don't know if you'll need to clear off sharpish at any moment.

The girl is curious about where she is, and Pop Tart is being curious right along with her. She doesn't appear to be afraid, just curious. Or wary. Nick has tucked away what she'd mentioned about the black shapes around the car. The spirits of the Murdered. Katy mentioned she'd seen one before she was kidnapped. She didn't mention the one in the back seat, though.

That one is just for Nick.

It has a name, too.

Harvey squeezes Nick's shoulder and the sausage-fingered gangster whispers, "I told you you might need a favour one day."

It's a playful warning that let's Nick know that whatever he needs will come with a price.

Two goons wearing glasses inside shut them in, the bang reverberates down the corridor. Katy picks up Pop Tart and walks next to Nick.

Harvey says, "Can you believe this place was once a shithole, just like your flat?"

"Yeah," Nick replies.

"We purchased it on the cheap."

"I don't care, Harvey," from Nick.

Harvey looks at Nick. "Where have your manners gone? You never were great with them. Anyway, this used to be all concrete and brick, most of it on the floor. We saw the potential right away, and with business ventures coming up, we couldn't say no."

"Is this before or after you bought out Frank?" Nick grunts.

"Before," smiles Harvey. "Frank was very recent."

Harvey runs his fingers through his hair, which, since his surprise visit, he has tried to style in a way that hides his bald spot.

Harvey glances at Katy, "How're you doing, Cherub?"

Katy puts on a fake smile and nods. Nick knows it's a fake smile, because he wears it a lot, too. You can tell by the way the rest of the face stays smooth. A genuine smile creates creases.

Nick can't hold his tongue. "Looks like you're doing alright for yourself then."

Smiling wide, Harvey replies, "Yes. We aren't doing too bad."

"Works out okay for some, I guess."

"Could've worked out for you too, Nick."

They reach the end of the corridor. Two more goons open a door without command. Well-trained dogs.

The room they enter is large, a repurposed work floor. It has a very high ceiling, and the brothers have kept the original steel stairs and walkway that lead into what must have once been a supervisor's office. In that office, Nick see's Walter George sneering down at him.

Furniture is posted around in groups of threes and fours, coffee tables with thick books act as hubs. There're other goons talking in their own little sects, just like at Crane's. Bulbs on lengthy chains hang down to fill the ex-factory floor with warm light.

Harvey leads them up the stairs. Everything here is a boast. The topiary bullshit is a boast, the art is a boast, the goons with their Ray-Ban sunglasses and their suits is a boast. The enormous globe Nick can see in the middle of the room which has been opened to reveal the alcoholic contents of three pubs is most definitely a boast.

Harvey opens the office door and holds it. If you didn't know the bloke, you'd think he was being a good host.

"Good morning, Nick," says Walter, lounging on a leather settee. "How're you feeling?"

Nick replies, "Always a pleasure, Walt."

Flames ignite in Walter's eyes. It doesn't take much to excite his anger. His nose is only slightly crooked, now. Almost unnoticeable, but not the same. Good.

"Come on now, you two." Harvey closes the door, strides over to one of two large desks sat next to each other at the end of the office. "Let's not jump to any aggro. It's not even midday yet."

Walter holds out his left arm. "I was only showing concern for our guest, Harvey. Word has it he bumped into a bit of trouble about a week ago. It's our duty to show concern for his wellbeing." Into that open arm comes a woman, almost curling into Walter's embrace. She's wearing a dress meant for evening events that compliments her olive skin, her hair done up with waves in all the right places. Nick knows she is either one of two things to Walter. A plaything, or someone he wants to *become* a plaything.

Harvey sits at his desk, the one on the right. "I know what you're trying to do, Walter. You can't stay away from it. Remember, I can read you like a book."

"You're an easy read y'self," says Walter, eliciting a smile from the woman by pinching her arse.

Harvey ignores his brother. "Care to sit, Nick?"

There are many chairs to choose from. Nick takes one and drags it out into the middle of the office. Katy is already dragging her own over without being asked. She doesn't know how foolhardy she's being. Harvey chuckles at her naivety.

Before Katy can sit, Harvey says to Walter's woman, "Find this Cherub some fresh clothes, will you? She can't go around looking like that. Pick out something nice. Don't make me send you back for something else."

Rolling her eyes – she's only able to get away with that because of her Kevlar Walter Vest – the woman stands. Walter playfully tugs her hand whilst she straightens her dress. She laughs, Walter lets go, the same hand going to his moustache to twiddle one of the curls.

As the woman saunters past Katy, swinging her hips for Walter's pleasure, Harvey adds, "The young Cherub can go with you, if she likes?"

"No."

Nick and Katy say it together. The pleading look on her face softens as she realises that Nick won't let her be taken.

"No?" from Harvey.

Just Nick this time. "No."

Harvey shrugs. "Fair enough, as long as you don't mind the young girl listening in?"

Nick doesn't want to drag this out. He wants to tell the brothers what he needs, pay them the fee that Crane's money will take care of and move on to the next part of whatever the hell this is.

"Where I go, she goes," says Nick, folding his arms.

"Settle down, nonce," Walter says.

"Walter!" Harvey snaps at his brother, who shows no signs of backing down. "Enough of your shit, okay?"

"Whatever."

"Sorry Nick," says Harvey. "Walter is obviously having an off day."

Katy speaks up, "I'd rather stay. Please."

It's good to hear Katy is on his side. This morning she didn't want to be anywhere near him, and the feeling was mutual. A lot has happened in the last few hours, perhaps they've managed to establish a level of trust, one that's only there when they're around other people.

"And what about that ugly thing?" Walter says to Katy, pointing out Pop Tart, who's booping his head on her chair.

"It's just a cat, Walter," Harvey says. "The Cherub is allowed her pet."

Nick interrupts, "Can we get to it, Harvey?"

Anger flashes across Harvey's face and is gone again like a shimmer of light. Harvey doesn't like being the one to be pushed along.

"Certainly," Harvey grins. He moulds his fingers together and rests them on his stomach. As if by cue card, Walter goes to his own desk, taking his time to make himself comfy in the plump chair.

Harvey asks, "So, Nick. What can we do for you?"

"The girl and me need to get out of the city."

"Can't you do that y'self? Just hop in a car, a bus or train and fuck off?" replies Walter.

"No. We need to be smuggled out."

"Why?"

At this juncture, Harvey is allowing his brother to conduct the business. They've always done it like that. Before long it'll become a two-pronged interrogation.

"There are people looking for this girl, they've got eyes and ears everywhere, including the police. It needs to be done carefully," Nick explains.

Harvey drums his fingers on his desk. "We're always careful, Nick."

"So just shove her in the boot and get driving. I don't see why this is so hard," Walter continues.

"They're after me as well," says Nick.

A smile flashes on Walter's face. "Ah, I see. You're covering your*self* as well?"

"I only need to be covered whilst I get the girl to safety. After that, I'm good."

"Yes. You always were good at looking after yourself, weren't you, Nick? Sometimes you needed," Walter pretends to search for the word, "help, a little bit of influence from outside your own little bubble, but yeah, you could say you were looking after yourself. That young lad wasn't, mind."

Nick sets his attention on Harvey. "What is this?"

"Not now, Walter," Harvey sighs. He's rubbing the flabby skin that acts as his second chin. There's a greasy shine to it.

Walter leans forward. He isn't wearing his suit jacket, rolled up shirt sleeves are tight against his forearms. "Apologies. Well, still, at least you can look after yourself in broad daylight walking down alleyways. Oh, wait."

"Fuck you," Nick bursts.

"Enough!"

Katy jumps.

Walter backs off at the sound of his brother's boom, but does so with a slowness that secretes defiance, resentment. For a while the office is silent. Walter smirks at Nick, and all Nick wants to do is smash his face in. One-on-one, he could do it, but in the manor of the Georges one-on-one doesn't exist.

Anyone who knows Harvey knows Walter knows how to press all his buttons. It's been suspected before that the younger brother sought to overthrow his elder sibling's throne. All hearsay.

"Nick," Harvey stands, strolls to the front of his desk. "I know my brother paid you an impromptu visit not so long ago" – Walter sniggers – "and I would like to say sorry for that. It certainly wasn't ran by me." He throws his brother a scowl.

"Yeah, well, what's done is done. Still," Nick glares at Walter, "it's always easier when you've got help."

"And I hope it didn't cause you any…grief?" Harvey picks up a silver globe from his desk, a paperweight, inspects it whilst he awaits the answer to the *real* question he just asked.

Nick mirrors Harvey's body language. "I didn't grass."

Harvey thuds the paperweight back on the desk. Nick notes the same paperweight would make a decent weapon…should the need arise.

"Good," smiles Harvey.

A tug on Nick's jacket.

Katy whispers, "What happened?"

Nick waves her off. She doesn't need to know the details. Is she going to be this inquisitive the whole time? She cares a lot about things a teenage girl has no business caring about.

When Nick looks back, Harvey isn't there. Instead, he's being faced by the Figure. It stands in front of the desk, arms at its sides, legs shoulder-width apart. Two tainted-star eyes stare him down, wisps of hair hanging like soggy straw from its head. It's body, a black void. He can hear the shadows swirling around it. Walter is a statue, Katy is a statue. Pop Tart is…the cat is washing itself, unaffected by the manipulation of time.

The office drops in temperature, Nick's breath plumes. Keeping his rising fear in check, he keeps his eyes on the Figure. It isn't his own fear, but a fear being injected into him. It's different.

"You were in my car," says Nick.

A split opens in the Figure's face, a horizontal crescent moon filled with mismatched teeth, some long, some flat, a graveyard crammed with too many headstones.

It nods.

"Leave me alone," Nick tells it.

It stretches forward with a leathery creak, seizes Nick by the throat, causing him to gargle. Its icy grip burns into his flesh, the breath on his face is chilled. He tells himself it isn't real, but it *feels* real. As its fingers tighten and its grin widens, this is, Nick realises, the most real this thing has ever been, more real than when it had been the young lad on his way to the top of where Nick wanted to be. He'd been afraid the young lad was going to rob him of his opportunity, that was all, just afraid and vulnerable to bad ideas. And now it had him by the throat.

It speaks with a zombie voice. "Can I…join…in?"

"Nick?"

The office is back to normal. Nick gawks around for the Figure. It isn't here. It always vanishes. Harvey stares at Nick like he's a troubled youth, Walter is on the edge of laughing and Katy is keeping her head down. If she saw the Figure, she isn't acting like it. Pop Tart isn't finished with his paw yet, licks noisily between his toes.

Harvey repeats himself, "Nick?"

"What?" Nick answers with more impatience than is wise.

"Are you listening?"

Nick stretches his neck, still feeling the cold fingers etched into his skin. He sits back down, weary on his feet. "Yeah," he says, unable to shake off the Figure like normal.

Harvey continues, "What's the danger in this, Nick? Say we help you, are we putting ourselves at risk?"

What do they want to know first? That a rampaging South African giant might stampede into their manor? Or that a band of shadow people – the Murdered – are prone to sieges?

"You know we can't have the Old Bill sniffing around us more than they already are," Harvey finishes.

Oh, yeah. Them, too. Nick clears his throat, rubs his neck. "I'm not an idiot, Harvey. The police won't get involved. Trust me on that. Not the real police."

Walter's questions smears into one word. "Whassatmean?"

"Tell us," says Harvey.

Nick inhales a long breath, holds it for a couple of seconds before letting it go. "The people looking for the girl are connected. A number of them are police if the threat is real, and for definite at least one of them is a higher-up, which is probably enough."

"How'd you figure?" asks Walter.

Tossing the younger George a glare, Nick answers, "Because it was him or her who allowed one of their officers to be murdered."

A thin sweat cools Nick's forehead as the Figure's presence lingers. Is it still here, hiding?

Walter leans back, eyebrows raised. "That's a strong word to come outta the blue. Serious outfit, is it?"

"That's why you need *us*." Harvey drums his fingers. "Old Bill've got connections everywhere. If people are after you and they have police intel at their disposal, they'll be able to keep tabs on you as you move through the city, which you don't want. That your thinking?"

"Pretty much," replies Nick.

Walter pipes up. "All I'm getting' from this is that police are involved."

"Not the *real* police," Nick replies.

"These are *bad* police," Katy adds. Pop Tart has moved from the floor to her lap. "Friends of bad people."

Walter scoffs. "The girl has an opinion."

Harvey puts his hands in his pockets. Grinning, he tells Katy, "Cherub. To us, *all* police are bad."

"Then you must be bad men," she says.

Nick tries to keep her quiet. "Katy…"

"We *are* bad men, darlin'." Walter runs his thumb and index over his moustache, checking its shape like all people with hairy lips do. "So you'd best keep quiet."

"Walter, for fuck- " Harvey stops himself. Apparently running a criminal empire is okay, but using harsh language in front of a child is a no-go. Harvey addresses her, "Cherub- "

"Stop calling me that," Katy says.

"Cherub?"

"Yes."

"Will you tell me your name instead?"

"No," Katy shakes her head.

Harvey snorts, a smug smile on his face that Nick recognises. It's roughly the same these days, only with a different kind of grit. "Then we'll stick with Cherub for now."

"The police who're involved," Nick interrupts the two of them, "will not be interested in you. Not police business in other words. They'll have to be careful or risk exposing themselves."

"And who is the*mselves*?" Walter asks.

"The people who want the girl."

"And you."

"Thanks for reminding me. I might've forgotten," Nick responds, unable this time to hold his sarcasm.

"Why're you sweating, Nick? Scared?"

"Go fuck yourself, Wally." Extra points for *that*. Nick wipes away his perspiration, the beads wet the back of his hand.

"Nick," Harvey walks to the window, the whole office groans under his weight. He gazes down over his converted factory floor. "I'm not really concerned about the police, real or not, good or bad. Just knowing if they're around is all I need."

"It's not like we've never smashed the granny outta some coppers before," from Walter.

Harvey goes on, "And these who you're running from, I'm not really fussed about them, either. Look at this place, Nick. My brother and I have made a successful habit out of not being fussed by others. But, the more I know, the more it helps."

Hopeful, but not trusting it, Nick says, "So you'll help us?"

Smirking over his shoulder, Harvey replies, "I didn't say that."

"Then what *are* you saying?"

"I'm saying that perhaps we can work something out. Make a deal."

Katy is loud enough that Pop Tart leaps from her lap. "What kind of deal?"

Nick shushes her, she doesn't take any notice, her attention locked on

Harvey. She's close to finding a way home and she wants to grab it before it fizzles away, only she doesn't know the Georges well enough to be accepting any deals.

Harvey chuckles. He walks away from the window.

"It's all black and white, Cherub. Nick," Harvey taps Nick's shoes with his own, "you remember the night I came visiting?"

"You mean when you broke in?" Nick pulls his foot under the chair.

Spreading his hands, Harvey says, "I don't remember anything being broken. I used a key, didn't I?"

"You know what you did, Harv."

Nick can see the twitch hook the corner of Harvey's lip at the abbreviation of his name.

"Nothing a new lock can't solve," dismisses Harvey.

"No need for a new lock anymore."

Harvey ignores it, probably didn't even hear it. He's at the start of one of his tangents. "Anyway Nick, you'll remember on that night I tried to talk you into repaying a certain favour we did for you a while back. You refused to hear me out, didn't even want to know what the opportunity was, or the rewards involved, which I knew you could use. I'm guessing the flat is still a shithole?"

Apparently fuck was a word Harvey wouldn't use in front of children, but shithole was.

When Nick doesn't answer, Harvey goes on. "Here's the deal, Nick. I'm prepared to reoffer you the option to repay the favour. If you do that, we'll help you and the girl get out of the city without a soul knowing. Hell, we'll get you to exactly where you need to be. Thing is, you carrying out this favour for us is already a backlogged payment, meaning that we'd be doing you an *extra* favour. Meaning that you…"

"Would be indebted," Walter finishes. At some point he's moved back to his settee, sits with his hands between his knees, a joyless smile spread across his face.

This is how the Georges got you in their pockets. They offered help, offered you a way out of their bad books, yet it always resulted in you being deeper inside. It's why Nick has tried to avoid them, because he knew this kind of greasy business would lead to something like this.

"Do we have a deal?" Harvey holds out his hand.

Nick doesn't shake, only stares at Harv's hand. If snakes had hands, this is what they'd look like, nails done all perfect, moisturised skin. After a few more seconds, Harvey drops his arm, clicks his teeth together and paces in front of his desk.

"What is your attachment to the little Cherub, may I ask?" says Harvey.

"She needs to go home," answers Nick.

"And that falls down to you?"

"It isn't ideal, but yeah. It was me who got her away, so I s'pose it's up to me to see it through." He glances at Katy, sees her hiding a smile behind Pop Tart, who she's just picked up. It's not the smile of a happy child, but one who knows she has someone to trust. Arguments and all.

"Hero now, are you?" Walter sneers. "Makes a change."

Harvey leans on his thighs, gets down to Nick's level. "So make the deal, Nick. You repay our favour, we'll help you and this little ray of sunshine, then you just have to do one more tiny job for us when it's all done and dusted."

Nick asks, "What'll *that* favour be?"

"Might never happen."

That's a lie. Whatever they have in store for Nick if he makes the deal is already set in stone, and what's more, he has to take it. Or…

"If we leave now?" asks Nick. "Just walk out and pretend this meet didn't happen?"

Harvey says, "What if you *do* leave? Makes no difference to me. I'm no worse off."

"But there's a lot of distance between here and the front door," says Walt, standing. He has the same deranged look on his face he wore in the alleyway. Nick should've thought this through before entering the villain's paradise.

Katy holds onto her furry talisman. "We're not leaving, are we?"

"Katy," Nick pauses, then, "these men are dang- "

"Offering you the help you seek for a small price," Harvey interrupts. "Nick, I won't make my offer more than twice. Do we have a deal?"

Harvey holds out his hand again.

A small price? If a life is small, what qualifies as big? Only the devil will know that.

"Time's ticking," Walter squints at his wristwatch, taps it.

This is typical of the Georges, particularly Harvey. Putting people under pressure has always been one of the ways in which they get what they want. Even back in school, Harvey had chiselled out the technique into a fine art. This had been back when Nick enjoyed life, when he wasn't repulsed by other people and their natures. It was only into their adult years when Nick had witnessed how devastating Harvey's technique could be when employed malevolently. In a twist of fate, it had been Harvey who implanted Nick's repulsion, the cynicism that made Crane all giddy. Little Walt had learnt the trade by proxy.

Katy pleads with Nick. "It'll be okay."

Tightening his lips, Nick thinks, *So naive.*

Jumping to her feet, Katy says, "He'll do it."

Before Nick can protest, Harvey grabs his hand and yanks him to his feet, shaking on the deal with gusto. A handshake with Harvey George is a legally binding contract. Cheers, Katy.

Tightening his grip, Harvey says, "It's settled then."

"Little girls always make decisions for you, Nick?" Walter teases.

Nick's had enough Walter's lip. "You wanna sort this out, Walt? How's the nose?"

Walter sneers, "Careful what you wish for, Nick."

"Always am." Nick pulls his hand from Harvey's pasty grip. "Go on then, what've I gotta do?"

"All in good time, all in good time. First, we eat. It's late for lunch and the Cherub must be starving," says Harvey, jolly as they get. He always comes over jolly when he gets his way.

"Don't fuck me about, Harv. What's the job?"

Harvey sighs, unbuttons his suit jacket, flicks it open to his hands on his hips.

"You never could wait, Nick," from Harvey.

"No," Walter joins. "Always wanted things done immediately, didn't you, Nick? What was it you told us? 'Just put him outta the game', I think it was."

Knuckles crack as Nick tightens his fists. Walter smiles at the scoring of a point.

"Let me do the talking, Walter," Harvey tells his brother, then turns his head back to Nick. "Nothing huge, just a little visit to someone who owes us money, that's all."

"Debt collecting?"

"Sure, why not?"

"I'm not hurting anyone."

"Hopefully you won't have to."

More bullshit from Harvey. Nick isn't going to break any bones or black any eyes for the Georges, they're more than capable of doing things like that themselves.

"When?" Nick walks from Harvey to the window, looks out at nothing in particular. Katy follows, cradling a purring Pop Tart in her arms.

"Tomorrow night?" suggests Harvey. It comes out as a question, but really there is no bartering here. What Harvey says, goes. Nick isn't pleased, wishes it was tonight. The sooner, the better. He's starting to realise how easy it is to wish for things, and without being careful about it, either.

"Fine."

"The girl will stay here whilst you make your visit," says Walter.

Nick spins around. "No. She goes where I go."

"You'd have her witness a debt collecting?" Harvey laughs. "Hasn't she been through enough? You know how this works. Consider her staying here our insurance. Now we know you'll do a good job. And Nick?" Harvey places his hand on Nick's shoulder. "I do mean a good job."

Harv is right. Katy can't come with him, plus if she's outside she'll be in more danger. At least she'll be here and hidden. He doesn't trust the Georges as far as he can throw them, and Harvey would definitely be a lump to try and throw, but it's the best option he has.

"I'll be alright," Katy assures him.

Harvey drums his fingers in a neat little Mexican wave. "See? She'll be fine. But until then, try and relax. Eat, wash yourselves. Our home is your home."

Harvey is being way too friendly.

Walter walks up to Nick. "We'll fill you in on the details later, don't you worry."

Nick looks down at Katy. "I hope you know what you've gotten us into."

"I was hoping you did," she replies. Pop Tart is undoing the last of her ponytail.

The office door opens and the woman waltzes in with a selection of folded clothes in her arms and two pairs of trainers to pick from balanced on top. Curls of her hair have come loose, she has to puff them from her eyes.

"I've told you to knock before you come in," Walter approaches her. She apologises with a worried smile, maybe expecting the slap she'll be getting later right now.

When Nick looks back to Harvey, his old friend's eyes shimmer as if the Figure has found its way inside him, like cat's eyes catching light in the night. Nick's neck turns cold again, he can hear the frostbite sizzling in his ears.

Scrunching up his brow, Harvey asks, "You alright, Nick? Look like you've seen a ghost."

And with that, the words it had spoken ring in Nick's ears, bringing a wave of bad memories.

Bad, bad memories.

Can I...join...in?

Walter says, "By the way, we never asked who it is you're running from." He takes a moment to comb his hand through his hair. "Who is it, Nick?"

Katy starts, "A man and- "

Nick covers her mouth, squeezing maybe a little too hard. Katy glares at him. "People who want to hurt the girl. That's it."

Narrowing his eyes, Walter tilts his head back, as if doing so might reveal a side of Nick and the girl he hadn't before noticed. The true story, perhaps.

"Simple explanations require simple solutions," says Harvey.

"You heard your brother, Walter. Simple." Nick removes his hand from Katy's mouth, ready to shut her up again if needs be. All she does is hold her glare.

Shrugging, Walter says, "Simple."

CHAPTER 19

Th-WHIP!

The swish of the whip slices air as easily as it slices flesh.

Th-WHIP!

As each knotted end of the cat-o-nine-tails opens up new wounds above old scars, it sounds like a straight razor being stropped.

Th-WHIP!

In the confines of the Secret Room, this act is neither an atonement or a punishment for Ulysses Crane. He has nothing to atone for, nothing to be punished for.

Th-WHIP!

The flames of the candles veer towards him with every stroke. The Secret Room is, as always, lit only by their glow.

On a pedestal, the book sits open on a blank page. The paper is ancient, but hasn't yellowed much. The corners are tattered, the binding strong. Ulysses gazes at the page, his eyes heavy. Hot blood flows down his back, and though he does not break concentration on the book, he knows the cat-o-nine-tails is drenched in his blood, for it is heavier than when he started.

Th-WHIP!

A few more and the night's flagellation will be done.

The book craves tribute. Ulysses' blood may not be the ultimate payment it desires, yet it still demands performances of loyalty if it is to, upon receiving the offering, return the same level of loyalty to its subject.

Th-WHIP!

The blank page stirs, moving fluidly, like ripples. The flagellation is working. That is to say, the spilling of blood. It came as no surprise to Ulysses Crane, at a time when his balls and armpits were bare, that the inner workings of magic all come down to blood. It is the greatest sacrifice, to offer this natural magic that created life here, in this place, in this time, in this universe. An eye for an eye, magic for magic.

Th-WHIP!

And now he sees it, clear as crystal.

The page is showing him what he seeks.

Th-WHIP!

It is the hardest strike of the whip all night, and succeeds in slashing deep, reaching muscle. Lodging. It hurts, but a good hurt. This final whipping is his gratitude.

Ulysses smiles softly. Many surprises await his friend Nicholas in the coming hours.

In his private quarters, cleaned up and dressed in a wine red silk robe, Ulysses sits before the fire, flames throwing twitching shadows around the room. He doesn't blink as the flames dance, permitting the heat to dry his eyes. The majority of his room is in darkness, his bed a solid hunk of shadow. In a tumbler he swirls around brandy, uninterested in the comfort it has to offer.

His age once more begins to best him. The joints of all the important bones are solidifying, his back in a constant state of pain, the folds in his skin deepening with each passing day. He felt much better only days ago. That's how it works without the full power of the book, it comes in waves, teasing what may be. It is still attainable. Upon the girl's blood dripping on the book, which slumbers now in the Secret Room, there started a time limit which he neglected to tell his society, and the sand is falling, though not fast enough to cause a panic. If all goes as it should – and it will – then there is nothing to fret over.

A knock at the door. Without waiting for permission, Juniper enters the room. She is the only one who needs not wait for Ulysses' leave. She brings a tray of food with a thin candle stick and a rose cutting. Her feet whisper on the carpet as she approaches him. He is not hungry. Spittle pops in his throat as he grumbles, he knows he must eat. The act of chewing, of swallowing, even digesting, has become a chore which he enjoys little.

Neither of them speak, they don't have to.

The Black Rose. There is something elegant about it, yet frightening at the same time. It has been a long time since Ulysses experienced anything resembling fear. It is an effective reminder of his humanity.

Juniper sets the tray down on a table. "Is everything alright, Mr Crane?"

Dismissing her question with a flick of his hand, Ulysses replies, "We are alone, Juniper. Call me by my name."

She straightens, clasps her hands in front of herself, a pose that makes her look like an awaiting maid. She says, "You aren't looking so well."

"I don't feel it."

He looks at her, shoots her a smile that is painful to draw. She is wearing her trademark face this evening, as she does *all* evenings, and all days and always. Those red lips that look like they are hiding vampiric teeth, the powdered face, hair pulled back tight enough that her eyebrows try to follow it. She is a beautiful woman. Ulysses examines the brandy, turned brighter by the fire, before downing the last of it, his throat immune to the smarting of the alcohol.

"I'm concerned that you're pushing yourself too much, Ulysses," she says.

Ulysses snorts, "Do not be concerning yourself with that. I am doing what I have always done. What is necessary." Sitting the tumbler on his arm rest, he points at the fire. "Place another log on, would you?"

Juniper takes a log from the stack next to the hearth, places it in the flames. Many moons ago, she might have awoken desire in Ulysses, a desire strong enough to best the book. It is not to be, however. The libido he may have once possessed was banished when he committed himself to knowledge, to the wielding of magic, to becoming the Wishmaster. Back then it had not been such a high price to pay, nothing ever is when you've set your mind on something, when desire is little more than a stiff penis in the mornings. Now, though? If ever Ulysses were to wish for something selfish, he might ask back his concupiscence.

"You have to eat something," says Juniper, turning her back on the fire.

"I know."

Ulysses glances at the plate of food with scorn. A steak which is too moist and overcooked vegetables that are swimming in the meat's tangy flavours. Splotches of oil wonder within the juices.

"Do you really think Schaeffer will be able to carry out his task?" she asks, moving to the tray.

Ulysses queries, "Are you doubting my order?"

"Never, Ulysses," she bows her head.

Chuckling, he replies, "I know, Juniper. You never have done, which is one of the reasons you are so vital to me. You have always been loyal since I took you in off the street." His brow furrows, loose skin bunching. "You have also never requested a wish. Why is that?"

Juniper begins unwrapping cutlery from a napkin. She speaks in her customary deadpan fashion. "I have never had anything to wish *for*."

Dubious, Ulysses says, "And yet you have remained by my side even though I have done nought for you?"

"You already said what you did for me." Juniper picks up the tray to place it on his lap. "You gave me a home. I suppose you could say *that* was my wish, and that being my wish, you granted it to me long ago. No offering, no blood." She smiles, her face powder cracked in the style of a renaissance painting, adding to her beauty, which is aging as might a fine wine.

Ulysses smiles back, takes his hands off his lap to make room for the tray. Ulysses would tell her to take a seat, though will not this evening. Juniper should know by now she can act freely when it is just the two of them.

Pink juices squeeze from the steak as he cuts into it. He says, "To answer your question, Juniper, I have what faith I can muster in Mr

Schaeffer. I believe he has already made his first move. We shall just have to keep an eye on him, is all."

Juniper looks away, her lips twisting. "His face…"

"Yes," Ulysses swallows, "that is rather unfortunate."

"And yours. The cut, it's gone."

Calling what the girl gave him a cut is an understatement, but an appreciated one. No man wants to feel undesirable. "A trick of mine. It is still there underneath the guise. Back to Mr Schaeffer."

"He's not altogether there, in my opinion. I do not like the trust you are placing in him."

"And I am grateful for your opinions, but let us look at it this way, if *you* lived in a world where the dead flocked to you, where you could hear their voices everywhere you went, do you believe that *you* would remain altogether there?"

"It was his wish."

"Yes it was," Ulysses playfully points the fork at her, "so let us trust that he can handle that better than he can handle his wounds. Besides," the knife scrapes the plate as he cuts off another chunk of steak, "he is only performing a simple task. At the nucleus, he is not doing much at all. Not really. All he need do is make sure Nicholas underperforms from here on out. He is strong man, is Nicholas, and it is a shame that he did not see my way of things in the way I forecasted. Much he could have understood if he just waited, if he allowed himself time." The next bit, Ulysses speaks more to himself, caught in the memory of a dear friend. "But, I suppose, desperation does not afford time, nor does seeing an opportunity to metaphorically save yourself."

"And what of Apollo?" asks Juniper, trying to conceal her hatred for the man who ruined what was to be the most glorious gathering of the society. She apprehends Ulysses' tumbler, glides to the hearth where a near empty bottle of brandy sits on one of the stones. It warms the brandy, which Ulysses likes.

"Apollo is healing nicely. He shall be back on his feet tomorrow, and not a moment too soon." Seeing her with the brandy, Ulysses says, "Please, take a nip. It is being wasted on myself this evening."

After draining some of the drink, Juniper asks, "What is our next move?"

"I am glad you asked, Juniper," answers Ulysses. "Our eyes have served us well. The opportunity for reclamation is not far off, all the chess pieces shall be in their correct positions."

Juniper sets the sampled brandy next to Ulysses', making sure to put it on the coaster so as to avoid any stubborn ring stains. From day one she has understood the importance of avoiding contaminants. She has never tried to hold him, to take his hand or embrace him even after he had performed what the Bible would dismiss as black magic but what was actually miracles. However…to feel the arms of the Black Rose wrap around his brittle frame might be…might be…

…rejuvenating?

"Would you like me to make the call?" she asks.

Ulysses adjusts himself. The lashings on his back cling to the chair, blood sticking through his robe. The book had stitched the fibres of his flesh back together, though it will still take a couple more hours for the wounds to fully heal. The book also has the ability to take away his scars, though he would prefer them to stay. They have been earned, and each of them he wears as if a war medal.

"Yes," he answers her, his attentions on the brandy glass. "Please, make the call."

With an unnecessary bow, Juniper leaves his room and Ulysses is left staring at the glass. Juniper's lips have left a fine print of her lipstick around the rim of the tumbler. He pushes himself to his feet, shuffles to the table where he picks up the glass and holds it aloft. Then, his heart rate climbing, making him dizzy, he drinks from the glass, his tongue licking up the print of the Black Rose's lips. These are the only germs whose attack he surrenders to.

CHAPTER 20

Nick leans on the windowpane. From two floors up, he watches the overdressed henchmen patrolling the grounds outside, torches tracing their routes in the dwindling light. Those who don't carry torches can be seen by the glowing ends of cigarettes. Voices swap jokes that must be funny because Nick can hear them laugh. When a light shines up to Nick's window, he backs away into the room the brothers have set him up in.

With a flat-screen TV mounted on the wall, adjustable lights and even a fridge stocked up with anything he might need, it's better than any hotel he's crashed at. This room doesn't come with the bugs, damp, or the smell of those five-quid-a-night hovels. Hell, it's better than his flat. There's more junk that cost more than its worth, too. On two walls are shitty looking canvasses that the artist has just thrown paint onto and hoped for the best.

Showered and shaved, Nick is back in his clothes from the morning. The Georges have decked his room out with a collection of clothes in a walk-in closet, not to mention a few fine suits to choose from. Nick doesn't want to wear anything they offer him. He'd rather wear the dirties, nothing a few blasts of deodorant can't fix for an hour or two. At least his chin isn't spiky to the touch anymore. He lumps down on the foot of the double-bed, the memory foam mattress shaping itself to his arse.

Katy and Pop Tart are in the room next to his.

At least…Katy is.

Pop Tart has just walked into Nick's room. The cat makes itself at home, rubbing its head on just about everything in the room that can be claimed. Fridge, chairs, toilet, plants, and, of course, the bed. At long last the cat rubs itself on Nick's leg, leaning into it, tail catching like a hook before it lets go and Pop Tart turns himself for another pass.

"How did *this* relationship ever happen?" Nick asks the animal, to which Pop Tart answers with a trill.

The way Pop Tart acts isn't the way Nick expected a cat to be. Shouldn't he be hiding in dark corners, contorting his shape in unnatural ways to squeeze into crevices that defy the limitations of a spine? Pop Tart, since day one, has never shown any of these typical feline traits. Rather, the cat is able to make himself at home wherever it goes, even in the car when the windows had been shattered and the tyres screeched.

Nick bends, pats Pop Tart's flank.

Come to think of it, when the dark figures had surrounded the car, when *the* Figure had been in the back, Pop Tart had not reacted even a little. Weren't animals supposed to sense those things? Bark, snap, spit and hiss?

"Stroke him gently," says Katy, peeping in from behind the door.

Nick replies, "He can handle it." Again he pats Pop Tart's side, the cat's purring juddering as he does so. Sitting back up, Nick says to Katy, "You can come in."

Katy bites her lip, mulls it over, then pushes the door open, gravitating towards Pop Tart. The cat springs over to meet her. She's changed her clothes, opting for a baggy pair of jeans that cover her trainers and a yellow tee-shirt that's about three sizes too big, a cartoon character that Nick doesn't recognise grins on the front. She has also redone her hair, the braid neat and tidy.

"Everything okay in your room?" asks Nick.

Katy, rubbing Pop Tart's belly, glances around. "It's fine. Kinda the same as this one."

Remembering Frank's plea for him to find common ground with her, Nick tries a joke of sorts. "Same crappy art?"

"I like it."

You swing and you miss.

"Well if there's anything you need," says Nick, "just shout."

"I'll be okay. There's a lock on my door." Katy picks up Pop Tart, brings him to the bed and sets him down on the duvet.

"No don't- " Nick protests too late. Bloody cat hair will be getting up his nose all night, now. As if sensing his annoyance, Pop Tart shows off his gall by padding to one of the pillows to knead it.

Katy giggles. "He's making biscuits."

"Making biscuits?"

"That's what we call it at home, when our cat does that. Making biscuits."

"Whatever," Nick grumbles. Then, "Just make sure you keep you and the cat locked in your room whilst I'm gone."

"That's what I was going to do anyway," says Katy, sitting on the bed close to Pop Tart to watch his ongoing primping.

Nick stands from the bed – the memory foam courteously keeping the shape of his behind – and returns to the window for a quick inspection of where the patrols are. From what he can tell, it's the same people doing the same rounds. Again, a torch flicks up to his window. It's obvious the Georges have tasked someone with keeping an eye on them. This time, instead of just backing away, Nick flips the bird, holding his hand to the window as long as his arm will allow before it comes with him.

As Nick opens up the fridge for a water, Katy says, "I see why you don't like those men. They're...scary."

Nick replies, "You didn't seem very scared." He takes a gulp of tap water that reckons it comes from a highland spring, which is, of course, bollocks. "I'd say you've been holding together pretty well through everything."

"Thanks."

Katy blushes, tries to hide it by pushing her nose into the cat's fur. It's sweet, although Nick doesn't know what to do with sweet. "Back at Crane's, what did you use to- "

"How'd I get a blade?" Katy finishes for him.

Nick nods, takes another swig of Tap Water Springs.

Smiling, apparently a little proud of herself, Katy answers, "I was allowed to draw in my cell. The woman who brought me in made sure I had all the stationery, including a pencil sharpener. When she came to...to take me" – she swallows – "I accidentally stood on it. The blade got stuck in my shoe. I took it because I thought I'd need it."

"Good thinkin'," Nick commends her. No child should be using a blade, yet the girl's circumstances had been...what had Crane called it? Preternatural?

"I guess," she shrugs. "I wish I never had to think like that in the first place."

"But without it- "

"You were there," she says, without accusation.

She looks at the floor, her hand on but not stroking Pop Tart. Unblinking, her eyes are seeing everything that happened all over again. Nick sees her shudder. It looks like she's about to cry, something that makes Nick's chest thump because he hasn't got the first clue about how to handle that. Do you just let them cry and hope it stops? Let them lick their own wounds in the same way that Pop Tart licks his-

Katy snaps herself out of it, wipes her eyes. Thank God.

"I...um...I want to thank you," she says, speaking to Nick through the cat, though the words must be falling on deaf ears. Pop Tart is asleep. "For doing whatever it is those men want you to do."

"Thanks?" says Nick. "You pretty much fed me to the wolves back there."

"You would've done it anyway."

"What makes you say that?"

"Because there's no other choice, like you said. And because you're a good person."

Nick smiles, "You didn't think so this morning."

"What did I say?" Katy asks.

"You called me mean."

Katy chews on her lip, then says, "Being mean every now and then doesn't make a person bad."

Nick scoffs, "You don't really know me enough to be saying that."

Katy ruffles between Pop Tart's ears, making the cat stretch out. "Pop Tart thinks you're okay. Cats always know when someone's iffy."

"You seem to know a lot about cats," Nick points out.

"Not just cats, and not just animals. I like nature. I want to travel the world and make documentaries."

"That's quite a dream," Nick says, surprised by Katy's sudden confession.

She shrugs, pouring her affections onto the cat. "We all have wishes."

Nick's smile melts away. He's heard someone say that before, or something similar to it. It doesn't sound sweet coming from the girl. Ulysses Crane has soured any talk of wishes.

It's clear that the girl is still processing everything. They both are. Not counting the experience at Crane's, she's been nearly re-kidnapped, been in a car smash up, dumped the same car into an offshoot of the Thames and been dragged around the city to end up here. To top it off she can't even let her parents know that she's alright. It's hard to believe that it all started last night.

Katy says, "I'm still not sure why you're doing what you're doing to help me, but whatever reasons you have, I just want you to know that I'm grateful."

Nick squeezes the bottle in his hand, causing the plastic to crinkle. How else are you supposed to sift through all this…emotion? "You're, uh…you're welcome. I guess."

Katy asks, "So…what do you, like…do?"

"Sorry?"

The smile returns to Katy's face. "I told you what I want to do. So what is it *you* do? You know, when you're not rescuing people from cults."

Smirking, Nick says, "That the word we're using for them, is it?"

"It's the word *I'm* using," Katy replies.

Nick mumbles, "If the boot fits."

"So...tell me?" Katy lifts her legs onto the bed, crosses them, resting her hands in her lap. She leans forward with the bad posture that comes with genuine interest.

Nick stumbles around the question, then settles on, "I do a bit of this and that."

"Like freelance?"

He snorts. "I don't think you can glamourise what I do by calling it freelance."

"How come?"

"I punch people for money."

Katy averts her eyes. "Oh."

"Yeah." Nick manages a smile. "Oh."

Spinning from the bed back onto her feet, Katy explores the room she's already said is the same as her own. "Is that how you know those two men?"

Nick watches as she tries to act interested in different things, including the bad art. "No, but I s'pose you could say it's related."

"In what way?" Katy smells a flower, not realising that it's a fake one until it's too late. She glances over her shoulder to see if Nick noticed. He pretends he didn't.

"What I do for money now is kinda the same as what I did back when I considered Harvey my friend," he tells her.

"Which one's Harvey?"

"The big one."

Katy nods. "And then he wasn't your friend anymore?"

"That's right."

Katy turns to face Nick, her back to the window. Parking herself on the sill, she asks, "Why?"

Nick sighs, "Aren't you tired?"

"Not a bit."

Suddenly, Nick wants to be alone again. "It's a long story, Katy."

"What happened?" At least her mind is off home for now.

His foot drums a beat on the floor, Nick stands to stop it. He doesn't want to talk about the favour between him and the Georges. It's ancient history that doesn't need to be dug back up. A part of it already follows him from the great fucking beyond, so why dredge up more?

"Did they…hurt you?" asks Katy.

"No." After a pause that feels like minutes, Nick adds, "But they hurt someone because of me."

"Did you do something to them?"

"No. I was stupid, shoulda known better."

"Is the person okay now?" Katy continues.

"They're dead," Nick says abruptly.

"Oh."

"Oh, again."

She begins to ask, "Because of- "

"Because of," Nick nods.

Nick can tell Katy is growing uncomfortable. He can hear her swallow, and if he listens hard enough, her heartbeat. Or it might just be his own. Briefly, she is backlit by torchlight sweeping over the glass.

"Did you mean for the person to…to die?" she says.

"No," answers Nick. Wanting but unable to stop himself, he carries on, anger straining his words. "But that's what happened. If I didn't tell them to- "

"Then it wasn't your fault," Katy cuts in. "If you didn't *mean* for the person to die, then- "

Nick shoots her a glare that just might destroy every bit of bonding they've gone through up to now. "I still wanted broken bones, still wanted the guy hurt. I wanted him out of action…" He faces the floor again. "And that's what I got."

When he finally looks back at her, Katy is staring at Pop Tart, desperate for her safety net, her talisman. Guilt pushes against his chest.

It's not fair of him to be bringing all this up, whether she asked for it or not.

"I'm sorry," he says.

"No," Katy takes the opportunity to go to the cat. "I'm sorry. I shouldn't have been nosey."

"It's okay. I haven't talked about it in so long, kinda just…I hope I didn't scare you."

"You don't scare me."

"Well, I'm sorry, anyway."

Nick tosses the empty plastic bottle into a wastebasket. It startles Pop Tart, and is so far the only time Nick has seen the cat act normal. It makes Katy laugh, and Nick laughs, too.

"What did you want to do?" she asks.

"About what?"

"Before, when you were young?"

"I don't remember being young," Nick says. "Only that I was lost."

Katy hops off the sill. "Lost how?"

"Never had a role model. I had people, too, y'know, at school. I binned them off like you did, only they had bloodied noses." Nick turns away. "It was Harvey who taught me to fight. That's how it started, 'cause I'm good at it."

"You can't solve all problems with your fists. That's what my dad says," says Katy. "Not everything has to be a fight."

"But most things are."

"You can always run," she suggests.

Nick replies, "That's what we're doing."

After a moment of silence to rival the armistice, Katy says, "You really had no dreams as a child? Astronaut? Rock star?"

"Yeah," he replies, disgruntled. "To be left alone."

Katy looks away. Nick has destroyed the topic.

"Nick?" Katy asks, scratching the cat's ear.

"Yeah?" he sighs.

"When you go, what if those...things...come back?"

It's tempting to go the route of playing dumb, asking the obligatory what-do-you-means and what-are-you-talking-abouts. It'd also be useless to insult the girl's intelligence. After seeing the ranks of dark figures creeping slowly towards the car from a fog that seemed to follow them, to be *of* them, how could anyone get away with not knowing what *things* meant?

Hands in his pockets, Nick answers truthfully. "I don't know."

"Do you think it's likely?"

"I dunno, but...I guess anything can happen."

"You're not really helping."

Inhaling first and holding it, he says as he lets loose his breath, "I know."

"Do you know where they come from?" Katy lifts her head, eyes pleading for a logical response that Nick can't give her.

"I'm not sure," he answers. "Somewhere we're not s'posed to know about."

"I'm...afraid that one of them will take me again. Back to that place. To my cell." She faces the window.

Until today, in the Georges' office, Nick hadn't known that the Figure could touch him. Thinking about it sends a shiver up his spine.

"I think you're safe enough here."

It's more than ironic that safety is found within the belly of a crime duo's safehouse. Well, not *safehouse*. Safehouses are meant to keep people hidden. This place straight up points them out.

Sounding once again like the lost girl back in the flat, Katy asks, "Have you ever seen one before?"

Not answering straight away, because he isn't sure how, Nick glances at the window, ice begins to blossom in intricate patterns. In the corner of the ceiling, attracting shadows that slide in from anything that makes them, bundled up like spider silk, he sees the Figure, arms and legs pretzeled out of shade, clinging to the flat surface. It's eyes shine. He cannot see its mocking grin, rather he feels it. Then it's gone in a blink, shadows reattached to the things they should be.

"One," Nick replies.

"And…" Katy gulps, furrows her brow. "Do you see it often?"

Pop Tart is listening, his radar ears pointing at Nick, Major Tom(cat) ready to receive transmission.

"Often enough."

"Do you know what it is?" she says, unaware of her voice dropping to a whisper.

I know who *it is*, Nick thinks. He responds with, "It's the past."

"Does the past have a name?"

Nick clenches his jaw. "It doesn't matter."

"If you talk about it, you might- "

"Enough," Nick snaps. A button has been pushed, one whose depression holds Katy in cold static. "I don't want to talk about it, you won't make me a better person, I won't be fixed. I don't *want* to be. I don't want to share my life story with you, or hear yours. You're what? Thirteen? What do *you* know?" Nick wants to stop, but can't. "You don't know me, so stop trying to. Neither of us wants to be here, so let's just get on with it. I'll get you home, I *promise*, but that's it. I don't need saving. This mess is just that. An accidental mess."

An accident. The words visibly knock the girl, only now it's too late to take them back. This is exactly why he keeps people at a distance.

Katy utters, "I was only trying to help, and I'm thirteen and a half."

Nick moves so quickly, Katy gasps. He holds the door open, Pop Tart has already leapt off the bed and is out in the corridor before he says, "I think it's time for bed. You need your rest, I need mine."

She makes no attempt to coax anything else out of him. Enough words have been spilled that shouldn't have been. They'll need to be gathered up and buried all over again, you can't have unwanted memories dirtying the floor. Shoulders hunched and bottom of her tee-shirt clutched in her hands, Katy stares down at the floor as she leaves.

"Goodnight," she murmurs.

"Goodnight," Nick says harshly, shutting the door without another word.

For a while he leans with his back against the door, catching breath that he didn't realise had gotten away from him until now. The corner of the ceiling is empty, his third visitor has also checked out. He's sweating, too. He'll have to shower all over again.

Letting himself drift in the hot water as it soaks his body, he echoes the first words spoken to him by the Figure when it was still alive, droplets of water trickling from his lips.

"Can I join in?"

CHAPTER 21

Fog is back with a vengeance.

The entrance to the block of flats is identifiable by the big illuminated lie above its doors: Paradise Heights.

It might've been once, but you wouldn't believe it.

There are buttons in the entryway with faded names scrawled on bits of paper. Water damage has blotted the ink, making them unreadable. The holes of the speaker have something mashed into them that looks enough like shit to come with a placebo smell.

Buzzing in isn't required. The handle hangs limp. Pushing the door open, the overhead closer wheezes like an old man trying to breathe. Automatic fluorescent tiles flicker on, and left in the door's wake is an angel wing in the grime. Nick suspects that Paradise (to be read: Parasite) Heights is missing its maintenance man. That, or the welcoming committee need new jobs.

Why can't he ever wind up somewhere nice for a change?

He pushes the button for the elevator. A light comes on and he waits, hearing the trundling winches.

Ding.

Even the ding sounds like it's troubled.

The elevator doors slide open, the left one sticking before it opens all the way. The light inside works properly, but that's about it. In one corner is a second-hand needle. Curling his lips, Nick decides he'll take the stairs. As long as he can avoid touching the banister, Plan B – the stairs – should go off without a hitch.

He peers up the stairwell, sees the bulb at the top. There are eight floors in total, he needs the sixth.

Flat 6C. The Georges had repeated it enough times.

Nick begins the climb, litter crinkling underfoot. The task shouldn't be too hard or take that long. If it goes smoothly, and there was some wishful thinking, it would take up less time than it took for him to get here. Whoever said paradise was around the corner, anyway? And the job was simple. Bring back money or bring back a finger – method of removal optional.

"Dealer's choice," Walter had grinned.

A bucket of sand doubling as an ashtray is tipped on its side at the top of the first flight. And why not? Who'd want to stop a fire *here*? Nick steps over it, glances down the hallway at the sorry doors of Floor One. A few optimists have put welcome mats in front of their homes.

The third floor is the last to show any signs of tenants trying to make the best of a bad situation. Flat 3B has popped artificial plants outside their door, though still the fake shrubs manage to appear dead.

Ascending the rest of the way, Nick worries about Katy. He'd gotten angry with her, scared her even if she wouldn't admit it. Plus it wasn't like him to let his mouth blab like that, it takes him out of his comfort zone, a turreted mind castle that keeps all the bad shit in.

Talking to her about very personal matters wasn't as foreign as he'd expected. Maybe he should've been more appreciative. She'd only tried to help, didn't matter if she floundered or not. She had no idea of the nerve she was poking.

The rattling of the entrance door opening downstairs brings Nick out of his thoughts. Leaning over the banister, being careful not to touch it, he peers down the stairwell. He can't see anyone. He listens for footsteps, waits. Again, nothing. Only the torn first page of a newspaper rustles into view.

Time to focus, Nick. Get the job done and get the fuck out.

Past the fifth floor, passing a bronze-nozzled fire hose that zigzags down the steps like a fat albino eel, Nick reaches level six. The wonders of Paradise Heights' penthouse will have to remain a mystery, and hopefully shall remain so forever.

A television turned up too loud blasts soap opera omnibus from one of the flats, and in another a couple argue about something or other, she screams as loud as he shouts. This is all to Nick's advantage. More noise means less chance of being heard, especially if he has to break in by booting the door open, not that he expects the goblins in Paradise Heights care enough about each other to have a functioning neighbourhood watch, but you can never be too conveniently drowned out by background noise.

Calling the people trapped here goblins is a bit unfair. Not everyone is to blame for their situations, some people fall into a funnel and can never seem to get back out of it. He knows this as much as anyone. So maybe not everyone here is a true goblin, but Jesus Christ, would you look at this place? Fuck.

The walls are drab, grey and flaking. Walking down the hallway under the hum of fluorescent strips (tiles are too good for here), Nick counts the doors. 6C is going to be closer to the far end, near the fire exit.

Fire exit – quick means of getting the fuck out. Noted.

6C is next to the flat playing the soaps. A fist sized hole in the door has been covered by duct tape, and the lock is a blatant replacement that's been fitted to the door like arse. A botched spot of DIY. There's a reason that shit is so…shit.

Nick has no idea who's on the other side of the door. The Georges had, for some reason, refused to divulge that bit of information.

He takes a look down the hallway, left then right, just like crossing the road. Taking a deep breath first, Nick knocks on the door of 6C.

Simon Schaeffer presses his back to the dirty wall, trying to breath quietly. It helps to hold his eyes wide open, but still hurts his chest. He hopes Master Crane's man Nicholas didn't hear him come in. He'd had to run to catch up, the fog which had been so helpful to him yesterday was being a royal pain tonight.

The busted door closes itself with a hiss, dragging a dune of filth, shutting out the weather. Tonight the outside world is busy with spirits, Simon can see them ambling through the haze. In this fog, it's hard to identify who is actually dead and who is alive. One of them is in the building, hunched over in an open elevator poking a used syringe. Simon wants to say hi, no matter how many of the passed over he speaks to he never gets bored of it. And it's common courtesy. Just because they're featureless and deceased doesn't mean they're unworthy of manners. However, talking to this wandering soul would only take up time, and Simon wants to catch up with the Master's man. He touches his staples, trembling at the pain.

Nicholas's spirit – not literally his, but the one attached to him – is a peculiar spectre born from remorse. It performed well when commanded through the ether, haunting Nicholas almost immediately without concern of when and where. Simon wants to see it up close, like he did when one of the sprits took the girl from the forest.

The spirit keeps on at the syringe, poking it as if it should come alive any second, hoping to learn how to pick it up. Simon could teach the spirit, it wouldn't take much, especially not for a spirit like this one. These lonely spirits are always the quickest to learn. Teach it he could, then it'd be a different story when telling the spirit that it couldn't use the syringe.

Footsteps echo upstairs. Excellent. Nicholas doesn't know he's here. Simon creeps to look up the stairwell. Empty…and brooding. Buildings come with many auras, only a handful of them could be labelled as brooding. This one broods with an intensity that excites Simon.

Two at a time, Simon starts up the stairs.

A knock on the door makes Katy jump. She's lying on her front, halfway under the bed, searching for Pop Tart. She was positive he'd hidden under the bed, but with strands of dust now tinselling her hair, maybe it's time to accept that he's elsewhere. Before she has slid her way from under the bed, there is another knock at her door. Her response for whoever is there to wait comes out as a sneeze that excites dust into the air and makes her sneeze again. As nice as this room is, the cleaners had obviously neglected moving things aside to get under them.

Pushing herself to her knees, Katy brushes herself off. She wonders where Pop Tart has gotten to. She didn't see him dart out of the room before she locked up. He isn't like any other cat she's had the pleasure of meeting. He's wily, like that cartoon coyote Dad still laughs at. At any rate, she's sure he'll make himself known when he's ready, though she'd been looking forward to having company whilst Nick was out.

"Hold on," she says to a third knock at the door.

She stops as she's about to grasp the gold doorknob. Before leaving, Nick gave her strict instructions to keep her door locked, don't answer to anybody. Anything that needs to be said can be spoken through the door.

She *should* cast his words to the wind. She's still mad at him from last night. He'd turned mean again, said some hurtful things. Really, all she tried to do was know him better, but he'd slammed the door on that figuratively and literally. He's had a tough past, is obsessed with it, believes it defines him. But it doesn't matter to Katy what he did, or what he *thinks* he did. The past is the past, it's what you do *now* that counts. Her frustration with him doesn't stop her from wishing he was still here, though, especially now the door is knocking. Yes, he'd been spiteful, but amongst all that, he'd also promised to get her home. She believes him, even if he made the pact in anger.

He'd also said this was all an accident. Did he mean saving her?

The question comes as her fingertips brush the doorknob. A voice inside her says something, too quiet to hear. She thinks it said, "Don't answer it."

Taking her hand away, she says, "Who's there?"

No one answers.

They might've gone away by now.

Either it gives her the chills or the bedroom has gotten colder.

She starts putting together the three ingredients for a Katy coffee. Freeze-dried, one and a half sugars, milk. By the time the granules turn the milk brown the water will be boiled. Mum and Dad don't like her drinking coffee, they say that a young girl doesn't need any extra caffeine, but that's such an outdated attitude. Coffee's just coffee.

Hopefully it'll keep her awake for the whole night. She's tired but doesn't feel much like sleeping, especially whilst Pop Tart is out. She's afraid those shapes will come back. There's a bookcase full of everything from literary fiction, horror fiction (might be best to give that a miss), romance and also a few non-fiction books, at least one of them about birds. That one could be cool, she has to brush up on her ornithology. Yes, the books will take her mind off the shapes.

Pouring the water, the lights dim on their own. She looks up, accidentally letting the water spill over the mug, flooding the tray.

She takes hold of her hair, stroking with her thumb, starts to hum, but the melody drops away. The room falls into a blackout when there is-

-another knock at the door.

Nick can hear shuffling feet inside 6C, things being knocked over. Whoever's in there is taking their merry time. At last they reach the door. As the lock is being fiddled with, they yell at something. A pet, maybe.

The door is yanked open.

Nick keeps his mouth from dropping. Instantly he recognises the woman holding onto the doorframe with her left hand, though he doesn't think that she recognises him.

Until, that is, she says, "Oh, look. It's th' insy winsy spider."

Her milky eye has a faint spiral instead of a pupil. He doesn't think that was there when he'd first seen her under the bridge, then again, it'd been darker that night.

She doesn't give him the chance to say anything. "Might as well come

in."

Retreating into her gloomy flat, she blurts out a fragment of nursery rhyme. The Tourette's, if that's what it is, is still alive and ticking.

Before entering Nick glances up and down the hallway. The couple have stopped arguing, though there are now thumping sounds that don't sound like the product of violence. As for the soap addict, a whole new episode is in full swing.

Nick steps into the junkie's flat, closes the door. The smell assaults his nose before the rubbish attempts to trip him. The flat is dank, has mould in just about every corner. Wallpaper peels away from the walls and a radiator has flaking paint revealing a colour that was given to it before people cared about what colours matched. There's a light fixture on the ceiling, a strand of cable with frayed wires sticking out.

"Y'wan' somethin' t' drink?" She calls from…where the fuck is she?

Her speech is slurred. Drugs or alcohol. People fucked up on anything are a nuisance. It's also an indicator that whatever money she might've had is well and truly up the vein.

"No," says Nick, then adds, "thanks."

Kicking through discarded food packaging and empty bottles with fungus growing comfortably in the dimpled bottoms, Nick comes into the living room. A lamp with a red sheet draped over it colours the room a pinkish hue, which does little to hide the squaller.

"Don' judge me," she says behind him.

"I'm not," Nick unblocks the doorway.

Walking past him with both hands cupped around a medicinal smelling brew, the junkie says, "Who sen' you? Crane or Georges?"

"Georges."

She lumps down on the settee with her back to Nick, the tie-dye throw peeling away and falling behind her neck. In front of her is a television, turned off, most likely doesn't work. On whatever shit she's plunging into herself, she maybe sees her own brain broadcasting back at her. It's one of those old bulky things that the kids today would call a fuck-is-that.

"They know I don' 'ave their money," she raises the broken-handled mug to her mouth.

Nick approaches the single chair to the right of the settee, an empty rectangle pressed into the carpet where a footrest once sat. He says, "Didn't expect to see you again."

She squints at him, her neck working hard to keep her head balanced. She's not wearing a hat tonight, thinning hair on show at the top of her head.

"*I* knew I'd see you again," she says.

Dust squirts from the cushion when Nick parks himself. He wafts it away, asks, "How could you've known that?"

"Hm." She grins, brings up her mug again. "There's lots I know."

She blows away the ribbons of steam that curl over her face, then as she is about to take a sip she barks, "Along came a spider!"

The drink sploshes into her lap. Steam rises from her ripped jeans. She doesn't realise that with steam comes pain, doesn't notice or care.

"Got a thing for spiders?" says Nick.

"Can' help wha' comes out, can I?"

The junkie looks much older than she did the night she passed along the package. Drugs work fast, they don't clock out, don't take a day off.

"Y'still best buds with" – she exaggerates the next bit, showing all her teeth in a brown sneer – "Yoolisses Crane'?"

"That's not your concern."

He'd like to lean back in the chair, doesn't dare. Must be crawling with lice.

The junkie cackles, "I'll take tha' as a," she growls the last word and drags it out, "yessss."

"Don't take it as anything." Her, Crane and the Georges are intertwined somehow. Small world, that's what they say. Not small enough. "You know what I have to do if you've got no money to give?"

Grinning, the junkie waves her fingers at Nick. They're skeletal, pronounced arthritic bumps at every joint. If he waits long enough, one might fall off on its own.

She says, "Y' won't do it though."

"I think you underestimate what I'll do," he answers. *What I have to do.*

"I'm sure you'd do it t' someone else. But y' won't do it tonigh'."

The junkie sounds arrogant. She takes a sip of her brew, testing the heat with her cracked lips.

Newspaper has been stuck over the window to her right, multiple layers that block out the sunlight, when it's there. Pictures and type can be made out on the yellowed paper. A curtain rail is on the floor, plaster encrusted screws scattered around it. There are many items littering the floor, though strangely, there doesn't appear to be any drug paraphernalia. Left in the elevator, maybe?

Nick sits forward, morbidly curious. "How'd you get in the Georges' bad books?"

Throwing an egg carton off the settee, the junkie pulls her legs up under herself. "It's easy t' get in their bad books," she eyeballs Nick, winks. "You know that."

"You don't know shit."

"Bu' I know piss, an' snot an' blood an' tears. I know a lot of it."

"What's your connection to Crane?"

She stares dead-eyed into her mug. Nick is about to say something when she chucks out of her mouth, "Fetch a pail of water!" Then she slurs, "Tha's a long story."

"I have time," Nick says.

"No you don'," she tilts her head. "I don' know why, but you don'." She smiles at him, strokes the crease of her meatless thighs. "Maybe we can make time?"

Nick's face twists.

The junkie shrugs. "No? Don' blame you. I know I'm not as hot as I was un'er the bridge, bu' you don' have to make tha' face. I was'n always like this, y'know?"

Coming from the kitchen – a coffin of a room with urine-yellow walls that Nick passed in the hallway – is a munching sound. So there *is* a pet. Sounds like it's rummaging through a cereal box.

"So...how's Mr Craney?" she continues her babbling. Producing it from apparently nowhere, the junkie has a cigarette in her hand, places it between her lips.

"I don't have- "

"Time?" She drops the lighter down from the cigarette before the tobacco can catch. "Thought y'said y'did?"

"Thought you said I didn't?"

The junkie cackles, enjoying herself. She lights the cigarette, chucks the lighter on the floor, lost forever, now. She scratches her arm, loose threads of wool catching on chipped nails.

"How's the society?" she asks, blowing smoke through her nostrils.

"Don't give a shit," says Nick.

"If y'say so." She sets her mug on an upside down crate acting as a table, the slats bowing. "I use t' be one o' Crane's groupies. Talkin' a year...year an' a half ago now, t' answer y' question."

Just after the favour, then. The Georges had expanded rapidly after that.

"Was this before or after you knew the Georges?" asks Nick.

"Why d'you care?"

"You're wrapped up with Crane and now so am I. You also know more than I do. I want to find out what I can." He wants what information the junkie has on Crane. Might be something he can use against the old murdering fuck. The junkie has already stated she doesn't have the Georges' money, and Nick isn't about to go searching through this roach motel. Her fingers are safe from him, too, which she already apparently knows.

She rolls her eyes, there's something flirty about the gesture that definitely isn't in the dark clouds framing them. "Don' you care abou' the money the Georges wan' you to take from me? I tol' you I don' have it."

"Never did care."

"Y'sure?"

"Sure."

The junkie exhales smoke, sucks it back into her nostrils, not wanting to waste precious tar. As if she wasn't fucked enough already. She says, "O' course, you mus' know by now wha' Craney is all about."

"I've seen some stuff."

"What you- "

She cracks her neck, grimaces, then shouts, "Black sheep!" Twitching a little more, she gets back control of herself. "Wha' y' wish for?"

"I didn't," Nick answers.

She looks confused. "You musta. Gotta have a wish t' get in."

"He guessed at something." Nick remembers the alcohol, the illusions, those accusing masks. Had all society members been seduced that way?

"Bet he was right. What've y'been doin' for 'im?"

Nick sighs. "Pick-up and drop-off guy. Same as this."

"The more things change," she laughs. After a drag on her cigarette that barely touches it, she goes on. "When he accepted me, my wish was t' be able t' see the past and the future. Mos'ly the future. I could make the right choices, avoid getting' raped or mugged, avoid the world's rotten core. The past, so I could look back on things, learn from mis'akes, of which there've been many. Like reruns o' some messed up drama, or com'dy."

Nick asks, "How'd he find you?"

"I found him." She's looking at the television as if something is playing. "I had a life of hardship. I was damaged. I always wan'ed more, was greedy. Reckoned I knew how. I thought if I could see ever'thin' I could alter my own path. I started asking around occult haunts, sinkin' deeper into th' swamp until it swallowed me down t' him. I was a willin' partic'pant. It's easy t' fin' darkness if you wan' it."

For Nick, it was the darkness that found him, in the form of jealousy and two brothers.

Nick asks, "If you wanted more, why not wish for money?"

"It's not abou' money!" Her twirled pupil opens out. "It's abou' the *soul*. I wan'ed to protec' my *soul*. Wan'ed to ensure it wouldn' go through more shit."

Seems Crane has a habit of recruiting the vulnerable, the desperate.

She goes on. "So I did th' thing, took part in tha' year's offering, he spoke 'is words an' granted my wish."

"You kill a child?" Nick asks in an angry whisper.

"The blood is a must," she answers coolly.

"Same as the sex?"

"Acts of depravity prove your subservience."

"You're as sick as the rest of 'em," says Nick.

"Maybe I was. Maybe I still am. Pocket full of posies!"

Nick delves deeper now the junkie is off on one. Perhaps she knows more about the book. "Didn't plan out as you'd hoped, I'm assuming?"

She snorts. "Does it look like it? It worked okay forra bit. Yeah, I could…can…see backwards and forwards, bu' only sometimes, an' sometimes the pictures are fuzzy, or wrong, like a broken telly that can't be tuned. An' it was'n jus' me. It was ev'rybody."

"What do you mean everybody?"

"Ev'rybody I came into contac' with. I could see wha' they'd done, what they were gonna do, wha' had been and would be done to 'em."

"But not all the time?"

"Not all the time, enough though." She's forgotten about her cigarette, the ash slowly droops towards her legs. "It started t' drive me mad. Only so many times y' can watch someone else's life run through y'head. In the end, it's all I saw. Other people's suffering. So I turned into a fuckin' hermit, never leavin' my cave." She hugs herself. "My soul more damaged than when I star'ed."

"That's how you knew you'd see me again?" says Nick. "And how you know I won't cut your finger off? 'Cause of what Crane did for you?

You're…what? A mystic?"

"You're not jus' a han'some face. Did'n think you'd believe any of it," she replies.

"Not sure if I do, but I'm starting to question reality" – *Crane knew the cynic in me would* – "and I know what Crane is capable of."

"An' you've also jus' admitted that y' won' hurt me," she grins.

"You said you knew that already." Nick wonders what else the junkie knows about him, if she's seen any visions of his future, or his past. If she has, she's not letting on.

"That was all me. Does'n take a lot to see you're not a malicious man. It's y' eyes. Baa baa black…black SHEEP!"

"So what next, after you got your wish?"

"I was afraid of my wish, afraid of Crane. I didn' wan' outta the club, but I wan'ed away from Crane forra little while. Clear m'head. That's when I prop'ly acquain'ed myself with th' Georges. Walter set me up with a room, helped me cope. I returned the favour by givin' him the results o' business ventures e'ry now an' then. Helped 'em build 'emselves."

That explains the brothers' rapid criminal growth.

"His brother didn' seem t' mind. O' course, he didn't know Walter was usin' me as a human eight ball. It was peachy forra bit, 'til I discovered the slots."

"Slots?"

"Fruities. I loved those rollin' fruit. Still do. It became an addiction." She slurs the word, spilling every letter. "It wasn't abou' th' money. Those gamblin' machines somehow drowned out ev'ythin' I was seein'. Started with an app on my phone, then…it wen' from there. Problem is, I suck at gamblin'. Made up quite a debt, then started takin' Walter an' his brother's money without 'em knowin' t' s'stain it. 'Ventually, I lost enough that Walter couldn' overlook it, enough that makin' me suck 'is dick wasn' enough. But…I couldn' help it. Playin' the slots, distractin' my out o' control visions was too good to pass up. So I ran away from the society an' th' Georges. Holed up here 'n there 'til I wound up at Paradise Heights. Haven't seen a fruit since. They foun' me not too long ago. Maybe a couple months. Bidin' their time 'fore sendin' a collector my way." She winks at Nick. "Jus' like I saw they would. I tried to prove my own visions wrong by runnin', I shoulda known better. Walter might be a frien', o' sorts, but he's also a serious gangster, or wha'ever they call 'emselves, and they wan' their money back."

Nick doesn't come equipped with a sixth sense, but something taps him in the skull, a warning from himself to himself.

"You never said how you knew the Georges in the first place," he says.

"Jus' Walter, really, obviously because…" The junkie looks him square in the eyes, her spiral pupil circling slowly, losing any hint of playfulness. "You…you don' know?" she asks.

"Know what?"

"I thought…because o' Crane…you'd know…"

"Well, I don't. So tell me what I don't know," Nick knocks the crate with his knee, spilling the tea.

"Walter George," she says, her head shaking, "he looked after me forra while because…because he's part of the society."

In the darkness, heart pounding, Katy opens the door. The chain keeping it locked underlines her eyes. They peel wider as she recognises who she's looking at. Her throat closes, throttled by the air around her, stops her from screaming. Deep down, she already knows that screaming is useless. By the time a note claws its way passed her locked throat, it's already too late.

"Good evening, Miss Robbins," says the surprise visitor. "Or shall I revert back to- "

KATY!

Nick boots over a stack of magazines leaping from the chair, kicking up a tornado of dust. He makes it a few inches into the hallway when he hears the click of a gun being cocked. It's a surprisingly loud sound, unmistakable even if you've never heard it before.

Slowly he turns. The junkie is on her feet, knees bent inward so that they almost kiss. In her right hand is the gun, heavy enough to cause her arm to droop a couple degrees. The black eye at the end of the barrel is aimed at him.

Streetlamps turn on outside, shining through the newspapered window, projecting fish and chip-greased headlines all around the room.

Nick speaks carefully, aware that words too heavy might just set the gun off. "Why're you pointing a gun at me?"

"My name's Danielle," says the junkie.

"Why're you pointing a gun at me, Danielle?"

A pretty name for a junkie. She wasn't always a junkie, though she looks as if she was born for it.

"I'm not a druggy," she says. "I know y'think I am."

"I haven't hurt you Danielle," Nick tries to keep her level, she's most likely been on the tipping point for quite a while.

"An' I haven' hurt you. You need t' stay jus' a bit longer," she says.

She's trembling, red rings around her eyes are getting redder. The right one swirls with shades of grey, clouds meeting in a storm. It crosses Nick's mind, but it wouldn't do any good to rush her. Too much distance, and even with sweat-slippery hands and one blind eye she'd be able to sink a round into Nick before he reached her. Factoring in that she's a wreck, her finger is probably already putting pressure on the trigger. At this range she'd be hard pressed to miss.

He turns his body to face her, hands open to show he poses no threat. He flicks his attention between the three eyes on him: teary, cloudy, gun.

"You have to let me leave," he tells her, keeping his breathing steady. His lungs want to pump in and out and hyperventilate, but he won't allow it.

"I know," she sniffles, "but no' yet. I know how this meetin' ends. I've seen it. There's no other way it can go. You…" She gulps. "You h-have t' list'n t' the res' o' my s-story."

"There's no time," keeping his tone level.

"We've back-and-forthed abou' time too much. This won' take long."

Nick considers making a dash for the door.

It might already be too late.

But what can he do? If the junkie (he cannot accept that she, in some form, isn't) shoots him, Katy's as good as…don't think it.

He steps to the side, his back to the wall. The light through the newspapers tattoos the word *search* across the bridge of his nose.

The junkie uses her gun arm to wipe her nose.

Nick listens, his mind a tempest, too jumbled to make a reliable plan. Reliable – that was one of his and Crane's words.

"Desperately," Danielle continues, "I wen' back to ol' Craney. I asked him f' help, said I couldn' take it anymore, the bein' scared, the Georges on my arse. I thought he could get Walter off my case, bein' our 'lustrious leader an' all. Tol' him I was sick an' tired of what my life had turned into. Even as I tol' him this, visions swirled through m' head. It has a radius, like an old radio, bu' I don' know what it is."

She waves the gun as she talks, using it to enunciate her words. Each time the barrel passes over Nick his arsehole nips up.

"He gave me help o' course, but not before makin' me beg forrit. Made me bark like a dog. Said I should be punished f' leavin' the society behin'. I tol' him I didn' mean to, but he wouldn' listen. In the en' though, he asked what I wan'ed." Her body shakes. "Down came the rain. DOWN CAME THE RAIN!"

Nick holds his breath until he's sure the tick is over. He tries to placate her. "What'd you ask for?"

Danielle closes her eyes, smiles, exhales through her nose. Probably some meditative bullshit. "I asked forrit t' be over. I asked for Walter t' leave me alone, an' for my visions t' be gone."

"You wished away your wish?"

She coughs a wet laugh. "Ain't that a bitch?"

"Crane must've been offended," says Nick.

A human-shaped shadow glides across the newspaper on the outside. *Can I join in?*

"He was upset," Danielle answers, "angry, bu' switched on his charm, shiftin' the look on his face the way he does. Y'musta seen it. Able to appear younger in the right light or somethin'."

"Maybe," says Nick, thinking back to when he first saw Crane step out of his Rolls-Royce, how his features had been like mercury.

"He said he'd help me, that he'd grant my anti-wish, bu' only if I was willin' t' help him firs'. Gave me tha' shitbox car," she sneers. "Said I had t' pick somethin' up forrim."

"The book?"

Nick steps forward, a stupid move too late to take back. Danielle stretches her arm fully. Nick stays put.

"Yeah. The book. How'd y'know?" Her face sags. "You didn' *look* at it didya?"

"Not on the night, but I saw it before long," replies Nick. "Put the puzzle together myself."

"When you saved the girl?"

"You know?"

"I saw it in a vision."

Nick swallows. "Is she going to be okay?"

She drops her eyes for a second. "I can't see."

"Broken telly?"

"Broken telly," she sniffs. "I had t' go through a few people t' get it. Swappin' money an' other kindsa shit that Craney loves. He gave quite a lot t' get it, spent a lot o' money. Crane tol' me I should look when I had it, said it'd be good f' me."

"Danielle," Nick starts, "if there's anything you can tell me about the book- "

She shakes her head. "No. I don' know nothin'. Only that it needs young blood an' displays o' gross loyalty. I don' know wha' it is or where it came from or wha' it's called. It's alive, I *do* know that. It's, like, the cen'erpiece of Crane's magic. He needs it to make himsel' stronger, to achieve all he ever wan'ed. To be the Master of Wishes. I...I also know it doesn' like me." She prods the bag under her blind eye. "It's getting' worse. It'll spread t' the other before long. Crane knew it'd happen if I looked inside the book. I only managed t' read one line before it did this. I don' know how...bu' it did. I think he set it up t' do this t' me. Tha's why he sent me. It coulda been anyone, bu' he wan'ed it t' teach me a lesson. Another punis'ment for the society dog."

"Sorry."

"Don' be. Fas' forward a bit and I han'ed the book over t' you t' give t' Craney. I know he didn' tell y' anythin' about me. That's okay. He likes knowledge, an' bein' the keeper of it. He loves people askin' questions. You gave me a parcel tha' night, too. 'Member?"

Nick remembers.

"After that," she continues, "I came back here an' opened your special deliv'ry." She nods at the gun. "There was a note with it."

Danielle reaches into her back pocket, tosses a ball of crumpled paper at Nick. He catches and unravels it.

On a post-it square are two words.

Wish granted.

Danielle scratches her arms again, catching wool in her nails. "It was then tha' I knew wha' I had t' do. A final cruel joke by Craney. I knew wha' it meant. I've been waitin' f' this momen'. Been waitin' f' you."

There's that arsehole nip again as Nick realises that she means to shoot him. That's what the note means. If she jumps through this final hoop, she's free.

"Danielle, I don't know what you think you have to do, but this isn't it," he says. He feels helpless. Confronting people with knives is one thing, a gun is another. Is there anything he can say? His muscles contract, tighten in all the important places.

"Oh, Nick," she laughs. Nick doesn't recall telling her his name. "Y' can' change what will be. I've seen it, like I said. I know what I have t' do, it don' make it any easier, though."

Her tears start up, cradling streetlamp light. Her ticks are a thing of the past.

"All you have to do is let me go," Nick says, holding up his hands. "Just let me walk out the door and forget me. Forget Crane."

"No can do. Don' y'see? This gun is how Crane is gonna make it all end f' me. The magic, the Georges."

"I can stop him."

"There's only one way t' stop Craney, his society, an' tha's t' kill him." "How do I do that?"

Danielle chuckles. It's a pretty sound that would sit well on a summer breeze. "You can't." She smiles. "He ain't all human." *Hooman*. "Can't kill him conventionally."

"Calm down, Danielle." Nick's heart is an engine.

"I'm more calm than I've ever been," she says, tears dripping to the crumby carpet. "Because I made it here, an' it'll all be over soon an' I'll be free of these damn visions. I'll say one more thing about Craney t' y'though. If y'get t' him...go f' the heart."

Nick's brow crinkles. "What?"

"The heart," she reiterates. "Not his, though."

"Whose heart? You said he can't be killed."

"Oh, Nick," she says again. "I said not conventionally."

"For God's sake, let me go. I have to help the girl," he pleads. It doesn't feel good to be practically begging, but he finds that, for Katy, who he met ever so recently, it comes easier, a willing action in this shit show.

"I can' see your future," Danielle says, readjusting her grip on the gun, "because I cannot see beyon' the end, bu' I've seen some of your past. It's hazy, dark clouds hang over it. Y'need to let go of the sufferin'. The girl…the girl spoke true."

"Don't shoot, maybe I'll give it a shot."

Danielle lets fly another summer breeze chuckle. "You'll get that chance," she tells him.

Huh? "But…I thought- "

"Y'thought this gun was for you?" She smiles. "I jus' needed someone t' hear my story. Needed to clear my head, set matters in order. I was tol' to stall f' longer, but I'll cut it short. Go fin' the girl. Go for the heart, it may be broken. See ya han'some."

Danielle turns the gun on herself, smiling the smile of the girl she once was, presses the gun's muzzle against the soft pad of skin under her chin. Her left eye turns cloudy, the blindness finally infecting both eyes, then she closes them.

She whispers, "Wish granted."

"WAIT!"

Danielle pulls the trigger. The back of her head explodes, smearing over the newspapered window. Her body drops to the floor.

Paradise Heights falls silent for a moment as the remaining tenants consider the bang. Before long, having sussed it out as only one of a hundred gunshots this year, they return to their lives.

Simon has had his ear pressed up to 6C since about five minutes after Master Crane's man entered. He followed Nicholas tonight to run more interference, and he'd gotten some in, telling the spirit to make itself known by being omnipresent. He could have had the spirit literally walk up to Nicholas inside 6C, kick him in the bollocks and rip his throat out, but theatrical had been better. Building tension is always a hoot, kind of like salting the meat. Normally, once a spirit has been given a new purpose, it takes to it well. This one having a past with Nicholas only serves to beef it up.

Simon's focus is somewhat tarnished, though. His target has come all this way and gone into Danielle's home. Or as Simon knows her, Dani.

She's about the only person of all Master Crane's followers who Simon truthfully likes. She hasn't ever said hurtful things to him, nor about him when he's not around. He hopes. She also didn't take one look at him then cast him off as a loser. They even talked, once. It broke his heart when she just up and disappeared. That's a fissure that can't be stapled.

All speech on the other side of the door is muffled. It gets intense, then simmers, then intense again. How does Nicholas know her, anyway? What business does he have with Dani? What does Master know?

Picking at a staple in his cheek, Simon pulls away from the door when a gunshot shakes the wood. Footsteps thud closer, he throws himself to the left. As he hits the cold uncarpeted floor the door bursts open, tearing off a spine of doorframe with it. Without noticing Simon, the man Nicholas dashes for the fire exit, kicks it open, and is gone into the night fog. His face was white, *ghost* white.

No one comes out of their flats to investigate. The hallway is now a cold, windy tunnel, the fire exit door banging against the bricks.

Simon stands, doesn't bother to brush himself off. Where he'd been picking at his face is a scrawny streak of blood.

He enters 6C. The hinges are fucked. Dani's home. It's like being invited into the house of the prom queen, only she doesn't know you're there, which kinda makes it more exciting. He doesn't see the mess, not in his eyes. To him, cautiously treading to the living room, it's as beautiful as he'd always imagined. He runs his hand along the wall, playfully flicking at a curl of paper. Peering into the bedroom, seeing the unmade bed with all its stains and…are those feathers? Dani really has a feather bed! It's hard not to let the excitement get to him, hard to not allow the childish squeal to explode from his lips. What is also hard presses painfully against his beltline.

The smell, it's wonderful. The kitchen is full of decomposing treats, the mould within bite marks is like fuzzy icing on a cake. Dani really is living in a dream, and all Simon wants is to be part of it. He'd like to go into her bathroom and rummage in there, but that might excite him too much. Just thinking of piles of discarded damp clothes and an unflushed toilet…he moves along, the staples in his face vibrate in tandem with his sadistic pleasure.

He reaches the living room. His smile retreats instantly. The first thing his notices is the moist lumpy stuff sticking to the window and wall. Chunks of it slide down, plopping to the floor. Then he sees the body, lying in a classic chalk line pose.

Simon knows it's Dani by her shape, having watched her enough. He kneels by her side, confused by his lack of tears. They're there, but aren't breaching. There is a certain emotion though, an odd one.

Blood glugs from the back of her head. When he lifts it, there isn't a back of it to look at, just a bone cave where her brain used to be. Gently letting her head down, a shard of bone cuts his finger open that sends a trill through his muscles. He licks the cut, paying special attention to the blood that isn't his. He's never before had a desire to try what another person's blood tastes like. This seems like a good a time as any, especially seeing as it's his special girl Dani.

With quivering, excited fingers, he picks up a length of bone that has a sharp edge. Simon begins making slices in his forearm from his wrist to his elbow, creating a companion ladder to go with the one on his face. Every cut is a pleasurable symbol of his love for Dani, a reminder that Nicholas caused this to happen. If he'd never come here, then…

Then what?

Would things have gone differently?

As Simon gazes around the flat, the rose-tinted glasses begin to wear off. Clearly, Dani wasn't in a good place. She could've come to Simon. He wishes she knew that, wishes she had done. But it's too late for wishes. Even Master can't wish the dead back to life. It confuses and agitates the spirit.

He administers an extra cut as punishment for his blasphemy against

Master, then throws the bone away.

The odd emotion spurs him to do what happens next. The emotion, he realises, is victimhood. He is the victim, a victim of stolen love.

Simon removes his clothes, undresses Dani with as much care as he can. It's still pretty awkward. Laying on top of her, letting his fingertips grip the empty back of her head for support, he directs himself inside her. Still warm, still lovely, still Dani.

He kisses her, then begins to cry.

Whilst he makes love to her corpse, a spirit manifests silently behind him, watches the deed that is happening to its former body.

CHAPTER 22

The road unrolls out of the fog. Adrenaline turns his legs into pistons, works them until his knees are set to explode. His breathing comes out lumpy with the rhythm of his sprint. Unsure if he's running towards Katy or away from the suicide, the images of both melt together in his head to show Katy shooting herself.

He could've taken Danielle's affectionately named shitbox, but he hadn't thought. His legs are taking control right now and they command that he keeps running.

He stops only once to haul in more oxygen before continuing to charge his way through the fog. Streetlamp bulbs are stemless, appearing as floating halos that guide him through the various streets towards the old industrial estate.

Arriving at the converted factory, Nick stops, drawing breath in ragged gasps, not one providing enough air. He grabs his chest, spits out a wad of phlegm. From his bent position, he looks up, the gates are open, the guards away from their posts. All that's left of them is piles of cigarette butts.

Nick navigates the grounds, shins like hot razors cutting into his legs, making it seem as if he's walking on jagged boulders rather than packed gravel. Through the haze the topiary animals appear as freakish forms, observing his approach. Fog fingers wrap around the factory possessively, unfurling at the entrance.

The corridor isn't in total disarray, but is altered enough to be suspicious. Framed paintings are off kilter, plant pots are spread out or emptied of their contents, a few tipped over to spill their soil. It's too organised to be a real job, it's a play that reeks of the Georges and their rich cologne. Could, actually, be pinched straight out of the conman's handbook, How-To-Make-It-Look-Like-You've-Been-Burgled 101.

Step One: Mess shit up.

Step Two: Now some more.

Step Three: This is *your* shit, don't fuck it up *too* much.

It's not a hard job to spot.

It seems as foggy in the corridor as it does outside, and it's too quiet. Nick treads carefully, grit crunching underfoot. He doesn't know what he's walking into, running on fumes. He calls out for Katy, gets nothing, calls out for Walter, expecting and getting nothing.

Harvey is sitting on a brown leather settee when Nick comes to the factory floor, leaning towards a coffee table with two drinks on it, one with ice, one without. A lamp on the coffee table with its shade askew is the only light, casting Harvey in a yellow glow.

"Harvey," Nick growls. "What the fuck is going on?"

Without facing Nick, his hands dangling between his legs, Harvey mumbles, "I asked the same question."

"Bullshit!" Nick's voice echoes.

"Why don't you come sit with me, have a drink?"

"I'd sooner shoot you."

A voice to Nick's left says, "I think you should have the drink."

Walter, hands in pockets, walks into the subdued light with the complacency of a man strolling in the park. "Might be your last."

Though his body is a doctor's poster of aches and pains, Nick moves to strike Walter. Before he can, tree trunk arms wrap around his neck and waist, clamping his arms down. He gags as his throat is squeezed shut.

"Ease up, Apollo," says Walter. "Remember what we were told."

Apollo grunts, slackens his grip.

"Good to see you again Apollo," hacks Nick. "No hard feelings?"

White flashes in Nick's eyes as Apollo headbutts him from behind, skull cracking on skull. "None taken," the South African replies.

"That's enough, Walter," from Harvey.

"I'll say when enough is enough," his brother responds.

Drunk stars in his eyes, Nick asks, "Where's the girl?"

"She's safe," Walter says, undoing his tie. "Well, I mean, for *now*."

Nick clenches his fists, the energy he exerts trying to break from Apollo's grip is absorbed by the big fuck's arms. "You bastard."

"I suppose I am," Walter whips the tie from around his neck, "but you knew that already, to some degree." The change in Walter's accent is jarring, sounds like an imitation of Crane. He takes meandering steps closer to Nick, swinging the tie in circles, his shoes tapping on the floor.

To Harvey, Nick says, "You in on this? You one of Crane's too?"

Standing, his belly stretching his white shirt, Harvey replies, "I don't have a fucking clue what's going on. On my life. And I don't know who this Crane is. Hooligans charged in and- "

"*Mr* Crane," Walter shouts at Harvey.

"Eh?" Harvey scowls, perplexed by his brother's disrespect.

"That's *Mr* Crane, to you. And Nick, my big brother isn't telling porkies. He's just as ignorant, just as stupid as you."

"Harv, you really had no idea?" asks Nick.

Harvey grits his teeth, glaring at Walter. "About what?"

"Your cunt brother is in a cult."

"Oh!" Walter claps. "Big man words like that deserve big man reprisals!"

Walter lassoes his tie around Nick's neck, makes a tight knot, then punches Nick in the gut, winding him. Apollo chuckles, a sound like floating logs bumping against one another.

Harvey lowers his voice. "What's he talking about, Walter?"

"Oh, come off it, you know I have other friends," Walter removes his suit jacket, lays it over the settee.

"I know you have other friends, Walter, we all have our ventures on the side, but it all comes under *our* umbrella. If you're up to something that ignores that rule- "

"So what's your problem?"

"My *problem*?" Harvey turns to pick up his drink, spilling liquid over the rim of the glass. "My problem is that you're involved in something I had no idea about. My problem is that your friends came barging in here, apparently under your orders." Harvey becomes more agitated. "You also took it upon yourself to send *our* men away, then you had the girl under *our* protection taken away, after I promised Nick she would be safe. I've never claimed to be a saint, but a liar I ain't. And there's mention of a *cult*?"

Undoing his cufflinks, Walter says, "That's quite a problem."

Harvey sips his drink, then asks, "Who exactly are your friends?"

Nick croaks, "Tell him, Walt."

For that, he receives a slap that leaves a red print across his cheek. Apollo's square jaw digs into Nick's crown, hot bullish breath parting his hair.

"Cult shmult." Walter rolls up his sleeves, his back to Nick. "I'm not in it for the crazy shit. I have other intentions."

"I've been patient with you," Harvey starts. "When this kicked off tonight you told me to keep my calm and you'd explain everything later. Well now is later, Walter, so off you go."

"Why do you even care?" Walter asks his brother. "It's not like we're in any danger."

"Maybe so, but I need to know *who is*. I need to know who's involved, what's going on, where the girl is and why the hell this ape has Nick in a headlock. We started this together," Harvey indicates everything around them, "we're a team and that's how it's always been."

Walter responds with a confidence that worries Nick. "You know what? I know what your *real* problem is. You care about this dickhead too much. That's your weakness, that's what happens when you make an enemy of a friend, or friend of an enemy. So why don't you let it go? Let me handle my business. You won't have to lift a finger."

"I didn't get us here by not lifting fingers. Your business is *my* business," Harvey bites, showing teeth, a bubble of spittle on his chin. "What cash is being spent, and what's being made? Any police involved, on our payroll? What?"

Walter laughs, hands on hips, "That's another one of your problems. You've got so many problems you should see a doctor. You think business means money, that's all you think about. Money, money, money. But business is more. Don't you get it?"

"I don't think I've ever really gotten you, Walter. How can I *get* anything when I don't know what extra-curricular shit you're dealing in?"

"No," sighs Walter, "I don't think you've ever gotten me, either."

Harvey necks the last of whatever alcohol is in the glass, throws it across the factory where it smashes again a wall. "A cult, Walter?"

"I wouldn't use that word myself." Walter spreads his fingers over his chest.

"What word *would* you use?" Nick manages. Against Apollo's forearms, speaking hurts his Adam's apple. "Child Murderers Club?"

The blow this time comes from Apollo, a swift punch to the face that gives knuckles to Walter's handprint.

"For fuck sake." Walter shakes his head.

"You had your turn," Apollo grunts.

"Yeah, but I'm bruising a peach. You're more liable to breaking eggs."

"Walter?" Harvey stares deep at his brother, brow furrowed with many lines. "Kids?"

"Whoah, hang on," Walter waves his arms. "We're getting into dangerous territory here. *I've* never killed a kiddy. Why don't we all just relax, yeah?"

Through clamped teeth, Harvey asks, "What the fuck're you into?"

Throwing his hands up, faking exasperation, Walter argues, "So your old mate says some shit and you instantly take his side?"

"No, but tell me why I shouldn't. So far all you've done is dance around my questions."

Seconds pass in which Walter processes what Harvey has just said. "I've always been the better dancer. How about this? I'm your fucking *brother.* Surely that counts for something?"

"And I've known Nick since we were kids. We may have our differences, but he's always been an honest man, more…more than I've been to him. I've been able to trust him more than I have you."

The sentiment is dead wood floating to Nick. Only a few weeks ago Harvey had been putting pressure on him to repay a favour gone awry, going so far as to break into his flat and threaten him. Maybe ideals change when your empire crumbles around you.

Disbelief pinching his eyebrows together, Walter snorts, "Sounds like you're taking his side. That hurts. He may be honest with you, telling you where to stick things if he dislikes what you have to say, but he's never been too honest with himself."

"You have a lot to answer for tonight," Harvey tells his brother, attempting to soften his voice. "I shouldn't have allowed it, it's only because you're my brother that I did. Had I known that you've been supposedly associating with child killers and devil worshippers- "

"It has fuck all to do with the devil," Walter barks.

Harvey goes on, "You've always had a flare for going off on one, going where your dick pointed. I've been at my wits end for ages, worrying that your lack of discipline will get us nicked. I don't *want* to believe Nick over you, but all this…I dread to think where your friends are taking the poor girl, and what she and Nick have to do with it. That boulder there attacked Nick before any of us had a chance to talk."

The boulder, Nick gathers, is Apollo.

"Don't worry yourself, Harvey," says Walter. He unbuttons the top of his shirt to reveal a segment of tattoo reaching up to his neck. He carries on with a smile. "I can see how all that's happened here would arouse suspicions, cause you to question allegiances. I think you've said all you have to say. Truth is, brother, that I never really needed you anyway, or your approvals. You were safe, though. I mean that."

Walter snaps his fingers. Three hooded people materialise from the shadows. They grab Harvey before he can defend himself. A big man, power still coursing through his muscles, though not big enough to handle an ambush of three. He does his best to break their grasps, but once they have him all it takes is a kick in the back of the leg to bring Harvey to his knees. They hold him before his brother, who is checking his nails.

"You're a little shit," Harvey grimaces. "What is this? A takeover? Think you can handle all we've built? You're nothing without me."

The hoods have to hold him back, clearly Harvey is giving them a run for their money. He has his teeth, should he get the opportunity.

Walter bends down, hands on knees, to talk to Harvey. "You're missing the point. I don't want what *we* built. Yeah, it's fun, there's no denying that, and I have to say, the fear slash respect that comes with it is a nice bonus, but this game we have going on here is so…" Walter gives time for the right word. "…unimportant. There're far greater things than city streets and money. Far more things to *wish* for. Make no mistake, I shall continue to endorse the benefits, run things as usual."

Harvey spits, hitting Walter on the cheek. Casually, Walter wipes away the saliva with a handkerchief.

"I guess I am a little shit, yet I'm a little shit who isn't on his knees." He glances over Harvey's shoulder. "You're scuffing up your shoes. That's good money your fucking up, mate."

"You'll pay for this, Walter," says Harvey.

"Oh, really? You're friends are my friends. But not all of *mine* are *yours*, evidently."

"Maybe not."

"Don't fucking lie, brother. What on earth will you have to say at the pearly gates about that? Oh! Before I forget." Walter is walking with his hands behind his back, ignoring Nick for the time being. "I'm sorry about messing up the place. I know it wasn't strictly necessary but, I never liked it here."

Nick slowly raises his arm, intending to ram his elbow into Apollo's ribs. The big fuck grabs his arm, squeezing tighter around Nick's neck.

In three strides Walter is back in his brother's face. "Notice how Nick came back from the junkie empty-handed?"

"She…wasn't…a junkie," Nick rasps.

Harvey's chest heaves, tendons tense in his neck. "You're prattling."

"A skill handed down to me from you. It was a distraction so we could nab the girl. You were both just too stupid to see it. A while ago, yeah, it was about what she owed, cash or pieces of herself, but circumstances change all the time. How do you think I met her in the first place? Imagine my surprise when I got the call telling me Nick and the girl had to be detained! In the end, her scummy money didn't mean shit." Walter laughs. "She served her purpose, though, and got her wish."

Harvey keeps his face concrete, a stern look born in the playground, seasoned on the streets, yet Nick sees the realisation chipping in, sagging his features, aging him ten years in ten seconds.

"It's true, isn't it?" Harvey asks. "This…cult, the kids?"

Patting Harvey's cheek, Walter says, "There's so, so much more to it than that. But, if it makes you happy…yes."

Harvey grits his teeth. "That doesn't make me happy. It pisses me off."

"I'm quaking in my shoes."

"Three hours ago you were my troublesome baby brother, now you're a stranger."

"You gonna kill us, Walt?" says Nick, face inflated with blood, purpling.

Walter tuts, reaches into his back pocket. "Oh, Nick. I almost forgot you were here, you've been so quiet."

The three hoods titter. The society emblem is pinned to their cowls, weighing the fabric into a widow's peak over their glistening foreheads.

Harvey turns to Nick. "I promise, I had nothing to do with this."

"I believe you, Harv," Nick replies.

"I had every intention of holding my end of the deal."

"Yeah." *So now we're friends?* Nick thinks.

Scratching his chin, Walter interjects, "We haven't got all night. To answer your question, Nick, no, I ain't gonna kill you."

"So what then?" Harvey bites, sweat sticking under the folds at the back of his head. "You fuck off and we're supposed to forget all this? You know I won't allow it."

"You think I never listen, Harvey, but as it turns out, it's *you* who needs to clean out your ears. I said I'm not going to kill Nick."

"Then- "

Walter whips a blade from his back pocket, flips the straight razor from its handle to noiselessly slice open his brother's throat. Harvey gurgles, eyes wide and pleading, fighting to suck in air. For a couple of seconds there is only a red seam across his neck, then the blood pours out, opening the wound right to left, spurting onto Walter's face, over his moustache, his grinning teeth. Harvey tries to swallow it back into his body, unable to keep pace with the red tide. It slops onto the floor. The hoods hold Harvey up as he bleeds out, jolting with every bodily spasm, all of them laughing from mouths beneath shadow. The sound of Harvey's scuffed shoes kicking the ground will stay with Nick forever.

When the spasms stop, the hoods release Harvey, retreat into the gloom with serpentine motion. Walter doesn't move as his brother's body slumps over his knees, smearing blood over his trousers.

"Ah, fuck," he whines. "These're only a week old."

Frowning, he shoves his brother's body away. It lands on the floor with a thud, shirt buttons popping to reveal a rotund belly.

Nick doesn't mourn as the pool of blood spreads from Harvey's throat. He isn't upset. He's pissed off.

Walter stands, makes the blood on his trousers worse by trying to rub it off. "This shit'll never wash out." Red shoeprints are left behind as Walter drags his feet to Nick, clacking a rhythm on the floor. He tilts his head sideways, grins, licks blood from his teeth.

"He was your brother," Nick says as Apollo renews his hold.

"He was a barrier," Walter shrugs.

"You're a coward."

"Cowards live."

"What kinda life is that?"

"A living one." Walter makes a big show of sinking to his knees, groaning, puffing out his cheeks. He grasps Nick by the chin, squishing his cheeks, hard enough for Nick's teeth to bite his tongue. "Can you even hear with that freaky ear? Doesn't matter. I have to come clean."

"Dirty cun- "

A fierce slap from Walter cuts the word short. Again, he clutches Nick's chin.

"I was shocked if not overjoyed to learn of your involvement with Mr Crane. It may be hard for you to believe that until tonight I had no idea. Back in the alley, when I uglied your face, not a clue."

Nick pushes gloopy blood from his mouth to purposely drain over Walter's hand. "You tellin' me you didn't know who the girl was?"

"Was I at the last gathering? I was held up with other business that night, which I would've rescheduled had I known how important it was going to be. Actually, you've done me a favour. Consider us even." Walter flings his hand downward, blood splats on the ground. "We don't stay in constant touch, Mr Crane gives me plenty of wiggle room. I'm informed as and when I need to be. I was called about an hour before you set off. I already knew the junkie no longer mattered in the sense that Harvey thought she did. As far as he was aware, she was a friend of mine who toppled into our pockets. I kept her close because I knew her through the society, to help further my career, 'til she started with the gambling. I didn't tell Harv. He thought it was all good villainy. Some of it was, I suppose. Gotta give him that."

Nick splutters, "How?"

"How what?"

"How'd you pull it off?"

"Ever hear of telephones? I was called, like I said, told about you, the girl. It's that simple. Told Harvey some associates of mine were coming to discuss business. Shortly after, they arrived and the girl was taken back to where she's needed. The Black Rose did the honours herself."

"The fuck's that?"

Apollo twists Nick's neck to the threshold of breaking, skin ready to rip.

"Calm down, Apollo." Walter waves his hand. Apollo obliges. It's not clear who holds authority between the two of them. For the meantime it's Walter, though with every order he hands Apollo, the resentment ripples the big fuck's muscles. "You'd know her face," he dismisses.

"If you didn't know before tonight," Nick says, "how'd *Crane* know me and the girl were here?"

Walter grins, gnaws his bottom lip, then, "Oh, fuck it. I've told you enough already, might as well divulge some more. "*Mr* Crane has had tabs on you from day one. He's been watching you day to day. He knows all about you, Nick. He knew about *our* relationship weeks before I knew about yours and his."

"But- "

"He sent Apollo to your flat because he knew you were there, he saw you in the car, saw you dump it, saw you go to that slag Frank's, then watched you come here. Knowing that you'd be away, he struck, using me. I knew how unhinged that junkie was, knew she had the gun and what she had to do. I assumed she'd keep you long enough for us to do the job. Tell me, were you ever going to take one of her fingers?"

Nick blinks rapidly to stop his eyes rolling. Blood squeezed into his head is starting to make him light-headed.

"I'll take that as a no," Walter chuckles. "Then again, who knows? There's never any telling with you, Nicko You're an enigma to most, but I know different. You're just as fucked up as I am. Does the boy still haunt you? All he wanted was to join in, wasn't it? You put an end to him ever joining in, didn't you? We all did. You were fucking scared of him, scared he'd steal your dreams, fuck the wife you never had. I'm sure he had his own dreams that didn't concern you. You were the one doing the fucking, *we* just..." The smile on Walter's face doubles in size.

"…granted your wish."

Nick bursts into another breakout attempt, veins bulging in his arms, his face flushes red, he snorts, foaming at the mouth. It's pointless. Apollo has him tight, relishing the moment, baiting him with soft whispers.

Walter continues, "It's funny, really, how long we've known each other, ended up socialising in the same circles. I always thought our relationship would end with me personally putting a bullet between your eyes, burying you under an airport runway and reliving the memory over and over with a cocktail in one hand and some pussy in the other. I never, *ever* considered that it would be because you fucked with Mr Crane."

Nick struggles. "How…did…"

Smacking a palm on his head, Walter interrupts, "Oh, yeah. You wanted to know how Mr Crane knew where you were. Sorry mate."

Walter looks to the shadows, rubs his fingertips together, making squeaking noises with his lips. From the murk emerges a shimmering Pop Tart, casual in his approach, moon eyes split by vertical pupils. With a trill, the cat jumps into Walter's arms.

Facing Nick, Walter says, "Ever heard of a familiar spirit?"

The cat.

The fucking cat.

Both it and Walter stare at him, the cat purring with a strange sense of triumph. If cats could smile, this one would be the Cheshire. It's been spying on him all this time. It's a good thing they didn't try to escape the city themselves, the cat would've lead the society straight to Katy's home.

The fucking cat.

Katy is going to be devastated.

Nick lets his hands slip from Apollo's forearms, knuckles on the floor.

Walter puts down the cat. It saunters to Nick, sits on its hind quarters a few feet away from him, purring.

Walter starts to explain, "You see, Nick, a familiar spirit is- "

"Don't care." Nick shunts his elbow into Apollo's ribs, the cracking bones sound like colliding marbles. Apollo is winded long enough for Nick to take Danielle's gun from his waistband. He lunges forward, aiming at a snarling Walter. As he squeezes the trigger, his knee skids in blood. Suddenly the gun points at the cat. Yellow muzzle flash lights up the familiar before the round pierces its skull and ricochets off the floor. Without a sound, the cat topples on its side, spilling gunk from its obliterated skull, popped eyes sagging from their sockets. Nick retrains the gun on Walter, but Apollo chops down on his elbow with the force of a crane arm, knocking the gun from his grip. The big fuck kicks it away, wraps his arms and legs around Nick, bearhugging his spine into a question mark.

"STOP!"

The factory falls silent. Nick freezes in the four-limbed grapple.

Walter takes the gun, blood-spattered, from the floor. He wastes little time in smacking it across Nick's face, splitting open his eyebrow. Nick spits blood, his eye begins to balloon.

"Why'd you go and do a dipshit thing like that, Nick?" says Walter.

Too weak to fight back, Nick says nothing. His face is a crimson mess.

"You don't know, do you?" Walter says. "You never know why you do the things you do."

Before Nick's eyes, the cat drunkenly stands, its fur wet with its own blood, whiskers zigzagging, moon eyes pumping up with life. Its skull cracks as it rebuilds itself, leaving brain matter on the factory floor. Nick's eyes dilate, the word zooms out and in at the same time. Panic sets in. Nick draws quick, ragged breaths, tries to kick the zombie cat away, red spume dripping from the corners of his mouth. He chokes when he inhales his cascading blood. When the cat has finished its resurrection, it has thick scars protruding through its fur, most noticeably an X on its face.

Walter kneels to stroke the cat, washing itself. He chuckles before he says to Nick, "Don't you know cats have nine lives? This is the sort of thing you can expect when you dabble in this occult shit."

"Shit?" Apollo challenges.

"Don't look too much into it. Just a figure of speech."

A ragdoll in Apollo's custody, Nick says, "So it *is* a cult."

Walter stands, letting the cat prance into the shadows. "A cult and the *oc*cult are separate things, Nick. Don't confuse the two."

Walter's manner has been playful. It makes everything more discomforting, not that it's possible to get much more uncomfortable. It's crossed Nick's mind what they plan to do to him. Walter has already stated that they won't kill him, but that doesn't mean much. Nick has heard of methods employed by villains to hurt people they *want* to live. A little of this, a little of that, a smidge of torture, a dash of rape.

"How is it then, Walt? You all have nine lives?" asks Nick, searching for the undead cat.

"*Christ* no," says Walter.

Without looking, he points the gun into the darkness and lets off a round. Momentarily, the factory floor is illumined with the hot flash, revealing the hoods. After a few seconds, one of the hoods tumbles facedown into the light. The concrete crunches their nose into their face. The others hoods, confined to the umbra, don't react.

Nick stares at the bodies, Harvey's eyes held open by Death's hand. The hood's face is still hidden.

Walter asks, "What do you think we are. Gods?" He invades Nick's space again, face to face, twiddling his moustache, using droplets of his brother's blood to glue up the tips. "Now listen up, Nick, and listen good because I do *not* enjoy repeating myself. You're going to leave this estate alive. Tomorrow, you will be given the briefing of what to do next. You might experience a terrible headache, but you don't have to go pussying off to the hospital. I suggest that as of tomorrow you leave this alone, do as you're told, and fuck off. If I have another opportunity, I will end your miserable life as slowly as I can. Is that clear?"

"The girl…"

Walter tuts. "She's not your problem, anymore. Forget about her. Now," he stands, tosses the gun onto the settee, "I'm afraid I must conclude tonight. It's been a long one, and I, for one, am knackered."

Nick starts to speak, "I'm gonna kill y- "

He can't finish. Apollo's grip tightens, he can feel sleep being forced upon him, his vision darkening from the outside in. His heartbeat becomes tinnitus. He isn't sure what's coming next, though he finds himself welcoming this sensation. It's going to be a good sleep.

I'm gonna kill you. He's not sure he means it, but it's a pleasure to dream.

That fucking cat, he tells himself again, his inner voice an echo in the distance.

He watches Walter flip his suit jacket over his shoulder, walking away with the two remaining hoods obediently at his tail. As he passes out, the Figure, from the office overlooking the factory, reminds Nick of its presence. You've killed before, it tells him.

As if he…

…could…

…

…forget…

CHAPTER 23

Katy awakens.

For a few seconds that are the cruellest of her life so far, she has forgotten everything. For those few sweet seconds, she could be waking up in her own bed, fresh sheets with that fabric softener smell, the same one that Mum always buys because it's not only cheap, but consistent. She uses her left hand to wipe the crumbs of sleep from her eyes. Through the bleary cracks she can see the posters in her bedroom, they've shuffled themselves around slightly, for some reason.

Then the sweet seconds come to an abrupt halt. Opening her eyes fully, Katy finds herself not in the luxury of her bedroom, not even a cell, but the ruin of a dank old room that smells of wet soil, fungal and mouldy. There's no carpet, only warped floorboards with nail heads poking up. What she thought were posters in her bedroom are framed paintings depicting black scenery, cold oceans and grey faces.

They have her again. They found her.

Nick said she'd be safe. Does he know she's gone? Is he okay?

Her pulse quickens, beats at her wrists, her eardrums. She wipes her eyes again using her left arm. Trying to use her right hurts, as if someone is sawing into her skin. She gawps at it. Her arm isn't dead, it's handcuffed to a flaking radiator. She flips her legs around, starts kicking it. The bangs are loud. She cries as she drives her feet into the steel, hoping that she will break through the wall if nothing else. Of all the things in this room that are old or broken, the wall is solid, does not budge.

Look for another way, her brain tells her.

Katy has small nimble hands that might one day play the piano if her music teacher has anything to say about it ("fingers made for the keys," he'd proclaimed with a raised finger). She clamps her hand over the handcuffs, pinches the fingers of her right hand into a cone. She tries to slip her hand free, cutting a bloody bracelet around her wrist. The gruesome thought that her blood might act as a lubricant is all too real for her, yet drives her on until she can't continue because of the pain. Her hand has become purple with the effort.

Look for another *way, then.* It's not her voice.

She scans around the foetid room. There won't be anything like a pencil sharpener handed to her this time. Maybe there's a crusty toolbox bundled away up here, or some rope. She has no idea how she'd use anything she might find or how she'd even reach it, being handcuffed to the radiator and all. One step at a time, though. That's the way you accomplish things. One step at a time.

The ceiling is slanted, suggesting Katy is in a top floor room, or an attic. Wooden beams hold up the tiles and insulation. What remains of it, anyway. Most of it has been stolen by rodents and birds who've found a way inside to make their nests. Birds are clever, if there's a way in and out that no one else knows of, they'll find it. Unfortunately, that secret will belong to them, too.

Tears are replaced by a primal urge for survival. She's in the den of the predators, at the heart of the spider's web. How strong this survival mode will continue to run she has no idea, or to what lengths it'll push her. Against Mum and Dad's wishes *and* their knowledge, Katy watched one of those franchise horror films a few months back. In it, a man had sawn off his own foot to survive. Gazing at her handcuffed hand, she hopes it doesn't come to that. Suddenly, this survival instinct frightens her, because she knows she would.

At least there are no hacksaws up here.

She flips her legs around so they're stretching out in front of her, leans back against the radiator, the icy cold now a relief for the sweat dripping down her back. She closes her eyes, and thinks.

The room is quiet. The rats are asleep, the birds tucked in their nests, though the insects are still scuttling around under the floorboards. She can hear them, their chitinous bodies clicking. She opens her eyes. Where her feet are she can see a beetle lolloping to the top of an exposed nail. It's not the beetle that's important. After defeating the climb, the beetle continues on its path to the other side of the room. Katy grunts onto her knees, reaches out as far as she can, shoving her tongue into her cheek for extra motivation before the handcuffs hold her back. She manages to grab the nail head. Though it's half out of the plank, it's still in a fair way. She wobbles the nail, blanking out everything else. It's just her and the nail in a spotlight.

CHAPTER 24

Walter had lied to Nick. Surely what he has now is a fucking concussion and a half. He's lying on his front, head turned to the side.

Prepping himself for further pain, Nick peaks through his lids, keeps them narrow, unable to work out the various shapes in the pale place where he finds himself. A ray of sunshine spears through a boarded up window, warming a patch on his chest. Another conspires to blind him. He coughs, blowing a cloud of dust into his nostrils. The oncoming sneeze tickles him to an upright position. His head pounds once, twice, then the pain relaxes.

His throat is a desert, his tongue sandpaper. Dust has crammed up his nose. Sucking saliva into his mouth, Nick can at least take the prickles from his tongue. Once Nick opens his eyes beyond slits, he quickly recognises where Walter and the big fuck have dumped him.

O'Reilly's is where Nick used to train, before the favour, before the subsequent scandal that closed its doors forever. Not much remains, though there are some remnants of the gym's former success. In the middle is the sparring ring, blanketed by dust. The ropes loose, dangling smiles. A bucket sits in the centre, a couple of stools in the corners. Around the edges of the gym are punching bags, mended and re-mended with duct tape. One of them has fallen from its hooks. A few speedballs remain, and a training manakin covered with a white sheet, it's nose giving features to its hidden face.

Nick uses a crumbling wall to help him to his feet. Maybe there'll be a box of painkillers in the old locker room if they haven't been cleaned out by enterprising junkies. A wave of dizziness sends his head on a loop-the-loop. On legs made of jelly, he stumbles to the ring, gaining more confidence with each proceeding step. Anything he can use to assist his balance is taken advantage of. A training dummy offers the most help in spite of its beaten body.

Pressing handprints in the dust, Nick uses the ringside for support. The structure creaks with the added weight. O'Reilly's logo, a green clover beneath a golden glove, tags the centre of the ring, colours washed out. It turfs up memories Nick has tried for years to avoid, not only because he is scared of them, but because they remind him of when everything was good and right in his world. That's a distant dream, now.

He knows Walter dropped him here on purpose. Nick didn't realise that psychological warfare was Walt's bag, the bastard has never shown any enthusiasm or trust in anything that doesn't include physical violence. Unless…the nutter considers this a breed of *mind* violence. That would pass in Walt's deranged head.

Nick bends his mind to Katy. It's worse, the dark images of her fate, how he'd failed, how he'd broken a promise that, although said in anger, was exactly what the tin says it is. A damn *promise*. He clamps down his eyes, rubs his head, the concussion pumping sewage around his skull. The ring reclaims his attention, and the echoing rhythm of shuffling feet.

Dancing around the now vibrant green clover, in a clean ring with all the ropes where they should be, Nick sees himself shadow boxing, moving in slow motion, an imprint of himself trailing behind. His body is trim, toned. He's agile, ducking under the blows of an invisible opponent. Sweat drips from his body as he throws a jab, an uppercut, a right to imagined ribs, another jab. All these standards he's still able to execute, at the peril of pulling a muscle or putting his back out if he moves too quick. No one ever said getting older was fun. Youth gives speed, age bestows brute force. Nick is in awe of his younger self, jealous of the smile he once wore, envious of the potential.

Young Nick, who has floppy hair because he's rebelling – in good humour – against O'Reilly's wishes, stops and stares straight at Nick. In a moment his heart solidifies, sure that he is about to communicate with a phantom of himself. Does it count as a ghost if you consider that part of you dead? Before he has time to question further, Young Nick vanishes in a soft cloud, the clover loses its colour, the ring is broken again.

Nick turns his back on it, a cold sweat pebbles his forehead. The wall where he regained consciousness is filled out by hundreds, if not thousands, of promotional posters. Most of them in tatters, overlapping each other, duplicates tacked over originals. He recalls some of the faces, unable to remember names, and vice versa. His own face isn't up there. O'Reilly had ripped him from the wall of fame immediately after the cops came calling.

A second phantom appears to the left, announcing itself with panting breathes. Nick double-takes, yet Young Nick remains, this time going to town with impressive blows that smack like lightning against a free standing punching bag. This version of himself has cut his hair, giving in to the demands of his trainer after a year and a half of leg pulling. O'Reilly had taken a keen interest in Nick ten minutes after he'd first entered the gym, it had been these same lightning strikes that grabbed the grouchy Irishman's attention. Days later, Nick was being managed by O'Reilly, who promised him the top if he was willing to start at the bottom. That seed embedded itself in the soil of Nick's heart, festering instead of growing.

Behind Young Nick is a poster with the Figure's face on it. It's watching Nick relive the memories of his younger years, taking enjoyment in his misery. A row of sharpened teeth glitter as its face splits open. Young Nick bounces on his toes in front of the poster for all of a second, and the Figure is gone. It's around, though. This is its home. It was born here.

Another ghost materialises into the memory. A young lad, shorter than Nick, field-blonde hair sitting wig-like above his ears. His hands are in his shorts pockets, a pair of gloves dangling around his neck and a sleeveless shirt that makes him look skinnier than he really was. He's smiling, but it's a nervous smile, a smile that wonders if he belongs here. Young Nick takes a break from punishing the bag, looks at the scrawny newcomer, measuring him up, taking stock.

The young lad asks, "Can I join in?"

Both ghosts deteriorate, carried off by a wind that isn't blowing. Having the memories rerun is a taunt that only history can deal out, a mocking of bad decisions. He wants to shoo them away, yet Nick doesn't think they'll leave him alone, not yet. He's had years to play back everything, to seek out forgiveness that refuses to be found. Now the memories are massing an assault, tired of being held in the waiting room.

"Water," he croaks.

The locker room door cracks loudly against the wall, springs back. Nick stops it. Nothing's changed in the locker room. The lockers themselves are still blue, chipped at the corners, scratched up in front. Some have been personalised with stickers. A gym bag is stuffed on top of one, drooping down the side. A long slatted bench runs down the middle of the room. At the far end is a vending machine that O'Reilly said didn't need replacing because it worked fine if you rammed it with your hip now and then. Just don't let him catch you doing it.

An elbow to the glass shatters it. Treacly liquid spills from the corners of Nick's mouth as he upends a can of Coke, able to glug it down as it's gone flat. Chucking the can away, he grabs a second and downs that, too. When he turns, catching his breath, he isn't stumped by the sight of his younger self again, sitting on the bench tying his shoes. This time, Nick doesn't intend to watch the memory. Thirst quenched, it's time to leave. There's a lot to dissect.

When the phantoms of the Georges enter the locker room, dressed in suits that even then were worth more than he was, Nick finds himself unable to run from the show. Harvey hasn't yet put on his weight. Walter doesn't have his moustache, though the shadow under his nose alludes to its growth.

"*How's it going, Nick?*" says Harvey. He claps a gossamer hand on Young Nick's translucent shoulder.

Nick remembers the entire conversation as it happens before his eyes, moving his lips along with every player.

"*Got several fights coming up, so not too shabby. You?*" Nick answers, finishing the lace up.

"*Business is good.*"

"*Getting better,*" from Walter.

All their voices echo.

Harvey asks, "*Going to knock 'em all out, I hope?*"

"*Always do, don't I?*"

Walter says, "*I hear that young lad is knockin' 'em all out, too. Catching up to you, Nick. So I hear.*"

Harvey cuts his brother off. "*Don't let yourself get distracted, Nick. A few more wins and you'll go pro. I'm surprised it's taken this long. You heard much more about the scouts?*"

Nick answers, "*No, but O'Reilly says they'll be there. Contracts in hand, he says.*"

"*Scouts're eyeing up the other lad, too,*" Walter teases.

It's easy now for Nick to see where the manipulation started. It hadn't been at the time. He no longer queries if he really is or isn't seeing these phantoms perform. They're here whether he likes it or not. This sort of thing usually happens to people who've gone mad, doesn't it?

Harvey and Walter – mostly Harvey – prattle on with their small talk, Young Nick nods along. As he knew it would, the talk darkens.

"*Listen,*" says Harvey, nudging Nick's arm. "*I've been meaning to talk to you, you know...the kid...Walter's right, he isn't doing all that bad himself.*"

"*So?*" says Nick. "*He's a good kid. Good fighter.*"

"*Good? He's the prize horse,*" Walter says.

"*Walter's right,*" Harvey continues. "*He's about three fights away from matching your numbers. Zero losses, all wins by KO. Aren't you concerned?*"

Nick asks, "*Should I be?*"

"*You're both middle weight. I've been talking to a few people I know and they say the head hunters are looking for the next champion. That's champion, Nick, not* champions."

Young Nick goes to his locker, reorganising the items inside. "*What're you getting at, mate?*"

Harvey gets defensive in the same way a lawyer gets slimy. "*Nothing, nothing really. But Nick, you've put a lot into this. God knows I've watched you put your body and mind through hell to get where you are now, I don't want to see-*"

"*The kid's set to take it away from you, Nick,*" Walter interrupts. "*Younger. More handsome, no offense.*"

Harvey sighs, bites his tongue. Even then he was at war with his quick-mouthed brother tearing down whatever foundations he was laying.

"*You don't know that,*" Young Nick laughs, shutting his locker. "*We've both put our work in, can't do any more.*"

"*So, you're not worried at all?*" from Harvey, raising an eyebrow.

"*No.*"

Walter sifts through the pockets of hanging coats, discarding thin wallets. "*We've got a lot of plans in the future for you, Nick. Management, promotion. All of us stand to make a lot of money. My brother and I have as much at stake in this as you do.*"

Young Nick scoffs, "*I don't think so, Walter.*"

Harvey puts a hand on Young Nick's shoulder, each finger decorated with thick rings that wouldn't fit him today. Not that they had to. The dead don't wear rings. "*That's fine, Nick, that's fine. All we're saying is there are ways we can ease the competition for you.*"

"*I'm a boxer. I like competition,*" Nick objects, hanging a towel around his neck.

"*But not at the cost of your career, Nick,*" Harvey stresses. That had been key in Nick's manipulation, making him believe his whole life was about to succeed or fail if he didn't do something about it, convincing him to tip the scales in his favour.

"*It'll be fine,*" says Young Nick, smiling at his old school friend. "*O'Reilly believes in me. So do I. And he's my manager. That's enough.*"

"*I believe in you too, Nick. I just don't trust chance,*" Harvey says.

"*We'll be in touch,*" grunts Walter, who leaves.

Harvey says goodbye to Young Nick before following his brother. The phantoms disappear and Nick is alone again, the rivulets of Coke down his cheeks are sticky.

He remembers how the seed of ambition O'Reilly had planted had been corrupted that day.

The gym is cold. He kicks a boxing glove across the floor, leaving a skid mark in the dust. Taking one last glance around the place, he decides it's time to go. Before he's able to get near the front door, more voices arrest his attention. They come from behind, crawl up his spine. He already remembers this one as if it were yesterday.

The phantoms occupy O'Reilly's office, which the Irishman told Nick he could use if he wanted. Young Nick is pacing, the Georges perched in place, knowing smiles spread across their faces.

"*I'm losing everything,*" Young Nick says. "*It's being taken right from under my fucking nose. Even O'Reilly is giving him more attention, now that he's number fucking one.*"

"*Told you this'd happen,*" from Walter, checking his nails.

Young Nick pokes a finger at his own chest. "*I've worked too hard for fuck knows how long. He's younger, he can afford the luxury of time, my chances for a professional career are limited.*"

His younger self has a fat lip and a juicy eye, a memento from the match he'd had against the kid. He remembers the match, recalls how bitter the defeat had tasted, how the hatred had birthed itself on the canvas then and there, blood gushing from his busted nose.

"*There's still time, Nick. Still a chance,*" says Harvey.

Young Nick continues to pace the office filled with trophies and boxing memorabilia, black and white photos of O'Reilly in his prime.

Harvey goes on. "*Nick. Athletes have accidents all the time, falls that put them out of action for a spell. What if something like that were to happen to the kid?"*

"*I ain't that lucky,*" says Young Nick.

Walter purrs, "*You're misunderstanding us.*"

Young Nick gawks at the brothers for a while before it clicks. "*Oh, fuck no. No, I couldn't do that.*"

"*You wouldn't have to do a thing.*"

Harvey gestures heavily with his hands to add gusto. "*Something easy. He won't be able to fight, the scouts will forget about him, you'll be number one and you'll get your career back.*"

Nick hesitates. "*I don't know…*"

"*Look what he did to you, Nick. He fucked up your eye, burst your lip, your nose. He's stealing your dreams. I don't want to see that happen. I don't for one second believe he's a better fighter than you, not for a second, but he's doing something right, and it's ruining you in the process.*"

"*I dunno, Harvey,*" Walter joins. "*Maybe Nick wants the life of a failure?*"

That had been a low, cheap shot. Nick can't believe how easily it riled him up back then, how easily it riles him up now.

"*Fuck off, Walt,*" he says.

"*You want another sore eye?*"

"*Shut up, Walter,*" Harvey says, drumming his fingers.

"*Harvey,*" Young Nick is close to tears. "*I…look, if…if you do something to…to help me, only do the bare minimum. I don't want the kid hurt too badly.*"

But he *did*. He'd been lying to himself. He'd wanted to see the kid hurt. Hearing himself tell that lie is a punch to the gut, he wishes he could bang on the glass and alter the course of time, only this isn't an interactive film, and memories cannot be altered.

"*Bare minimum,*" says Harvey, hand on heart. "*And you'll get that life you've always wanted.*"

"And we'll be in touch," adds Walter, ominous enough to be threatening.

"But Nick, you have to ask us. You have to ask us to do this favour for you."

That had been the barbed hook. It's possible the Georges would've made a lot of money off Nick if he'd gone pro. They would've had this dirty secret to hold onto. They were setting Nick up for lifelong blackmail, they could've used him to rig fights. He's ashamed that he never saw it, blinded by a friendship that was never genuine. The promise of a professional future in this sport he had so loved was the final ingredient needed in making the worst choice of his life.

"Can you do this favour for me?" he asks.

"Of course," the Georges say in unison.

The phantoms dissipate. O'Reilly's office is empty.

The Georges did what they said they'd do. The kid got hurt. Nick doesn't know, to this day, if they did it personally or if they hired their goons to do the dirty work. It was likely that Walter made himself apart of the action, which would have pissed Harvey off something royal. Only, the kid didn't just get hurt. The kid got killed.

They did a number on him and multiplied it. Nick saw the pictures, shown to him by the two officers that came calling at O'Reilly's. Police involvement hadn't been a factor he'd expected. It had also been how he learned of the kid's death. He remembers their faces. One of them was a woman, attractive if not for her too-short hairstyle, the other an arrogant bloke who thought he was the dog's bollocks. The pictures immortalised the kid's mauled body, a yellow number standing by his head. His face was swollen, puffed up eyes and a split in his lip so bad that you could see teeth. The officers had said both legs were broken, multiple ribs had been fractured and smashed wrists and dislocated shoulders added to the roundup. Not to mention the semi-crushed skull. The list was long. Nick remembers how his stomach had churned at the news, how his head spun and suddenly jumping from a tower block seemed appealing.

How the cops came to suspect Nick in the first place remains a mystery. He guessed they had a motive. Whilst he had a hand in it, there was nothing at the scene which could be used against him, nothing that could prove he had, as the officers said, "put the hit" on the kid.

The Georges involvement never saw the light of day. They told Nick to keep his cool, the cops had nothing that would stick and pretty soon it would all wash away. They'd been right in that regard. The cops, who backed off eventually, had only their suspicions, and suspicion is not enough to condemn a man.

Money, perhaps, passed between two bent parties, is enough to save him.

Though he was found not guilty, the police involvement was scandal enough. O'Reilly had disowned Nick the same day, telling him whatever he was close to was going to fuck up his life, that he didn't want that kind of aggro inside the gym, and that those George brothers could go fuck themselves and no he didn't give a whistling shit who they were.

For O'Reilly, in the end, kicking Nick out of his gym didn't save his business. The gossip was already ink blotting the grapevine. Promising fighter on the cusp of turning pro suspected of brutal slaying of rival to further career. Rumours continued to float around like the plague. Before long, O'Reilly saw a drop in business until it got so bad that no one came through the doors. He had to close the gym, go back to Ireland. Nick hasn't forgiven himself for that, either.

The pros wouldn't touch Nick, on the grounds that, guilty or not, it was too much for them to take on, that in doing so they would jeopardise their own reputations. Even if they handled Nick with a ten foot pole, the poking end would still get shitty.

And so began the life of taking odd jobs which would eventually turn Nick on to the world of door work and unlicensed boxing. The Georges said they would sort him out, that it would take time and they should all lie low until the fan had been cleared of the shit. They promised Nick – Harvey promised him – that the kid's death was an accident. Having seen the photos, it was apparent that more than an accident had occurred that night. They must've accidentally battered the kid over and over.

Their chances of using Nick's pro career as a money-maker had been ruined, but they'd performed the favour in full, and Nick was in their pocket. Their property.

It took almost a couple of years for the Georges to come collect. Nick had turned them down time and time again, not wishing for a repeat. They still had dirt on him, but Harvey championed the long game. At any time, they could have fed Nick back to those suspicious wolves. It was his and Harv's very strained friendship that kept it from happening. The Georges always kept ways of incriminating a person, which is why they never had the need for fall guys. If they wanted you to do bird, you didn't have a say.

Of course, the Georges aren't the Georges anymore.

It's just the George, now.

The worse of the two. The one who had always tortured Nick. Now, thanks to another stupid decision, the George and his psycho friends have the girl.

Katy.

Life hasn't been good since that initial choice he made with the Georges in O'Reilly's. The best choice he'd made since then had been to work for Crane. The money had been easy, the jobs easier. What a pile of shit that all turned out to be. It had been one more bad decision in a long line of them. Saving Katy, he still can't say why he did it other than moral obligation, which should be good enough. There was something else there, though. A driving factor that wasn't merely the fight between right and wrong. Is the matter of his redemption the only reason she's still alive?

Is she alive?

Does…does he care?

Picturing her face, he thinks he does. Isn't sure.

And look what all that led to. Beatings, shootings, ghosts, conspiracy, home invasion, murder, the occult, responsibility. The cherry on the cake had been going to the Georges for help and leaving her *alone*. Nick's life choices are starting to have their own lineage, maybe they already have a coat-of-arms.

His fear is that he's incapable of making the right choice.

Nick has had enough of O'Reilly's. Where to begin, he doesn't know. Frank's? The flat? There might be some answers at Crane's building. It's got to be swarming with his followers by now. They won't take a chance on Katy being taken from them again.

"One step at a time," Nick tells himself.

The heavy glass front door grates open. It's covered in posters broadcasting the gym's availability. All of them are stuck over older posters advertising classes, hours, equipment.

It's cold in spite of the radiant sun cresting over the roofs of the businesses lining the street. Its glare erupts another headache behind Nick's eyes. This road used to be so familiar to him. The café directly across the street, Pudgey's, had been a frequent pitstop, and the pub at the end of the road (The Glove and Ref) had been where most training nights ended as a kind of ritual. Now, Brentworth Road is another planet, contaminated by O'Reilly's ruination.

"Got a delivery for you."

Nick doesn't know the hick puffing on a sorry looking cigarette that must've been pinched off the pavement. His face has to be the result of a botched surgery. In a second, when the hick lifts his stapled face, recognition arrives. Simon, dabbing ash onto the ground, doesn't get a chance to say anything else. Nick grabs him by the collar, drags him into the recess and rams him against the wall. Off his feet, Simon's lack of weight isn't a surprise. He pushes out his chin, lips scrunching together.

Nick presses his forehead up against Simon's. "The fuck *you* doing here?" Ignoring Simon's disfigurement proves too hard. "What happened to you?"

Unparallel staples scale up the right side of Simon's face, turbid liquid oozes from them. The top one, not fully in because it can't break past the skull, holds down threads of hair. Leftover smoke from his last drag plumes through the gaps between the staples.

"*You* happened," Simon replies, lifting the cigarette to his mouth.

Changing his grip, Nick pins Simon by shoving his right arm across his chest. Nick slaps the cigarette away. Simon stares after it as if it was his only one left.

"You did that to yourself," Nick says. "Don't tell me I'm capable of doing *that* to a man."

"Cut me down to the bone, you did."

"I didn't turn you into this!"

"Don't shoot the messenger." Simon raises his hands in surrender.

Applying more pressure, Nick asks, "Where's the girl?"

Straining, Simon answers, "You think they tell me anything? Jesus, I'm the bottom of the barrel!"

"There're more ways to hurt you." Nick bumps his forehead against Simon's.

Simon moans, "Put me down. I have to give you something. A message. Master Crane said if I return to him and he sees you've hurt me, the girl will lose a finger."

Spraying spittle on Simon's face, Nick demands, "Why should I trust a single fucking word that comes outta your mouth?"

Simon cocks an eyebrow. "You wanna take the chance?"

Reluctantly, Nick lowers him.

A empty-eyed passer-by glances at them as she drifts by the gym, doesn't stop or show any concern. In this neck of woods, where the jungle is at its thickest, people like her see this sort of thing all the time. As far as she cares, Nick is a dealer pressing a client to cough up. She passes.

Nick catches Simon smiling. The urge to launch a punch into the prick's gut is almost overwhelming. *Is* overwhelming. Nick rockets his fist into the glass behind Simon. A smooth, curving crack divides the pane in two. Nick knows his knuckles are bleeding, they're getting warm.

Simon's confidence has been revived now he isn't restrained. He smirks, pats down the sleeves of his military cast-off jacket. On the left arm, below the shoulder, a German flag hangs on by its last stitches.

"Deliver your message and fuck off," says Nick.

"Don't wanna chat?"

"No."

"We need a catch-up. Last time we saw each other was- "

"You're pushing it, prick."

Simons grins, the staples writhing in his face. "I haven't *began* to push yet."

Cold hands seize Nick from behind, claws digging into his shoulders. He's thrown through the door in a hailstorm of glass. The burglar alarm sobs once, then the batteries run flat.

Nick is on his front, glass pebbles jab into his palms. Footsteps approach, crunching on shards. Rolling over, expecting Apollo, he draws his leg back to kick the big fuck, intent on busting his cobblers. When he sees the Figure looming over him, he freezes. There is no definition to its body, an empty space cut out of reality where a human should be. It chuckles, a reptilian click from the back of its throat. Circular lamps for eyes shine down on Nick, unable to convey emotion.

Does the past have a name? Katy had asked.

It speaks. "Can I join in?"

"That'll do." Simon walks into view from behind the Figure, a cocky spring in his step. He kicks large pieces of glass across the gym, slicing through the grime.

The Figure takes a submissive step backwards. Why is it listening to *him*?

"You know each other, I believe." Simon reaches into his jacket, produces a plain white envelope.

Does the past have a name?

Nick stutters, unable to look away from the Figure. "How…how can you…it…"

"I told you it can be made better, or worse, didn't I?" Simon replies.

"But…how?"

"It was my wish, my gift, from Master Crane. You really should have stuck by him, Nicholas. You could've had the world if you wanted, and if he likes you enough."

Nick jumps to his feet, slipping on glass chips, holds up his fists. Blood leaks from the clenched creases. His head spins, dosing up the nausea.

"You can fight it, if you want," Simon laughs, "but it won't do you any good."

Not listening, Nick puts all his power behind a right hook. It goes clean through the Figure without resistance, as affective as punching mist.

Simon tuts. The Figure shoves Nick with one cold hand. He slides backwards, crashes into a pile of rubber mats. Winded, he struggles to catch his breath. Simon is quickly upon him, an insect over its prey.

"I can make it do worse," he says, balling Nick's tee-shirt in his fist. "Don't forget that. If I had my way, I'd let it slaughter you right here. It'd be ironic, wouldn't it? This is where you and it first became friends. That's what *I'd* do, but Master has expressed no such desires. I'm supposed to give you this." He holds up the envelope, tucks it inside Nick's jacket. "And now I have."

Too stubborn to show vulnerability, Nick grunts, "We done?"

Simon lets go, licks puss that has dribbled from his staples. Backing off, he says, "Almost. I know you killed Dani."

"Danielle?"

Simon's lip twitches. "You shot her."

"I didn't shoot anybody," says Nick.

Face flushing red, Simon shouts, "You put one through her head!"

The prick slaps himself across the staples, doubles over, clutching his face. He pants. Nick hears more than a man in pain. It's the ecstatic gasping of an orgasm.

"I reckon you need to investigate closer to home on that one," Nick suggests. Using his elbows that pestle glass into grains, he props himself up.

"You're a liar." Simon nails his eyes on Nick, the right one filling with blood.

The Figure stands guard, its lamp gaze on Nick the whole time.

"It was Crane, Simon."

"Now you're trying to be my friend?" A couple of staples hang dislodged. The gash widens, threads of sticky blood stretch like gum. "You didn't wanna be my friend before, did ya? When Master Crane's through with you, I'm going to find you. It'll be easy." Simon points at the Figure. "He'll tell me. You made him, he knows how to find you. I'll let it drag out, you'll wish for death long before you've paid back what you owe for Dani's life. Stay *DOWN*!"

Parking himself back down, Nick's refractured rib sends a paralysing shock through his torso. He doesn't let Simon or the Figure see his pain, though something tells him the Figure is aware.

He explains, "I didn't shoot her. I didn't do anything to hurt her. Crane didn't give a toss about her and doesn't give a toss about you. All he cares about is his book."

"You're so wrong about that," Simon scoffs.

"You know who's wrong about what? You thinking that haircut would look good. You've delivered your message, so leave."

His tongue protruding through the gash like a pink slug, Simon slurps up his own gunk. It makes him quiver, Nick is left sickened by the prick's twisted nature. Or is it nurture?

"I'll do that," Simon turns. "But remember what I said. When Master is finished with you…you're mine. I can wait. Shit, I might wish for me and you to live forever, that way the fun will never end." Opening the front door instead of stepping through the frame of smashed glass, Simon faces Nick before leaving. "Read the letter, Nicholas. Don't leave until you do. And, by the by, you've gone viral. That kinda makes you famous."

Viral?"

Simon exits, a stiff breeze feathers his mullet. The Figure remains.

It doesn't do or say anything, only watches him. The air turns glacial, the gym darkens. The Figure knows O'Reilly's, remembers it as well as Nick does.

Does the past have a name?

Nick wets his drying lips.

"I'm, uh…I'm sorry."

The Figure is unmoved. In the dead of night, the Figure is a harbinger of guilt, of dread, and in the sunlight hours, it is a monster. But behind the Figure, underneath its darkness, is a promising young lad who only wanted to join in.

Bending his knees, pushing himself upright against the rubber mats, Nick adds a word he has been afraid to speak for many years.

"Callum."

The Figure flinches. It fades away, taking the cold and darkness with it. Nick drops his head back, catching breath that he didn't realise had gotten away from him until now.

Nick wonders when the last time it had heard its name was.

"Callum Granger," he says to the empty gym.

Hurting in corners of his body he didn't know he had, Nick drags himself up. He stumbles into O'Reilly's office, falls down in the wonky swivel chair behind the desk. He picks the letter from his jacket, drops it on the desktop. On it is his name written in calligraphy, the back sealed up with a splat of red wax. It's a personal letter from Crane if ever there was one.

Before he opens it, Simon's parting words come back to him, and Nick asks himself, "The fuck does viral mean?"

Have Crane's followers injected him with a sickness?

He doesn't feel ill.

CHAPTER 25

As the teabag turns the water brown, steam spirals with the delicate stirring of the spoon. To avoid any drops, Crane taps it lightly four times against the rim. This musical chiming to signal that a perfectly balanced mug of tea has been brewed is a compulsive behaviour.

Crane spills a selection of plain biscuits onto a dish, fans them out. The dish goes into the centre of an oak table.

"You needn't go to this trouble," says Juniper, hands in her lap.

"Nonsense," Crane replies, sitting down. "How often do we get to have a humble cup of tea these days? I fear I have forgotten the taste."

A gentleman, he waits for Juniper to take the first sip. Her tea is a shade darker than his.

They sit at opposite ends of the table, a king and queen. Though the table – fit for Vikings if their barbaric decorum can be forgiven – is grand, the rest of the kitchen is in a state of disrepair. The work surfaces need replacing, the cupboards and the cooker, the plumbing is a dripping mess and the fridge is incapable of keeping anything cold. Fixing these problems shouldn't take too long. The only redeeming feature is the diamond leaded windows, which throw a criss-cross pattern over Juniper's face.

Juniper starts, "The girl- "

"Is secure," Crane stops her.

"She's clever. Sneaky. I'd prefer if we have someone keep an eye on her. At all times."

"Not necessary," Crane says. From his pocket he takes a tube of cream, rubs a dollop of it into his hands. Mountainous calluses are getting worse, dry skin has turned his hands into scorched riverbeds, itching and stinging more with each passing day. Only a few more to pass, then he can finish the offering. In the meantime, the cream – as a bonus – is antibacterial.

"How long are we going to keep her up there?" Juniper takes her mug.

"Until she is needed. She is quite safe. A diet of buttered bread and water will keep her going. Please, Juniper," Crane gestures at her tea. It'll start going cold if she leaves it much longer, and that just won't do.

Juniper sips without a sound.

"I grew up here, you know," says Crane. He looks over the kitchen, remembering. "This building shall replace our old one. I can make it nice again, should I wish it, better than the last. I do not envision the society complaining too much. Not with the future we are facing." Crane shuffles in his chair before he can glance over his shoulder enough to behold the brambles climbing up the window. "A spot of gardening shall do wonders, and there is a stunning drawing room that shall make a more stunning library. It is time my books had a worthy home."

"It's beautiful," says Juniper.

"Thank you. It was in this house that I first discovered the journey my life was to take. A tiresome story, one I shall not regale you with fully. I am needed as an educator, though the need is not yours. My parents were not simpletons. They had money. I had access to much that other young men did not. Mother had always shown a keen interest in forbidden literature. Father was unaware. I feared him as much as any young man should fear his father, but I kept Mother's secret from him. They had their differences of opinion. Mother's and mine could coexist."

Juniper puts a pause on Crane's story. She always brings the conversation back to business. He doesn't mind, he knows he's waffling on. The family home is a nostalgia pit that sings a siren song imploring him to reminisce.

She asks, "What happens next?"

Crane takes a hearty draught of tea. A biscuit to dunk would be nice. They are out of reach in the middle of the table. His own fault as the placer.

"What *we* do next is wait." The aftertaste of sugar clings to his tongue. "As for our nuisance, Mr Schaeffer has delivered my letter. The rest is up to Nicholas."

"What do you think he'll do?" asks Juniper, dillydallying with her tea.

"A great deal has happened to him. He has been chased, coerced, formed attachments, witnessed a" – Crane smiles – "suicide, betrayed and beaten. His mental stability is being tested. He shall be weak, and I am offering great generosity. I anticipate no further trouble. I have to concede, however, that all of this I unleash on him regrettably."

"Can't we kill him?"

Crane sighs. Ordinarily, this would be the protocol for troublemakers and heathens. There are plenty in the society who have the requisite skills for such a task. Mr Walter George is one of them. That man, ruthless as he may be, is unreliable. Crane briefly recalls his and Nicholas's exchange on the topic. Nicholas had a good handle on the matter. Still, the crime boss has his uses, and now Crane has permitted the younger brother to become top dog, perhaps he will simmer.

"I don't think so," Crane answers.

"Any reason?"

Averting his gaze, he says, "Nicholas is not the only one who has formed attachments."

Juniper takes a sip of tea. It is all Crane needs to understand her concern.

"Call it old age," he chuckles.

"Is the book safe?" she asks.

Taking some offense from the question, Crane reminds Juniper of her place. "Of course it is safe," he snaps, slapping the table. A biscuit bounces from the dish. "Do not dare think me a fool. It is sleeping, so do not awaken its ears to pointless questions about its wellbeing."

"I only ask out of concern." She bows her head.

Crane's lips tremble. He feels awful for scolding her like that, yet the temper remains. "Well," he says, "you need not. The book is our portal to greatness. It is more than safe."

She backtracks, a form of apology. "What do you believe Nicholas will do?"

"I believe he will listen to the fire in his heart and the grit in his belly. He is a man who had nothing until all of this, he shall want to retrieve the girl again. The letter will do little to deter him."

"You said you expect no further trouble from him."

"I said I *anticipate* no further trouble from him," Crane corrects her, unable to shake the caustic tone in his voice. "And I still do. I never stated that he would not *try*."

"If you believe he'll ignore the letter, come for the girl, but you won't have him killed, how do you surmise that he'll be no trouble?" asks Juniper.

Crane grins, his teeth have started to stain, hang crooked, loosen. "He has no clue where we are."

§

It's the best pop in the world when the handcuffs click open, a party popper – congratulations! – without the confetti. Katy drops her lockpick, the nasty nail which had been as smooth as a stick of coral. Rubbing her scored wrist, she searches for the hundredth time for any electric red eyes watching from the corners of the attic. Surely if they have been keeping tabs on her, they'd have stopped her when they saw what she was doing. Katy can't bring herself to trust that logic.

She sucks on her thumb and index, the saliva stings the cuts gouged by the nail but feels like cream on the blisters. Katy had been close to giving up before the cuffs popped open, the nail had caused a lot of damage to her fingers. It had been hard enough working the nail out of the floorboard. The technique she chose was to jab the point of the blunted nail into the keyhole and hope for the best. It worked, didn't it? And it only took the best part of three hours.

Fingers in her mouth, tasting dirt and the irony zest of blood, Katy gets to her feet. The planks groan.

She treads cautiously towards the one way out of the attic she can see. Weighty spiderweb hammocks cover most of the wooden door. They appear to be vacant except for the husks of flies, which is good because she's never got on with spiders like she does other creepy crawlies. One or two is fine, three at a push, but a horde of them would have repelled her fingers back before she could touch the handle. Spiders and injections, those two things she dislikes. And wasps, which are basically nature's needles.

Katy takes hold of the handle, which has a coarse green patina. There's no keyhole. When she twists the handle the door opens inwards. It doesn't creak so much as it clunks. Cold air rushes at her. A short flight of stairs leads down to another door, this one ajar.

The walls between are open, tatters of insulation are falling out, dust encrusted spiderwebs hang like bunting, the worn steps are littered with mice pellets. Katy listens for voices, any indication of the cult, certain that at any second she will hear them laughing before they cuff her back up to that horrible freezing radiator.

Her gut tells her to stay put. New friend Survival has other ideas. She's known Gut longer. Survival is fresh, eager to take her fears and turn them into bravery. Gut plays it safe, tells her that help will come. Survival says that help comes to those who find it. Katy wishes she had Pop Tart with her. He'd help her make a choice.

Having Nick would be ideal. She wonders if he's close, if he's coming…if he knows. He's most likely dead already. The thought sends a knife through her heart.

Go on, Survival encourages. *Think about that later.*

Katy descends the steps, ducking under the webs and exposed wires, using her arm to umbrella herself from falling eight-leggers.

"One step at a time," she whispers to herself.

She spies through the crack of the lower door, sees a hallway with great framed paintings as far as peaking allows her to see, candelabras holding waxy nubs separate each piece. The wallpaper may once have been red, age has stripped it of vibrancy. It smells, gives the impression of a museum left behind. There are, Katy notices, more cobwebs. Nowhere close to what the attic suffers.

More importantly, there are no cultists.

Steeling herself, sure that she is alone for now, she opens the door and sneaks out. The hallway is lifeless in both directions, and just like in the attic she searches for any cameras, finding none. Following her dominant hand, she heads to the right.

A continuous threadbare rug runs the length of the hallway, dampening her footsteps. Plenty of natural light filters through curtained windows, but lacks all essence of colour. It's cold, grey light that, as soon as it enters into this place, begins to rot.

This is where light comes to die. The thought startles her.

She takes her hair and begins to knead, hums a song about reaching for the stars.

Let go, Survival says. *Girls who play with their hair don't get out alive.*

Hide, says Gut.

Survival says more than Gut. Gut has always been around as a cautionary advisor, but it's only with the appearance of Survival that it seems to become a voice unattached to Katy.

At the end of the hallway, where it bends with a right angle, Katy tests the window. It's sealed, and she assumes the one at the other end of the hallway is, too. It's always been drummed into her to never assume anything. In this case she's going to make an exception. Outside, where the light is still alive, she sees grassland, and a little further abroad, a forest.

Around the bend is another stretch of hallway, longer. At the far end she can see a rocking chair, covered by a throw, with a pillow. Between here and there is a banister and some stairs. Down must be the best way to go. Survival agrees, and even Gut can't defy the reckoning, though it reminds her with a nudge that *down* also leads to crypts. She moves on, keeping her feet to the outer edges of the rug where it's thickest.

A chest of drawers that comes up to Katy's stomach rests against the wall halfway to the stairs. On it are black and white photos behind glass so dirty nothing can be identified other than faint outlines of people behind the crust. Set around them are weird sculptures that bear no resemblance to anything Katy knows of. Twisting shapes that go nowhere.

She examines a sculpture, a humanoid form with a melted body. Must've been expensive, it has some weight to it. There's no origin when she turns it in her hands. An original? Quietly, she pops it down again, lining it up with the dustless spot it came from.

This place doesn't seem very…culty.

Quite what to expect from cultists she has no idea, but it certainly hadn't been this quaint, if not majorly spooky, manor house. Come to think of it, didn't pop culture tell her that cults congregate in the woods, or dark cellars, and they all wore oversized cowls and flowing robes, dancing around satanic symbols and singing awful songs? So far she's found not one upside down cross, or a pentagram, no ominous candles, and she hasn't heard any voices singing songs about the devil.

Gut yells at her, *Don't wish for it!*

Above the drawers is a leering portrait. The frame has more detail engraved in it than the others. Within poses a man, a tall painted figure. He appears to be as austere as he does successful, with a stony face above a wide chin. His hair is slicked back, his nose beaky. Not beaky like a crow, beaky like a puffin. From the look of him, he never smiled, which the artist has captured perfectly. Next to him, shorter and wearing the smallest of smiles is a woman in a fine gown. Her hair is done up in a bun with loose ringlets curling down the sides of her face. A pearl necklace around her neck isn't the only jewellery she wears. A contradiction to the man, she gives of a friendly aura that goes so far as to make the painting easier to look at. In between them is a boy, about eight years of age, dressed to replicate his father whilst lacking the flinty expression. His mother's hand rests on his shoulder. The boy looks innocent, smiling, yet has in his painted eyes a countenance of menace. Katy is certain she's seen those eyes before.

A noise disturbs her. Footsteps, downstairs? She quietly and quickly tiptoes to the top of the stairs, peaks around the corner. At the bottom is a cultist. She assumes (two times, now) the person is a cultist, anyway. They aren't wearing a robe or a cowl, but instead jeans and a fleece. It's entirely possible that the person isn't someone who wants to hurt her, and it's also entirely possible that the wind can blow sand from a beach to have it form a perfect sandcastle when it lands. Slim odds.

Don't let them hear you, Survival whispers.

No shit, Gut responds.

Gut can swear, it seems. Katy is more used to it telling her to be careful of algae on rocks, or nettles hidden inside bushes.

Keeping herself low, she prepares herself to crawl past the stairs. She gasps aloud when she sees Pop Tart staring at her from the rocking chair, perched on top of the pillow. Clamping her mouth shut, she ducks behind the wall. The cultist listens…ignores. Katy lets go of her held breath, releasing it so slowly it hurts.

She wants Pop Tart, to run to him and hug him and never let go. Survival reminds her to not be an idiot. Gut concurs. The two get along rather well when they want to.

Pop Tart sits on his hind quarters, washing himself. There's something different about him. His shape? Katy knows for sure it's Pop Tart because of his yellow moon eyes. Even if the way down wasn't guarded by a cultist, she'd want to fetch the cat first. On her hands and knees, she crawls across the landing, licking her lips with every inch gained, constantly looking at both cat and cultist. Pausing once to peer through the banister's slats, Katy can't see any means of exit from here, though there's a vase full of umbrellas and canes by a massive window that has its curtains drawn.

As she clears the landing her foot snags on a section of rucked up rug. Her shoe thuds the floor. Pressing herself against the wall, she holds her breath again, listens for footsteps coming up the stairs. Pop Tart mimics her, paw held aloft with his tongue hanging dopily from his mouth. Katy looks at him and holds a scratched up finger to her lips.

Shhhh!

A heavy footstep, followed by a second.

Pop Tart continues washing. Katy edges around the corner, making as little noise as possible.

The cultist keeps coming.

Run at them, catch them by surprise. Push them down the stairs! Survival puts the idea forward.

Run anywhere else! Gut argues.

The pair of them are the angel and devil on her shoulders.

Thud…thud…thud…

The cultist takes their time. Maybe they already know Katy is here and they're turning it into a game. Maybe this whole escape is a game. Maybe this *house* is a game. Something for them to do whilst they kill time before they kill her.

Actually, why *haven't* they killed her yet? It would've been easy for them whilst she was unconscious.

Pop Tart sails from the chair past Katy, chirps when he lands. He gives her a glance over his furry shoulder before prancing off down the hallway. It's like he's asking her to follow him.

So follow the cat, says Gut.

Push the bastard down the stairs, from Survival.

Both of them swear.

She peeps around the corner, heart pumping. The cultist appears, looks both ways before coming left, towards Katy. If their attire wasn't very culty, their face looks positively suburban. A monopoly player's face. It's a man with a neat beard, no overhang of stubble on his cheeks or chin, reddish hair cut close to his scalp. That's all Katy sees before she pulls herself out of sight.

She prays to the wall opposite. There's another painting, this time only the austere man is in it, glaring down at her. He doesn't give her any ideas, in fact, Katy reckons if he had any ideas, the man in the painting would try to sell them before giving them up.

She could try to run, but the cultist will hear her and come running himself, there's no way she can outrun an adult. If she crawls she won't be nearly fast enough, only delaying the inevitable.

It's over.

Nowhere to go, nowhere to hide.

She squeezes her eyes shut, wills herself to become invisible. Grabbing her hair, Katy chokes it. This time Survival has no objections. Three or four more steps and the cultist will find her cowering around the corner against the wall.

Thud…thud…

…thud…

Static screeches into a feedback that hurts her ears.

The cultist fumbles the walky-talky from his back pocket, drops it on the floor. Katy pulls her feet in, hurting her ribs, certain that the bearded cultist will see her trainers.

But he doesn't. Has willpower actually worked? Is she invisible?

Survival and Gut speak in unison. *Stay still.*

"Everybody report to the library," a female voice says over the walky-talky. It's a voice Katy now knows, hearing it causes the hairs on her arms to stand up.

Without responding, the cultist retreats down the stairs, walking with more haste. Katy makes sure she hears his footsteps disappear completely before she gives herself permission to breathe.

A harvester spider stilt-walks over her shoulder. She lets the harvestman pass. All of sudden spiders don't pose much of a threat. If she could choose to have a year of daily injections (needles or wasps) or spend an hour in this house, she'd be first in line at the doctor's.

Releasing her hair, Katy gets back to her feet, fear makes it an awkward task. Down the hallway, Pop Tart pops his head out of a room. After a last glance at the man in the painting, whom she can't help but feel is disappointed at her evasion, Katy goes after the cat, who rewinds himself back into the room he's leading her to. That *is* what Pop Tart is doing, it's strange, but can't be anything else.

Dithering at the threshold, Katy looks inside. It's a bedroom, with a dresser next to a grand wardrobe with swirling patterns carved into the wood that, amidst the dustiness of this place, is polished to a slippery sheen. *Everything* in this bedroom is polished and clean. Pop Tart is nestled on the bed, his backside sinking into the plush feather duvet. It's a four poster bed, too many pillows piled up on it.

Katy goes to Pop Tart, holds out her arms. She barely notices the sharp drop in temperature. Being near him brings a smile to her face, an action this house tries to repress. Smiles aren't welcome here.

Pop Tart hisses, showing his fangs. He lashes at Katy with claws that catch her left arm, drawing four searing cuts across her wrist. She pulls back, shocked at the cat's sudden aggression.

He darts past her, leaps onto the dresser. He's back to back with his reflection in the mirror fixed to the furniture, fur spiked up. Katy tries again to go to him, assuming (that nasty habit) that he's only scared, and all he needs is a friendly presence.

Pop Tart hisses again, this time shooting spittle from his jaws.

Katy flinches away, doesn't know how to react. She's sees now that Pop Tart's head is slightly misshapen, bands of scar tissue poorly concealed beneath his coat.

Something's wrong, Gut tells her.

Pop Tart jumps down, races out the bedroom, his tail attempting to take the lead. Before Katy can follow him – and she wants to – the door slams shut on its own. After a couple more seconds, the lock clicks shut. Like a party popper…without the confetti.

CHAPTER 26

Nicholas,

I hope this letter finds you well, and Mr Schaeffer has treated you with the respect that is your due. I am awfully regretful that events have unfolded the way they have, not one bit of this dreadful fiasco had been in my reckoning, however, such things as "planning ahead" are never to be relied upon.

First and foremost, Nicholas, I do not want you fretting over the girl. She is safe. A few minor luxuries have been denied her, but I promise you that she is in no way uncomfortable.

Secondly, it is not wise for you to come searching for her, it would only result in putting the both of you in danger. Especially the girl, whom I should like to keep from mischief. You would be wasting your time should you choose to partake in such an endeavour. You will not find me at my previous residence, which has already been stripped bare. No books, no Orphanage, no-

The waitress sets Nick's coffee on the table. Nick hides the letter against his chest, offers the waitress a weary smile that he knows isn't convincing anybody. She offers him milk and sugar, to which he declines. Before leaving him be, she squints, tilts her head, as if trying to place his face. She's at least ten years younger than he is, so it wouldn't be from school years. Could be because he looks like he's missed the last three days of sleep, covered in the marks of fists and broken glass. His eyebrow is sore, fuck knows how bad that looks. He smiles again, offers a nod. She shrugs, moves on to take the order of the booth two tables away.

When he's sure no one's attention is on him, Nick continues to read

Crane's letter. It's his second readthrough.

-trapdoor. You would also, should you choose to discard my word and go snooping, find my office naked of décor. Where I have taken myself is of no concern to you.

I fear I am rambling. You know I revel in the use of words, Nicholas. I mourn our discussions.

The purpose of this letter is to present you with a choice.

Cease your pursuit. By Sunday, a sum of £50,000 shall reach a bank account set up for you by my associates. There is no catch, no ulterior motive. It shall simply be your reward and forgiveness for what has happened. In eight months after the first instalment, you shall receive a further £100,000. With this money I trust you shall move on with your life and let bygones be bygones. Think of this, Nicholas, as your way out.

The other choice is this: Seek her, futile as it would be.

I shall be aware of the path you choose. I can see you even now, though do not search for prying eyes, you will not find them. Do not worry, if you choose incorrectly, the girl will not be harmed ahead of schedule. What will happen is your unfortunate death upon the same hour as the girl's. That may have been something you would have welcomed not so long ago, though I do not think that is the case anymore.

Whichever choice you make, I know it shall be the right one for you, and I can ask no more than that. One path leads to salvation, the other to the grave.

Salvation.

Is that not, for long years, what you have pined for?

Choose wisely, Nicholas. I have faith that you will.

Your friend,
Ulysses Sebastian Crane

Nick turns the letter upside down on the table, scrunching up the corners. His options have been made clear.

Become mildly wealthy, let the girl die.

Try and find her, both die.

Crane can't guarantee that, of course, though calling his bluff is risky at best. He can probably *wish* Nick terminated. And can the offer of money be trusted? To Nick, a purse like Crane's promising is a new life, a fresh start somewhere where his past – and the ghosts that come with it – will be lost. He could erase the mistakes of the past simply by pretending they never happened. He could become anything, start his own business or some rags-to-riches crap like that, make money like any other average joe. More importantly, he could begin the process of forgetting. It's bogus to comprehend. The prospect of gaining capital to get him started and keep him running in less than a year paints it in realistic colours. Crane is an exploitative bastard.

At O'Reilly's, he'd been ready to go after Katy, but back then, giving up didn't mean making bank. But does money mean anything when a life – *her* life – is in the guillotine? Would money mean shit if it was gained through the feigned ignorance of her murder?

Nick shifts in his chair. He balls the letter, stuffs it inside his jacket, surveying the place. The owners have attempted to give it an American diner vibe. He looks for anyone standing out as suspicious. Men wearing glasses reading newspapers, a woman with a plate of food that's gone cold, a child playing on the pinball machine without putting in coins for new games. He sees no one except the waitress taking an order from a moan of teenagers in the booth two down from his.

A brand new life. The allure of that shakes its arse at Nick and asks him to stick a fiver in its knickers.

A fiver of blood money. Child's blood.

He'd tried his best. Made a real go of it and…and still failed. He's failed himself, and Katy, in less that seventy-two hours.

Even if he decides to, he'd never be able to find her. Trying to think of a place to begin, nothing comes to mind. Nicks rubs his forehead, takes a sip of coffee that he lets spill back into the mug from his lips. It's not that the coffee is bad. It's because he's sick of mulling over problems with a mug in hand. Coffee ain't no miracle elixir.

He doesn't think he can just allow Crane's society to kill her. Can he? That's the real question, one he doesn't know the answer to, or one that he's afraid of lest he sees who he really is. Fortune, as it has done once before, tempts him. It has powerful strings, knows how to pull each and every one.

He hardly knows her, yet…has gotten to. A little, anyway. He can't lie to himself and say that the two of them, for all their gripes, hadn't bonded, perhaps with fractured adhesive. Not a brother-sister bond, or that of a father and daughter, but more like an uncle and his niece.

But they're not! And that aside, he owes her nothing. Nothing, except…

Humanity.

Though he keeps trying to sabotage his own compassion, he isn't convinced keeping out of this from here on in is the lesser of two evils, appealing as it is. Maybe the lesser of the evils is to strive against the odds, to keep his promise to Katy, to get her home.

Weighing up choices is hard work, which isn't helped by the swing music that some twat has just slapped on the jukebox.

Start a new life. There'd be additional guilt, but Nick is adept at carrying that, it wouldn't be much extra. Yet, he cannot help but wonder if running away from himself is really possible. It certainly isn't the road to redemption. He wants that more than paper with a royal face on it.

Redemption. Sounds like a town, doesn't it? The lonely streets of Redemption, population: few and far between.

Or, attempt to find Katy.

She is Redemption, he realises. Always has been, before he even saw it. She is his talisman in the same way the cat had been hers, only he doesn't plan on betraying her trust. In her he sees the kid wanting to join in, he sees reconciliation. In her, he sees the real way out.

Her fate may be partially sealed, his isn't. Crane moved his chess pieces, went for the checkmate. Now the move is Nick's to make. He's allowed people to manipulate his destiny before, won't let anyone else do the same again, and if Crane thinks he can then the old geezer can go fuck himself. Only reason they'd offer Nick a way out is if they see him as a threat, and if they see him as a threat, that means there's a chance.

If he had the money right now, Nick would burn it. What's a life if it's born from another's death?

But the on his brain is a twister cutting up the landscape. *Where is she?*

Shunning the coffee, he says aloud, "One step at a time."

Assuming there *is* a step.

The café – its Americanisms are something straight from an imagination that isn't native to the U.S. – is quiet. The swing music has been turned down to a volume that disguises it as any Glenn Miller number. A waiter, behind a counter surrounded by swivel stools, chews on gum whilst poking his smartphone. The waitress is still at the other booth. Nick notices her furtively glancing at him, as do the four youngsters she's waiting on. He straightens up, winces. They turn away, continue to steal glances over their shoulders. The waitress's pencil is pressed to a paper pad but isn't writing anything. Aware that Crane may have spies in the most unlikely places, ready to snitch to their Fuhrer, Nick isn't taking any chances.

He clenches his fists and snarls, "Can I help you?"

The outburst doesn't get the reaction from the waitress and the booth boys Nick expects. One of the teens, a hotshot blonde who is one lettered jacket away from being as Yank as the diner, smirks.

"That's the guy," he says to his mates.

The others mumble appreciatively, stretch their necks to get a better look.

"*Help* you?" Nick stresses. He stands with an outlaw's tilt to compensate for the pain in his ribs.

"You sure?" asks another, uglier teen, taking out his phone. In unison, the rest of them produce their smartphones, swiping the screens.

After a couple seconds, the blonde hotshot holds up his phone for the others. "There," he says, knowing he's loud enough for Nick to hear. Probably never taken a crack on the chin before, thinks he can be as obnoxious as he pleases. "He looks like microwaved arse, but that's him."

His mates approve, chuckling at the insult. They're one cliché away from high-fiving each other. One of them, a pig-faced marvel whose skin folds at the bridge of his nose, gives Nick a thumbs up before continuing to snort at his screen.

Katy isn't a kid lost in her phone. She realises there's more to everything than having your attention glued to a world of drivel.

Nick lumps down in the plump red leather seat. He hasn't got time to deal with arsehole teens. Could be they're older than they look, though everyone under twenty-five looks like a child to Nick. It's an age blindness that hits when you turn thirty.

He catches his stretched reflection in the chrome panel around the front counter. What he sees is a sorry sight. Stubble, grey before forty. Pallid, dry skin. Eyes that are struggling to stay open. The hotshot is right, Nick does look like microwaved arse.

He turns from his dishevelled reflection, seeing it as a strong argument that maybe he should just let it go, give Crane what he wants. What's a failure like Nick going to do, anyway?

He shakes off the thought, concentrating on one word. The town. Redemption.

Population: one, maybe.

The antique jukebox churns over the record.

Again the waitress approaches his booth, preceded by her perfume. Nick wraps his fingers around the handle of his coffee. Anyone in the diner could be a member of Crane's society. The waitress? Pig-face?

Hotshot? The fucking *lot* of them? Mulling it over, this whole get-up is like a stage set designed to fool him, that can surely be the only reason this gaff looks like regurgitated America. The street signs on the walls are a bit much. A giveaway, really. There's no telling how young Crane recruits them, provided they aren't selected to have their throats sliced open. It makes sense that he would keep youngsters in the society. Kids are full of wishes, having them follow him would be like tapping a vein of ore.

If the waitress tries anything smart, she'll get a face full of hot coffee, then Nick can use the mug to lamp one of the booth boys when they undoubtedly spring into action. That oughta even the odds.

All she does is offer Nick a smile. "Sorry about those dick'eads," she says.

"S'okay," Nick replies to the opposite seat.

Getting the hint that Nick isn't going to make this easy, she asks, "You *are* the guy, right?"

Nick tightens his grip on the mug. "Depends what you mean."

The waitress, whose tied back hair is the colour of spice, dips into her waistband pinny. Out comes her smartphone. Nick was more than half convinced she was about to pull a weapon.

She taps the screen. In seconds the waitress has what she wants and holds the phone for Nick to see.

The sound is tinny, at first the video isn't clear but when the camera operator gets a good spot Nick has no difficulty viewing the footage. It lasts fifteen seconds.

The waitress grins. "That you?"

Watching the clip replay itself, optimism swelling, Nick shakes his head. "No," he lies.

"Are you sure?"

She finds another video of the same noisy scene but captured from a different angle.

"Not me." Nick breaks from the video.

Shaking her head, the waitress returns her phone to her pinny. "I was sure it was you."

"You and the dickheads?"

She sniffs a laugh. "Yeah. Me and the dick'eads."

"Sorry to disappoint you."

"I'm not disappointed," she fibs. "Just never met anyone from a viral video before. Well, semi-viral. Are you sure there's nothing else I can get for you?"

Nick views his darkened reflection in his coffee, swirls it around to disturb the image. "Don't s'pose you have any painkillers?"

She shows two empty palms, smooth and as yet undamaged from work. "'Fraid not."

"Then I'm good. Thanks."

Nick budges out the booth. The waitress keeps a wide berth, doing her very best to not come across as rude. He probably smells like microwaved arse, too. The booth boys spare a few more looks, Pig-Face gives another thumbs up, seeks the approval of his mates by grinning at all of them. "See ya later, hero," says the hotshot.

"Careful of them. They're trouble." Nick reads the waitress's uniform tag, her name written in bubblegum pink letters. Staci with an *i*. "Thanks, Staci," says Nick.

"For the coffee?" she asks as he walks away. The bell jingles when he pulls open the door and Staci with an *i* adds, "You didn't even drink it."

There's a chemist a few shops down. Nick pops in to get a couple of boxes of painkillers, the strongest he can get over the counter. He receives some strange looks on account of his appearance, and the clerk can't get rid of him quick enough. Outside, Nick dry swallows more than the recommended dose, throws his head back to help them on their way down. *Pain-Away*, they're called, promising *Max Relief in Minimum Time*.

The breeze, mingled with the acrid waft of exhaust fumes, is sobering. Nick thinks clearly. There's a step to take. How he's going to put it all together isn't entirely clear right now, but he has a starting point. As it turns out, Crane gave him the answer some time ago, it had seemed so insignificant back then, so peculiar.

I have also made a nemesis or two in my time, Crane had said that night at The Cross.

"Yes you have," Nick says to himself.

Hands in pockets, he weaves through the crowd and out of sight, ducking into the narrow alleys where it's quiet.

CHAPTER 27

For fifteen minutes, Katy has been stuck in the bedroom. No amount of fighting with the door is going to persuade it open. A dusty voice scratches her spine.

"You are a curious worker bee, my dear."

Katy spins around, hair unfurling, sure her heart has stopped beating. Only ghosts can close doors when there's no one around to close them, and only ghosts can speak when there are no people around to speak.

There is no ghost. An old man relaxes in a chair by the bed, an inviting smile deepens the wrinkles around his mouth. Tucking away his silver pocket watch into his waistcoat, he rests his hands in his lap. Something else is there, too.

"I apologise that we did not speak when first we met," he says. "I knew then that you were a wonderful, curious girl, and so smart as well. Just not how much."

Katy tries the door again, twisting the knob until it begins to squeak. The door holds fast. She recognises the old man. At the altar, the one who had attempted to cut her throat. She traces the bump on her neck where the knife had nicked her skin. She can't see the scar she gave him.

He touches his forehead. "Oh, you fetched me decent. However, I have seen to it that no scar shall mar my flesh. Just one of the gifts I have acquired over the years. Make no mistake, it had stung a fright on the night." He chuckles at his rhyme. "I trust you have no secreted weapons on your person at the moment, though I would ask that you keep a distance. I pride myself on learning from my mistakes, of which there are not many. That, and you are rather filthy."

"How did you- "

"How did I get in here?" The old man lets his eyes wander around the room. "I know it might seem odd, seeing as mere seconds ago you were all by your lonesome. Put it down, my dear, to me knowing this building better than you ever will, that way we can avoid any questions that you may not appreciate the answers to. Having said that, I will stress that you must, *please*, continue to ask me any questions that may pop into your head. I, too, am an inquisitive fellow, and understand the need to know where one is wearing one's boots. You will of course allow me to ask of you as you ask of me? Trading, if you like."

Crane, Gut quivers.

Crane, growls Survival.

"Where is Pop Tart?" she asks, hoping that the cat is safe.

Crane chuckles again, it's a bubbly sound, a cough being kept down by too much mucus. "Pop Tart. Yes, I heard you refer to him by that name, thought up by Nicholas. A peculiar name, I must say. Actually, if you are interested, the cat is neither a he nor a she, though I have for a long time now called it Solomon."

For a second the name Nicholas doesn't register, until it dawns on her.

As for the cat, a piece of her heart breaks. To attach herself to a cat, only to learn that it was against her, a member of the cult with fur. She looks down at her feet. "He…it's…yours?"

"A familiar," Crane waves. "Animals have their uses. Tools that we can call upon. To be completely honest, this is the first case of needing the aid of a beast companion since before the Second World War. Solomon will be around for as long as I need him to be." Crane pooches his bottom lip. "You grew fond of the cat?"

Katy nods.

"My sincerest apologies. I know this may be hard for you to understand, my dear, but I do not wish for you to suffer."

"Where am I?" she asks, hoping he can't see her distress.

Crane titters. In his lap is a book. It makes Katy queasy. It's the same book he had her bent over before Nick jumped in.

"Excellent. More questions. Brain food." Crane's fingers tap dance on the cover. "This is my childhood home, my dear. A beautiful place that I rather disliked coming back to, yet now it is as enlightening as it is essential." He leans forward. "Do you know what I mean by enlightening?"

Katy gives no response. The book, she sees, *thinks*, is reacting to the old man's petting.

"Of course you do," he says. "Uncouth of me to question your intelligence, you have already demonstrated on at least two occasions that your brain is a factory of smarts. I have to ask, how did you break free of the handcuffs?"

Don't tell him, Survival commands, but Gut wins on this one, telling her that by keeping the old man happy she *might* escape harm.

"I…used a nail. Picked the lock."

Slapping his thigh, Crane laughs. "Clever," he praises her. "Very clever. I can see that your fingers might need some treatment, though. Must be careful of germs. Nasty blighters get everywhere."

Katy hides her hand.

"I doubt you have had much time to explore the house. A crying shame, if you ask me. I trust that you have seen the beautiful paintings in the corridors?"

"You're family?"

"Precisely," he pets the book again. This time Katy definitely sees the front cover move under his touch. "My mother and father."

Katy dares to take miniscule backwards steps back towards the haunted door. "And you."

Crane glances away. His smile remains, but twitches as he holds it. "Actually, no. The child is not me. Father did not want me in any of the family portraits, and thus you shall find none in this house. Mother had a handful of private pictures. Alas, I have not been able to recover them. And, dear?" His smile, the same but different, locks her in mid-step. "You will find the door quite locked. There is no roaming this house without my leave. I would like to give you that permission, however, you must hold your patience for the time being. I am enjoying our talk. The whiteness of your skin betrays your fear. Please hold it in check."

Katy takes a deep breath, swallows nothing. Her bones are chilly, her stomach hot with boiling nerves. She asks, "W-who is the boy?"

Don't stutter! Survival's reprimand comes with a snap.

"The child in the portrait is my brother. Older. Father always had a soft spot for him. Phillip was everything Father wanted him to be. Charismatic, athletic, a good mind for enterprise. In short, he was everything I was not. Mother loved me, though she was helpless to persuade Father to allow me into what he called the family legacy. He did not want me, a strange boy, to reflect badly on himself. Everything I learned in life was because of Mother. She was beautiful, yes?"

"She looks like a lovely lady," Katy replies. It comes as a shock to hear herself utter the words.

Crane flashes her a smile that someone who slits the throats of children shouldn't have access to. "A lovely lady," he parrots. "Yes. She was."

"Is he still alive?"

"Father?"

"Brother."

"He…" Crane pauses, eyes ping-ponging as he considers his reply. "He's not terribly well, these days."

Katy waits for him to expand upon his answer.

He lifts the book, which doubles the sickness whirring in Katy's stomach. She hugs herself, wretches in her throat, leaving it with a sting. Crane notices.

"You get used to it," he tells her. "Do you know what this is?"

Gut chimes in with the most ominous thing Katy thinks it will ever say. *Death.*

Gazing at the sickly book with a twinkle in his eyes, Crane explains. "It is what Mother left me. Not the actual book, you understand, but knowledge of it. She was always aware of the forbidden fruits that humanity has denied itself for centuries, arts of which are forced into practise in cellars and sewers and caves the world over."

"Your cult worships the book," blurts Katy, swiftly covering her mouth. The sickness rises to her gorge.

He lays the book back in his lap, its pages tasting the air. "We are not a cult, my dear. I will not hear it. Cults are for fools and pretenders. Nor do we, as you say, worship this book. The book is one and the same as us. It may seem to the uneducated eye that the book is our deity. Or myself. I may be the one who grants the wishes, yet only through the teachings and allowance of the book."

"Wishes?"

"Yes, my dear," Crane warms. "Wishes. Do you have any of those?"

"I wish I was home with my mum and dad." She wipes under her nose.

"That is not a wish. That is a desire. Desires and wishes are as separate as snakes and ladders. I shall ask again. Do you have any wishes? I would very much like to hear them."

Katy stays silent for what feels like minutes. Through each ticking second, Crane smiles. His thin hair flickers between grey and deep mahogany, his wrinkles fade, too quick to be sure it actually happened. A trick of the light?

Gut pleads, *Don't tell him.*

"I wish…" she starts.

Survival: *Let him have it.*

"I wish you were dead."

Crane marinates in the dreadful quiet, strokes the book with bony fingers, overgrown nails curl into scoops.

"I applaud your honesty. It may hurt me, yet it is a truth, and the truth is something that we all must hold sacred. Too many deceivers in the world today. You know, I do believe I like you, Katy. Is it Katrina? Something else?"

She finds a length of hair, runs her fingers through it.

"We shall stick with Katy, then." He thumbs a jewel of spittle from his lips.

Crane grunts to his feet. Katy retreats towards the door, presses her back against it. It's cold, neither rattles or shakes.

"Are you going to kill me?" she sniffs.

Tucking the book under his elbow, Crane answers, "Yes."

He hobbles to the wardrobe using a black cane. It's an act of defiance against age and the impending reality of a wheelchair. Seeing him like this, knowing his sad history of a father who never loved him and a mother who tried her best, it would be easy to forgive who – *what* – he was. Both Gut and Survival have to remind Katy that this old man wants her life.

Searching for anything to help her escape, she asks Crane, "Why wait? Why keep me here?"

He stops, straightens his back, spine clunking into place. "You know, my dear, you really do not have it so bad."

With sluggish movement, as if his wrist has a band of weights around it, Crane opens the wardrobe. Inside, at the base, is a flat pillow and a wafer thin cover. There's barely room for a child.

"This was my bedroom," says Crane.

Katy peers at the dirty little nest.

"I used to get terrible splinters in the backside. Mother begged Father to give me a proper bed but he would not concede, decreeing that I was already receiving a luxury. When I think back on it now, all I can do is thank Father for what he *did* give, though I cannot understand why he could not *learn* to accept me." Crane faces Katy. "You at least had a room when first you were brought to us. I am sorry that we shut you in that mucky old loft. I am glad you Houdinied yourself out. Do not believe that you will have the same luck escaping the walls of this property, however."

Taking a step forward, she says, "You didn't answer my question. If you're going to...to kill m-me" – *DON'T STUTTER!* – "why're you keeping me in this house?"

For a while Crane appears to not have heard her. Hypnotised by the cramped sleeping space, his face performs that weird thing again where, for a flash of time, his age becomes running water. Katy snatches a glance at the book, gags on fiery bile.

"I should thank you," he mumbles.

"Why?"

"For that," he says. "For asking your questions. And, for answering mine. I appreciate, even if you do not believe me, how distressing this must be for a young woman."

No one, not Mum or Dad or anyone, has ever referred to her as a woman before.

"It has been a rather extended period of time," Crane keeps on, "since I have spoken of my childhood, and you somehow managed to coax it out of me. I enjoy talking with you as much as with Nicholas. There is not enough good discussion in today's landscape, no mystery, no Pharoah's tombs of the mind to uncover. You have unearthed a part of my tomb this day, Katy."

She replies, "I didn't ask you about it."

"You showed interest in the contents of the portrait," Crane turns to her, closing the wardrobe behind him, "and that was enough. Sometimes the slightest slip of sand can reveal the entrance to a tomb."

He keeps calling his mind a tomb. Is it because all of semblance of humanity in there is dead? Katy imagines it's a cold place to be, a place where the walls, pointing in all the nonsensical angles of a bad dream, are covered (to continue the old man's analogy) in hieroglyphs.

"I don't accept your th-thanks," Katy stutters again. Survival doesn't tell her off this time.

"You do not have to. I shall not be offended. I am sorry, but can you pose to me again your last question?"

The rage rises above the fear. Katy throws her hair from her hands. "Why the hell are you keeping me here?"

Moving with the speed of a corpse, Crane rubs his chin. The cracks in his face stretch and contract. His skin is gummy. "It is necessary."

"Why?"

Crane laughs. "I suppose I owe you an explanation. I am, though, going to keep it short. My time in this room is nearing its end, and I am sure you shall want to get about the place and push your curious little nose in corners it might not get to go again. We have to hold you here because now is not the right time to complete the offering. It was, as I'm sure you well remember, interrupted. We can only commence on the same night it began."

Katy glowers at the book, tightening her abdomen. "Is that what it says?"

"It is what it *needs*." Crane taps his cane on the floor. After a silence in which the house has time to breath, he adds, "It must be the same day its heart started beating."

"What does that mean?"

"How I wish – yes, I have them, too – that I could answer further questions and ask some of my own. Now, I must repair to my private quarters."

With a click the door opens on its own. Katy spins around, cold air wafts in her face, her shoulders and knees quake. She's desperate to run, both Gut and Survival urge her to steal the chance. After all, the cult needs her alive for now. What're they going to do?

"You can flee, if you like, from this room. You can run anywhere in this house," says Crane, shambling past her. "I beseech you to stay for a while in this room. It was my mother's room. Her and Father, after a while, slept apart. There is much you can learn from this house if you give it a chance. I shall even have Solomon..." Crane winks. "I shall send Pop Tart up to you, if you would wish it? Do you wish it?"

Pop Tart isn't Pop Tart anymore. Pop Tart never *was* Pop Tart, she tells herself. The cat Crane calls Solomon is, in its own way, as much a member of the cult as the man with the walky-talky on the stairs is. But...to not be alone in this place, to have a companion, the thought gets the better of Katy. If she can't have what she believed to be the real Pop Tart, she can pretend.

Wimp, says Survival.

If it helps you, from Gut.

Will these two ever shut up?

"I…I wish it," she says.

Crane approves with a warm smile. "Then it shall be so." He walks through the door. In the hallway he pauses and, without facing her, tells Katy, "We might need you alive for the time being, my dear, but do not attempt to purge my trust in you. There are things that can be done to a person to keep them in line."

On its own, the door closes with a soft clack.

Click for open, clack for shut.

CHAPTER 28

The visiting room is a thrum of emotions; love, joy, despair, anger. The tables are honeycombed, spread evenly so the officers can keep a close eye on any wandering hands.

Nick waits at a table, hands knitted around a Styrofoam cup of tea he has no intention of drinking. A badge pinned to his chest says in big capital letters, VISITOR. The person he's here to see is running late, apparently.

It's crossed his mind that a handful of the officers could be on Crane's books, men and woman who've made wishes yet to be fulfilled. Or have been, if working with the incarcerated was their wish. So far, none of them have shown Nick any extra interest, nor any of the inmates. Still, he remains vigilant.

There are all sorts in the prison visiting room, including families. A boy and girl, about six, chase around Nick's table. He's patient with them, is thankful when he hears a stern voice call them away from 'that man'. When Nick sees the mother, he believes these spirited tykes will have no shot at a future. Call it judgemental, but the father with his scarred scowl and marked up arms only affirms the assumption.

An officer brings a prisoner to the table. Nick nods his thanks, the officer nods back, hiking up his trousers. The inmate, who's wearing a pink vest that Nick supposes is designed to humiliate the hard men, watches the officer move away over his shoulder.

"That one's trouble," the prisoner says, turning to Nick.

He looks different without the beard. Older, too. For a moment, Nick wonders if he's got the right man. The prisoner frowns. It's because of this frown that Nick knows he's got his bloke.

The prisoner asks, "Do I know you?"

"We've met."

An inmate, on the other side of the hive, explodes to his feet, throwing his chair out from under him. The visiting room suspends itself as three officers bundle on the shiny-domed giant and drag him away kicking and roaring, leaving behind a crying...wife? Girlfriend? Sister? As if nothing has happened, the visiting room resumes its chatter, a few laughs shared at the expense of the drama.

"You looked fit to scarper there," the prisoner observes, folding his arms. "You in danger being here?"

Surveying the visiting room, Nick answers, "It's possible."

"You going to offer me a drink?"

Nick raises his eyebrows. The prisoner is upfront, more together, well-spoken, confident in a way that would suit a butler. That alone, however, hasn't made him invulnerable from other cons. A scimitar shaped scar curls under his left ear, stitches only recently removed.

"I've grown rather partial to a tinny of lemon Fanta, if you don't mind." The prisoner rubs his bulbous nose, pores big enough to resemble a cleared minefield.

Nick grabs the attention of a passing officer, a young woman. She wears the same hairstyle as all the other female officers; a tight bun sitting atop raked back hair. Nick hands her a quid, asks if she can grab a can of lemon Fanta, please and thank you. She obliges with a smile that her job hasn't yet dampened. It will one day. A smile like that is too bright for prison.

"You say we've met. I don't remember you."

"Didn't think you would," from Nick.

"What's this about, sir? I wasn't expecting visitors today, nor *any* day. I'll admit it's a nice surprise, a break from the monotony of a life behind bars, though we aren't actually behind bars as such, but hefty doors- "

"Ulysses Crane."

The prisoner fastens his lips.

The can of Fanta is placed in front of Nick, who slides it across to the prisoner. The can goes ignored. The prisoner dissects Nick with one eye narrower than the other.

Waiting first for an officer to saunter past the table, Nick says, "I was hoping you could help me."

"Has he sent you?" The prisoner keeps his voice subdued.

"No. He doesn't know I'm here."

The prisoner scoffs. "Of course he does."

"I'm taking the chance he doesn't."

"Then you're a fucking fool." Derision flashes over the prisoner's face. He leans forward. "So go on, how have we met?"

Nick answers, "I stopped you from stabbing him."

The prisoner sneers. "I knew it. A fucking fool."

Nick thumps the table. "I need to find him. Can you help me or not?"

An officer approaches. Nick holds up his hand to apologise. The officer, after giving them a warning, returns to his post by a water fountain, where he continuously checks his wristwatch.

"If that man is out of your life, the last thing you want to be doing is finding him. I don't have that blessing. He visits me even now."

"You said you don't get visitors?"

"I don't. There are…other ways to visit on a man." The prisoner looks away. "I apologise for my bitterness."

"You look different. Older but…better," says Nick.

The prisoner relaxes his frown. "A shave and three square a day will do that for you. I've had my share of troubles in this dump, though life is on the up."

There's something about the prisoner that reminds Nick of Crane. It's the way he speaks, the way his mouth shapes words.

Nick edges the Fanta closer. "Help me. Please."

"No. I shouldn't. And *why* should I, for that matter?"

Nick makes sure no ears are probing into their conversation. "I need to find him. If I don't, a girl will be killed."

Pity invades the prisoner's features. "Still doing that, is he? I would have thought he'd needn't do that anymore. So why do you believe I can aid you?"

It jumps into Nick's head out of the blue, an expression learned and stored for just such an occasion. It's exactly the kind of hand-me-down wisdom Crane would preach. "The enemy of my enemy is my friend," he quotes.

"Young man." The prisoner accepts the Fanta, cracks the tab. "I am more than that man's enemy." He takes a gulp, a strand of fizzing lemon juice trickles from the corner of his mouth, magnifying his stubble. "I am his brother."

§

Nick is sure there are words to speak, though he can't find them. How do you reply to something like this, other than repeating the man before you?

"You're his brother?"

"Older brother."

"*Older?*"

He's old, but not nearly as old as Crane. It's possible that Nick is being had, unfortunate enough to get lumped with an opportunistic conman. He doesn't think so, though. The prisoner and Crane have too many similarities.

The prisoner grins. "It's complicated. I remember you, now. I'll admit I was going mad by the time I tried to kill Ulysses, but I retain some memory of the night. You shouldn't have stopped me."

"Tell me about it."

"Okay then. I will." He takes another slurp of fizz. "Ulysses has left insurmountable grief in his wake, he disguises it with words and whatever else he studies from a thesaurus. He thinks his band of followers and himself will be the next great superpower. A breed of illuminati, kept hidden and feared by the guesswork of conspiracists. He will leave behind further pain and misery. You shouldn't have barged in like you did."

"I was just doing my job at the time. I didn't know."

"That's no excuse. What's more," Nick receives a glare, "I fear if ever he has the book, his vision might be realized."

Nick sits to attention. "You know the book?"

"Of course I know the book. I had to endure Ulysses' ramblings about it for years. He and Mum were inseparable, she was the one who filled his head with all the mystic crap. Don't be influenced by my chagrin, know the powers are very real. I had to learn that the hard way. I don't believe Mum would approve of him using them on me, though."

"Who was your mother?"

"What is this, twenty questions?"

"As many as it takes," says Nick.

The prisoner takes time to consider what he's getting into. His breaths are measured, his wide flat chest prominent under his prison greys. Before long, he says, "If we are going to do this, the least we can do is know the other's name."

"Fine," Nick replies. "Nick."

"Phillip."

"Call you Phil?"

"No."

"Phillip. Who was your mother?"

"She was a fanatic of the dark arts, Nick. At an amateur level. The occult." Phillip knots his hands together on the table, circles the pads of his thumbs together. "She joked that she was a modern witch. Really, that's as far as it went for her, an interest, obsessive as it might have been. Unable to talk to Father of her hobby, he would simply dismiss it as silly woman stuff. She would show Ulysses texts and scriptures and tablets and other assorted pseudo-religious tripe, letting his own interest flourish. He never connected with Father like I did, and I suppose it was this rejection that led his mind into stranger tides."

Nick says, "What about the book?"

"The book was simply part of the magic lore he became attracted to. A legend. It was said that sects around the world all had their own magics, and whilst the vast majority rejected the magic used by their rivals, a pragmatic few saw the potential if all available magics were pursed together in one, all-encompassing bible. Essentially, the book was written to govern all other magics, grant the reader unlimited potential, make them able to do almost anything within the realms of sorcery."

"You know all this how?"

"We grew up in a house of literature, so it was only natural that I stumbled upon some of his reading material. Mainly, though, I studied his obsessions after…after things changed for me. I studied them to understand my brother more, coming to the conclusion that he was mad. And dangerous."

"Did you know what he was doing?" Nick asks.

"His society? I learned of it after a time. After the deaths of Mum and Father."

"And you never reported it? Your brother was killing children!" Nick keeps his voice low, his teeth a cage for his anger.

"He's my *brother*," replies Phillip, as if that's the only answer needed. "I only wish I *had* put a stop to it. Father, in spite of his contempt towards Ulysses, ground into me that family is family, whether we like it or not, and we must never betray the other."

"Daddy sounds messed up. Treating each other like shit is okay but remember to stick together."

"I think he tried to love Ulysses, in his own way. Father had a keen radar built into his head, and with it he detected something foul in my brother. He made sure, at least, that he had a roof over his head, food, adequate bedding. In hindsight, it only served to fuel his ambitions."

"How did things change?" Nick finds himself invested.

"Years later, when he was more adept than I realised, Ulysses laid a curse on me. He'd collected enough scraps of knowledge to perform a number of magics by then." Phillip says this like it's general knowledge. "When I was approaching my fifties, my feet firmly in the world of business and feigning ignorance to his silliness, he somehow paralysed my age, decreed that further success would elude me, bad luck would hunt me, and that I would wonder aimless for an eternity."

"Revenge for being the favourite?" asks Nick.

"Sorry?" Phillip's brow crinkles.

"Sibling rivalry. Getting back at you for the father's love you hogged."

"Perhaps," Phillip blinks. "I don't think Ulysses cared much about Father in the end."

Nick isn't sure of the theory, either. He can't imagine the Ulysses Crane he knows being the kind of person who would let themselves be influenced by something as trivial as revenge.

One of the children in Crane's photographs had died for Phillip's curse.

Curse. A wish gone rotten.

"I didn't have you down as being so perceptive," says Phillip.

"I didn't have you down as being cursed."

"Touché." Flicking the pull ring on the Fanta can, Phillip says, "No offense, but after getting mixed up with my brother, I thought you might be a member of his stupid brigade."

"Stupid?" Smirking, Nick replies, "Found you, didn't I?"

Phillip sniggers. "Yes, you did. May I ask how?"

"There's an action video of us floating around. Lucky that today was visiting day."

It's Wednesday. The wait through Tuesday had been like chucking seconds over a cliff. For each one that was thrown, Nick believed a little more that he might not be able to find Katy. When the prison opened it gates, he'd been amongst the first in the queue.

"And lucky that you saw this evidence of you messing things up. Luck favours," Phillip winks.

"I'd say things were already messed up. I'd also say luck has nothing to do with it. Breadcrumbs I didn't know were there, is all."

"All this back and forth. Ulysses must've loved you."

"We developed a rapport."

A pause, then, Phillip adds, "Yet more luck for you that this generation feels the need to document everything they think, say, do or see. In a way, similar to the Egyptians."

"Can we continue?"

"You caused the tangent." Phillip cocks an eyebrow.

Nick prompts, "Your brother used magic on you?"

"A curse," Phillip's face curdles. "Of course, I didn't believe it, laughed him off. I was wrong, and here I am. Slowly going crazy, I found him and made an attempt on his life. I knew how dangerous he was. Is. I won't age beyond this point. I haven't for decades. When they turn me loose, I shall look the same, and there will be no future waiting for me. Still," he says with a glimmer of hope, "at least my mind has reverted back from madness for the now."

Decades? That explains why Phillip looks younger than his little brother does. "Age everlasting. Isn't that something Ulysses wants?"

"Not necessarily. He wants to hold back the ravages of time without the torture defiance of it brings. To him, youth is a tool. Means he can stick around longer to be what he really wants. There are types of immortality. He gave me the worst. He wants the type on the opposite end of the spectrum."

Nick barely contains a scoff. "You're telling me there's an immortality chart?"

"Of all the things you've learnt, you're questioning it?"

"Sorry. How old are you? Actually?"

Scratching the back of his neck, Phillip answers, "Would you believe me if I told you I've forgotten?"

"Take a stab."

"Is it important to you?"

"No."

"Carry the zero, divide by two and multiply by pi…" Phillip mumbles. "…I must be close to, if not just tipping, one hundred and thirty."

"Jesus."

A call goes out over speakers announcing visiting time will end in fifteen minutes. It repeats, fifteen minutes. There is a static punch as the speakers go dead.

"Jesus can't help me unless he can gift me death." There's a sadness in Phillip's voice. The plight of the immortal.

"Does the book have a name?"

Phillip ponders, popping his lips together like a fish. The knowledge is there, only he has to dig for it. It dawns on Nick that for the rest of his life – eternity – Phillip will have to arrange and rearrange the things he learns. There will never be enough room, the data will never stop coming in.

Finding the name, Phillip says with a rolling accent, "Liber Votorum. Book of Wishes." He nods, sighs. "Look, I am sorry that my brother has this girl of yours. Daughter?"

Nick shakes his head.

"Well, whatever. Truly, you have my sympathies, but there is little you can do now, especially if you've lost him. Being in his company, I assume you would know his place of business, that disgusting building that once belonged to Father. A law firm I think it was, one that operated on the fringes, anyway. My father was not all the way corrupt, though he did understand the way the world worked. If Ulysses is no longer there, it means he's gone to ground."

"Do you know where ground is for him?" Nick shimmies his chair closer, then leans back when the officer, not moving from their post against the coffee machine, shows an interest.

"I can think of only one place, though I doubt it'll help you. I'm still not sure I want to. Has a clean slate been offered to you? My brother, cruel and unusual as he may be, has always been one for affording second chances."

Nick explains. "I had a letter yesterday, offering me money to stay away. After Saturday, it's all over."

"Do yourself a favour and take it. You don't want to be in my shoes. If he wishes, he can lock you in time on the edge of death. Imagine that, if you will. Perpetual, eternal, living death."

Nick hangs his head. The table is covered in the bruises of frustration and anger, inmates who couldn't control themselves. A name has been carved into it that Nick can't decipher.

He says, "I'm not taking the money. I'm helping the girl. I've done it once, I can do it again."

"I assure you, you can't. If he's gotten her back, he won't make another mistake. Let it go before he gets the book, *when* that happens, I don't want to imagine what- "

"He has it," Nick says.

For more than a few seconds, Phillip cannot speak. His jaw drops, revealing decaying teeth, meaning that for all his grandeur before the curse, the older Crane had little care for dental hygiene.

Before long, he asks, "Why didn't you tell me? You're back to being a fucking fool."

"Would it have made a difference if I'd told you sooner?" asks Nick.

"How'd he come by the book?"

"I picked it up for him."

"Jesus."

"He won't help us." Nick manages a humourless smile.

Phillip – his nose filling with blood – says, "If he has the Liber Votorum then hope is already lost. Your girl is as good as dead already."

Five minutes. The speaker repeats, five minutes. Time to start saying goodbye to your loved ones.

Nick hurries things up. "I don't think so. He's giving me until Saturday to think things over."

"That long?"

"Luck favours, as you'd say."

"It seems there's a chance she'll be okay. Luck in the presence of my brother is akin to syphoning blood from a stone," says Phillip.

"There's been a fair amount so far," Nick says. "Blood, I mean."

"That's unfortunate."

An officer starts to float around. Inmates are being rounded up. With at least three minutes left on the clock, it's easy to see how prisoners can become so irate when precious seconds are stolen from them.

Nick asks, "Any idea why he's given me time?"

"Should I have?"

"You know all the *other* shit."

In spite of three minutes about to become two, Phillip takes his time searching for an answer, rubs his chin. "Magic is finnicky. It has its own set of rules. When did you first steal the girl?"

"I *saved* her last Saturday." Nick harbours some resentment at the use of the word *steal*.

"Ulysses is waiting. Could be that the offering has to be completed on the same day it was started? I'm not entirely sure. I'll admit, I've retained more information about his exploits than I ever expected to, what with being a puppet to a curse, yet I do not know everything."

"How do I stop him?" Nick holds up his palm, with a smile, for the officer to allow just one more minute. The officer shakes their head, but with crossed arms they allow the extra time. The visiting room is half full, anyway.

Phillip laughs. It's a sad laugh. "You can't. If he has the Liber Votorum, he'll already have too much access to its magic. The offering is the final key for the final lock. It will make Ulysses and the book as one, but is not wholly essential to use the book's magic. He's been using that for years. If the lock is opened...you'd do well to not be anywhere near him."

"I don't get it. If he could already use the book's magic, why does he even need it?"

"Greed." Phillip nods at the officer who is waiting to cart him off. "When people are rich, they still want more money. My brother simply seeks greater magic."

Nick crams in more questions. *Knowledge is motherfucking power.* "If he had some use of the magic, why didn't he just wish for the fucking book?"

Standing, Phillip chuckles. "You'd want him to have had it *sooner*? Listen, Nick. Can you ask a genie for more wishes? It's a clever little firewall, isn't it? Look, I'd like more than anything for Ulysses to be put to rest. Any magic he has performed would be null and void if he were to die. I'd be free."

The speakers declare that visiting hours are over, and for all visiting family members and friends to please get their arses up and leave.

Nick rises. "Where is he? I don't care what you say, I don't care if he's got magic coming out of his backside, I can't let him kill the girl."

The officer speaks under his breath. "What the fuck're you twos on about?" It's a good thing he was barely listening. Any talk of killing could be reported, which could land Nick in here with Phillip.

"You're efforts will lead to nought but pain." Phillip warns with sympathy showing through the cracks.

Nick practically hisses at Phillip. "I don't care if you say he can't be stopped. If that's the case then so fucking be it, but I can still get the girl if I can't stop your brother. You said you knew of one place, so where is it?"

The officer takes Phillip by the arm. Phillip resists for a millisecond before saying to Nick, "He would go to my parent's old house, the family homestead, in the Surrey countryside."

"Tell me where it is!"

"That's just the thing," says Phillip as he's being led away. He looks over his shoulder at Nick, sympathy gone in a face which is now full of dark enjoyment that stinks too much of the little brother. "It doesn't exist."

CHAPTER 29

Katy has been given her own room with books stacked as if by supernatural hands. It's a pain to take out the ones she's interested in, resulting in smaller stacks spiking up around the room.

A clock ticks, a relaxing metronome trying to hypnotise Katy. She's fought off the effect through constant study. All the books are about mysticism, ancient religions, all kinds of magic craft. One she read the first three wordy chapters of was called Magic Craft: The Craft of Magic.

An F- for the person who thought *that* up.

Crossed-legged on the floor, she leans against the bed. The wooden frame is an effective neck brace against what Katy calls homework-neck. The book she's reading is a thick slab of non-fiction entitled Rituals. The chapter currently being absorbed is a small segment called 'Interruptions.'

Her eyes glide over the last sentence. She drops the book in her lap with a blank stare on her face.

"I'm dead."

By her side is Pop Ta…

Solomon. Curled up in a neat ball, fur spiralling into a fluffy centre bulls-eyed by the cat's nose.

She hates that it's not Pop Tart anymore. Never was. It's hard, though, for her to imagine the cat as anything but. Every now and then it will do something so genuinely loving Katy cannot help but think of him as the same cat she attached herself to in Nick's kitchen. Whether a boop on the head, or a sandpaper lick. Most likely the cat is doing it on purpose. It's probably been *ordered* to do it as much as keep an eye on her.

She strokes Solomon anyway, seeking solace, thankful, if nothing else, for the company, especially after what she's just learnt about her position on the rungs of interrupted rituals.

The cat stretches itself into a new position, giving Katy maximum access to all the best places to pet. He purrs. Solomon has more cat in him than evil.

Gut and Survival haven't made themselves known for a while now, especially Survival, which seems to have gone AWOL. The only word from Gut has been to keep herself alert and calm. *Calm girls get out alive*, Gut had said without much gumption, obviously trying to emulate its stronger, braver cousin. Katy wishes it wouldn't. She's tired of being brave.

"Settling in nicely?"

Katy jumps, upsetting Solomon's spa evening and throwing the book off her lap, denting a corner of the binding. Solomon sprints around and under the bed, claws marking the floorboards.

Standing in the doorway with one leg relaxed is Walter George. He hasn't bothered to keep himself as well dressed as he'd done previously.

Katy backs up, sits on the bed, then moves to the other side of the room where there is an antique table full of old beauty products, all of it covered in powder that smells of many perfumes. She doesn't know exactly why she moved away from the bed, only that Walter George makes her uncomfortable, and whilst he is around, so does a bed.

He has both hands in his pockets, no jacket and a loosened tie. His hair looks wet and is combed back, enhancing the arrow of his widow's peak. "I asked you a question," he says with utmost politeness.

Katy grabs her left arm. "You betrayed us."

The comment amuses Walter. "Betrayed is a strong word, but I'm afraid you're wrong on that score, Cherub."

Her lips crumple at the nickname his brother used.

"Stay away from me," Katy orders.

Walter walks into the room. His moustache, a waxed symbol of pride the last time she saw him, now sags to either side of his mouth, acting as a magnet to the rest of his facial features, pulling everything down in a way that makes his face longer. His eyes still burn bright with mischief. He tries a smile, which fails to raise his moustache.

Jingling the change in his pocket, he tells Katy, "You haven't got to worry about me. I ain't your enemy."

"I'll decide that," she answers back, wanting Survival to make an appearance. That corner of her brain is silent. Gut has stiffened because Gut is a scaredy cat.

"Reckon you already have." Walter takes in the room, nods. "Nice digs."

Katy repeats herself with more force. "You *betrayed* us."

"You've gotten your words mixed up, Cherub. I didn't betray you, I sold you."

"There's no difference," Katy argues.

"Of course there is," Walter brings a hand to his moustache, strokes it. "Betrayal is personal, something you do to someone because you hate them, or they hate you and you have to punish 'em for it. What I did was make a business transaction. Believe me when I tell you there wasn't anything personal about it."

Katy replies, "You hate Nick."

"That easy to tell, is it?"

"Yes."

"You're right," Walter replies. "But I didn't sell *him*. I sold *you*, and not for money either. I'll soon have no use for money. Actually, scratch that. I'll have no use for *gaining* money. The business transaction wasn't for Mr Crane. He's not the only fella who needs you."

"Where's Nick?" she asks.

"He's no longer my issue. I had some fun, put it that way."

The way Walter winks is all Katy needs to clarify her fear. People like Walter don't wink like that if there isn't some hidden message. She's not even sure why Walter and his creepy personality came wandering in her room this time of night. She decides to tell him to, "Stay away from me," again, blocking thoughts of (*dead*) Nick out of her mind. *Good idea*, Gut agrees.

Walter smiles wider, which succeeds in altering the position of his moustache. He glances around the room, strolls to a desk. He lets his hand glide over the wood, then traces his index finger around a lamp, nudges a wicker basket bin with his foot. Spraying a quick laugh, he says to himself, "You'd really think it was all real."

He awaits a response to his strange observation, but Katy doesn't give one, meaning for the last thing she said to stay as it is. For him to stay away.

Hands back in pockets, he asks her, "How long you got?"

Survival mumbles something from a great distance. Katy shrugs.

"Shame."

Solomon is on the bed, has reconfigured himself into a position more comfy than the last, resembling now a black meringue. Walter strides to the bed, scoops his hand under the cat and flings it off the duvet. Landing on all fours, Solomon bares its fangs, hisses. Its hair punks into spikes. After Solomon's tantrum, it stalks from the bedroom, into the halls of the labyrinthine house.

She takes a step forward before Gut objects. "Why'd you do that? Leave him alone!"

Walter points to his ear. "Cats listen. In this place he's a directional microphone. I don't like being listened in on."

"Get out!"

"Fine, my interest in you, for now, is wearing thin anyway, but I have to say, you speak of betrayal without knowing what it really means. There's plenty more time for betrayal. If you hold on, you might get to see."

That last, ominous statement is what he leaves her with, sauntering out of the room in carefree fashion, almost dancing.

Katy dashes to the door, slams it shut, pressing her back against it. There's a keyhole but no key to lock it with. If only, she thinks. If Pop Tart wants back in he'll scratch for entry, if it's Solomon he'll howl. Katy hopes Walter doesn't come back.

You'd really think it was all real.

She peers around the bedroom as Walter had done, then at the damaged book on the floor, recalling what the pages had taught her. With luck, what's written inside won't turn out to be real, either.

Through her own mouth, Survival speaks with a whisper. "But it is."

The dam cracks and the implied killing of Nick is the skimming bomb that knocks it down. Katy slides to her bottom, legs curled up underneath herself, and she cries into her arms.

CHAPTER 30

If you had your ear to the ground, you'd hear Juniper Abraham stomping through Crane Manor end to end. Hard-soled, schoolmarm shoes clomp on the planks. Mr Crane has charged her with seeking out Simon Schaeffer, for his services may be required again in the coming hours. A shame that his services come with his personality. And that face, already annoying to behold before it became a hideous mask of one man's depravities.

Staples, indeed.

Schaeffer is a pain to find. As Juniper stomps through the grand house she is struck, not for the first time, by how impressive the structure is. Not just the house either, but what Mr Crane has accomplished by its being here. Time and time again he has proved that her loyalty, and the whole society's reverence, is duly afforded, yet this house, able to be touched and felt, is a step up. A sign for sure that his and the book's connection is growing steadily stronger, especially now the offering can be completed in a matter of hours, minutes and seconds. Each second, passing so slowly, is a moment closer to the final offering that shall be a world apart from those that came before. Not that the children before this were any less important, their sacrifices had been appreciated, their unmarked graves adorned with gifts for the first year after their deaths. Katy Robbins shall play her part, too. There will be a photograph of course, it shall be the centrepiece on the table the society feasts from after the ceremony.

They no longer have to concern themselves with the man Nicholas and his meddling. If he isn't dead, he's scared. Let the meddling mouse drive himself mad, it's all he deserves for the trouble he's caused. She knew he was effort the day she watched him on the bus, sent by Mr Crane to gather an opinion of the newest prospect.

Mr Crane had been preparing to knight Nicholas with his new name. He only handed out new names to people he really enjoyed. Apollo himself had once carried a common name from his country. She's quite forgotten what it was. Something with a J in it.

She herself had been Bridget Carmichael, a name she now associates with misery. Oddly enough, she had won Mr Crane's favour by stubbornly refusing to make a wish. Her fortitude had enchanted him.

Where *is* Simon Schaeffer?

Juniper, hand on the banister that morphs into a carved bulb at the bottom, descends the house's main staircase. At the bottom are two members of the society. They stand to attention, nervous in her presence.

"Schaeffer?" she asks them. Her tone one of reprimand.

One of them, a frail man who hasn't yet wished for his vision to surpass his glasses, answers, "I saw him a few minutes ago. He went that way." The poor-sighted man points to Juniper's left.

Without thanks, she crosses the threshold of the foyer into another hallway, this one wider, more decorated. As she leaves them behind, their mouths start running. She is aware of what the society calls her. She lets them keep it, for it gives her strength amongst the clan. That had been one of Mr Crane's sayings, one he hasn't used since then, as if he meant it just for her. Juniper knows she holds some mystique over Mr Crane, it's readable in his eyes whenever she enters the same room. She doesn't exploit him though, that would be the dumbest of follies.

A voice hooks her attention. Not far from her is a door that's been left ajar. She stomps to it, pulls it open slightly, stops herself when she sees Schaeffer sitting at the foot of an unmade bed. He is in conversation with a ghoul. The black shape stands before him, seemingly unaware that it's being spoken to. Just who the ghoul is, Juniper cannot tell. They all appear the same once they pass over, only attaining – she has it on good authority – individuality when they are given duties to attend to in the afterlife.

Schaeffer unzips his trousers and begins to fondle himself, whispering sweet nothings to the indifferent ghoul. He plucks at his deformity as if each staple is a string with a different note, heightening his sick pleasures. She prepares to launch into the room, catch the pervert with his wilted member in hand.

"Didn't figure you for a peepin' Tom," Mr George whispers in her ear.

Juniper doesn't gasp or make any indication that she has been caught out. What she can't hide are the roses blooming in her cheeks. Moving away from the door, leaving Schaeffer to himself, she turns to Mr George.

"Back away, please."

Mr George steps back, palms up. He gestures with his chin at the ajar door. "Sick fuck isn't he?"

"Mr George, I am trying to make preparations for the coming events, so if you wouldn't mind…"

"Christ," Mr George's lips twist, "you can hear the bastard at it."

This one doesn't like to listen, it seems. The society is filled with a cabaret of personalities. Juniper is used to dealing with them. Mr George has only a teenager's deaf ear to contend with.

"Mr George- "

"You can call me Walter," he says, offhand.

"Is there anything I can help you with?"

Walter picks up a lamp from a set of drawers, flips it over in his hands and seems surprised when he gazes at the felt base.

"Problem?" Juniper holds back the venom.

"Reckoned this'd be made in China or something. Then again," he thunks it down in the wrong position, which will upset Mr Crane, "nothing in this house was really made *anywhere*."

"Mr George- "

"Walter."

"*Walter*. I must insist. I am busy."

"Busy peekin' at cocks." Before Juniper can retaliate, he goes on. "Is everyone where they're meant to be?"

Juniper blanches from this question, more so because it is not his place to ask. With a sharp tongue, she says, "Not that it's any of your business, but yes. Those that aren't will soon be informed of their roles, if any roles are left."

"What about those who don't have roles?"

"They can enjoy themselves."

"Where's the god of war?" he asks, meaning Apollo.

"Security," Juniper answers.

Narrowing his eyes, Walter says, "Can we really be sure? An operation like this, who can you really trust?"

Pointing a spindly, red-tipped finger at him, Juniper warns, "You and I have never exchanged words until now. Your face is new to me, but don't you dare come sowing seeds of suspicion- "

Walter slaps her hand away, a crack that, for a second, stops the pervert in the room from spoiling himself. Juniper looks up at Walter, if that's what he *must* be called. His snarl is that of a dog with rabies.

"Listen, tart," he says, doing the pointing now. "I might not've been in this as long as you're crusty arse has, but spare me the bullshit and talk to me like an actual human for fuck sake."

She isn't scared of his bark or his rapier-quick bite. Dogs can easily be neutered.

"Very well," she says. Standing prim, she lets him have it. "I think you being here is wrong. I'd have said erroneous but I'm not sure you'd understand it. I know your type, I see through your front. You are a crook, a liar, a deceiver and a rogue that this society could do without. I am *never* wrong in my opinions of people. The last man who rubbed me wrong is the reason we are here in the first place- "

"Wherever *here* is."

"-and I do not intend to allow Mr Crane's destiny to be delayed further. I have my eye on you, and that is where I shall keep it."

"Better. Can't shake that posh accent though, can you?" Grinning, his swift rage obliterated, Walter gestures at the door behind Juniper.

"Anyway, I thought you had your eye on Chuckles in there?"

Grumbling moans of pleasure come from behind the dark oak door.

Looking over her shoulder, almost growling, Juniper replies, "He is needed by Mr Crane."

Walter fake shudders. "That make you mad? I dunno why he keeps that freak around."

Passing close and on purpose, wafting his cologne up her nose, Walter passes Juniper for a peek. Heat flushes her cheeks. Never in her years has a man affected her composure, but *that* had. He'd moved like a serpent laying its scent. At sixty, the sensation is discomforting.

Keeping to Mr Crane's words, she says, "It matters not who a person is. There are many colours and creeds in the world, a wish does not care for them. Wishes carry weight here, anything else is inconsequential or put to use."

"You hate him, too?"

"I believe *that* specimen belongs on a whipping post. My feelings are irrelevant. The value of a wish is universal."

One eye closed as he peers in at the pervert, lips drawn over his teeth, Walter replies, "Yeah, but…fuck. *This* guy? Some wishes come from better people."

"What makes a person better?" asks Juniper, actually intrigued to hear the answer.

"You tell me," Walter winks at her, breaking any spell of a relevant reply. "You're the one with the good judge of character."

She crosses her arms, asks, "*Your* wish? Are you *better* than Schaeffer?"

"Sorry love. My wishes are bound. I'm not about to grass them up to you."

Juniper considers her response, drawing on what she's learned from both Mr Crane and her own experiences. "That's fine, I don't need to know. Your wishes, Schaeffer's wishes, my wishes" – *which don't exist* – "are all the same when you separate them from the physical mind. In essence, it doesn't matter what the wish *is*, but that it *exists*. A person could wish for a bar of chocolate or the death of a politician, yet the important factor is the wish itself, the words spoken, the thought. That is the energy Mr Crane, and the Liber Votorum, craves. To put it simply, who the wish comes from doesn't matter."

"And if someone wished to fuck a kid, would that be okay because the act is not the important thing?" Walter asks as if something fowl has touched his tongue.

"Mr Crane would never grant such a wish."

"So there *is* a moral compass here," says Walter. "Sometimes the person making the wish *is* taken into consideration. Sometimes a person's ethics weigh more than the wish."

"Perhaps." Juniper tilts her head.

"Does the book share this compass?" he asks.

"No. The book doesn't care for morals. It will listen to whoever has proven themselves worthy of its delights."

"Good to know."

She doesn't like the cockiness in his voice, his bulletproof arrogance. "What are you getting at, Mr George?"

"Only what I already said. Some wishes come from better people, and you and Crane know it, too. I've just proved myself right. Though I find it strange that he would condemn the molestation of a child but has no problem slicing their throats."

"That's different," Juniper counters.

"Yeah, yeah, because it's an offering, I know the drill. Guess that magic of his needs more than *just* the energy of a wish, huh?"

"Are you questioning the forces you've seen at work?"

"I'm questioning nothing, just makin' an observation. I'm enjoying this."

"And I am growing tired of it," Juniper revokes.

Stepping away from the door, Walter leaves the unsuspecting Schaeffer to his fetishes. He approaches Juniper, a glint in his eyes that's as charming as it is ridiculous.

"You know," he begins, "for someone I've, quote unquote, rubbed the wrong way, you're being awfully chatty with me."

"It's called manners, though I cannot reason why I'm affording them on you," Juniper says.

"Could it be that I'm rubbing you the *right* way?"

He gets closer, playfully twists his moustache, wets his bottom lip with a thick tongue. This is a man who identifies sex as a weapon, is proficient in its use. Don't let this excuse for a man get under your skin, Juniper tells herself.

"Mr George- "

"Would you like me to?"

She straightens herself, stiffens her lips, feet glued together. "You are vile."

"Some people like vile. I think you're one of 'em."

"And now you're wasting my time," adds Juniper.

"Just *now*?"

"What do you want, Mr George?"

It's a question she should've made herself ask long before the conversation got this far.

"Don't get upset." Walter steps back, tickling his belt buckle with his forefinger. "I'll backtrack. All I'm saying is I'd keep a closer eye on people. Word is there's a big prize when this is all over- "

Juniper interrupts him, which she enjoys. "This won't ever be over. It progresses."

"-and I wanna give you fair warning."

"What you are suggesting is not only an imbecile's notion," Juniper says, "but also treachery."

"I prefer mutiny," Walter offers. "This house feels like a ship. Mutiny is a pirate thing, right?"

"Mutiny is mutiny, Mr George. Whomever performs it is irrelevant."

"Kinda like a wish," he winks, adding another point he thinks he's gained. "Who'd've thought that wishes and mutiny would have so much in common?"

Imploring him further, hoping he will take his leave, "Mr George…"

"My money's on Apollo. He has motive, and the physicality to inspire a following. Only takes a few."

Juniper scoffs. " Motive?"

In the most serious voice since he barged into her evening, Walter replies, "There's only so long a powerful man can take being *under* someone. They are two kinds of powerful, him and Crane. Power doesn't do well in bed with itself."

Glaring, she responds, "If anyone here is planning treason, Mr George, it sounds like you. As for Mr Apollo? Nonsense." She splutters a laugh. "His loyalty stretches to match my own. Any attack on Mr Crane would be met with unpleasant ends. Nobody would dare, and whilst you insist on speaking rubbish, what has filled your head with it?"

Thrusting his hands in his pockets, Walter kisses his teeth, then answers, "It's not me Miss, I can tell you that. My brother and me have run this city together for a good bitta time now. You get to know the subtle signs when something's amiss." Inhaling deep and letting it slowly go, he finishes, "You can smell it."

Patience nearing breaking point, Juniper says, "If anyone was planning anything of the sort, their plotting would be discovered. Nothing remains hidden from Mr Crane. He has eyes and ears almost everywhere."

"Almost. There's always a way to keep things hidden." His voice is almost a purr. "Could be as easy as chasing a cat out of a room."

"Your assumption is idiotic, Mr George."

"You've been letting all that up-tightness get the better of you, Juny."

Her eyes blaze. "*Juny?*"

"I asked you to talk to me like a regular human, but you've been letting all those posh, archaic words slip in like the men you wished could've slipped inside you." Ignoring her frustration that Juniper imagines is cartooning her eyes with spirals of red and yellow, Walter forges on. "You're a powerful woman, Juny. I can tell, got a sixth sense for it I do. I have power too, believe it or not. Influence. But unlike Apollo and Crane, I wouldn't mind being under you."

He winks, licks his lips.

For an instant, the mental image of the two of them together, naked, flashes in her head, she on top, he on bottom, a passionate entwining of her hate and lust for this no good scoundrel. How did he plant this lust? In the image she is young, her body unafflicted with the ailments of age. For the second or two it lasts, it empowers her hate for him.

Chasing it away, she tells him, "If you're done, Mr George, you can leave now. I have to see Schaeffer, and if this pointless conversation between us has done nothing but give the degenerate man time to finish, I shall consider it worthwhile."

With ferocity, Walter kicks open Schaeffer's door, nearly ripping it from the hinges. The ghoul vanishes in an instant, Schaeffer, naked but for his socks, unhands himself, stunned into an awkward silence.

Schaeffer stumbles over his words in an attempt to defend himself, makes no effort to cover his erection. His body is a collection of scars, some red, others wine-coloured. There are also fresh wounds which are trickling blood.

Walter laughs, finds it all very amusing.

Schaeffer groans, clenches his teeth and eyes shut as his orgasm finally bubbles out of him. What an awful thing he is. It's reasonable to consider that Mr George has a point on *this* one. Out of all the people to keep around, why Schaeffer?

The answer, of course, is a simple one. Because of what he can do. Surely, if Mr Crane saw anything like this he would keep Schaeffer on a very, very short leash.

"There you go." Walter turns to her, steps closer. "You can see him now."

He leans in close to her ear, his breath making her skin tingle. All her muscles tighten as she fights a reaction. He sniffs a couple of times. When he pulls back he smiles at her, looks her straight in the eyes, piercing her.

"That's a curious smell you have, Juny."

He brushes past, whistling as he strolls down the hallway. She listens as his footsteps fade away, his forest-scented cologne going with him. Juniper will treat him with kiddy gloves from now on, won't let him get too close. His portents to an incoming mutiny are laughable, of course.

"Miss Juniper?"

Schaeffer is stumbling towards her, fumbling into his stained jeans. Thank God he has a tee-shirt on now, a faded one depicting some noisy band or other. She takes a step back, not wanting him any closer, stopping him before he can cross into the hallway. Her disgust for him looms on the edge of pity.

Holding back her sneer, she tells him, "Mr Crane wishes to speak to you. Make yourself presentable for all our sakes."

"I'm sorry about- "

Reptile-quick, she lunges forward and slaps him hard across the face, leaving behind a perfect red imprint of her hand. She chose the side without the staples.

"Do as I say, Schaeffer. I don't have time for your empty words. Get yourself to Mr Crane. I trust you can find your way without ejaculating on everything."

It's clear he took some enjoyment from the slap. It felt good to strike him. "Yes, Miss Juniper, right away. I shall...I shall just..."

He backs into the room and closes the door, following her orders to make himself not so pathetic.

At that, Juniper dismisses herself, eager to be away from his aura, resuming her stomp through the hallways of the house. Her next port of call is the girl, Katy Robbins. Juniper is glad the girl has better accommodations, now.

She has to be prepared.

PART III

' The House That Crane Built '

CHAPTER 31

The quiet life never will suit Nick.

Constable's Heath, a set of coordinates on the satnav and straight from the lid of a puzzle box, should be, for a man like Nick, a holiday resort. But it isn't. When he'd arrived a short while ago in the grassy sitcom village locked deep in the green of Surrey, the quiet was nice enough, and not having to barge shoulders to get around was a welcome gimmick, but it quickly wore thin, and when he noticed the hustle and bustle – the *action* – operated at zero, he reasoned that every country village was and is a rustic, walled-in, dystopian wasteland.

Okay, dystopian *flowered*-land.

There're flowers everywhere.

Initially peaceful, the quiet is now too empty, the lack of physical interaction is making his mind too sleepy. The slowness of life here is too…snaily. Everything is *too* something.

Places like Tutt's or Estelle's don't exist in hamlets like this. The high point of entertainment here, if it doesn't get too boisterous, is probably the am-dram club.

Walking faster than the speed limit – unsure of what he's searching for or how he'll find Katy here – Nick passes a bakery. In its windows are lumps of fresh bread, rolls and pastry bakes, all trays full to the edges. A duck lands on a nearby pond surrounded by bulrush, drawing Nick's attention. The green-headed yapper quacks, the loudest thing in the village above the twittering of songbirds. Why can't they have pigeons instead? A good city noise.

This place, it's all too fucking perfect, pristine. Too…*nothing*.

For a long time Nick has entertained the thought of leaving the city, believing that this kind of *nothing* is what he craves. To leave behind his history, the faces that hound him, he thought the best place to attain that is in vast areas of *nothing*. And maybe it is, to a degree, yet he now knows he can never leave the carnage of a cityscape. He's just another bee, the hive calling for him to return, even if the other bees piss him off. It is, it turns out, the city's buzz of activity – the wailing sirens at night, the grinding roadworks during the day – that acts as the white noise that soothes him. If he has to deal with the past for the rest of his life, seeing those faces and places, then that's the way it's got to be, because here, in places like Constable's Heath, he is not soothed. Here, he's a fish out of water. He'd happily get back in Frank's loaner car and fuck off right now if it wasn't for Katy.

Jesus, they always say going somewhere quiet helps you clear your mind, but damn. The sensory deprivation here has kicked the shit out of any half-baked plans for the simple life. This place should be called Epiphany Heath.

Rustling through the reeds, disturbing Nick from epiphanies of character, the duck waddles up the bank towards him. It fixes him with beady black eyes and honks. Probably knows he's an outsider. Outsiders didn't bring bread.

Further up, there's a pub across the road, a white and black building with benches outside. There's no pathway, no parking area, the grass reaches right up and kisses the walls. The Toasty Stoat, a name as brand new as the table umbrellas. The hanging sign shows a pipe-smoking stoat by a fireplace.

Landlords, regulars, they always have their noses in the air and ears to the ground. That fact stretches beyond city limits. If anyone has any info regarding the Crane house, they'll be in there. Nick still has no idea what Phillip Crane meant when he said the house no longer existed. How can a man move a society to a location that isn't there? Perhaps prison hadn't ironed out all his madness.

Pulling open the door, Nick takes another glance at the village. He wonders how the Cranes ever came to live in a place like this. A family with a dominating patriarch and a witch mother must've been hard to miss, not to mention their psychotic progeny.

Inside, the pub isn't really a pub at all. It's family friendly, bright colours over what should be deep red carpets and beer stained bars. It's tobacco-free smell is clean air boosted with fresheners. Fancy signs direct patrons to the beer garden, the toilets, the play area. Any inn traditions have been shed. This same happy horseshit is an epidemic in London. Nick reckoned the outback pubs'd have more spine in chasing off this kind of bollocks. Country dreamer or city slicker, a person should always have a pub as an escape pod. Nick doesn't drink, yet he still appreciates a sombre watering hole.

Nick wonders what will happen to Frank now that one half of his business partnership is weighed down at the bottom of the Thames. Is Walt going to pick up everything that Harvey handled? It's possible that Estelle's future is now up in the air, bait for sharks.

Before his feet have left the welcome mat, a member of staff flaunting a smile way too wide to be genuine appears behind the bar, a necklace of cards and keys jingling as they open up the cash register. She spots Nick and winks one heavily made-up eye.

"Be with you in a sec," she promises.

"Thanks," replies Nick.

He sits on a barstool. The Toasty Stoat is mostly empty. Tenacious pre-lunch drinkers are the only ones to have claimed their spots, pint mugs acting as flags on their chosen tables. It's a biggish place, Nick doesn't think there'll be a shortage of tables come the Heath's rush hour – and he uses the term lightly. There's only five drinkers in all, old guns with thoughtful faces that would definitely take a traditional pub over the Stoat. Being the only pub in the village, they're stuck with what they've got. They eye Nick with a suspicion only bumpkins possess.

The barmaid comes back, curls loose from her hairband. She's in a bit of a flap. "Sorry about that, had to run some inventory. What can I getchya?"

"Lemonade, please."

She winks again. "No problem." Fishing below for a glass, she asks, "Pint of?"

"Whatever's easiest." Nick smiles, then asks, "Where're your toilets?"

"Just follow the signs," she tells him, hiding that everyone asking instead of following the signs pisses her off something royal.

"Thanks."

Nick doesn't really need the toilet. He wants to scope the place without sticking out. On his way, he passes a wall of pictures showing off the pub throughout the years in glorious black and white.

Liar's Heath, it used to be called, as the photograph from 1820 tells it. A horse and carriage carts a group of youngsters in a field, all of them mischievous. Any one of them could be a Crane, or a branch of the family tree.

Nick already knows the village went through a name change in 1902 after the constable sought to have the name improved, citing that Liar *'glorified contemptuous behaviour in a world wrought with abhorrent morals'*. He'd had a stick up his less than perfect arse, and though he was remembered in the history books with little affection, the name of the village stuck, continuing the legacy of that egotistical, unfaithful lawman.

Nick knows this because he'd found it all in a library back in the city, on the internet.

Nick had chosen a library tucked away in a lesser known area, reasoning that if any of Crane's followers worked in a library they'd be in the upscale sort with glass architecture and listed bricks. As far as he can know or tell, he'd been correct. No one in the Hemingway Library gave a toss he was there. This'd been the day after his meeting with Phillip Crane.

Into Google, he'd typed the name Ulysses Crane, which came up nothing (not a coincidence, he reckoned), before typing in Crane. Taking away the first name hooked him up with myriad options to choose from, including a restaurant, an oil factory, and a plethora of HGV hire merchants. Nothing jumped off the screen, and when he'd been about to pack it in to try some books, he spied a link on the sixth page that simply said: CRANE – A Family History.

It'd been an independent article by some trumped up uni student with more vocabulary than knowledge of prose, not that Nick knows anything of prose himself, only that bad prose is as easy to spot as a city bloke in a country pub.

The article didn't have much of the Crane family in it at all, no business associations, no residences, only that they spent their twilight years in a sleepy village a couple of hours outside London before all trace of the family disappeared. Of the village itself was what most of the information went into detail about; the name change, businesses, pubs. Still, it'd given Nick a place linked with the family name, so here – after borrowing a steaming banger from Frank – is where he came. It isn't what he expected. After a family like the Cranes had inhabited a place, he'd thought there'd be a perpetual dark cloud blanketing the land, especially after what he'd learnt from Phillip.

It had been what happened at the conclusion of his library visit that shook Nick the most. The maggots have left an aftertaste.

§

Two days ago…

The Hemingway Library smells of moth balls and empty wallets. The décor is mostly brown, with windows that have a matching tint. The aisles, which only have room enough for one-way browsing, are comprised of shelves on wheels, bookended by swivel racks neatly lined with hobby magazines. There's an upstairs, but that's been cordoned off with a sign reminding people who aren't staff to keep out. Gladys behind the desk will fuck you up otherwise.

Nick sits at a computer, an outdated, blocky bit of kit, yet one that earns its keep by working for all its worth. Almost finished with his research, Nick types slowly, checking after each clack that the letter has jumped correctly into the screen.

He looks over his shoulder, then up at the top floor where the landing overlooks the library. In the shadows, he at first believes he catches a glimpse of one of the Murdered, which turns out to be a coat hanging on a hook.

No one's watching. Good. In the back of his head, he reserves concern for the Figure, which hasn't shown itself since the attack at O'Reilly's.

Nick enters *cult* into the search bar. The results are too plentiful. A bombardment of names are flung his way.

Heaven's Gate, Angel's Landing, Children of God, The Manson Family, Synanon, Sons of Sam, all of them begging to be clicked on to take the reader on a conspiracy rollercoaster. He narrows the search by adding *UK*. One of the first he sees is the Process Church that Frank talked about, though most of the rest are questions aimed to lure the reader in. *Is Satan turning your family into a Cult? Is my Church a trafficking Cult? Are you Trve Cvlt?* All a load of bollocks. Nick goes to the images, finds nothing, not so much as a pixelated picture of Crane's society symbol.

He begins typing in his next search.

L-I-B-E-R V-O-T-O-R-U-

The M key doesn't work. Nick presses it a few times, bangs the side of the computer. The library lights flicker, the sun disappears outside, plunging Nick into brown darkness. If there were others in the library, they've gone, or aren't aware of what's happening. Distant thunder rattles the bookshelves, vibrates through the floor. Nick pushes away from the desk to stand, is shoved back in by an invisible force.

His face is lit up by the computer screen cramped with scrolling ones and zeroes, moving horizontal and diagonal. It cries like a broken fax machine, a screech that drills into Nick's skull. The screen bulges, glass crackling without breaking. Nick tries to pull away, but the invisible force is holding him in place. He sees a face forming behind the binary code, pushing its way, painfully it seems, into being. When it succeeds, the numbered face speaks to Nick with a sizzling electric voice.

"Good afternoon, Nicholas. How was my brother?"

So he had *known.* "Crane?!"

Wires spring from the computer, twist themselves into thick cable that wraps around Nick's head, dragging his face closer to the living monitor. Exposed tips scratch his skin, with a life of their own they attempt to find orifices in which to plug themselves. He's powerless against them.

"Let it go, Nicholas," Crane urges, sparks lighting the inside of his mouth.

"I can't!"

"Yes, you can," Crane titters. "You must."

Nick can smell burning coming from the computer. "I won't let you kill her."

"How are those wounds, Nicholas? Still troubling you? Perhaps you need a reminder of the pain caused by injury?"

Gripping the sides of the desk, Nick pulls back. More wires shoot from the monitor, joining the already powerful rope enveloping his head. Something pops inside the computer.

"I'll find you," Nick grunts.

Crane's face sinks back. "Nicholas, you should know by now, I am a master of keeping myself hidden. Still, good luck and all that. You have my best wishes, and you know those are reliable."

The screen explodes, shattered glass machine-guns into Nick's face. He falls backwards off the chair, wires gone. The computer is still in one piece, stuck on the list of UK cults. The library is once again full of natural, albeit filtered, sunlight. Frantically, Nick touches his face, expects to find shards turning him into a pin cushion. There are none. This isn't the first time Crane has fooled him with an illusion. It will be the last, Nick tells himself.

When he rises to his feet, Nick doubles over, clenches his stomach, his arms, legs, head. Everywhere. The world around him blurs as pain rings through his flesh. A voice, Crane's voice, echoes inside his skull.

"Let it go."

Every injury Nick has sustained since he met Crane flares back anew. His ribs, the beating Walter gave him, his split eyebrow, a multitude of cuts, scrapes and bruises. All of them throb with a searing pain that throws Nick into a bookshelf, knocking over paperbacks. It's like fire beneath his skin, maggots inside his guts.

Crane's voice says again, "Let it go."

Nick staggers from the library, retching, his face red, eyes bloodshot. Pedestrians avoid him. He manages to get himself to Estelle's – paying an Uber double the fee for a no questions ride – where he collapses through the door.

§

He'd spent the rest of Thursday and all of Friday in a feverish sleep, brought food and water by Frank. Saturday morning – today – he'd finally felt well enough to leave. It was still an hour or two more before the maggots left his stomach, though. They'd witnessed the sweaty nightmares, the trauma of the attack, feasted on his anxiety. Driving to Constable's Heath, he'd used Crane's computerised words to spur him on. He says them again, now, knowing he'll ignore them.

"Let it go."

Nick rubs his eyebrow, the scab itches. He returns to his seat at the bar, a pint of lemonade with ice and a slice waiting for him.

The barmaid skips over. "Two pounds, please."

Digging in his wallet, Nick says, "Quite a lot of history in the village."

"I'm not sure myself, I don't live here." She takes the two quid. "But the photos on the wall might be able to tell you a bit."

"I've seen 'em. They're good." Nick takes a slug of lemonade, giving his throat pins and needles.

"Cool. Well, I won't be any help to ya with more'n that, but the museum's open every day 'cept Mondays. You stopping or passing through?"

"Just passing." He gives her a smile.

"Just as well." She opens up the cash register, drops the coins in. The tray dings when she closes it. "Constable's Heath doesn't have anywhere to stop over. Used to be a B & B a couple of years ago."

"Thought you said you didn't know the history?" Nick jokes.

The barmaid laughs. "Two years isn't history."

Taking his chances, Nick asks, "Anyone here called Crane?"

"Not to my knowledge. I've worked here about three years and I know the villagers pretty well." She crosses her arms and leans back, bored.

"Okay," Nick sighs. "No worries. Just wondered."

"Lemme know if there's anything else I can get you. Lunch starts in half an hour, but you can order early if you like. S'not like we're rammed or anything."

Off she goes, finding something else to whittle away the oh-so-slow hours.

Taking a second gulp of lemonade, Nick sees, in his peripheral vision, he has a companion sitting at the end of the bar. It doesn't have a drink, nor is it interested in one.

"Wondered when you'd show up again," Nick says to it.

The Figure sits on a stool of its own making. It should scare him more, knowing it can breach the rules of reality to attack him, but it doesn't. This feels more like it used to, back in the good old days when it would randomly show up to remind Nick of what he'd done. It doesn't have Simon Schaeffer around to act as a power booster. Around it, the air is distorted in the same way black holes warp light.

In a way, the Figure being here is a comfort.

No one else sees it. The exclusivity of it to Nick is confirmed when the barmaid stops where it sits. She looks straight through it, shivers. Uneased, she moves away, puffing out her cheeks as she thinks of something else to do, all the other things she could be doing with her life.

Tough it out, kid.

"Buy you a drink?" Nick asks it.

Asks *him*.

"Callum?"

The Figure twitches, understanding its own name yet unable to speak it. The spirit of the young boxer has been defiled by Nick's unrelenting guilt, and for that he carries a second burden. Not allowing someone's soul to rest in peace.

He continues speaking to it.

"Don't s'pose you drink. You're here alone, I take it? Haven't got that annoying little prick with you? You're not much more than this without him, are you? We've got our own shit to sort out, and I'd rather do it without him around. Right now, you can stare all you like, because I'm telling you now, I ain't in the fuckin' mood."

For more than a minute, the Figure enchants itself on Nick, living off the guilt it's been made from, connected by a chain forged in the fires of a mistake.

"I'll ask again," says Nick. "Buy you a drink, Callum?"

"Excuse me?" says the barmaid, one drawn-on eyebrow raised.

Nick smiles at her. "Sorry. Talking to myself. Been a long week."

She smiles back, rolls her eyes in sympathy. This girl knows what it's like to have long weeks.

An old man dodders over, leaving his table open for the vultures. Wearing what Nick considers typical country attire (tweed, flat cap, welly boots), his back has him curved into a comma. In his right hand is a pint and in his left is the hoop of a fraying dog lead. The dog follows behind, taking measured steps so as not to overtake its master.

The old man, a codger of the finest degree, takes a seat where the Figure had been, is for a moment annoyed by the icy temperature of the upholstery. He turns his neck enough to give a tight-lipped nod.

Condemned by his wrinkles, the codger scoots over, almost gliding, until only a single stool stands between them. The dog, a black Labrador, wiggles by his master's side, a bib of grey fur rises up its neck into a wizened beard on its muzzle. Once the codger stops his scooting, so does his companion, sighing after the exertion.

Lifting his ale, though not drinking from it, the codger says, "Name o' Crane ha'nt much bin said round 'ere forra while." The *i* in *while* is drawn out.

"You know it?" asks Nick, hooked in. The old'n had been listening in, it seems.

Driving here, speeding through red lights and breaking about a million other bullet points in the highway code, the urgency had been a burning stove, yet upon arrival, the urgency – or the desperation that Crane seemed to get so hard on when they'd first talked – had evaporated. Not only is there an energy in Constable's Heath that tames any form of urgency, it's also because he doesn't know where he's going, and you can't be urgent if you have nowhere to go. Urgent people get hysterical if that urgency is left unvalidated. Hysterical people get other people – a teenager perhaps – killed. Causing death by hysteria is on par with death by way of shitty life choices.

Now, however, the urgency tingles his gut.

"I know it, can't say I thought anyone else did." Again the last *i* is abused.

"Wish I didn't."

"Y'don't wanna be wishin' anythin' with name o' Crane tacked onto it. Tend t'go wobbly they do."

"Don't I know it," says Nick. "You, uh, have experience?"

As if reminiscing a war story, the codger answers, "Back in the old days, when things weren't s'bad, like."

"So bad with what?"

"Young'n Crane, o' course. Knew 'im an' his brother when I was a lad, the father, too. Mother kep' to herself." The codger's accent isn't regional to the Heath, might be from the east, or somewhere close to it. Knowing the Cranes when he was a lad means the codger's been here nearly all his life, yet not a shred of his accent, which is as broad as his wiry shoulders, has been lost.

A dark band of shade under his flat cap, the codger takes a pull from his pint. Dark dregs spill from corpse-like lips which sink back into his face. The wet doesn't moisten those purple strips.

Spinning the lemonade on the bar between thumb and forefinger, Nick asks, "They still around?"

Tapping his chest, he says no in the most unique way Nick has ever heard.

"Nop."

Nick sighs. Thinking of the family home Phillip mentioned, he asks, "Is there a family estate in Constable's Heath?"

"A mouthful, that," says the codger. "Call it the Heath, like the resta us."

"Is there?"

"What you" – *yoo* – "wanna go creepin' 'round the Heath's hist'ry fuh?"

"Personal interest," is Nick's answer.

Raising his eyebrows, perplexed by anyone's personal interest in village matters, the codger replies, "Not mucha be int'rested in. Yud need t'be a architeck up at their ol' patcha land, now."

"So there's a place? Like a house?"

The codger raises a finger to the barmaid. She reaches down, comes back up with a metal bowl with the word DOG scribbled on it. Dropping it at the Labrador's front paws, the codger empties his ale into the bowl. The dog guzzles at the alcohol, spilling it over the edges. Laughing, the codger gives his greying friend a pat on the head.

Nick taps the bar. "Hey."

"I'nt there n'more. Han't bin for years," explains the codger.

Shit. When Phillip alluded to the family home's non-existence with cryptic delight, Nick had been optimistic that the older brother still had some of the curse's madness on the tip of his tongue.

It could be this ale-wasting old boy is also as cooky as a bag of frogs, heard a name from bygone years and started running his flaccid gums. His experience with Crane could've left him as wacked out as Crazy Phil. If Ulysses has done it once, who's to say he hasn't done it before or after. That, and the old boy looks like he should've dropped dead just lifting his pint. It crosses Nick's mind that, quite possibly, this man might be living a never-ending life.

Or…the codger might know – as most old folk who live within their borders do – exactly what he's on about. They're like cobwebbed community boards with all the old guff still pinned on.

Watching the silver-faced clock behind the bar, Nick persists. "Where'd it used to be?"

The Crane estate, there or otherwise, is the tap that Crane poured from.

Facing Nick, the codger grins, tobacco-stained teeth like oak blocks. His right shoulder dips lower than the left, as if the weight of a hunched crow sits there, cawing directions into his dangly ears. "Worth much to yer?"

Wherever the wind blows you, or wherever cultists bring you, there will always be someone who wants something from you.

"See you're short a pint," Nick observes. "Refill?"

Pretending to be pleasantly surprised, the codger nods. "Thankee kindly, suh."

Nick orders an ale, the darkest the Stoat serves.

"You in the habit of holding information to ransom?" Nick asks after the ale has been sipped at.

"Information dunt come free, m'lad."

Crane would agree with that logic.

At its master's feet, sniffing the possibility of more ale, the Labrador licks its chops.

"Tell me how to find the Crane estate," says Nick.

Lips loosened with more drink, the codger answers, "'Bout a half mile to the north o' the Heath."

"But there's nothing there?"

"Never said there was *nothin'* there. Just not a house n'more. There's a residue a'right, somethin' in the dirt. Only way t'get there's by foot. Follow where the ol' bridge takes you into the woods an' keep" – *kep* – "on a-goin'."

"Reckon I could've found that myself," says Nick, preparing to get up.

"But you didn't. You came to wet y'whistle first." The codger taps his glass on Nick's lemonade. "With that girly drink."

Better than your tar, Nick thinks. His stool squeals on tiles as he pushes it out. He heads for the door. As Nick gives his thanks, the codger, in his tweed blazer, stops him, turning on his stool quicker than his bottom half can move.

"Not wise t'be muckin' 'round up there. You be careful. Strange stuff happen' at the ol' Crane estate."

"I'm counting on it," Nick says, opening the door. The light outside is pale.

The codger continues to warn. "Not long 'go some outta towner come muckin' up at that place, some arrogant sod she was, treatin' us all an' the Heath like some sorta pagan freak village. Always had a camera on she did, shinin' light in our eyes. Ha'nt bin sin since."

"Long ago?"

Turning back to the bar, the codger mumbles, "Couple month back."

Nick tries his luck, very aware that the wall clock is eating away what may be precious seconds. "Has an out-of-town girl passed through in the last week?"

Shaking his head, feeding his dog the pint, the codger answers, "No girl t'my knowledge. People don't pass through 'ere." This time, *pass* has the honour of being stretched.

The message, whether delivered with malevolence or not, gets through. The old codger isn't expecting to see him again, another interloper pig-ignorant of wild superstitions. Then again, when village superstitions are born from the likes of the family Crane, perhaps they qualified as real threats. Guess the old boy thought a pint bought for him by a dead man would carry some novelty.

Nick walks back in, stoops to give the Labrador a rub between its ears. "See ya later," he says to the codger.

As Nick exits, the barmaid does her duty and bids him farewell with a hope-to-see-you-again-soon thrown in even after the lack of a tip.

When the door closes behind Nick and the bell has jangled its last, the codger, who would have introduced himself as Sam if Nick had asked, smiles down at his dog.

"You're the best wish I ever made," he says.

With the content squeak of a newborn baby, the dog gazes up at its master, a simple wish thankful for a simple life.

§

The bridge resembles a fairy tale metaphor of foreboding, a rotting structure built from mismatched planks and rope. Nettles grow through the cracks, reach over the edges, stinging from existence any blooming flower.

Across the bridge, over a dry stream, the woods are dense, wearing a canopy congealed enough to block out the day's silver light. A disused path with flattened long grass is slowly reclaiming itself, though for now acts as a good enough trail for Nick to follow. Just keep on a-goin' the codger said. Nick wastes no time, the reality sinking in that if the trip to Constable's Heath leads nowhere, Katy won't stand a chance.

Dew wets the bottoms of Nick's jeans as he brushes through the grass, not quite seeping through to his socks. Kicking through a knot of brambles, he steps into a small clearing the local kids have anointed as their bin. Drinks cans and food wrappers half buried in the dirt have lost their colour. Fag ends seed the soil, an anti-compost. Sticking out against a downed log smoothed by weather and arses is a brand new (ish) backpack, only a frosting of dried muck at its bottom where boots have kicked up mud.

A twig snaps.

Nick whips around, his knees bending as his legs prepare themselves for violence. Fists balled, he has to relax his jitters, though is glad to know his muscles have woken up even if he's struggling to shake the lethargy of the Heath. Surveying the woods, he sees only vertical strips of different barks. The trees make a tight wall.

An appearance from the owner unlikely, he unzips the backpack, finds an array of...

Shit.

Just shit.

Nothing he can use.

A video camera comes out first, the cracked screen unfolded. The battery seems to be missing as well. Placing the camera on the trodden dirt, the next item to emerge is a torch that doesn't work. A Zippo lighter is also present, as well as another electronic device that might be a voice recorder. There's a can of beer with three empty plastic rings still attached, and a variety of snacks. Goofiest by far is a palm-sized manual that claims to the be the Ultimate Guide To Paranormal, Supernatural, Preternatural And Other Unexplained Phenomena.

Wait. Hold on.

That's the *second* goofiest thing. First place ribbon goes to the rubber-banded stack of business cards that've had too much money invested in them.

Paranormal Investigations Co. Ready to prove or disprove any of your paranormal problems. And hey, you can also check out and subscribe to the Youtube channel – HauntsWivHanna – and sign up for the monthly newsletter. All enquiries taken seriously, it hastens to add in the small print.

Nick drops the cards back in the bag along with the video camera and torch. Flipping through the manual without actually looking, he tosses that back in the pack, too. The Zippo stays, and the voice recorder, which he switches on.

Piercing static screeches, forcing Nick to cover his ears. It doesn't sound like it's coming from the device but from all around him, as if the woods are screaming, similar to the screeching computer that tried to eat him at the Hemingway Library. The voice recorder hits the floor, shutting itself off.

Reluctantly taking his hands away from his aching head, glaring at the device, Nick taps it with his boot, recoiling in anticipation of another sensory assault. Wary, he picks it up, fingers hovering over the buttons.

Another twig snaps, and this time when Nick's muscles jerk him up, he sees them.

All of them.

The Murdered.

They surround him, emerging from thin air, closing in. They zombie-sway, a million whispers united in agony. Where the moist woodland ground meets the spoiled campsite, the figures stop in a cold circle, sealing Nick inside. Still they moan, still they sway. Their eyes are a constellation of stars, none of them burning with life.

The voice erects the hairs on the nape of Nick's neck.

"You should've taken the cash."

CHAPTER 32

That'll put the shits up him.

Through the trees, Simon Schaeffer watches his dark servants close in on Nicholas. It's delicious, seeing the lamb surrounded by the wolves. A drip of saliva warms his chin.

The moist smells of woodland invade his senses. So contaminated by his own hellbent excitations is he, he swears he can hear slugs slime their way around, and roots eat the earth beneath.

Simon can hardly wait to make the man suffer for what he did to Dani. Nicholas had tried palming the blame off onto Master, spewing some shit about suicide. But the Master wouldn't do something like that, and suicide just wasn't Dani. Beautiful people don't take their own lives. If it'd been suicide, then why was their no weapon? The murderer had taken his tools with him when he ran, that's why.

Nicholas thinks he's stupid, thinks he can be manipulated so easily. Most people share the sentiment. In school, Simon may've had his head shoved in a toilet more than in a book, but he had different smarts. An intelligence that you couldn't develop. One you were born with. If it wasn't for Master Crane's orders to not hurt Nicholas (too badly) in that dump of a gym, Simon would've had him torn to pieces, slowly, sensually. Plucked tendons like fingers on a cliff edge. Then the task had been to deliver the letter, nothing more. Now, the orders were more open to interpretation.

After the Black Rose and the gangster had snuffed out his pleasure, Simon went to the Master. On his way, he'd noticed that a number of the corridors had changed places, like bad memories correcting themselves. A couple had shifted in a way where they should have glitched together. All roads went to where they should, though. Rome or otherwise.

Master Crane had been waiting for Simon in the library, a room which had undergone more treatment than the rest of the manor. It looked like the ribbon had been cut only hours ago, the spines of all the books close to sparkling in the light of the grand chandelier that hung from the ceiling. A spiral staircase swirled around the fixture, taking whoever climbed to greater heights of books that never seemed to end. Master has always treated books with a unique kindness, if the book is *worth* it.

The Master had had his bare back to Simon, reading from the book that turned the air around it into caustic fumes. The light dimmed around him too, as if it also found the book repugnant.

On the Master's back – skin paper thin against his spine – were many open slices, opening and closing in silent, bloody conversation. Simon wondered how he might attain such a level of ecstasy, to experience what the Master felt at that moment. It would most likely come with Simon's ascension, when he took the rank over the dead promised him by Master Crane. Such a generous man.

Foreign words, decorative, came from the Master's mouth. Words like that are not meant for Simon. Hearing them was wonderful enough.

Covering a sticky patch on the crotch of his trousers, Simon spoke. "Master?"

With the sound of tiny smacking lips the wounds sealed, scared into hibernation like clams on the seabed. Master Crane ended his recital, carefully pulled his white shirt back over his shoulders. Leftover blood blossomed in the cotton. The Master's voice was velvet tobacco. "Thank you for coming, Mr Schaeffer."

Gulping, Simon asked, "What were you doing?"

He expected reprimand, though the question had ached too much to hold it.

Facing Simon, adopting that gentleman smile that he so often had, Master Crane answered, "Letting it suckle."

Youth shivered along the Master's arm, through his hair, rippling the fibres as if wind through a wheatfield. His stomach tightened, too, before the muscles released again. Often the Master took rapid jaunts through his ages, though that had been the first time Simon had seen it up close. He also saw the book softly close itself. The chandelier trembled, a chime in which none of the glass notes had been musical.

There'd been no time for Simon to bow and ask what was wanted from him before Master delivered everything in two short sentences.

"He's arrived. Bring him in."

"Bring him in," Simon whispers to himself amongst the trees, caressing the sharp bark a little too hard.

An order like that can be pulled apart and read in so many ways. Master Crane himself enjoys dissecting words and phrases. All Simon is doing is claiming inspiration.

You can pin any number of words to the end of that phrase.

Bring him in *dead*; bring him in *alive* (*lame*); bring him in *screaming*; bring him in *choking*; bring him in *bleeding*; bring him in *dismembered*; bring him in *gutted*.

A rhyme comes to mind so sweet that Simon has to chuckle:

Bring him in raw,
Bring him in scalped,
Bring him in with his eyes poked out!

With so many flavours, *bring him in* is the Ben and Jerry's of execution orders!

Bring Him In Ice-Screaming!

Nicholas looks confused as he spins around, searching for gaps to escape through, wondering where Simon's voice came from. The spirits leave no means of exit, the closer they get, the tighter the circle becomes. It's only a matter of time, which Simon is deliberately stretching out, before they're upon him.

Knowing Nicholas was so close is yet more testament to Master Crane's abilities. Anything that has a pulse, the Master is able to see through, be they two, four, a *thousand* eyes, and when the book gives him total servitude, so shall he stick ears and mouths on those things. The Master shall be everywhere.

A centipede distracts Simon. It crawls up his thigh, rears its two-pronged head. Is Master seeing him through the insect? Making sure he's doing what he's supposed to? His thumb hovers over the creature, thoughts of crushing it pass. Taking his thumb away, Simon raises his hand. It's time to give the spirits the final command. This bunch are a demented lot, handpicked from the dungeons of the dead.

The flavour of the day shall be…

Bring Him In Skinned.

Behind Simon is a wall of deadfall. A bulky, dense structure, it sits nestled between two great fern trees that once came with greenery and a scent, now they're just posts to hold up the dam. The branches within the tangle almost create a malevolent face, keeping watch over its patch of woodland. Over the top climbs a gorilla form, muscular, tall and wide enough to be a bigfoot. It speaks clearly to Simon with an accent that grates on him immediately.

"What are you doing?"

This breed of Murdered, far more physically grotesque than the others, are relentless. Their shoulders melt together. They bring with them an unnatural cold that freezes Nick's breathe. Hyperventilation squeezes his throat, adrenaline pumps his lungs faster than he can keep up with. Regulating his breathing is impossible. How do you fight something you can't punch? For once, his fists are useless.

They're here because of Simon. These things follow him like a bad smell.

Around the car they'd been a part of the mist, here they sport beards of moss, limbs are creaking branches, wooden faces twist and bleed. Nick kicks up mud, throws rocks, tells them to stay back. None of them listen,

353

they only lurch closer, groaning.

Forcing himself to catch his breath, Nick notices their legs rooting into the ground, turning loose soil that churns up worms rotting with ghoulish decay. One by one, they snap away from their sinking feet. Sporous breath geysers from unseen mouths whilst they take their last urgent steps towards him, then they are inanimate, a circle of scarecrows. One, Nick sees, has leaves stuffed into its mouth. No longer whispering, the ghouls have given themselves to the forest.

Spinning on his heels, he checks there are no stubborn Murdered pushing on. His thighs are weak, vision rattles with each sharp beat of his heart. He hears a voice again, not Simon. Two of them, now. Agitated. On stiff knees, Nick bends down to pick up the voice recorder, then pokes at one of the scarecrows. It's solid, but can, with some effort, be pulled apart.

If ever there was a man to hate, Apollo is that man. Simon glowers at the giant ape as he descends the deadfall, feet never missing their mark in spite of the hazardous fungi that boobytrap the timber. A shame, it'd be funny to witness the giant slip on his anaconda-sized spine.

Simon glances at Nicholas.

The spirits are beginning to lose momentum without constant direction. Some are bound by stricter rules than others. It's these most deplorable spectres that must be kindled into life by the energy around them, causing them to appear in unique ways depending on the location. It's a punishment that they cannot roam or pass over as the others can. Even the afterlife comes with judges, juries. And executioners.

Damn Apollo and the fucking distraction that he is, and damn the noise he makes as he jumps onto a cushion of leaves.

"I asked what you're doing," Apollo says.

Simon flaps a hand to shush the giant. "The Master's bidding."

"You're the only idiot who calls him Master." Apollo's shins part the leaves like an ocean liner through waves. "This is not what Mr Crane asked of you."

"What do *you* know of it?"

"Your orders are to bring him in," says the ape man.

Still crouched at his vantage point, Simon looks up at Apollo. The giant has never said this many words in all the time they've known each other, though the term *known* is a stretch. Wiping the saliva from his chin, Simon replies, "That's what I'm doing. You're slowing me down!"

"Alive."

"Alive was never part of the arrangement."

"I'm making sure you're doing as you're told. Evidently I was right to do so." Crossing his arms, Apollo's width inflates by at least thirty inches.

"You shouldn't have followed me."

"I do as I wish. There are trust issues."

"Trust issues?" Simon steps away from his hiding spot. "Then why didn't Master Crane ask you to do it? Or anyone else? I think…" He glances away. "I think you're jealous."

Did Master really not trust him? The thought is…hurtful. He doesn't believe it. Though he can't pretend Master Crane hadn't given him those looks from time to time. Those looks of contempt. Simon had wanted people to notice him as they never had before, to feel sickened at the sight of him. Kind of like a walking rendition of the Master's book. A tribute, now that he thinks on it. But the *Master*, sickened by his most loyal, doting servant? It's so stupid it has to be a lie.

Apollo smirks. "Jealousy is for the miserable. I have other duties to attend to."

"Then sod off." Simon bares his teeth. "I need to concentrate or- "

"The trust issues aren't Mr Crane's."

Apollo's right fist becomes a sledgehammer across Simon's jaw. A flash of white punctuates the fracturing of bone. Staples come loose, spilling watery red ooze. His head bounces off bark before he lands face down in the dirt, a gash above his eye plugged by soil. Already he can feel his jawline doubling in size.

Straddling over Simon, Apollo growls, "I've had enough of you. You're a thorn in many sides, and I mean to take out the prick."

Turning over, forest detritus sticking to his face, wedged in his nostrils, Simon replies with wide eyes. "You've come to kill me?"

"Maybe you aren't as stupid as you look."

Shoving away with his feet, Simon tells Apollo with a stutter, "Y-you'd better not f-f-fuck with me. You h-have ghosts, too."

One swoop of his arm and Apollo has Simon dangling in the air by the throat.

"I'm the wrong man to threaten with your ghosts," Apollo snarls. "I don't fear them. They can't do a thing to me."

Simon tries to respond. The grip on his throat is too much. His windpipe is being crushed. Any second now his eyes are going to pop from their sockets. He's slammed against the tree he was spying on Nicholas from, its base drifted by mulch.

"My ghosts don't rule me," Apollo adds. "I have no guilt, no shame. Know what your problem is, Schaeffer? You think everything's a toy. Something to play with. You could have grabbed the bastard over there and brought him in, but you had to make him a plaything. There's too many of your type involved already, one less since that crazy bitch put a hole in her head. Wish I pulled the trigger myself."

Dani's memory, insulted by the giant ape, infuriates Simon. He flails, foaming at the mouth, no longer caring if Nicholas hears them. If he's as clever as the Master says, he'll be gone already. Simon quits thrashing when his left eye is pressed by Apollo's thumb.

"I can make this quick." He applies pressure. "Or slow."

"I'll- "

"You'll what? Mr Crane sees value in your type, he says wishes are for everyone. He's wrong. Wishing *isn't* for everyone. Dignity, discipline, restraint, appreciation. You are a poor man when it comes to these things.

Your contributions have been minimal. You have the honour of being the first in the purge. But don't worry, I'll make this look like an accident. Better yet, I'll say he," Apollo nods to where Nicholas is, or was, "got the better of you. You're pathetic, no one will question it."

"I'll…tell…Master."

Pressing his forehead against Simon's, the ape responds with a grin. "You just did."

Closing his eyes, Simon accepts death. There's actually something exciting about it, tingly, a certain…that thing the French say. He thought his departure from this plain would be more romantic than this, but ho hum. Life has already given him bags of lemons, why not one more? Very soon, nothing Apollo has said will matter.

Death comes with a crunch. There's no pain, only a vibration. Then a fall. Simon always knew death would be a fall. Though…not this short. He hits a solid surface, crumpling as if he were a ragdoll.

Before he can open his eyes, there is a second death-crunch that catches him right across the forehead.

He feels this one.

CHAPTER 33

Nick didn't think he'd ever be trying to wake up Simon Schaeffer, but here he is. The prick's been out a while, now.

A slap does the trick. A second is administered for the trouble. Simon startles, as if he's had a bucket of water dumped on him. Nick whips away the blindfold, leaves the mouth gag in. The prick's eyes blaze. Realising he's tied to a tree, his arse in damp topsoil, Simon attempts to wiggle himself free. It's useless, of course. Nick has bound his wrists tight enough to not only chafe but to tighten when struggled against.

He doesn't stop, mumbles angrily through the gag. Nick slaps him again, this time upside the head.

Now that Nick has his attention, he says, "If I see any sign of your ghosts, I'll put you to sleep."

Simon is listening. His breathing is fast, wheezing as it filters through the gag.

"You've seen better days I imagine," Nick goes on. "Can't say I'm sorry about the bump on the head, though."

The bump is a golf-ball-sized molehill on Simon's forehead. Nick isn't responsible for the rest of Simon's face, a mud-sodden bloody mess. Where staples have fallen out looks like the lining of a mask.

And he smells.

Jesus he smells.

"I'm gonna remove the gag now, and you're gonna be a good lad. Don't test me today."

Simon spits out the gag as Nick pulls it off, stretches out his mouth, licks his lips.

"Where's Apollo?" he asks.

"Sleeping," says Nick.

"Dead?"

"I'm not a killer."

"Liar!"

A slap calms the prick down, chases away that chihuahua rage.

Nick calmly says, "I'll get right to it. You're gonna take me to Crane's house."

Simon replies, "Yeah? Why'd I do that?"

"You were going to take me, anyway."

"Uncomfortably. You're still alive."

"That Apollo." Nick rubs his chin. "He's a mean sort. I've seen plenty of 'em. Psychos. If you won't take me to Crane, I take you back to Apollo. Hogtie you. How d'you think he's gonna react when he wakes up to find you, the man he wants dead, wrapped up like a Christmas present?"

"You said you weren't a killer," says Simon, eyebrows knitting together.

"And you think I'm lying. Besides, it wouldn't be me doing the killing," Nick answers, flicking at the soil with a twig.

A fear sweeps over Simon's face that he tries to hide. Whenever he fought, Nick would know the sure things simply by looking at the opponents face. In a fight, you quickly learn how to read an opponent.

Simon pulls against his bonds. "I thought he was- "

"Dead? I said he was sleeping. I meant it. I'm not a killer. I didn't kill your girlfriend either, no matter how much you want to believe it."

Simon looks away. "Dani...wasn't my..."

Fucking Christ, is this prick about to *confide* in Nick?

"I don't care," Nick stands, snapping the twig in his hand. "You have your choices."

Simon gulps, puts on a bravado that's halfway impressive. His sweat gives him away. "You can't threaten me. Pain is a wank to me. Death means nothing, I'm not scared of it. Before you intervened I'd already accepted it. Death is my language, I thrive where death lingers. Death is my life."

"You're theatrical, aren't you?" Nick sighs. "You can take pain, I believe that, a person only has to look at your face to see it."

"I ever thank you for it?" Simon tilts his face, the remaining staples shimmer. "You won't kill, but you'll slice a man's face open."

"A man who has no qualms killing an innocent girl. Yeah," Nick replies.

"Hypocrite."

"You need to look up the definition of the word. You can handle pain, but can you handle Apollo? He'll give you pain and more. He's as sadistic as you. Leaving you to him, you might think the destination is your heaven, but he'll make sure the journey is hell. And it's a long road to heaven."

Simon looks down, eyes darting left and right. He doesn't want Apollo's wrath any more than Nick wants to subject him to it. The prick smiles as if he's hit the jackpot.

"You won't leave me. You *need* me. Without me you'll be lost!"

Nick paces slowly. "I think you care more about what the big fuck'll do to you more than I care about finding another way. I've tried to do this the nice way, Simon, but you're not leaving me much choice here." Here's hoping Simon falls for the bluff, because if he can't get him to the house, Nick really hasn't got any other ideas. Checking the time on his bare wrist, Nick tuts. "He'll be out for another couple. I can take you now, let the insects have a go at you for a bit before he wakes?"

Taking a while to unmuddle his brain, Simon replies, "I think I...see your way of thinking."

"I thought you might," says Nick. *Thank fuck for that.*

Behind the tree, Nick loosens Simon's bonds. The prick rubs his wrists, garnering some pleasure from it. He asks, "What's in it for you?"

"You'll take me to him," explains Nick, coming back around the tree, "and I'll propose a trade. You try to run, I'll knock out your teeth."

"A trade?"

"I heard everything Apollo said to you." Nick holds up the voice recorder, shakes it. "And so did this."

Seeing the silver device, Simon says, "So?"

Rolling his eyes, Nick says, "Crane values information above most things. This is damning evidence against one of his most trusted followers." He pockets the recorder.

The cogs are getting to work in Simon's head, unused gears that twist his face as he thinks. "Trade what?"

"The evidence for the girl."

Simon barks a laugh. "He'll never trade *that*, not even for the name of a traitor."

"*Her*."

Simon smiles, continues to rub his wrists. "She is the offering. There is nothing of more value to the Master, to *us*."

"He'll want to know who's plotting to take him out. I won't give it otherwise."

"He'll kill you and take it." Simon grins, digging his nails into his wrists.

"I'll destroy it before he has a chance." – *I hope* – "I'll be dead, but he'll be constantly paranoid. And if he has things his way, it'll be forever."

"The Master has no fear for his life," Simon argues. "When the offering is complete, any and all usurpers shall be vanquished. Apollo is of little consequence to the Master. Your information is redundant."

Nick waves him off. The smelly prick is grating on his remaining nerves.

Bringing his stench with him, Simon takes a step towards Nick. Defiantly, he says, "The Master will never give up his chance of ascendance. You won't stop him."

"I'm not trying to stop him, I only want the girl. If he's as wise as you believe, he'll find another offering. You'll be there to snatch one up."

"I'll tell the Master myself!" Simon blurts, pointing.

Nick delivers another slap, harder this time. "You'll tell Apollo first."

Simon backs away, clutching his face. If he should try anything to get away, or attempt to attack Nick, his efforts would be swiftly undone. Nick is the stronger, quicker man, and the prick knows it.

Nick says, "You bleat about your devotion to Crane, yet all it takes is the threat of one man to turn your coat."

"Call him *Master*," says Simon, diverting from the comment.

"I never will, so turn it in," Nick growls.

"I'm no turncoat," Simon sticks out his chin. "I've just decided this is best for Master. He'll understand, he always does. I'm still doing my job, I'm still bringing you back, so...I'm not losing."

"Yeah, okay. You're not losing, and I'm sure you've just decided you're doing what's best. All I want is Katy."

Frowning, Simon asks, "Who's Katy?"

The arsehole doesn't even know her name. Nick clenches his jaw, squeezes out, "The offering."

"Oh." Simon blinks. He sucks at his wrist, speech becomes muffled. "And Apollo? What'll happen to him?"

Nick shrugs. "He'll wake up and head back I s'pose. You do your job right, Crane'll know by then, and I'll be gone."

"Then that ape will get his." Simon swallows a mouthful of blood.

"Sure," Nick says, honest to God not giving a shit. "As long as I get the girl."

"I still doubt the Master will give her up this close to the ceremony."

"Just show me the way."

Simon tells Nick, "It's not as easy as simply *going* there."

Nick huffs. Groaning, he asks, "Meaning what?"

"It's not...really...there." Simon lets a bug crawl over his fingertips.

"Then where is it?"

Pointing a finger at his head, Simon squashes the bug.

"The mind?" Nick says with contempt. "So it's made up?"

Simon shakes his head. "It's there, but...only if the Master wants you to see it."

"How do I get in?"

"You have to be invited."

"Oh," says Nick. "Then I accept your invitation."

§

Back in the horrible grey tunic again, itchier than the first, tighter around the neck. Worse, when Katy scratches, it only makes things itch more. It's been an hour since she'd woken up surrounded by darkness, candles, and an overstuffed duvet that wanted to swallow her whole.

Katy had called out, no one answered. She searched for Pop Tart from the bed, calling his name, ps-psing at the dark corners. He didn't come, yet even now she believes he's in the room with her. She keeps seeing winks of yellow where the candlelight doesn't reach, a shadow darting this way and that. It's Solomon who's here, then. Not Pop Tart. It's okay, he'll come when he's ready.

When he's told, Gut speaks up.

Funny that Gut and Survival hadn't had voices until recently, funnier still that it feels like they've always been here. Katy knows their voices, how they think and what they're going to say. She just needs them to say it for her.

Funny, but not in the funny way.

Mingled with the aroma of burning wick is cooking food, creeping under the door. Chicken. Beef…or lamb. Sniffs of the banquet being prepared make Katy's mouth water. It's nearly enough to make her forget what she'd read in that book.

Nearly.

How long has it been since she's eaten?

How long has it *been*? Like…in general?

Could be Friday. Saturday? She thinks it's Saturday, can't be sure.

Wrestling over the duvet cover, she jumps off the bed, bringing feathers with her.

Picking up a thick candle, she explores the room, happy to distract her hunger that grows grumpier by the second. The melting wax runs over and glues her hand to the candle. It burns.

There isn't much to the room. In fact, this is the most plain so far. No paintings, no ornaments, no furniture bar the bed. No rugs or light fixtures. There's a coldness unlike any other, as if no love resides inside. If the walls could talk-

"This was my brother's bedroom."

They *do*!

Katy freezes, as does the flame on her candle. The voice came from all around her, in every pocket of this room's solitude. Crane, he's still with her in some form. His voice has taken on the cracks and creaks of the house, his words shake the beams.

Katy, swallowing the rock in her throat, asks, "Where are you?"

"Everywhere. And…nowhere. Think of me as Schrodinger's voice." A laugh that sounds like wood being sawn rumbles the bedroom. "Do you know Schrodinger?"

The last thing Katy wants to do is talk with Crane, yet she finds herself answering anyway. "Science isn't really my thing."

"Nor is it mine. However, it will never hinder your mind to know such things, even subjects you take no interest in."

He's a good talker. A *great* talker. Words slip from his tongue on a velvet chute. A silver tongue, she thinks it's called, even though right at this moment that tongue is made from coiling wallpaper.

"I thought I was allowed around the house," she says, "to explore as I wanted."

The walls respond, "You can rummage in here for the time being. There is nothing to find, I hasten to add. Phillip, my brother, had it all, so I have taken it away. A person who had everything does not need it twice. Nothing to find, that is, except for perhaps an etching in the floorboards hither and thither. A few of my early attempts in the use of secretive magic. None of them worked. I was too inexperienced."

Out of interest, she peers at the floor. Sure enough, there are two letters carved into the wood. UC. To the side of which is a strange symbol.

Katy argues, "I was happy where I was, wearing my own clothes."

"But they were not yours, were they?"

"Sorry?"

"Those ill-fitting clothes. You had them, but they were not yours. Interesting is it not? The meaning of possession. Take those clothes for example. You possessed them, yet they were not *your* possessions."

Sitting on the edge of the bed, the duvet flumps out around Katy. "What're you talking about?"

Wax drips from the candle.

"Merely some back and forth on the subject of words. I am pitching, I want to see if you hit back."

She eventually says, "You can be possessive of something you don't possess."

"Yes!" Crane marvels, the house trembling. "Or vice versa, you can possess something you are not possessive of. Or you can *be* possessed."

"Like Pop Tart?"

There is a silence. Katy thinks Crane might've left the walls. Then he responds. "Pop Tart, as you call him, was never Pop Tart. He has always been Solomon. *That* cat is not possessed, nor has he ever been. He does not possess, is not possessive, he is simply Solomon."

Fur brushes on Katy's shins. When she looks down the culprit has already gone.

Crane goes on, "I must apologise for taking you from your leisure, though I applaud the more appropriate attire. Preparations are taking a little longer than last time. Things are grander, more extravagant. I want to show the book I am mournful." The house groans as his invisible smile distorts the wood.

There had been a whole three pages on how a ceremony, or ritual, must be put together in order to please whatever god, power, deity or symbol is being called to. At the end of those pages, crammed into a small chapter, was a section explaining the course to take to restart a ritual. A genuine apology to the chosen power.

"And you also know," Crane continues, "*other* things, yes?"

She knows what he's alluding to. Talking with him has only provided a short respite from the thoughts she'd shoved to back of her head. They come flooding back, screaming over each other.

"You know where your life resides," the walls whisper.

"I know." Katy swings her legs, toes scraping the floor. The shoes she's been put in are the same grey as the tunic.

"I am glad we understand one another." The walls – *he* – add, "Time is short, I shall tell you that right now."

Standing from the bed, spilling wax on her foot, Katy asks, "How much time do I have?"

Her breath tickles the flame. Again, she spies the shine of yellow eyes that vanish when she turns to them.

"Let us see," says Crane. Although he isn't here in person, Katy imagines him stroking his chin whilst he thinks. "You have about seven seconds."

"Before *what*?!" she cries to the ceiling, expecting cultists to come barging into the bedroom.

"Is it not obvious?" Crane's voice becomes soft. "Tea, of course."

Katy jumps as the door opens, letting in a line of orange light that divides the bed in two. She'd have dropped the candle if it wasn't stuck in her hand.

Fatty smells of various meats instantly invade the bedroom. For crying out loud, the *sprouts* smell good.

Opening the door wider, a plate is passed through by a hand with blood red nails. On it is a cairn of roast potatoes crisped to perfection, vegetables that glisten in hot honey and a cut of T-bone. Steam ribbons from it, flirting with the air. Hesitant at first, Katy gives in, drops to her knees in front of the food. It all looks light years better than what was shovelled to her in the cell.

The steak if well-done, but the joke's on the chef. Katy prefers it tough. Within seconds her teeth strike bone, where she gnaws off any remaining shreds. Poison isn't even an afterthought. She'd have risked it anyway, powerless after her stomach took over the controls.

Wiping her mouth of grease, Katy drops the sharp white bone on the plate. On her arm is the grease she wiped off her mouth, which she sucks at, savouring everything.

Crane is no longer here. Katy can tell because the room has stopped taking breaths.

"Good to see you have an appetite."

Katy shoots up, knocking over the piled potatoes. There, at the crack in the doorway, is the woman with the white face. It's still unnerving how much her face and voice contrast.

Summoning all the courage she can, Katy steps to the door so their faces are inches apart.

"I don't want to talk to you."

"I would still like to be your friend."

"Nice try," she says.

"None of this is to hurt you. You understand that don't you, Katy Robbins?"

"Then *why* the hurt? Why all this? The captivity?" Katy can't believe she's mustering this without Survival. Maybe she's brave all on her own.

"Regretfully" – the regret sounds authentic – "hurt is an unavoidable part in the proceedings. As for the captivity…" The woman, Katy thinks her name is Juniper or Jun*something*, ponders her answer for a few seconds, then replies, "Birds are kept captive, aren't they? You, Katy Robbins, are a bird, a beautiful one, meant to fly to the greatest of heights. You are special."

"Then let me fly!" Katy grabs the door. "If you want to be my friend, let me fly!"

"Unfortunately," Junsomething shakes her head, "some birds who are meant to fly, do not. We understand your impulse to fly away, my dear. You have achieved it once, nearly twice, but there shan't be a thrice. We must keep you in your cage to keep you from flying higher than we can. Do you understand?"

Katy stares at Junsomething for a while. "No," she says. "I think you're sugar-coating everything."

"You can think that. Without you and your wings, Katy Robbins, we cannot fly, either. My dear, is there anything I can get you?" After a quiet moment she adds, "Within reason."

She's full of it, trying to make something beautiful out of being in a murdering cult, trying to make herself feel better for walking who knows how many other children into that shower room. That, or she really believes she's on the right team.

Thinking of Nick and what he might do if he were in Katy's shoes, she channels him, surprising herself.

"Fuck off."

She slams the door, snuffing out the nearest candle on the floor. With her back on the door she listens to the woman stomp away, heart racing with triumph. Telling the old hag where to go had felt good. *Really* good.

Katy's attention is drawn to her meal. Inspecting her plate, she has an idea, inspiration that only asks she is able to hide something.

She takes from the plate what she needs, concealing it inside the front pocket of her horrid tunic. The only question is whether she uses it soon, or waits.

Reaching the end of its vow of silence, Survival finally offers advice. *Save it.*

From the shadows plods Solomon, winding around the candles. He hunches down at the plate to begin his dinner, purring.

CHAPTER 34

A cemetery has more life to it than the path Simon has taken Nick on. It's tight. Trampled grass is mush in the soil, permeates the stagnant smell of cuttings left too long in the mower. There *is* a residue, like the old codger said. It's the sap in the trees, the sweat of the earth.

He's sure the prick is having him on, stalling for time. When Simon opens a curtain of damp foliage and the path cones open, Nick unclenches the fist he'd made.

"We're here," Simon announces.

From the mud stand two brick pillars completely tangled with thin, brittle roots that spiral up like veins. Atop them are huge Atlas stones, the colouration darker on the upper hemispheres, giving them the appearance of black and grey Christmas puddings. Well, *one* of the stones. On the right pillar, whose masonry has taken the brunt of the wood's claim of ownership, the stone has rolled off, punched a hole in the soil. Rusted pins stick out of the brickwork where a great gate once would have been.

"Doesn't look like much," Nick observes.

"You're looking wrong."

A crunch under Nick's foot brings his leg up. A broken pair of glasses stuck in the mud, the left lens hanging on by the last of its glue, the right giving a clear close-up of dirt. Others have been here, and Nick gets a bad feeling from the glasses.

Simon walks through the middle of the pillars, stroking his fingers between the bricks. He turns back to Nick. "Coming?"

Nick approaches the pillars. Static energy latches on, tries to pull him through on a beam. There is more than residue here. Whatever it is, is still at work.

"Once you cross the border," Simon explains, "there'll be no going back, not unless he lets you. The Master will make this place your personal Hotel California."

Nick pauses at the threshold between here and wherever there is, gazes into the empty space beyond. "You can never leave," he mumbles the lyrics to himself.

"You like The Eagles?"

"No," answers Nick, narrowing his eyes.

He passes through, ignoring the light feeling in his gut. The two of them continue walking at a slow pace, the pillars feeling almost like stalkers behind Nick, too arrogant to consider hiding. Distended mushrooms sprout from the path. When Nick flattens them, they make the same sound snow does under your feet, puffing out the last of their rank spore.

"I'm not into The Pigeons either. They're a bit soft. It's the heavier stuff I dig. Anthrax, Testament, Annihilator. I also don't mind some hair metal if- "

"I don't care," Nick cuts him off.

"Okay," Simon sighs, apparently upset that the guy he believes offed his missus doesn't want to make idle chit-chat. Also, Nick remembers him wearing a U2 tee-shirt. That's not the heavy stuff, though plenty noisy for Nick. "I hope you know what you're doing."

"I do, and one more thing," Nick stops him. "When we met, you said it can be made worse or better."

Simon catches on. "I did."

Looking Simon in the eyes, Nick says, "Make it better."

Simon laughs. He glances back at the pillars, not fifteen metres behind them, then back at Nick. Nick looks, too, sees nothing except discoloured trees and thickets of dry brambles.

"Only you can do that now," Simon says.

When Simon continues walking, he vanishes into a smog that cannot be seen, as if he's strolled through the face of a mirror.

Caught between shock and awe, Nick doesn't budge, stares at the space that used to hold Simon. The prick's voice comes from nowhere.

"Just walk."

Nick does, right hand cocked back and balled into a fist, should Simon try anything funny. He stretches his left hand out. If the smog means to melt him, his hand will let him know.

There is a shift in…is it air density? It becomes stickier, wraps around him. The woods themselves haven't changed, only the air, and perhaps the colouration, just a little, as if everything has been washed out slightly. Cautiously, Nick moves forward. There's no sign of Simon when he completely passes through.

It's darker here. Night dark, as if hours have passed. Maybe they have, which is bad. The sun, however, can still be seen through cracks in the canopy, a white disc that plates the sky silver. Trees have faces, leaves whisper, the wind passes along secrets to be held in the mouths of toads. Maybe the woods *have* changed, too.

Soggy grass bubbles under every footfall. Nick is sure any second now he will start being sucked slowly down by a bottomless bog.

But there's no bog-trap, and eventually the woodland retreats from a stony path.

Where the fuck is Simon?

Nick sees him. A silhouette in a light mist a few feet ahead. Catching up to him, Nick shoves his shoulder.

"Don't run ahead. Do it again and I'll clip your ear."

Simon's voice has taken on the lilt of a man hypnotised. "Isn't it amazing?"

Nick peers into mist, noticing that the woodland has almost completely fallen back. They're in a clearing, the treeline on the other side near non-existent.

The house does not appear in the gloom but sails sluggishly from it, a ghost ship with many pointed spires that reach above the treetops.

Crane Manor, a small castle if it had turrets, is every comic book asylum mixed into one.

"Homely," Nick murmurs.

"It's magnificent," swoons Simon.

It's magnificent, alright.

The unorthodox, impossible architecture is a physics defying representative of its lunatic sculptor. Windows cover most surfaces, are the eyes of stain-glass demons trapped in wood, brick and mortar. Light shines from some, others are asleep. Some watch without interest and a few appear to be faking nonchalance, peeping when they think no one is looking. How windows can convey all this, Nick doesn't know, but he knows it all the same. In one of those windows is Katy.

"There'll be special guests tonight," says Simon.

"I can go in now?" Nick asks.

"Mm-hm. You've been invited. As I was saying, the Master hasn't pulled any punches tonight."

"Nor will I."

Nicks grabs Simon from behind, locking him in a sleeper hold that's served him well at the clubs. The prick struggles. It's tempting to squeeze tighter, though that'd break his scrawny neck. Before long Simon goes down. He'll be out for hours.

A dumping ground for Simon's body shows itself in the form of shrubs. Nick conceals him, aware that eyes other than the house's could be watching him. A stupid move, in hindsight, to take the prick down in the open. A lesson learned is experience gained.

Nick crouches to the manor, ducking under fingers of fog as if they'll physically grab him. When he reaches the building, he clings to the wall, keeping below the windows. There's no front entrance, or any entrance, Nick can see. Not a porch light in sight. He'll have to search for one, a gruelling thought seeing as he's already wasted enough time. Where Nick is, the gravel reaches right up to the manor, making every step sound as if he's crushing beetle shells.

Nick keeps to the wall, bricks rough on his palms, reasoning that he has to find a door eventually, or an open window. He begins checking them, relieved that up close they have lost their watchful menace.

Through each window is a different scene, each one as empty and lifeless as its predecessor. The rooms have the same décor, albeit with new and uninteresting layouts. Tables, lamps, candles, desks, bookcases, paintings, not to mention the layers of dust the host has failed to have cleaned. Tsk, tsk, Mr Crane. Then there are the rooms left to their own emptiness, consumed by the darkness that swells inside them, and yes, they do seem to swell...somehow. Into these dark rooms, Nick is unable to look for too long.

Around a corner that's a little too sharp and a little under ninety degrees, Nick spies what he thinks might be a utility door, illuminated by a skittish oil lamp. He goes to it, not bothering to move around the flowerbeds, trampling the weeds. He takes a look in both directions to make sure no one is watching, then, taking a brief pause he can ill afford, gawks up at the height of the building.

Crane Manor, he thinks, then echoes the words of the cursed, imprisoned brother.

"It doesn't exist."

Under the shop he'd only glimpsed the madness. So...what waits in here? What else will he see, and on what scale? It dawns on Nick that this is where it will all end, one way or another.

He tries the handle.

Unlocked.

The stomping size fifteen boot drains the puddle.

Twice now, he's allowed himself to be clobbered. The fact is fuel to Apollo's fury, hot blood thumping through his head as he charges through the woods. Still regaining consciousness when he'd taken off, his run had a drunken gait, but now he's a freight train, tearing down all growth in his path.

At least the second time had been with something more befitting than a kettle. The dismembered petrified arm of a Hell's Reject carries credentials. It was almost impressive, though if the shoes were swapped, Apollo would have used the Reject's limb to thrust through Nicholas's back and stir whatever was in his belly.

Finally, Apollo thinks as he counts with his breathing, *I have a nemesis.*

He hadn't been sure at first, opting to observe Nicholas for a while. But now he's certain. Nicholas is a sneaky one, as far as fighters go. He utilises his environment, thinks ahead of his actions. Most fighters are bulls and the world is their china shop. Not this one. Apollo will have to get Nicholas in a straight fight, just their mitts and teeth as weaponry. That might be a while as yet. For now, there is so much more to worry about. Still, there is a fullness in Apollo he didn't have before finding his nemesis.

Nemesis.

On his back, mosquitoes ride the rollercoaster to suckle. Blood from his head wound adheres his shirt to his skin. The mosquitoes itch, the head injury stings like a motherfucker.

Finally being able to finish off Simon Schaeffer had been so exciting, it had temporarily blinded Apollo to any interference, which had been the reason, and the *only* reason, Nicholas had been able to get in his cheap shot. For that, Apollo will taunt himself always. Even when he triumphs over his Nemesis, he'll be unable to give the mistake to the wind.

Concerning himself with personal failures can wait. He must get back before showtime. His partnership is tumultuous enough without adding further strain. Mr Crane will be none the wiser. Nicholas, wherever he is, might cause some shit, though not enough to fuck everything up, not at this juncture.

Tonight.

Tonight, things change.

Ahead of him, puddles tremble in anticipation of his feet.

CHAPTER 35

Nick flicks on the Zippo he found in the backpack. Spiderweb is singed, expands in a glowing halo. He takes stock of his new surroundings. Dust rushes up his nose.

If the outside had been a madman's dollhouse, the inside is an eccentric's senility.

He doesn't find himself in a utility room, although there are utilities lying around, including an ancient washboard rubbed to ruin. This room is storage for the unloved. Bad taxidermy of animals stuffed into unrecognisable creatures, all mottled hair and glazed glass eyes. A banjo with its drum split open is strung up on the wall, seemingly by the strength of cobwebs alone. Advertisements on tin signs are hidden by years of dust and moth silk. Boxes stacked upon boxes of car-boot tat, unplanted hanging vases, hose lines, ropes, a couple of bicycles leaning on each other for support, not to mention the acres of books ripe for burning. Flotsam from the Orphanage.

Nick, in a cocoon of Zippo light, wades through the junk, careful not to knock over stacks of rubbish. The ceiling is low, uneven, cracked. This is what the inside of a mummy must look like, and those things have stuffed animals around and inside them. Not bicycles though, and he doubts a mummy has ever been found practising its banjo skills.

He coughs. The existence of the house might be up for debate, but the shit in the air is real enough.

Something grabs his thigh, turning his body rigid.

Without looking Nick grabs it, locks his fingers, pulls it free from a mound of rags. A hand comes away unattached to an arm, dry, cold and bloodless.

It's also hairy. Small.

Nick brings it into his cocoon. A monkey paw, coarse to the touch, all five digits point skyward. Of course Crane would chuck this out, wishes aren't granted by monkey fingers.

Using that logic, how many stars lay burning beneath this scrapyard?

Setting the paw down, Nick continues. At the top of some stairs a door is ajar, letting in a stream of voices riding on faint music. When they fade, Nick climbs. The steps bend under his weight, though there is no noise, as if the sound effect has been forgotten. He peers out, sees a wide corridor, dilapidated and candlelit, both ways clear. Moving out, Nick heads left, snuffing out the Zippo flame with a metallic ping. That's where the music – classical – is coming from.

Taking his time (but not too much), Nick follows the notes that flutter, sometimes crazily, down and around the bends of this confusing house. If not for the music, he sees himself getting lost all too quickly. The corridors might once have been grand, but now they look ready for the wrecking ball, a job that Nick would joyously take if given half a chance. There's a lack of sentries, considering that Crane, by his own declaration, would know if Nick was coming. Maybe the old geezer invested too much of his faith in Simon, believing Nick to be already dealt with. The voices he'd heard in the Storage of the Unloved had been the only sign of guard detail. Whether there's two or two thousand doesn't matter, if Walter has brought his loyal grunts with him, they'll be armed.

How many of the Walter loyalists believe in Crane's cult, and how many were just following their boss's orders and the next pay packet?

It still doesn't feel right to call it a cult. Cults are dangerous, sure, but there's much more at play here than Kool-Aid and cyanide.

Entering a foyer, Nick glances back at the corridors. There's something about them that makes him uneasy, the same something that pulled his attention back one last time before letting him leave. He hopes to not re-enter that maze.

A staircase that starts wide at the bottom and thins as it climbs dominates the foyer. The red rug running down it is in incredibly good nick compared to everything else. As for the foyer itself, well, if this were a hotel it wouldn't be winning any awards. Letting the music lead him, Nick starts up, quickly relieving the banister of his weight. Ravaged by woodworm, it can barely support itself.

At the top, Nick meets the head of the family. Daddy Crane glares under a heavy frown. Plumply painted lips refuse to show anything other than contempt, a pinstripe suit squares his frame. Despite Daddy's preference for his eldest, it's young Ulysses who resembles his father the most, especially in the eyes. Daddy Crane appears beyond old, though the artist – motivated by fear – has tactfully painted out any wattling of the neck. Men like this are precious about their necks.

In the glass that covers the portrait, Nick's reflection mingles with Daddy Crane's image, creating a grotesque face that forces Nick to turn away. Only then does he see the man watching him closely through pinched eyes.

Leaning against a set of doors, the bloke grunts, "Lost?"

If Harvey could see this guy, he'd have called him a *right sawt*, bringing out his accent. It's possible Harvey already did, before Walter slit his throat, which Nick still feels strange about. On one hand, Harvey was just as bad as his younger brother, and he too was manipulating Nick. On the other, Harvey and Nick had a backstory that could've helped or, dare it be said, *saved* whatever friendship they had. Nick will never know. To him, dead Harvey is the same kid he knew in high school.

The *sawt* is wearing a brown suit, the collar of his shirt starched to razor quality. Most of his features are hidden, his face in shadow.

"Yeah," says Nick, as if he's meant to be here.

Stepping out of the shadows, the *sawt* clumps a cosh in his open palm, weighing Nick up.

Who *uses* a cosh these days? Nick can see the *sawt* is carrying a pistol.

Stroking the cosh like it's an extension of his dick, the *sawt* nods at the painting. "Ugly cunt, inee?"

Going with it, his fist clenched into a cramped ball behind his back,

Nick says, "As they come."

Sneering his agreement, the *sawt* cocks his head back. "Party's through there."

"You joining?"

"An' mix with you nutters? Nah, thanks. Out 'ere's bad enough." He twiddles the cosh like a prison guard with a nightstick. "You'd best hurry up if you're lookin' to get in. Meal's finished, I know that much. Lotsa faces in there, if you know the faces to look for."

"Cheers," Nick says.

The *sawt* makes no effort to move, making Nick skirt around his bulk to get through.

When the door clunks shut behind him, Nick finds himself looking down from a balcony at a bright hall full of guests dressed to the nines and zeroes. All of them shoeless. They're in their groups, none of them remotely interested in integrating with others. It's in mostly good condition, the hall. What parts remain in disrepair have been concealed by enormous drapes bearing the society's insignia, including the entire ceiling which is all hanging fabrics. It seems the same playlist used the first time he'd seen Crane's society is cranking out the classical hits.

No one has seen Nick enter. No one appears to care. There are stairs to the right and left of him that pinch together at the bottom. Rather than take them, he crouches down behind the balcony wall, peering through gaps in the carved railing. At the same time, the music fades out, which in turn quiets the din of chattering voices.

At the far end of the hall, on a risen floor that doesn't qualify as a proper stage, is a podium with a microphone. To the left and slightly behind it is a plinth with an elaborately stitched blanket covering something. The book, Nick reckons, thankful that he's out of its perimeter of foulness.

All the guests – best dressed at the front – begin taking their seats. Red velvet foldouts fixed to the floor. They wouldn't have come stock with the manor, and looking around the hall, Nick isn't sure what did.

When the last seat is filled, the lights go out. A spotlight engulfs the podium, and to the patter of royal clapping, Crane enters on the stage, walking with but not relying on his cane to get him to the microphone. On the way, he strokes the covered book. Before the old geezer utters his first word, Nick fumbles in his pocket for the voice recorder. Taking it out, he presses *RECORD*.

CHAPTER 36

Is this how death row inmates feel?

Being marched along the corridor, which in this house is another copy and paste stretch, Katy feels detached from her legs. A drum militantly times her tread to the gallows. Or perhaps it's her heart? She hasn't yet resigned herself to die, though the tears are on the doorstep for when she does. Her head and vision blurred, she finds it hard to recall exactly what the ritual book had said, yet the words *heart* and *heartbeat* are as strong in her memory as the thumping drum in her chest.

Gut and Survival have retreated, no longer speaking except in her own voice with useless words of comfort, which are no use to her here. What does *she* know?

She'd started to think of them almost as characters in a Jim Henson film. In her head, they could have been gibbous-eyed shoulder fairies called Gut and Vival. Vival, because *Sur*vival isn't a puppet's name. The last advice Gut had offered was to keep quiet, which she employs now even though the lady behind her is making no effort at small talk, anyway. It's not the same lady as before. This one is smoother in the face with a nose that could peck seed. She's wearing a grey dress with a stale fur collar. If her wish had been to be attractive, it hasn't yet been cashed in.

Survival's words loop in Katy's head as she squeezes the hard lump in her tunic pocket.

Save it.

She clings to this splinter of hope.

The rug beneath her feet is an ugly, crazy paving pattern with none of the charm. She ignores avoiding the gaps. There isn't much bad luck can bring.

Rounding a corner, she sees a familiar face. Unsure if the powdery hag is glowering at her, Katy thinks now that the bitch's face was moulded like that, and any other expression is a farce. She's never thought of anyone as a bitch before, not even the bullies. However the woman looks, Katy isn't going to show any fear.

A muffled voice booms through the walls. A man well into the swing of an elaborate speech, the same man she'd heard the first time she was marched to a stage. Her stomach backflips. Katy swallows down a hot glob of vomit.

"Any trouble?" the hag asks the escort.

"None."

Solomon pads into the scene, flaunting his rump as he glides around the hag's stockinged legs. Katy hates the cat for it.

She meets the hag's eyes, determines that it's definitely a glower being shot at her. A sneer, too, the kind that taunts, *I tried to be your friend*. Katy squeezes the item in her pocket. Now would be a good time to go for broke.

Save it.

The voice in her head is both hers and Survival. Mixed together, they exude a demonic quality that makes her feel strong in spite of her numb knees. If *save it* is the only thing Survival has to say from now on, she reckons it's worth listening to. Maybe there'll still be a chance. As long as she chooses the right moment.

With a sleight of hand that could fool a master magician, a pair of handcuffs rattle from the hag's paws.

Crap.

She tosses them to the escort. "Put those on her."

Catching the cuffs above Katy's head with both hands, the escort whines, "But I'm missing the- "

"You are missing nothing you cannot afford to. Put those on her and your duties here are done."

The woman slinks in front of Katy, mumbling to herself. She's nauseated by her breath. It stinks of cigarettes and old tea bags. She doesn't put up more of a fight than what's necessary, thinking that maybe she can still reach into her pocket if-

"Behind her back," the hag orders.

I'm dead.

It's not the first time Katy has thought this, only…now it carries more weight, and not just because of the cold metal biting into her wrists.

The escort clicks the first ring a few notches too tight. For a cult counting on her as an offering, they're rough.

The hag gets down to Katy's level. Cigarette and old tea bag breath is replaced by elderflower, which makes her sick all over again. As the last click of the cuffs seems to echo down the corridor like the switch of an electric chair, she tells Katy, "No one's coming for you this time."

Helpless, Katy asks herself, *Use it?*

The recorder captures everything.

Crane drones on, addressing his flock with gusto. He feeds the recorder with verbal proof of the society's crimes, their clandestine activities including but not limited to the kidnapping and murdering of children. Crane announces the presence of a police commissioner, who rises to a standing ovation for his role in keeping the society a secret, raising his hands in thanks. Arrogant enough to wear his dress uniform, the commissioner wears the society's sparkling pin amongst his service medals. How many of them, Nick wonders, were the result of a wish? How many the outcome of a murdered child?

Time is taken for the commissioner and his grey, neatly trimmed Friar Tuck hair to climb the stage to kiss Crane's hand. When he retakes his seat, hamming himself up, the congregation silences itself.

Whatever the recorder swallows can be used against Crane. The girl in exchange for the survival of his society. None of them will be willing – will they? – to go to prison for their association with Crane, least of all the old geezer himself, who has dedicated his life to the magic he worships. Nor will he want word to spread out into the world. He has enemies, by his own admission. A number of those have to be rival cultists. With luck, Crane will hand the girl over, his secrets safe. They'd find a new offering, but Katy would be alive.

If Crane refuses the trade, Nick will share what he's captured with every media outlet he can get the attention of. The Sunday rags would be first. Seeing at least one news broadcaster in the hall, Nick knows that some companies would – nudge, nudge – lose the story, but not *all* media stations have a piece of Crane inside them. Surely. That goes for law enforcement, too. Yes, the commissioner was here, the very man, Nick assumes, who set up Vance, but he's still only one man in one branch of law enforcement. A person's influence can only stretch so far before ears stop listening.

If that bridge must be crossed, then second on the list will have to be considered: escape.

Battering through cultists doesn't pose a problem. From the top of the stairs, Nick will have a considerable head start, and as for Walter loyalists, he'd only seen one of them. That cosh-wielding bloke who Nick is sure he could knock sparko if he landed the right punch. Every bloke has a soft spot, the trick is finding it. So no, brute force isn't the problem, the problem is finding his way out. Those hallways are slippery.

Of course, there'd be an even bigger problem. It would mean the blackmail failed, which would mean he would've failed Katy.

That can't happen.

Before he shows himself, he wants to see her. Soon, they'll bring her onto the stage. Crane's speech is nearing its conclusion, judging by the crescendo in intensity.

"To be completely truthful with all of you," Crane steps away from the podium, leaving behind the microphone. "I excavate joy from my heart that this larger gathering of our society had to happen." The crowd listens intently. If there were binoculars on the backs of seats with coin slots, Nick reckons the fuckers would've used them. "Never before in this society's history has an offering been interrupted, and yet fate decided it was the final offering that was to be delayed, which is apt, for I concluded in my solitude that it *deserves* to be made a spectacle of, for it represents everything we have worked towards. What was at first a hiccup in our journey turned out to be a blessing incognito. It is now that I offer my apologies for not initially conducting the final offering in this manner, and my eternal gratitude for your attendance here tonight. At first, I thought that by making the offering as always we had done – without drawing special attention – things would play out as they always have. Alas, I was wrong. But those of you who have done your homework will know that tonight is not about us, or any of my apologies or thanks."

Nick's brow ruffles.

Crane stands next to the covered table, the encapsulating spotlight follows him.

"The book, with its many wisdoms, is thankful for your unconditional faith." Crane whips away the cover, exposing the Liber Votorum to his gasping audience. Even those who have seen it before cannot contain their marvel. They are under Crane's thraldom, now. Those who have little self-control are already squirming in their seats. Nick feels a claw jabbing at his insides.

"It is satisfied," Crane continues, "that you have gathered here in this place created by memory, and it is glad, too, that you have filled your bellies, partaken of the wine, and celebrated its presence. Now," a hand goes to its cover, Crane grins before he says, "indulge it. Allow its power to infect you, as so many times before has its words."

Steeling himself, Nick watches the full-to-capacity hall chuck its guts up on cue, recording all the grotesque sounds that come with it. Crane smiles over them, clapping them on. None of the flock flail into the aisle, though the rough lot in the back seats struggle to handle themselves.

Just where all the vomit is gathering, Nick doesn't want to imagine. Maybe there's guttering? He shudders.

On its plinth, the book quivers, begins shaking. Crane comforts it, is comforted by it, holds up a hand to placate his people.

"Let us pace ourselves. The pinnacle of our evening has yet to be reached," he tells them.

Shirts have been unbuttoned already, the books manifested poison turning them towards sexual acts. The police commissioner is receiving hand relief from both his female neighbours. It's not about sex, or the sickness, Nick thinks. It's about letting the book take control, showing it your willingness to let it have you, to *enchant* you. The book is a twisted collection of magics, it makes sense that it needs a twisted bunch to appease it.

The smell is almost too much to bear.

Holding the book, its pages lapping, skin all the more human-like, Crane approaches his microphone.

"You have all bathed in the book's power, seen it, heard it. Smelt it. Now it is here in the flesh!"

Nick sees the book judder. Crane has to strain to keep it contained, his flaccid muscles at max capacity.

"And now," he goes on, "you shall all witness it finally feast on the flesh of the offering!"

Another spotlight, from nowhere, shines on the stage. Katy is led out by the woman with the porcelain face from the bus. He has to stop himself from leaping up then and there, the urge to help is almost physically painful. He notices Katy's hands are tied behind her back. No...handcuffed. They glimmer around her wrists, shiny as bracelets. They're not taking any chances with her this time. Seeing her back in this position fills Nick with anger. He grinds his teeth together. Another round of royal claps fill the hall, sounding like hail on a rooftop. Amongst the hail is as handful of cheers and whistles.

Gazing out at her adoring audience, Katy stubbornly holds back her tears, though the red rings around her eyes cannot be hidden. However, there's a hatred for these people that ages her years beyond the child Nick had first met. In her is a lion defiance that conjures up a weird sense of pride.

Don't give the bastards the satisfaction.

As she gets close to Crane, the book lunges at her from his hands, every page biting as if a hungry mouth recalling her flavour. Katy recoils, the woman holds her fast, whispering into her ear. Around the hall, the drapes billow.

"Hold," says Crane, the audience captivated, leaving the hall in pin-drop silence. He faces them. "We have another guest."

A disc of light illuminates the balcony.

"Good evening, Nicholas."

Heads turn, a collection of ruffling collars that may as well be a cocking shotgun.

The only face Nick sees when he stands is Katy's. Her features drop with disbelief.

Bouncing his cane on the stage, Crane beams, "So delighted you could join us, my friend, though I do hope you will not be reprising your last performance. It was not a winner at the box office, I am afraid."

Laughter from the flock. Around the hall the drapes move as if wind is surfing behind them. Nick's skin becomes dotted with goosebumps. The breeze is not cold, or warm, but damp. Like breath.

"How'd you know I was here?"

"I have always known," Crane's smile cracks wider. "That is, I knew nothing I could do would make you stay away, not even our little cyber meeting, which I hasten to add was as delightful as it was hard for me." The maggots make a passing visit in Nick's gut. "You are a strong soul, Nicholas, more stubborn than you know, yet perhaps not as cynical as you had been. And have you not always sought redemption? Is it not presented to you here?" Crane makes a gesture around the hall. "You are as predictable as the moon is round."

Nick holds up the recorder. "All I want is- "

"I'm sorry, but…" Walter stands from his chair at the front, lets the seat clap back. Nick hadn't seen him. "I can't waste any more time."

"Mr George?" Crane sounds confused. The feeling is mutual for Nick with a little extra. Nothing involving Walter can be good.

Walter snaps his fingers, whistles. What takes place unfolds like a military operation, barely enough time to register what's happening. Walter loyals burst up from their seats, brandishing handguns. They shout at the congregation to shut up and do as they're told. Those who don't know how much shit they're in get a swift pistol whip across the skull. Walter pulls a handgun from a holster strapped to his torso, concealed by a silver-grey suit jacket. He uses the handgun – an ornate, engraved tool which has a tackiness the distance between he and Nick can't hide – to scratch under his nose.

The woman and Katy are apprehended by another woman whose coat looks like a dead animal. She takes pleasure in slapping the older woman, using the full reach of her arm. Pointing a revolver at the stung old woman's chest, she pulls Katy by the neck against herself, grinning a wicked smile.

Crane is seized around the neck by…

Apollo?!

The big fuck holds a dagger under Crane's throat, stretching the skin taut by yanking his head back. Crane raises his hands, the book drops to the floor, landing without a bounce, overripe with knowledge. A purple-green ring bursts around it. It makes a guttural sound, not pain, but frustration. The colourful blasts keep coming.

Behind Nick appears the cosh bloke, who only has to shake his head for Nick to know he's powerless. He looks back at Katy. She looks at him, too.

Walter takes the stage, hopping up playfully, a man who's found the lamp and tamed the genie. Disarray caused by the society and the surges of the book is a compact tempest inside the hall.

Nick whirls around swinging, hand primed to wreck the cosh bloke's jaw. Cosh Bloke sees it coming, damn near expects it. He smashes his cosh into Nick's fist at roughly double the speed, not only deflecting the sucker punch but destroying his knuckles, too.

Falling on his knees, Nick clutches his swelling hand, certain he can feel fragments of bone slicing into his flesh from the inside.

A voice calls his name.

Katy. He turns to-

A gunshot rings out, commanding the hall into silence. Walter is centre stage, pointing his gun to the rafters. A trail of smoke coils up where it meets the drapes.

Seconds pass. He lowers the tacky handgun, then, satisfied that he has everybody's attention, Walter says, "Slide it here." His voice carries with the clout of a Shakespearian actor.

Apollo uses his foot to shove the Liber Votorum to Walter, who stops it by stamping his foot on the front cover. A shock of purple dust cries from the pages. Nick sees Katy flinch.

Crane splutters, "What do you think you are doing?"

Walter spins on his heels. "Isn't it obvious?"

The porcelain woman tries to step forward, the revolver pressed to her chest reminds her to stay back. "*You?*" she says to Walter.

"I tried to warn you," Walter replies.

"Not just him," Apollo adds with a smirk. "Us."

Walter smiles at Apollo, then, condescendingly, he tuts. "Just me."

He turns his handgun on the South African, pulls the trigger. Apollo's head is thrown back in a haze of red.

Crane, with fluid motion, draws a hidden sword from his cane the second Apollo drops. From the balcony, Nick hears the blade whistle through the air.

He's unable to perform even one swipe before Walter puts a bullet in his chest. The congregation gasps as one, imitating the air rushing out of Crane's lungs. Nick can't believe what he's seeing. Crane goes down, wheezing.

"Hm," Walter lowers the gun. "So you *can* die."

CHAPTER 37

Fuck fuck FUCK!

Apollo claws for purchase of his earthly body, but the force with which the bullet struck his forehead pulls him away with the relentlessness of an undertow. He swims in a sea of darkness, watching his body get further and further away. Where the round crashed through his skull is a static buzz, slightly hot, without evidence of a wound. People die looking their best, do they?

It isn't long before that's disproved.

His hands evaporate, arms vanish, legs, then feet. One by one his organs pop out of existence, his eyes the penultimate disappearance before finally his brain ceases to be. Yet still he can think, still he can express rage as the other lost spirits greet him to their dark world in groaning song. Apollo beats them away, tells them he isn't supposed to be here. It wasn't supposed to go like this. They continue to hound him, he continues to fight them off.

That bastard betrayed him. Sold him out.

Walter George.

As the spirits inevitably close in around Apollo, drowning him, the world clears of shadow until he is back in the hall, a constant hiss of wind curls around his feet in the form of black gas.

Beholding his new body, somehow he is able to hold it together. It's no surprise that he doesn't go mad, he no longer has a mind to lose. Everyone is still in the hall. The society, Walter's people. His nemesis, Nicholas...or should that be ex-nemesis?

The hall is black and white, yet the living are vibrant with colour, a thin aura cartoons their image. That colour is a fucking brag, is what it is. An insult to the dead. Look at me and my life, they say. Bastards.

Apollo accepts his new world, seeing a division between he and the living as a boundary line separating countries. He can see them, they cannot see him…unless he chooses to be seen. Yes, he knows that already, instincts of the dead learning themselves into his vaporous mind.

He sets eyes on Crane, the old man bleeding out, then to Walter. They were meant to take over from the crusty old fuck, run the society how it *should* be. Apollo knew Crane had lost his touch when Nicholas was able to take the girl. Only a couple of years ago, the old man would have demonstrated his wrath with ruthless haste, would have made an example of Nicholas. But those days are gone. Apollo's own faults on that night are irrelevant. With good leadership it wouldn't have happened.

Crowding around him again, the spirits put hands on his shoulders. Apollo shrugs them off, and they heed him. Even in this dimension, he is an alpha.

He's dead but not gone. He has business. And there is still a way for him to conduct said business.

CHAPTER 38

The Black Rose wilts to her knees, face contorting as Crane attempts to plug his wound with skeletal hands, blood escaping through the gaps. The girl, who has closed her eyes, is held tight by the woman in the fur coat, who was eager to be a part of Walter's takeover from the beginning.

Leaving the flailing book, Walter steps over to Apollo's body, plays his finger through the twirl of smoke coming from the South African's head. It's like a chimney, he snorts to himself. Prising the dagger from Apollo's stubbornly strong fingers, Walter says, "Sorry not sorry, dipshit."

Crane gargles on his blood, coughs up a fountain that paints his face with red drops.

"You still breathing?"

Walter's question comes with a raised eyebrow. To take a slug to the chest and still be ticking is a hell of an accolade for an old bloke like Crane. Pity for him that he'll die soon enough, either way.

In the stupefied and beaten congregation, the police commissioner rises from his seat. One of Walter's men climbs towards him to deliver a smack, stopping when Walter commands it with a sharp whistle.

"Let 'im speak."

Straightening his jacket, the commissioner booms, "What're you playing at, George?"

"I'm not sure I can take a man with his cock hanging out seriously," Walter smirks.

His men join in with laughter. The woman, too, exaggerating to gain extra attention.

Red-faced, the commissioner zips himself up. "George, we've all made wishes, we all have more. We stand only to gain from Mr Crane's ascension. Can't you see that?"

"You can still gain everything promised to you," replies Walter, addressing the crowd. "This is simply a management shift."

"It's not that simple."

"It can be."

"George," the commissioner lowers his tone. "I've allowed you and your brother to thrive. I still can. Don't make me reconsider the status quo on the streets."

Is this clown really trying to *threaten* Walter? Oh, this could be fun. Walter plays along. Tapping his chin in mock thought, he says, "You're saying...what? Because of your position you have leverage over me?"

"I've always had that, George. It's why you and your brother have been as successful as you have."

"You're a bigger dumbass than I thought. A shame my brother can't hear this. He was a weak shithead, but he'd've had a laugh at your expense. You're saying you can take away whatever control *I* have in the underworld?"

The commissioner tightens his lips, puffs out his chest to emphasise his meaningless medals. "I'm saying what I'm saying."

"Hmmmm." Walter drags it out, looks to his men with raised eyebrows, then back to the commissioner. The flock shuffles, a pathetic, shivering herd. "I hear you. You're saying that, between us, the power is in your hands."

He and the commissioner duel with stony gazes. The crowd is stuck in a web of anticipation.

Pouting out his bottom lip, Walter announces, "I've thought about it. I can't have that."

Gunslinger-quick, Walter fires a round through the commissioner's gut. Blood bursts over the person behind right before the bullet tears through her, too. Both bodies crumble. Their friends scramble away, though the space made is quickly filled by those drawn to the messy scene. Two birds with one three-hundred-and-seventy metres per second stone. The engraved Luger is a nice piece, a little too German, but you can't argue with results.

No one dares to move, let alone speak.

"Anybody else have a point they'd like to raise?" Walter asks them. Answered with a load of nothing, he adds, "Lovely, then we can continue with our evening. Feel free to toss aside your programmes. We have until midnight to get this done. Make no mistake, if nobody tries fucking about you shall all get your dues. Some of you. My soldiers are armed, and are about as bashful as I am when it comes to cutting away the fat. Don't worry about the bodies, least of all the big fucker up here. He was one cook too many."

There's an atmosphere that could blunt the knife meant to cut it. The congregation is in shock, still computing the rapid, bloody change in command. They won't try anything, Walter is confident, now they've seen how easy it'd be for them to die. None of them wish that. Now Crane is debilitated, they will come to Walter, unwilling to give up their wishes. Because at the heart of it, everybody here is selfish, following Crane for something more than the old man's vision, something more precious. They're own needs, and they know it. It doesn't bother Walter, people should embrace their selfishness. Selfishness has accomplished many of the world's finest moments, most of the time dressed up as for the people, by the people, or some bullshit. Selfishness, Walter can use. Selfish people are easy to manipulate.

Holstering the Luger, Walter picks up the book, which nips at his fingers. "Nick? I know you can hear me. You just sit tight. I'll make time for you."

He sets the book on the podium, moves the microphone aside. A red glow warms his face when Walter opens the book, warping the shadows of his face to give him a devilish appearance.

Scanning over the words, he thinks, *So much potential, so much power. Infinite and at my fingertips.*

It'd only take killing one child, yet he'll do it a hundred times over, as

Crane had done, if it means obtaining these magics. The only difference between him and the old man is conflicting ambitions. Crane had no scope. He only sees as far as the society and himself, craving power without a plan of what to do with it except keep the society alive. When Walter sees the book, he sees continents of connecting webs, the impossible made possible using the arts of the book. There'll have to be screening processes for those coming with wishes. What can they do in return? It's all very exciting.

Laughing to himself, he flips the dagger from his right hand to his left. Without taking his eyes from the book, he extends his right arm towards the side of the stage.

"Bring me the girl." To his new subjects, he says, "As you were."

§

Better the devil you know, they say. Only Nick *does* know Walter George and there's nothing better about it.

It doesn't really matter, both Crane and Walter are madmen. What matters is Katy. Nick watches through the balcony as she's pushed towards Walter. He can see the worry on her face. Behind her back she's wiggling her hands for freedom.

Walter turns to Crane, the man who cannot die. He halts the girl, talks to the bleeding old man. Nick can't hear them. The audience has once again paused its perverse worship of the book. Now the stench of sick, blood and sex floats up to the balcony, gets stuck in the back of Nick's throat like turned honey. A rhubarb and custard sludge has started to flow in the aisle between the seats.

Nick gags.

There's no way out of this, the original plan is in the toilet. All Walter's cronies are armed. One wrong move and they'll turn him into

Swiss cheese.

Right now, no one is looking. He could surprise Cosh Bloke with a hit to the crotch, followed by a quick chokehold to put the guy to sleep. His right hand is fucked, but he's had to go southpaw before.

The question is, what *then*?

Hearing cries and gasps, Nick looks back to the stage. Walter has just done something beyond fucking mad.

Nick forgets to breathe.

There's so much blood.

As Walter is about to take hold of the girl's shoulder, Crane splutters, "It's not that simple…"

His head is cradled in the hands of the Black Rose.

Extending his index finger to press the girl back, Walter replies, "What's not that simple?"

The fur coat woman, whose name escapes Walter, takes the girl.

A chuckle bubbles deep in Crane's throat. "You believe…that" – pink foam spills from the corners of his mouth – "just because you…give it the offering, it will…listen…to you?"

Walter tuts. "Aren't you done being cryptic?"

"The book listens to me, because…I listen to it, have demonstrated countless times that I can be laden with its…treasures. I have…bled for it. I have shown it personal…hells…to prove myself. I maimed my body as I recited its words night after night. I…I have cut myself open in its presence to allow it to feed on my lifeblood. My life has been…dedicated to it." Crane swallows, his throat clicks.

"Looks like the book is really rushing to your aid there, Crane," Walter rolls his eyes.

"You are of no consequence to the Liber Votorum…because you have not agonised for it. It will…shun you…"

The Black Rose smirks. Truly, the pair of them believe Walter has already failed. It's actually quite amusing. Like many people before who didn't live to regret it, they have underestimated him.

"I suppose you've got a point," he nods.

Searching the stage floor around him, he taps Crane's unsheathed cane sword with the tip of his shoe.

"This sharp?" Walter asks.

"It'll take your nose off," the Black Rose spits.

Walter picks up the sword, inspects the glint along the blade's edge in the spotlight. Feather-weight, built for surprise, the point fine enough to split hairs. He bends the blade, reckons it'll be strong enough. He whips the weapon back and forth, unstitching the air, then marches to Apollo's body. With precision, he slices into the South African's meaty thigh, cutting easily to the bone. Blood oozes thick and warm from severed arteries, laminating the stage red.

Crane coughs. "It has to be your own blood. You are not...willing to lose any."

Holding the blade close to his face, Walter grunts. "Mm-hm." He steps out of Apollo's blood. "There's a lot to make up for."

"What are you...doing?"

"Testing."

"F...For what?"

"This."

Walter strides to the podium, plunges the blade into his left forearm, pinning himself in place next to the book. Over his shoulder, he growls at Crane, "I'll have to pay in full."

He begins hacking at his arm, slicing down on it guillotine-style. The meat of his muscles squelch with each butcher blow, bones grinds into splinters. Searing pain and lunatic humour join to create a screaming laughter that intensifies with each violent cut. Blood pastes his face, bringing out the white in Walter's peeled open eyes. Pints of it pool around the book, waterfalling off the podium. Faces in the audience are sickened...and entertained. Those who feared him are impressed, those who knew no better accept their new found fear. Walter's henchmen are captivated, though unsurprised. Those who know him well enough know never to assume his next move.

Getting through the tendons, the blade gouges chunks from the podium that go flying into the crowd, against Walter's face, scratching his flesh. After the last hack, he tosses the sword aside, picks up his arm and holds it above his head. Opening his mouth, he drinks the crimson tar spilling from the limb, moving his face around to make sure it's covered. His stump bleeds over the floor, spills into the centre aisle to join the thick gloop.

Thirst quenched and out of breath, he lowers his arm and smears the ragged mess over the book before throwing the limb into the congregation, *his* flock now. He's lost copious amounts of blood, yet feels more alive than ever. High as *fuck*!

The girl is slumped over, crying quietly with her eyes closed. Fur coat lady is holding her under the arms, licking her lips. Blood spatter sparkles like rubies in her fur collar. Crane and the Black Rose watch with a mixture of horror and awe. The blood has turned the spotlight a scarlet hue.

Steadying himself, taking a deep lungful of air, Walter leans down so that his face is almost touching the open book. Blood swims in a bulb of sweat dangling from his nose. A mist of colour perspires from the pages.

He whispers, "Are you listening?"

After a spell, the pages flutter.

Yes.

It's listening.

§

No one sees, for it happens quicker than the blink of an eye.

When the book acknowledges Walter George, Ulysses Crane exhales a gurgling sigh. The whole house flickers, just once. A lightbulb whose filament is about to expire.

CHAPTER 39

It's a nightmare.

Had the creepy man really just cut off his own arm?!

Vomit clogs Katy's throat. She manages to swallow it down, which in turn nearly makes her puke it back up.

He grabs her by the arm, fingers clamping like bulldog clips. He drags her away from the ugly woman in the fur coat, who claps as he does, the tip of her tongue poking out of smiling teeth. If Katy could think straight she'd at least try and pull herself away. Thinking straight isn't coming easy. If he lets go she'll collapse. Her torso – subconsciously bending away from the gory stump – lurches ahead of her legs before they catch up. The hall is spinning, faces in seats become featureless pebbles compacted together, jittering like so many cells. In the spotlight, her skin burns.

"I already know the first wish I'm bleeding out of you," Walter rasps in her ear.

He kicks out her ankles. With his body weight, he pins her down over the book, right arm curled around her to hold the dagger under her throat. Cold metal draws a gleaming line across her skin before it touches.

Tears pat the book's pages. Katy didn't realise she was crying. The book doesn't react to them, there's no flavour in tears.

She thinks of Nick.

He's alive and he's *here*. She'd convinced herself he was either dead or had given up, but here he is. A person who keeps their promise is a good person, no matter what they say about themselves. He can think poorly of himself all he wants, Katy knows he's not as dark as he paints himself.

Vibrating with energy, the book demands blood. A gravitational sinkhole slowly pulls at her face. The green-purple-red fog drifting from the spine smells like a cupboard under the stairs. Walter's stump is wetting her back, trickling down her legs, between her toes.

There isn't much Nick can do...but he's here. If not for that, Katy would be alone with these...these people. Neither of them are alone, now.

"IT'S NOT YOURS!"

Screaming, the old woman, Juniper, charges into Walter.

All three tumble. The dagger tangles in the chain of Katy's handcuffs and breaks them. Crawling away, she thrusts her hand into her pocket, listening to the combined voices of Gut, Survival and herself. It's her own voice that shouts the loudest.

Use it!

The hall has erupted, the pebble-faces clamouring.

Walter backhands Juniper, sending her sprawling on the bloody floorboards. "Bitch!"

He looks around, snarling. His men have already taken aim at the congregation infected with myxomatosis. A frenzied naked man climbs over the chairs using people's faces for extra footing, declaring that he wants his wish, he wants his wish, he wants his *WISH*. One of Walter's men shoots him, grinning as if he's just shot a pheasant instead of another human being. The naked body falls with raised arms, is buried beneath trampling feet.

When Walter sees Katy, his snarl vanishes.

"STOP!" he orders, holding up both his arm and phantom limb.

His men hold fire. Once again the crowd, confused and uncertain, comes to a standstill.

Katy is holding the T-bone from the steak under her neck, gripping it white-knuckle-tight between her middle and ring fingers. He takes a step towards her. She pokes the tip of the bone into her skin.

"I'll do it," she threatens. And she means it...she thinks.

Walter's hand creeps to the gun inside his suit jacket. "Cherub," channelling his sibling, wherever he is, "if you do that I'll hook you up and drain you like a pig."

A rattle.

It's Crane, he's trying to laugh. Juniper, with a purple bruise puffing up her eye, has returned to him, supporting his head so he can watch.

"She…has…bested you," Crane wheezes.

Walter blinks impatiently. "How so?"

"You must…make the offering yourself. That is the asking price when…the book…listens to you. It is stubborn…a child who wants…just its father. If she…or anyone else…takes her life…then," a grin filled with yellowing teeth, "so taken are ours."

The old man closes his eyes, the scar Katy put on his face starting to show. Seeing that untidy line across his face, she can scarcely believe she had been the one to give it to him.

"Oh, please," says the Walter. "Do fill me in on this nugget of information. We're learning all the time, aren't we?"

Crane splutters, then says, "Her and…the Liber Vo…Votorum are connected by…blood. It is why it must be…her. They share…the same…heartbeat. Should by a strange hand she perish…so does the other."

"And us?"

Nodding, Crane answers, "We are all connected to the book…all of us have made…wishes. Because of this…we are bound to…to its fate."

Crane's wound spurts, blood splats on his chest. He's too tired to talk any more. The old woman strokes his head, wipes blood from his lips.

Katy had read it, yet hearing the leader of the cult himself confirm what words had told her, the reality of it sinks in even more. If the reality sinks in any lower, it'll be in a grave.

Walter huffs, rolls his eyes. "So if she dies outside of sacrifice the book dies, and if the book dies so do we." He turns to Katy, she takes a sharp inhalation. "Reckon I could pop a round in your leg."

"If you touch that gun I'll put this bone in my neck," she says. Good God, she means it.

"You got the balls?"

"More than you."

He laughs, a disturbing sound straight from a stranger-danger video. "Reckon you can kill yourself quicker than I can draw a gun?"

"I've spent lots of time catching frogs and newts. They're slippery."

Who knew that one day her experience by the creek would be useful in a life-or-death situation? Still, she hopes the Walter won't test her.

Smiling, he says, "You knew about this, didn'tchya?"

"I've had time to read."

"Clever girl." Taking his hand away from the gun, he goes on. "Okay, Cherub, you have me at a slight disadvantage. What do you hope to gain from this play?"

Katy scans the audience, checks over her shoulder. She can't afford to let someone grab her from behind, this might be her only shot at getting out.

She answers, "Let me and Nick go."

He laughs, at first amused by her demand, then offended before being tickled again. He makes a display of his laughter, rubs his chin. It annoys Katy that he isn't taking her seriously.

"Nick! It slipped my mind." Up to the balcony he shouts, "Trev, pick 'im up."

The man hauls Nick up.

"Alright Walt," Nick grimaces. "How's the arm?"

"T'rrific. You hold tight." Back to Katy, Walter says, "If I let you go, I'd hunt you down."

"Then I'd kill myself then." Double-then, bad grammar. She can forgive herself.

"And so on and so forth. We can go in circles for hours," he smirks. "You know I can't let you go."

Katy starts, "Then I'll- "

"No, you won't. You won't do a damn thing, not unless you want a few of my guys to pay a visit to your parents."

For a moment her grip on the bone slackens. The images of her mum and dad's faces swim in and out of her vision. She'd forgotten to consider them.

"He's lying," Nick calls to her.

The man Trev grabs Nick by the head, primed to snap his neck should Walter order it.

"You...*are* lying," Katy murmurs. "How could you know- "

"Girly," he interrupts. "That dead man over there was one of the highest ranking police officers in the city." He points with his stump, tossing blood. "If we want to find someone, we can. And believe me, we *know* your parents."

The officer, Katy sees, is splayed over the chairs, arms by his sides, head tilted back with his mouth open, from which hangs his cold fat tongue.

"But..." Katy knows she's faltering. "You can't. If I kill myself, you'll die. You can't hurt my mum and dad!"

"I never said *I* would. My men have as yet to make a wish. They're not connected to the book. Upon my death, they will know what to do."

Nick cries, "Katy, he's fucking lying! If they knew where your parents were they'd have used it against you sooner!"

"Trev?"

Katy watches the man Trev lay into Nick with something he's holding. She looks away.

"A wise man never plays his trump card at the start of a game," muses Walter. Softly, he says, "Cherub? *Katy*? Think about what you're doing. You've been clever once, show me it wasn't a fluke. You can kill yourself and kill us, ending this whole thing, congratulations, you win and all that, but it would also mean murdering your own parents. Mummy and Daddy. My boys aren't quick, they can work as slow as they need to. They know how to keep people alive for days. It's you, or Mum and Dad. They don't need to be dragged into your mess, and only you can save them. If not they'll suffer, and suffer, and suffer. And when the end finally comes…they'll die blaming you."

Murder? Again, the tears break loose, her weak spot breached, battered. Katy hates herself for it, should have planned ahead better than this, should have waited for a better time to use the T-bone, her last hope. Its tip comes away from her neck, leaving a pink dimple.

"And I'll tell you what," Walter continues. "As a sign of good faith, if you give yourself to me, I'll let Nick go."

If Nick responds, Katy doesn't hear him. It's a lie and she knows it. Nick is as dead as she is. They're beaten. She lets herself accept it. She's been dead since she was first taken. It could only ever end with her death. She would be the last child killed, so at least there was that. Right now, if anyone has to die, who she'd pick between her and her parents was never going to be a question.

"He's lying! HE'S LYING!" Nick yells with desperation. "*HE'S LYING!*"

Slowly, Katy lowers the bone.

CHAPTER 40

The ice cream, a perfect, photogenic whippy (every time!), is dusted with multicoloured sprinkles. Simon takes it, marking the cone with dirty fingerprints. He licks the should-be-sweet treat.

"Doesn't taste of anything."

"Why, it never does, Si. It ain't really there." The *th* in *there* sounds almost like a *d*.

The ice cream man snaps his swinging jaw into place, whisks his mouth around to lock it in. This's been happening a lot more, recently.

Taking another joyless lick, twisting his tongue to the peak, Simon asks, "Am I lost, Wyatt?"

"Kid, look at me. I know a thing or two about bein' lost." With a white cloth, he keeps the ice cream pumps shiny. "You've never made a peep about it before."

"I just wonder what I'm really doing. Feels like I'm always getting shit on."

"Hey," Wyatt ducks his head to avoid the verbal bullet, gazes quickly around the woods. Against the dull backdrop, his striped bubblegum blue and pink shirt really pops. Leaning on the polished wood bar, he says, "Watch your French, pal. I could have kids come in any moment for their Snowies."

Snowies is what Wyatt calls snow cones – two for a dollah! – though Simon has never seen him make one.

On his swivel stool, Simon deflates, unable to sigh any harder. "Sorry, Wy."

Adjusting his matching hat to a Popeye jaunt, Wyatt goes back to his pumps. "No worries, Si. We all get a little forgetful of our tongues from time to time."

Wyatt is dead. Has been since the early fifties, Simon guesses. The ice cream man is starting to show signs of decomposition, the grave catching up. It takes a good long while before spirits start to resemble their earthly bodies. Not just the jaw, his eyes have started to sink into his face, and his skin has taken on a pale green pallor. For a seventy-year-old corpse, it could be worse. His uniform is always pristine, white collar starched rock solid.

Wyatt is also Simon's therapist.

The ice cream man isn't great at the job, and sometimes he gets confused, but he listens, and talks.

It can be weird having a spirit as your emotional fallback, but Simon's sitting at a make-believe ice cream bar in the middle of a foggy forest with the Master's house looming in the background, so what does weird even mean at this point?

"Talk to me, kid. We've got all the time in the world," says Wyatt.

Can't forget Wyatt's hair. Beneath his hat is a slicked back and parted black crop still as oiled as the day he bought the farm. Come to think of it, Simon has never asked Wyatt how he died. But, why *would* he? He wasn't the ice cream man's therapist.

"Wy?" Another lick. "How'd you die?"

"Milk lorry," he answers. And that's all the explanation Simon needs and Wyatt's going to give. Fifties ghosts don't gossip about themselves.

The chrome Wyatt polishes shines as if there's a scorching sun high above. It did burn for him once, the sun, back when the music was rockin' and rollin' and there were jars of sweets behind the ice cream man instead of a suffering woodland. Wyatt probably still sees the sweets, all colours clashing wonderfully with his shirt.

"Another?" Wyatt offers. For a second, his skeleton can be seen.

Simon holds up his hand, more than half the ice cream in his other. It hasn't started to melt yet, nor will it ever. "No."

"So tal…"

Wyatt's jaw falls loose again, droops down on the left showing half a mouthful of teeth. Skin is pulled down under the eye to give the ice cream spirit the look of a stroke victim.

Simon doesn't wait for Wyatt to correct himself. He knows Wyatt was inviting him to talk some more. "I'm not a good person."

Fixing himself, Wyatt speaks through crunching bone. "So you burned your mama to death, I get it." *Geddit.* "I once sold some hardboileds a week past their sell-by. Waitin' on some more right now." He cocks a thumb at where the jars would've been.

Who in Death's job office gave Wyatt this gig?

Simon tries again. "No, it's not that" – Mama deserved to burn – "I mean I'm not a good *person*. People…" For Wyatt's benefit he makes sure no kids are around, then whispers, "People always treat me like shit, even those who haven't gotten to know me. I get used, made fun of, shouted at, beaten up. I've been tricked. I'm…I'm not so sure Master values me like I thought he did. I have good ideas but still all I get is a carrot dangled in front of my face. If I was a good *person*, good to *myself*, I'd've stopped taking that shit long ago. Hell, I'm an asset! How many other guys you know can do what we're doing?"

"Pull ice cream?"

"No, Wy."

"I know, Si."

"I can't even experience pleasure without carving myself up. I'm alone. I'm a nobody."

Wyatt takes the old ice cream from Simon and puts in its place another. Mint chocolate chip, for all the difference it makes. "You ain't a nobody. Who told you that?"

"People don't need to. I'm a loser." Simon drops the fresh whippy. It lands ice cream first in the dirt, then decomposes to ash. It's ironic to Simon that not long ago he was imagining ice cream flavours based on different kinds of pain. You can't beat the classics though, even if they don't taste of anything when prepared by the hands of your therapy ghost.

One hand on the bar and the other balanced on a gleaming pump,

Wyatt asks, "What about that gal of yours? You've spoken about her a lot."

Simon buries his head in his palms. "She was…she was killed. But she isn't like you. She's one of the shadows."

Wyatt shudders, says, "That's tough, but hey, nobody likes a Gloomy Gus. Every guy and gal has their breakin' point. Seems to me like you've gone and found yours, pal."

Pal. Kid. Buddy. Tiger. Wyatt has called Simon every endearing nickname under the sun, all except for Your Royal Fucking Highness. Maybe the ice cream man and the shadows would call him that if Master had told the truth about Simon's future role over the dead. For some reason, and for the first time, Simon thinks Master might not have meant what he promised. Can a paragon lie?

Wyatt continues, "But if you want change? Well, slick" – that's new – "you gotta make it happen on your own."

Simon looks up.

"You gotta see what you want to change. Visualise the future you need. You're right, not just anybody can do this. You're the only guy from the land of the fleshies who *I've* ever had a conversation with. I mean, you get all those séance freaks, but they're just full of- " Wyatt catches himself. After making sure the coast is clear of young ears, he winks at Simon. "Full of crap."

Simon chuckles at the back of his throat. Wyatt isn't a good swearer.

"You've got talent, Si." The ice cream man begins polishing the same pump he's been polishing for seventy years. "Use it. No more carrots."

It's like the build-up to a singalong. Every now and then, Wyatt says something that really gets through. Normally, it's obvious stuff that Simon misses until it's scooped into a waffle cone.

"No more carrots," Simon repeats to himself.

"So what'll it be, kid? Double choc?"

Smiling now, Simon asks, "You got beer?"

"Ice cream flavoured like a bottle of suds? You gotta be kidding?" All around, not quite there, bells begin chiming an ice cream van's song. "Time's up, Si. I'll mail you the bill."

"You said we had all the time in the world," says Simon, tapping the bar. There's no sound.

"Maybe that's just me. For you, I guess time is gettin' cut short." Wyatt tosses the cloth over his shoulder, catches his jaw before it falls off. Shoving it up into a gurn, the goo from his green flesh glues it back on. "Remember, no more carrots. Don't let yourself be treated like no idiot."

The chimes grow louder, Greensleeves' haunting melody sounds as if it's coming from a blown-out speaker. The charade of an ice cream parlour is shattered. Wyatt is disintegrated into lumpy dust by a massive black shadow bursting through him, sending wood and chrome and ice cream flying off into infinity. Taking Simon by the throat, the shadow slams him into the ground.

Simon wakes up, lifts his head from a rough pillow of dry leaves. Red rings surround his eyes swollen from mosquito bites, a redder ring travels around his throat where Nicholas had grabbed him. His Adam's apple is sore, too. His neck is an iron brace, his head a hive of lazy bees that bump into the walls of his skull.

A few feet away stands the enormous spirit, heaving as it breathes even though it doesn't have lungs anymore. That means it's a new ghost, one that hasn't gotten used to its new form yet, which also means it'll be angry. One this size – the biggest Simon has ever encountered – is sure to be the worst kind of trouble when it's angry.

Simon asks it, "What do you want?"

"Don't you recognise me, Schaeffer?"

The voice is off but the accent is still there.

"Apollo?"

"You're already boring me. I need your help."

No more carrots, Wyatt's sing-song voice reminds Simon.

"*My* help?" says Simon.

"There's a man I need to get at," Apollo responds.

"What do I get out of it?"

Apollo's spirit growls, "What?"

Standing from his bed of twigs and leaves, Simon asserts himself. "You need my help. Tell me why I should, and make it good."

"How dare- "

"How dare nothing. If you need my help, that means you have no hope without me. So why don't you make an offer, and hurry up, wait too long and you'll start to forget who you are."

It feels much better to be dominant, boosts all kinds of confidence Simon didn't know he had. It's exciting, more exciting than a freshly stropped razor hovering over the most tender flesh.

Before long, Apollo grunts, "I'll tell you who killed that woman you were obsessed with."

His heart skips a beat at the thought of Dani. It's not a good offer, though. Simon shrugs. "I already know who did that."

"No you don't," Apollo snorts a laugh. "But you could. Help me and I'll help you."

Now it's a good offer, though he's inclined to warn Apollo. "This better not be a carrot."

Apollo doesn't answer.

Offering his hand to the dark spirit, Simon says, "Deal."

CHAPTER 41

Walter has Katy cruelly by the arm and is positioning her over the blood-soaked book. A soft wind blows through her hair, otherworldly dim orange light ages her significantly. She isn't resisting, sends an apologetic frown, mouths the words, "I'm sorry." Nick shakes his head. He should be the one apologising, wants to tell her she has nothing to be sorry for.

Chanting, at first hesitant, becomes stronger until it drones from the congregation with all the harmony of out of tune bagpipes. All but a curious two of Walter's men remain bystanders to the show. Bodies of the recently departed are being used like Halloween decorations to enhance the cult's sick experience.

Trevor kicks Nick in the stomach, beats the cosh against his thigh too close to the bollocks to've been an accident. He's been turned into a human punching bag. The pain is fuzzy. Nick focuses on Katy. A familiar guilt prickles his heart, memories of the young boxer whose shortened life lays at his feet, an injustice he has convinced himself he is responsible for. And now another, a young girl who he should have been able to save, who he promised he would. Not so long ago, fate had collided them together and she had been a fire-willed burden, a project Nick wasn't sure why he'd taken on other than his moral compass telling him he should. But when had that thing last served him well? Now, though, now she means so much to him, because she had made – *makes* – him feel normal, that he has nothing to feel guilty for. A person who can, even momentarily, take that weight away deserves to be cherished. After their first awkward breakfast, talking with her had been unnoticeably natural. Clunky and cat-oriented, yet natural in its own way. She'd even tried to find some common ground in the back of a van.

The last time they'd spoken, she'd tried to get to know him and maybe offer some new perspective, to make him see that he'd been manipulated all those years ago by the very people who called themselves friends. She'd wanted him to see he isn't the bad person he's chiselled out of himself. She'd tried to be a friend and he'd gotten angry when she least needed it, because she needed a friend, too. Then she'd been stolen again.

There's that wasp-sting guilt again.

It's because of Katy that Nick believes he can let go of that guilt, that persona, or at least see the light at the end of the tunnel, a shine that he hadn't seen until she'd shown it to him. And maybe that light is still there, but now it's almost extinguished. Only her words keep him believing that maybe he can still make it to the end of that tunnel before the end of everything.

It wasn't your fault.

You aren't a bad person.

Seeing her on the stage, this resilient girl defeated, defeats him. He can see it now, living or dead, her form will stand alongside Callum Granger, blaming him, a reminder that he should have done what he could not. And what could he have done with Callum Granger? Told Walter and his brother to leave the boy alone? Would they have listened, and would Nick have avoided all of his misery?

Maybe.

Yet, maybe not.

All he can do now is watch as Katy is bent over by one-armed Walter, preparing her for that Dracula book spitting and hissing on its podium. He rolls over, can't watch. He'd scream if he had any air to spare, all of it knocked out by Trevor via a devastating stomp to the abdomen.

Behind Trevor, Nick sees the Figure back from the pub. Its hair is a messy lightning shock, piercing lamp eyes sting Nick's retinas. It isn't smiling.

As unconsciousness draws nearer and thereafter – he *knows*, because Walter is Belial by another name – death, Nick's ears are filled with a shellshock ringing. No fanfare to the other side for him, just an atonal whistle.

He'd asked Simon Schaeffer how to make it better, to which the mulleted wonder had told him that only he could do that, now. Well, *now* is almost over.

Nick owes it to Katy to at least try before he fails.

You aren't a bad person.

He'd told the Figure he was sorry, addressing it by its name, but there's still one last apology to make.

"I forgive myself," he whispers.

And just like that, a weight is lifted from him. It's ironic that here, in the darkest of places, Nick suddenly wants to be in the sunshine. Unconsciousness doesn't come as he'd expected it to, nor a choked cry from Katy as her blood is spilled.

Instead, adrenaline kickstarts his heart, and the Figure attacks.

§

The Figure claps its hands around Trevor's head, imploding his skull. Brain matter and bone fragments hail down on Nick, who, keeping his mashed right hand against his torso, pulls himself up using the balcony railing.

With horror, and a strange elation, he sees that down below the hall is being assaulted by dark shadows. Society members are hauled from their seats, tossed across the room and through drapes shielding windows. Walter loyalists have their weapons wrestled from them, limbs torn away, bones bent in ways unnatural. What was already one chaos has further descended into another.

Turning around, Nick sees the Figure one last time before it too joins the attack in a teleporting haze. He watches it go, seeing it now not as Callum Granger but as the chain he'd padlocked to himself. A chain broken. It had recognised its former name, but that's all it was, an old identity long forgotten. It had only attached itself to Nick because he had invited it to do so. After forgiving himself, the invitation was void. A curse lifted.

For the both of them.

More ghouls tornado through the door, joining the others. Nick follows their path, sees Katy struggling to get free from Walter. He charges down the stairs, bashing shoulders with Crane's fleeing society. Midway down, a ghoul springs up in front of Nick and tries to grab him, missing by a hair.

Black shapes pop up from the floor, slice through walls, drop from the ceiling. Katy, unafraid of them, takes initiative as soon as Walter's grip falters. She stamps on his foot, brings her elbow back into his stomach. It doesn't wind him, but does catch him unawares enough that she can slip free.

She runs. He snags her wrist, twisting it. His hip bangs the podium, knocks the book to the floor where it leaps like a bug with a lost wing.

"You're not going anywhere," he growls with the dagger between his teeth.

The more she pulls the more it hurts. Around her, men and women are screaming, a number of gunshots go off, and the shapes are groaning. She catches a quick glimpse of Juniper, dragging the old man off the stage, her heels slipping in blood. Desperately, Katy searches for Nick. If he's still here, he's lost in the sea of panic.

"Fucking...get...DOWN!"

Walter yanks her arm down, hard, bringing Katy to her knees, nearly dislocating her shoulder. Using his foot, he slides the book under her neck, then comes the dagger, this time aimed to come down any which way.

Covering her head, Katy awaits the searing pain of the blade. When it doesn't come, she looks up to see Walter being pushed aside by one of the dark shapes. With a guttural roar, the gangster breaks loose, dives for the book which he tucks under his chest with his right arm, still holding the dagger, whilst using the ragged left stump to grab for Katy, snarling rabidly, eyes crazed.

A monster shows itself inside his throat. "Your whole family will burn after I slit your neck!"

By an unseen force, Walter is pulled away, off the stage and through a broken tunnel of shifting legs, into the crowd and broken chairs, his beastly glare fixed on Katy until it disappears behind the frightened cultists.

To her left, the fur coat woman is having her clothes ripped off by two shapes. To the right, a few feet away from the stage, a cultist has been transformed into a suffering, lolloping spider, his back bent the wrong way, head almost upside down. His arms and legs stretch beyond the length of his sleeves and trousers, the extra four limbs have been inserted into his body by way of any orifice available or created. This sight, of all the others, will haunt Katy for the rest of her life. Stumbling closer, the spiderman pleads her for help.

Wanting to be anywhere but right here, Katy kicks herself up, dashes off the blood-slippery stage, dodging both cultists and shapes that try to snatch her. She hugs the walls, imagines herself small, invisible. In her mouth lingers the taste of blood, her tongue bogged down with the stench of vomit and, sickeningly, excrement.

Making use of a large red drape, she conceals herself behind it. Keep your feet in, she tells herself.

Just hearing the God awful sounds are as bad as seeing what makes them. The spiderman, she hears, continues to beg for mercy.

Heat begins to press on her legs, then her stomach. It threatens to burn away the rest of her already tattered tunic. Suddenly, the drape has turned into a kiln and Katy, coughing, throws it aside.

The drape is on fire, flames hungrily eat away the cult symbol, climbing higher until the fabric is all burned up. The remains fall down like black snow, revealing the largest window Katy has ever seen. She cannot see outside, only the reflection of herself, bloody and barely recognisable, and the rest of the hell in the hall. An inferno.

Embers float down to burn her, little cigarette kisses. She beats at them, leaving smears of ash on her arms and legs and face. She notices she's still clutching the T-bone when she scratches her shin with it. In the pocket it goes, and not just because Gut tells her to.

Fingers dig into the soft part of her right arm behind the bicep, making her yelp. A dirty, porridgy face stares up at her. Who knows if it's a man or woman?

"Maybe *I* can kill you," the face slurps. "Then all the wishes will be mine. *I* can be the Wishmaster!"

Emerging from the crowd, Nick thumps the man-woman thing in the back of the head, knocking them out. The unconscious thing is dragged into and swallowed up by the crowd.

Arms outstretched, Katy throws herself into an embrace, holding tight around Nick's neck. He hugs back, his heart beating for the two of them.

"We have to go," he says, smelling of woodland and charred metal.

Crying, though she can't pinpoint when she started, Katy replies, "Get me out of here."

Holding her hand, he guides her through the madness. Amongst it all, the spiderman has died.

Katy doesn't feel sorry for him.

CHAPTER 42

Walter is dropped, his chin splashes in bodily fluids. The ichor gets in his arm stump, bacteria conspiring to infect it. He'll have the book take care of that. A trail of his blood follows him like a skid mark. The congregation is repelled into a circle around him they don't seem to be aware of, too involved in their own escape or dipshit attempts at fighting back against the attacking ghouls. They're hectic, panicked. It's become a dog-eat-dog bedlam. Invisible hands grip Walter's belly, spin him on his back, then rip off his moustache in one powerful tug, leaving a raw strip above his top lip. It's the kind of shit you'd get in a black and white comedy, and for a fraction of a second Walter thinks he might laugh, opting instead to cry "Fuck!" through the pain.

Something else laughs. More of a rumble.

Fire springs up across the hall, disintegrates a drape, then another, and another. The heat is immediate, sweat stings his raw spot, throbs in the gore where his arm used to be. He doesn't for one second regret chopping it off. What a fucking show it'd been!

The society is falling apart before his eyes, though he never truly cared for it. All of this is just an annoyance. It's also necessary, the dawning of a new era, making way for the future (and a new emblem) by means of a fiery purge. All that need remain the same is the offering. He'll get that fucking girl before the night is through.

The same invisible hands hoist Walter to his knees. He imprisons the book against his chest, damned if he'll let it go. The dagger is lost in the sludge.

Above, fire spreads to the ceiling, turning it into a volcanic sky, flames swimming like negative waves.

Walter hisses, "Had to come back, didya partner?"

A voice grates through the mania. "How could you tell?"

Walter snarls, "You stink, that's how." Dabbing the tender skin above his lip, he says, "I hope you kept the hair."

Apollo shows himself in his new form, a man made from bench-pressed shadow. A shark tooth grin leaks a smoky cloud, thick enough to dull the dead light in the South African's eyes.

He says, "I always knew you were unhinged. I didn't have you down as a double-crosser."

"I didn't have you down as an easy kill." Walter smirks, winding up Apollo's ghost.

"I accept death." Apollo's ghost rolls his shoulders. "Do you?"

Holding up the book, Walter says, "I don't have to."

A member of the society runs too close by Apollo. The South African pulls the man back, turns him inside out without breaking eye contact, or a sweat. The man screams like something stitched together in a laboratory, his new skin of veins and muscle audibly pulsing (*washa-washa-washa*), his organs glistening in the light of the fires before they begin to sag. With a powerful kick, Apollo sends the man away, his ridiculous banshee screech with him. The other right-side-out members stampede over the unfortunate's moist body.

Walter asks, "That supposed to scare me?" He waves his stump.

"It should. That's a vacation compared to what I'm going to do to you."

Up top, at the balcony, the doors explode open, slamming the walls either side, tearing through the wallpaper, handles anchoring the doors open in the plaster. A gale sweeps in a torrent of woodland litter. Members of the crumbling society fighting their way upstairs are blown back, bowling themselves down. A small horde of ghouls glide into the hall, preceding a lone figure strolling with arms by his sides. Faint heavy metal music thumps behind him. When it stops, firelight reveals his face, painted with charcoal to contour it into a skull.

HIM?!

Simon Schaeffer looks pleased with himself, surveys his ongoing desolation. Whatever you think of the rat, you had to get on board with his dramatics.

Schaeffer announces, "Gotta love the classics."

The society, what's left of them, is rounded up and held hostage by Schaeffer's ghouls, forced to their knees, bellies, faces. Walter's men, it isn't good to see, have all been dispatched. A journalist Walter recognises who once tried to bring down the George empire is on his back, legs gone at the knees. A ghoul plays with the stumps, probing its finger inside the mess.

Where're Nick and the girl?

Walter stands. Himself and Apollo are in the aisle. Chairs are torn out of the floor, leaving the two of them in a gladiatorial circle.

"Motley Crue, Dr Feelgood," adds Schaeffer, air drumming to the song even though the music has stopped. "And I do feel good."

The fires are beginning to burn out, still light, still hot, but cool enough to not roast a man alive. Walter can't fathom how this place is even burning. Usually, when something burns, it has to be real.

He barks, "So you set this up?"

"Who else?" Schaeffer poses with theatrical flair, twirling his fingers above his head. "Who else can do what I can? Who else can command the spirits of the dead?" Charcoal clumps crumble from his cheeks like cheap mascara. "They listen to me. I have always had this power, only had to see what I could really do with it! I am totally unique."

"Unique don't mean useful," Walter fires back. "You think I'm scared of you?" He looks back at Apollo, the other ghouls, back to Schaeffer. "Any of this?"

The rat laughs. He's grown arrogant. "It doesn't matter to me, either way. Not my fault if someone is too stupid to see how doomed they are. In fact, not being scared might make it easier for you."

Holding up the book, ooze dripping from its spine, Walter says, "Everything you are was given to you by this. It can just as easily be ripped away."

"Not the first time I've been threatened with that before. Honestly, it gets a little tiring. Besides, you wouldn't know *how*."

A ghoul lunges at Walter from the left, its legs morphed with the mess on the floor to create thick gelatine storks. Its mouth parts, a hole that goes all the way through to the other side of its head. Walter holds up the book, not as a shield but a symbolic weapon.

Immediately cowering, the ghoul backs away, an obedient mutt in the shadow of its angry master. Pleased but unsatisfied, Walter converts the book from a symbolic weapon into a real one, clubs it over the ghoul's head, making it evaporate into dust.

Spinning on his heels, he points to Schaeffer with his stump. The skull faced rat is rattled. "Even your creatures know where true power lies. I bet if I knocked you on the head with this, you'd pop too. So what now? You've banded together with Captain Dead here, formed your little allian- "

Schaeffer yawns. "Apollo?"

Too late does Walter hear the goliath footfalls running at him from behind. Apollo clasps him by the throat, hoists him up the air, shark teeth grinding in circles as if an industrial machine.

Skin is pushed up around Walter's neck, fold over fold, hurting like holy fuck. Scarlet flecks sieve through the raw patch on his face to grow another moustache. Using the book, he beats down on Apollo's head, laughing at the thought of turning the South African into crumbs.

Nothing happens.

Each blow sends purple and green sparks flying from the book.

"Oh, dear," Schaeffer purrs.

"Oh, shit," from Walter.

"The book doesn't scare or dictate to me," says Apollo. His accent isn't as strong as it had been. "I have spent years learning about it over Crane's shoulder. I know its teachings well enough. By knowing it, I am protected from it. Death hasn't fully taken me just yet. You made a mistake when you betrayed me, Walter. I shall punish you in the afterlife."

"Go fuck yourself."

"Hurry up, ape," from Schaeffer. "Finish your business and tell me who killed Dani."

Opportunity, it sweetens the bitterness – or is that blood? – on Walter's tongue almost instantly. Really, if people, or ghouls, want to get away with something, they should learn to keep their mouths shut.

He asks as loud as his squeezed windpipe lets him. "Is that what he's promised you?" He scoffs. "I can tell you *that* for free, and it won't be a lie, either."

Apollo growls, "You fucking..."

"HOLD!" Schaeffer commands. Fires flare up, forks of flame hissing to new heights.

Hot air races in to fill Walter's lungs as Apollo's ghost hand unwraps itself from his neck. Landing on his feet with a thick splash, he splutters. A frostbite claw still attempts to choke him.

Apollo is pushed back. Oily tendrils slither from the cracks in the floorboards, lace themselves around the South African's feet, rooting him in place. He struggles uselessly. The other ghouls are indifferent, keeping vigil over their pathetic charges. Seeing them bowed down, snivelling, Walter's opinion of the society needing some balls is reaffirmed.

"Schaeffer!" shouts the big dumb fucking ghost.

Walter winks. "Never count me out too early."

Schaeffer slides down the banister on his arse, arms outstretched for balance. He lets momentum take him to Walter when he reaches the bottom. "Tell me."

"Crane." Walter smiles. "He's the reason she's dead."

It's a joy to watch something inside of Schaeffer die. You can see it in the way his crooked smile droops. It's obvious he doesn't want to believe what he's just heard, and a stronger, better man may have questioned it. Schaeffer doesn't. Walter goes on, "I'm sorry to tell you, though, that the old man is already dead. Bled out before you joined the party. Where he is now…who cares? If it helps, I can tell you that putting a bullet in the old fuck was more enlightening than his speeches. But there *is* one other."

Apollo interrupts, "Let me kill- "

Snapping his fingers, Schaeffer, who has evidently found the balls in his abilities, takes away Apollo's mouth, which incidentally brightens up the eyes above. One sense compensating for another.

"Who else?" Schaeffer asks.

"It may've been your Master who engineered the whole thing, but someone else prepped the gun, and it was the gun that did the job."

"Who?"

Holding back that it was he and his brother who provided the gun in the first place, Walter tells Schaeffer, "You just took away his mouth."

Over Walter's shoulder, Schaeffer glowers at Apollo. Walter thinks he sees tears in the rat's eyes, but that could just be the heat drying them out. The big ghost makes no attempt to shake his head in denial.

Schaeffer asks, "Tell me why I should believe you, and don't give me any bloody carrots."

Carrots?

"You don't have to," says Walter, "but I reckon you know it's true, don'tchya? You've been treated like the company fuck-up for so long. Why would these people who claim to accept you be any better than liars and cheats?"

With another snap, Schaeffer frees Apollo, gives him his mouth back. In less than a second the South African's spirit ploughs towards both of them, shark teeth rotating like drill bits.

"I wanted to pull the fucking trigger," the ghost snarls. "You fucked everything." To Walter, "I'llkillyouyoufuckingbackstabbing- "

Schaeffer clenches his fist. Spiney, demonic hands spring from dark whirlpools that appear in the floorboards, hooking into Apollo's body with sharpened talons. Without trying they bring him down, sinewy arms sink him into the floor until he is gone. It takes only three or four seconds.

Society members gawk with terror, maybe only now realising they made some bad wishes in life. It's a new delicacy Walter didn't realise he had a taste for until now, watching people come to terms with everything wrong they've done in one tidal wave of regret. You can't get that flavour anywhere else.

"The fuck did he go?" from Walter, staring at the floorboards.

"Somewhere not good," Schaeffer answers. "They'll find a role for him, spirit his size."

"Brilliant, now take your ghosts and fuck off."

Dumbfounded, Schaeffer replies, "That's it?"

"Yeah, that's it," answers Walter. Finding it with his foot, he slides the dagger closer, not looking forward to having to pick it up. You'd think after mutilating his own body for his cause would harden him up to touching piss, shit, spunk and vomit. "Leave. Let me fix this and everything the old man promised you will be repaid a thousandfold."

"You've seen what I can do."

"You see this?" Walter holds up his stump. "Now you've seen what *I* can do, and your ghosties don't stand a chance against me as long as I have the book. So leave me be."

"I…I can help," says Schaeffer.

Jesus, has the fucker latched on already? A second ago he was a rampaging mystic, someone to be feared, respected, made use of in the coming days, but what worthwhile human didn't have their drawbacks? Now, though? Now he's back to being a sidekick, a clear sign for Walter to fuck him off quick.

"I don't want your help." Walter pulls up a broken chair, brushes off wood chips then rests the book on the plush red seat. A nearby ghoul backs away. "It's personal," his lip twitches.

Nick and the girl must've snuck out during the commotion. Not to worry. Crane's funhouse will keep them entertained.

Schaeffer asks, "How do I know you'll keep your promise?"

"I've proven my salt to you. I'll find you when the sacrifice is complete."

Quietly, Schaeffer corrects him, "Master Crane called it the offering."

"Well Master Crane is dead. I'll call it what I bloody well like, and until that time there's nothing for you here. I'm losing my patience," Walter glances at him. "Simon."

A moment of hard thinking in which Walter can see the twat's cogs working, then Schaeffer tightens his lips, frowns heavily. He has become that mystic again. At least there's still a shred of potential there. When Walter runs the world (it's ambitious, but you have to think big) he'll need a man with Schaeffer's talents, if he can keep them in check.

"If you fuck me," says Schaeffer, "I'll come looking for you."

The face-painted clown says no more, stands defiantly before the spine he's grown conks out. Schaeffer makes his way up the stairs, hand sliding up the broken banister. His ghouls, one by one, vacate the hall, dissipating on the spot or gliding away in a green-black smog that disturbs the guttering flames.

Taking a final look back, Schaeffer's skull face appears more genuine in the flickering light. Along with an entourage of spirits, he leaves the hall and, presumably, Crane Manor.

Rid of the rat, Walter addresses the remaining members of Crane's society. They all look disturbed, lost from their straightjackets. Funny, they could handle butchering kids, but ghosts have fucked them up. Load of loonies.

"All of you go."

At first they are hesitant, believing that he means to kill them after lulling them into a false hope. They're right to. If Walter wasn't pushed for time, he'd have made games of them. When they're sure he means what he says, they let their hopes spring. Some run, others wander until they find an exit. Eventually all that's left is Walter, a charred hall, and multiple dead, tortured corpses. It smells like the morning after a campfire minus the stale lager, plus the grilled pork.

On his knees – the filth on the floor wetting his trousers – he flips through the book until he finds something he can use.

"Are you still listening?" he asks the book.

It shakes, the chair vibrating. Magic dust coughs from it.

He chuckles. "Good."

Walter begins reciting from the book, words he didn't know he knew, rolling off of his tongue as if they lived there.

The stump of his left arm starts to pulse, flesh begins reknitting itself. Slowly…painfully…something grows.

CHAPTER 43

They'd slipped out when Simon had made his grand entrance. After that, they ran, and they ran.

And they run.

The hallways never end, or shift, or turn you around or vanish all together. Some take them higher, others on a slow descent. Doorways lead either to other hallways or void spaces that neither of them dare step into. Leaning inside these voids is like listening to the insides of a giant seashell.

Out of wind and sides stitching, Nick and Katy have to stop. Beneath an empty canvas of miserable grey paint, they catch their breath. Nick needs time, Katy has more left in the tank than he does, but she's more than half his age and hasn't had the shit beat out of her. Not physically, anyway. He's sure her mental stability has taken a hammering.

Grabbing a vase from a lopsided shelf, Katy throws it against the wall.

"I *hate* this place!"

Nick slides down against the wall to pick up a piece that didn't break, then he lobs it, making sure it shatters. "Me…too."

"You came back for me." She smiles.

Nick smiles back, for some reason it makes his mashed up hand hurt. "Nearly didn't."

"Fibber."

"I don't fib."

"How did you find me?"

A splinter pokes Nick in the behind, making him shuffle along a couple of inches. "I was in the area."

"Stop fibbing!"

"Luck, mostly."

"More than luck," says Katy. "I thought…I was afraid you might be dead. But I knew it."

"Knew I wasn't dead?" Nick keeps gasping in air.

"No. Something else."

Whatever she's on about, Nick doesn't know. "How are you?"

Her smile drops. She slumps on the opposite wall, dislodging dust, nudges the carpet with her foot, becomes that girl again who could only brighten up if she talked about the cat, only now there's no cat.

"I…I'll be fine."

No you won't, Nick thinks. *The bad dreams will just become normal.*

"What about you?" she asks, deflecting the attention off herself.

"Not so fine," he grimaces, "for someone who takes beatings for money."

Katy points. "Your ear's bleeding."

With a finger, Nick touches his cauliflower lump. No blood. Shit, then it's the other one. Now he'll have two ugly ears to take home with him. He peers right and left, either direction holds nothing but crusty old hallway.

He says, "Anyone follow us?"

"Not that I've seen," Katy answers. "I don't think there's anyone left. I think we're on our own."

"I'll take it."

Far away, a million miles maybe (*if only*), a crash shakes the entire manor. That can't be good. It's followed by many groaning floorboards, the manor shifting on its foundations.

"Help me up," says Nick, his heart revving up all over again. It hurts his chest, and for a second or two he has to decide if he's having a heart attack or not. Not, he decides.

She goes to him, slings an arm over her shoulder. The two of them grunt together as she helps Nick to his feet.

"You were fine a minute ago." She eyes up his mangled hand.

Fine is, apparently, a broad spectrum to the young.

"A minute ago I didn't have a choice," he tells her.

Another crash, closer. A hanging picture of a little boy comes loose, smashing on the floor. They both stare down the hallway along with the broken child.

"I don't think you have a choice *now*," she says.

"That's trouble. Jesus, there has to be a way out of here."

"We keep running?"

"Where?" Nick foresaw these walls becoming a problem. The house itself is against them. "There's not even a window to jump through."

"Well…we could fight?"

Her suggestion is the worst punch Nick has ever taken, and he's taken a right hander straight to the face from Robby 'Meathooks' Gulliver. He gazes at her to determine if she's lost a screw.

"Uh-uh," he protests. "Not a chance, we don't know what's coming."

At the end of the hallway a large unit is thrown into view, disintegrating into a pile of woodchip and glass, dust erupts around the wreckage. Snuffling, boar-like, can be faintly heard.

Katy talks fast, "If we can get hold of the book then maybe- "

By the shoulders, Nick takes hold of her, spins her around so they're face to face. On her left shoulder his fucked up hand resembles tenderised meat that she tries not to look at.

"I don't want you anywhere *near* that thing, hear me? I was told that to end this I had to go for the heart. I didn't know what the hell that meant. That was the *only* advice I got about how to end this shit. To go. For. The heart. I didn't know it meant *you*! I want that damn thing as far away as possible, it's- "

"A part of me," Katy stops him.

"Don't you understand?" asks Nick. "The heart is you, *and* that fucking book."

"I understand plenty," she says.

He stares, trying to work her out. Nick knows he's wrong when he says, "It might kill you." The only logic working in his mind right now is telling him that keeping the damned book as far away as possible is the best thing.

"It *won't*," Katy argues. "It's dangerous, but I'm connected to it, now. For it to live, it needs me as much as the cult do. It *wants* my blood. Surely the safest place for it to be is with me?"

Nick formulates his response, confusing himself in the process. "If you and the book are together, whoever wants you will have it all in a package. By keeping you apart they- "

"They only have- "

"Until midnight. I know," Nick sighs. "Change can happen in minutes. If we keep running, we can make it to midnight, then they'll be out of luck."

"I'm tired of…of…bloody running," Katy's face reddens.

Nick can empathise with that. Also, he sees the determination in her face, unshakable.

She says, "Maybe we can find something in the book that will help."

"Like what?"

"I don't know."

"Great, and if not?"

"Then we'll try the running thing. At least then I'll have all of my heart, and no one else'll have the book. Without it, Walter will have nothing."

"Unless he gets you, then he'll have everything," says Nick.

"He won't get me, because I have you."

Christ, this girl knows how to make a speech.

More furniture is tossed, destroyed, making a prickly dam at the end of the hallway. The snuffling is closer.

"I don't like it," Nick says, even though she's the only one with a real idea. "Are you sure?"

"About getting the book? Yes. About what to do after? No." She's consistent with her honesty, at least.

"How're we going to get it?" he asks. Katy shrugs. "Fuck." He let's go of her shoulders, glances the other way. "If what this comes down to is me destroying the book, I won't do it. I can't."

Katy touches his arm. "You won't have to."

It's a reassurance that Nick doesn't like the undertone of.

"Okay. Jesus. Fuck." A surge of adrenaline perks him up. "We need more room. What's coming is big."

"Lead the way." Katy damn near smiles.

Perhaps she wants some payback. Or maybe she's become like a soldier, unable to leave behind what she's gotten used to. A clock bongs on the wall, the gears inside whine as they spin. Doors open for a cuckoo bird that doesn't spring out.

"Half eleven," says Nick.

How has time passed so quickly? It doesn't make sense. Then again, in Crane Manor, nothing does.

Katy responds, "Until midnight, remember. We have to do this before midnight."

"What happens at midnight?"

"I'm...not sure." She glances away. "I don't think it's good."

"I hope we know what we're doing."

They run.

"We've already established that we don't," says Katy.

Cheers for that.

A slippery pink finger slithers around the corner of the hallway, peeling the paper, followed by a second, third and fourth. They appear sore, like skinned frogs, extra knuckle joints creak as they continue to grow. Leaving a track of slime in its wake is a forearm, longer than a leg, stringy with muscles that resemble raw chicken cuts. Half a face peeks out, the eye bloodshot, nose turned up and flattened, snorting.

Walter watches Nick and the girl run.

And he follows.

CHAPTER 44

Despite what she said, Katy takes the lead, peering inside every door she finds. Bruises cover the backs of her legs.

Behind Nick, the thing clump-clump-clumps closer, huge wet slaps that shake the floorboards. It laughs, a phlegmy snorting that bubbles on the nape of his neck.

"Pick a room!" he calls.

Flinging open another door, Katy replies, "I'm trying!"

She leaves the no-hope doors open. Each one Nick glances into holds either nothing or not enough space for taking on whatever's gaining on them.

She tries another. "In here!"

Following Katy, Nick turns into the doorway sharp enough to nearly be tripped up by his own feet. He grabs the frame with his bad hand, crying out in pain as the agony renews.

They're in a dining hall. Before them is a long table, immaculately set, which points to an unlit open stone fireplace which has another blank painting above it. Above the table is a deer horn chandelier that swings steadily from side to side, held aloft by rope. Everything in the dining room from the silverware to the walls wears cobweb veils. Cabinets holding glasses, plates and other hosting items are dotted against the walls.

"Plan?" says Nick.

"I don't have one yet."

Clump-clump-*CLUMP!*

"Quick," Nick orders.

They ram the door closed, putting their combined weight on it. Before it locks shut, a slimy pink arm thrusts around to stop it. Elongated fanned fingers jerk like animatronic claws. Whatever it is, is laughing, bashing to gain entry. Nick puts his back, literally, into it, shoving with his feet, sweat burning every abrasion on his skin. Katy grits her teeth, stepping over and over on the spot. The thrashing arm scrapes in further, grating off its own skin. Hinges squeak as the screws begin to wiggle loose.

"What is it?" Katy shouts.

"You wanna find out?"

"We're supposed to be fighting it!"

Nick can feel his head pounding. "We…are!"

The arm eels in more, curving around the door. It could reach behind them if it wanted to. A face butts itself between the gap, shimmies it wider, drawing back its skin into a distorted Halloween mask. The nose sniffs, right nostril capacious and discharging a yellow fluid.

Katy screams, repulsed by the porcine face. Nick pushes harder. Where's a fucking axe when you need one?

It looks at them. The left eye is a distended globe sponging up blood, wide open by default because the lid is no longer compatible. Swollen muscles on the same side bulge down its neck like tubing, disappearing into the shoulder. In a monstrous voice that burrows into Nick's chest, it asks, "Don'tchya recognise me, Nick?"

The voice is recognisable only by the sadistic enjoyment.

"Walt?"

The door detonates open, throwing Nick and Katy backwards. Katy tumbles under the long table, Nick lands on top, winding himself on the spread. Splinters quill his arm.

Walter…*floats in*?

His bare left arm is a grotesque tender limb of bone and muscle, coated in a layer of mucus. He uses it gorilla-style, propelling himself forward on doughy knuckles, lifting his feet off the ground with each arc. At the shoulder the mutation hasn't stopped. Oversized muscles bore into his neck like screws winding improperly through wood. Walter's face, half of it, is the last place the change touches. How the eyeball hasn't exploded yet is anyone's guess.

Holding himself aloft, Walter's body sits in the bracket of his new arm, his feet hanging freely three or four feet off the floor. He holds the book in his right.

Rolling off the table, bringing a racket of condiments with him, Nick lands on his front, dust wafting up his nostrils. He searches for Katy under the table but can't see her. His attention is fish-hooked by Walter's barbed voice.

"An improvement, wouldn't you say?"

Walter's hairline jabs down into an exaggerated widow's peak, skin stretched tight against his skull, bullying his flesh to rip.

"I had more refined images in my head, but without full mastery, I could only hope for so much," he goes on. "There's still time, though."

Nick wonders if this kind of mutation was in Crane's vision of partnering with the Liber Votorum. He kicks himself up, charges Walter without any plan other than to see if his southpaw is still any good.

Walter lowers himself, twists his arm around Nick to grab and lift him by the neck before he can deliver his punch.

Bringing him face to face, his breath foul with the book's black magic, Walter asks with sincerity, "Think anyone will still want to fuck me?"

The eye drowned in blood twitches over Nick, observing him. A chameleon eye.

"Not without the moustache." Nick lashes out with his left, catches Walter a literal cracker on the cheek. Walter doesn't flinch. That southpaw ain't so hot after all.

Nick steals a glance at the book. He might be able to grab it.

Walter sees. "Oh, God, you're pathetic."

Walter casts Nick aside. Nick's back jack-knifes against an armoire, knocking the wind from him, paralysing his spine. Ornaments of copper, bronze, porcelain and china crash onto him. The armoire rocks, falls forward. Driving past the paralysis, Nick crawls out of the way before it can crush his legs. It's a close, loud call.

It's too painful to stand, too painful to do anything.

Rubbing her head, Katy pops out from under the table, a gash on her chin. When she sees Walter, she screams. The monster swings its arm to catch her but she ducks, runs away towards the far end of the table.

"Run Katy!" shouts Nick.

"Yes, Katy," Walter mocks. "Run, run, run!"

Using his arm as a spring, Walter vaults over the length of the table in one fluid motion, upsetting whorls of grimy spider silk. He lands in front of Katy at the fireplace, creating an earthquake that unbalances her and the hanging canvas, which unhooks from its place on the wall, clattering between them. Walter smashes it in half, sweeps the remains into the mouth of the fireplace.

"Going somewhere?" he asks.

Katy windmills her arms to keep from falling back, then turns to run. Walter wraps his monster arm around her twice to draw her close, coating her torso with gungy secretion. She kicks and screams, hair glued down around her shoulders. Nick tries to get up, his spine says otherwise.

Walter sweeps aside cutlery, glassware and crockery on the table where he slaps down the book. On its front are two shimmering, amethyst eyes. It opens itself, a gale rocks the chandelier, rope creaking. Walter unfurls Katy, grips her by the back of the head over the book, teasing her and it. He's hurting her, squeezing out tears as if he's making juice.

Nick *has* to get up!

He tries crawling again, pushing his body over a limit of pain he's never experienced before. It lances his body, toppling him onto his side, spearing him in places. He shouts at the high ceiling.

Sheathed in his waistband, Walter takes the ornate dagger with his new hand, presses it against Katy's throat. Blood trickles over the keen edge.

He starts, "You're all out of luck, Cheru- "

From her pocket, Katy whips out the T-bone, stabs Walter's monster hand, twisting the makeshift weapon. Walter yelps, drops the dagger.

Katy goes to snatch the book but Walter yanks her back by the hair. She screams.

"You're a hard child to kill." Walter snorts in her face, spitting.

She grits her teeth. "What does that say about you?"

His face drops. Walter swaps her over to his right hand, holds her by the throat at arm's length. The monster arm draws back, back, back, until the elbow touches the fireplace. It makes a squelching fist that drips. The hole she'd punctured in it spurts viscous, glistening fluid.

Walter says, "Don't insult my pride."

He strikes Katy with a crack. Two teeth fly from her mouth, her nose a bloody mess. A second strike throws her head back with whiplash fury. The T-bone is knocked from her hand, skates on the floor just shy of Nick. When Katy lifts her head back up, she's laughing, the sanity beat out of her.

Walter brings his moist monster arm up, uses it as a sledgehammer for his final blow. Katy watches in a daze as it comes down.

Peels of wood coil under Nick's nails as he pulls himself forward, clenching his teeth so hard he's sure they'll break. Tears drug his vision. At the apex of his pain his fingers find the T-bone, and as if it were a magical rejuvenation trinket, feeling returns to his legs.

Katy goes down like a sack of bricks, unconscious, her face puffy, bleeding and bruised. Walter picks her up, drops her face down on the table. The book hops forward to nip at her hair.

Fishing the dagger up, Walter exposes her throat.

"Coward!"

Nick shoulder charges Walter in the ribs, hugging his arms around the monster's stomach. Beside Katy, Walter drops the dagger. The ferocity of Nick's charge knocks them both to the floor. In the two seconds Walter is vulnerable, Nick plunges the T-bone into the bulbous bloody eye.

Screeching in a way that resembles little of the man he used to be, Walter bucks Nick off. Blood spouts from the eye, deflating as if a balloon with a pin prick hole. His legs kick, arms flail unrestricted, flopping in every direction.

Nick rushes to Katy, kicking silverware across the stone slabs of the hearth. He turns her over, her face a mess, the gash on her chin split wider. Grabbing a tablecloth, Nick dabs hurriedly at the wounds, noticing that his hand is covered in eye-jelly.

She groans. "Get..."

"Katy?"

"...the...book."

Inches from the top of Katy's head, the Liber Votorum stares at Nick with its gemstone eyes, judging, *tasting*, his soul. A clump of Katy's hair is in its papery maw, chewing tobacco for the dark arts. Somehow, it growls.

"Quickly," she coughs.

Walter thunders, "*GET AWAY FROM THEM!*"

With his monster arm acting as a trebuchet, Walter fires himself at Nick, dropkicks him in the chest, sending him sailing over Katy on a slip and slide along the table. Cutlery and condiments gather over his shoulders until he drops off at the far end. Nick doesn't touch the floor for more than two seconds before Walter is on top of him, hoisting him off his feet by the throat.

Using his human hand, Walter smacks Nick's bleeding ear.

Nick cries out, the pain sears through his eardrum into his brain, a high-pitched whistle made from razor wire. He clutches the monster arm, unable to find a grip through all the slime.

Walter breathes deeply, snuffling his nose as if in search of something, snorting up a string of snot. The T-bone is still lodged in his eye, now an empty sack. A broken yolk is all that's left of the pupil.

"Thanks for popping the pimple," he sneers.

Nick replies, "Did I get the spot?"

"You always were a smartmouth."

"You always were a prick."

Walter smirks, "I should've killed you in that alley."

Nick taunts, against his better judgement. "Speaking of which, you wanna gather some of your mates? You're tough with a kiddy, but you always did need a hand with someone your own size."

"I think," Walter snarls, lips bending into a smile, "that you should have a better viewing platform."

"Hey!" Katy calls.

Nick and Walt both gasp when they see her.

She's rolled onto her front, barely conscious. Thick cables of blood from her nose stick to the table, her eyes roll from white to iris to white again. She has the dagger over the book. On her face, Nick makes out the smallest, happiest smile.

"It's the only…way," she says.

"Jesus Katy, no!" Nick pleads, kicking his legs, hammering fists onto the monster arm.

Walter begins, "What do you think you're- "

Katy spits a wad of blood on the book, sending it into a frenzy.

"That's the only blood of mine it'll get," she says.

Nick shouts, "Katy, NO!"

"NO!" from Walter.

"I'm going for heart."

The dagger plunges towards the book.

CHAPTER 45

Tock.

The dagger fails to pierce the leather cover.

Sobbing, breathing quickly, Katy lifts her arm for another stab.

Tock.

Again.

Tock.

She's too weak, struggles to make the knife land on its tip. Nick doesn't know how to feel.

She cries, unable to lift the dagger again. Walter chuckles, and fucking hell, so does the book. Maybe it takes on the personality of whoever it listens to. Crane was mild mannered, calm, calculated and intellectual, so the book too seemed to not be much of an entity. Walter, though, has gotten into it like a contagion, turning it physically into the monster he is.

"Too tough for you, Cherub?" asks Walter with a sting in his tone. To Nick, he adds, "Take a seat."

Nick is thrown at the chandelier. He grabs the creaking ropes, balances himself on the antlers. A couple of them break loose, shattering when they hit the floor.

"Try getting down from there without breaking your legs," Walter jokes.

Nick looks at the ceiling, hoping to see cracks. There are none, the chandelier is stable.

Walter lumbers towards Katy. She's lying flat, dagger loosely in hand.

Clomp-clomp-clomp.

Nick bellows, "Leave her the fuck alone!"

Walter lets the fingers of his right hand walk along the table, spinning knives and forks, whilst his left arm drags behind, leaving a sticky, steaming trail.

Breaking off an antler, Nick uses it to saw at the rope, but it's no good. When has a blunt tool ever been useful? Not to mention that if it came down he'd land inside a broken pile of things that could stab him.

Climbing on the table, walking on all-fours and donning a smile to freak out the creeps, Walter lets his left arm slither up to remove the dagger from Katy. She attempts to hold on, and Walter pretends with glee that, for just a second, he can't unlatch the dagger from her hand. With his right hand he reaches for the book, strokes it, then runs his fingers through Katy's hair.

Nick searches his pockets, hugs the ropes as he nearly falls backwards. He first finds the voice recorder. It's been recording this whole time, and goes back in his pocket. He then finds the Zippo he took from the backpack in the woods.

He flicks it open, that metallic ping so damn magic, strikes the flint for a flame, getting only sparks. It's hard to do with his mangled left hand.

He begs it, "Come on."

Looking down, he has Walter at an exact bird's eye view.

Katy yelps as Walter yanks at her hair, lifting up her head. He gets in close, rubbing his snout over her face.

"Yessssss," he hisses. "Crane certainly knew how to pick the best blood."

His awful arm worms the dagger over her face, head, lips, then finally scratches down to her neck.

Nick strikes the flint for the hundredth time and still there is no flame. He tries again and again and…

Fire!

He holds the flame to the rope, begins bouncing on the chandelier.

"Come *ON!*"

Walter doesn't hear him. The book opens itself, dehydrated and ready for its drink. Katy sobs, holds her eyes closed.

"I'll make it slow, shall I, Cherub?" Walter says.

The rope blackens, threads snap one by one. Nick jumps up and down, rattling antlers from their fixtures. Bones rain down onto the table.

Walter sneers at Katy. "You're a tough little bitch, I'll give you that. Tough *this* out."

SNAP!

The chandelier falls.

Nick watches the monster gawk up in time to see his face before the chandelier crushes him in a racket of snapping bone, splintering wood and ripping flesh. Just before it impacts, Nick jumps off to cover Katy, hauls them both to the floor. The table buckles, breaks in two.

The chandelier missed Katy by inches.

Nick, leaning over Katy, looks up. A plate spins on one of the chairs. The chandelier sits broken atop the monster in the gutter of the busted table, the end of the rope smoking like a doused wick. Blood trickles from the tangled nest, as if *it's* bleeding instead of what's buried. Out of the wreck hangs the monster arm, the dagger clenched in its impossible fingers.

Just outside of the crush zone is the book, snapping angrily. Leaving Katy for a few seconds, Nick bundles it in several layers of torn table cloth, then returns to her. She's curled up, covering her head.

"It's okay," he taps her shoulder.

She murmurs, "Is…he…dead?"

"I think so."

She breaths deep, exhales. "Not the…fight I had…in mind." She starts to cry and Nick hugs her, sure that at any second he'll cry himself. One tear does manage the great escape. It doesn't taste like salt, but blood.

"You have the book?" she asks.

Nick squeezes the package, wishing that he could crush it into a thousand pieces. "We have it."

"Can we go now?"

"Yeah," Nick replies. "I think we can."

Only, he isn't sure how they will leave. The house is still here, they're still lost inside it.

Katy's voice is weak, croaky. "I'm sorry I…tried to kill myself."

Nick knows she didn't really try to kill herself, but Walter and the book. The society. If she'd been able to, she'd be a martyr, which means more to the dictionary than it does to him. More tears cut tracks in his grimy face.

"I couldn't find…a spell," she adds.

He holds her close. "That's okay."

"Are you…crying?" she asks.

"Yeah."

"Wimp."

"I didn't ask for this," says Nick.

"Me neither," she replies.

Something cracks in the antler pile.

Katy yelps. "Did you hear that?"

"It's nothing."

Another, louder crack.

Nick looks over his shoulder. The monster arm is moving, the ruin of the chandelier is pulsing.

"We need to leave," Nick says.

"I thought you said- "

Walter bursts from his grave roaring, swinging his monster arm over his head. Stakes of wood and pieces of antler have given him horns. Gore tattoos his skin and clothes, weighs down his hair. The mutant muscles chug, twist, push the T-bone from his eye. He lashes at Nick, misses. Like a tentacle the arm moves without bones.

The monster howls, "The girl is mine! I am the Wishmaster!"

Nick drops the Liber Votorum in Katy's lap, picks her up. Catching and pulling off a nail on his hand sends his mind spinning. His busted hand is a throbbing lump, but at least he's able to use it with some degree of dexterity. He runs to the door, somehow managing to rally his legs into working together. Walter snaps his arm in front of them, an octopus whip, whomping a trench into the floor. It's grown longer, thinner, gunkier. Nick one-eighties, heading for God knows where. The monster is throwing chairs at them that Nick has to dodge as if he and Katy are insects in a meteor shower.

"Give her to me!"

Walter tosses one half of the long table, swinging it first as a bat. Nick ducks just in time. The half table volleys overhead, fracturing into a thousand pieces against the wall, taking out cabinets and paintings with it.

As they pass the mouth of the fireplace, Walter leaps in front of them, punching a hole in the great stone slabs. Using his new horns, he plays with them, butting his head forward, kicking his foot back, snorting. Nick falls with Katy in his arms. Clomping towards them, Walter lifts and throws away one of the broken slabs. Nick tries to kick away but his feet keep skidding, can't get up. Katy groans, blissfully ignorant of their impending doom. In her lap, the Liber Votorum shakes free of its wrappings, amethyst eyes now a searing emerald. Nick didn't think green could look so angry.

Walter, standing in front of the fireplace, wraps his tentacle around them, slowly pulls them closer.

"I've had enough fun," he says. His nose has been turned into alligator jaws, snapping open and closed as he breaths, strands of snot and blood bridging between the flesh. "I'll kill the both of you, give it some extra oomph." Walter once more brandishes the dagger. "And look, you prepared the book *and* the girl for me. How sweet. One quick slice and her blood will flow into its mouth like a pretty little river, and yours, Nick, will follow seconds after."

Around them the tentacle arm squeezes tighter. Mucus oozes from its flesh, sizzling.

So this is really it, Nick thinks. It's been it a number of times recently, but this is *the it*. The last of the fight has been sapped from it, but at least they had fought, to a degree, if you can call running a fight. Sometimes it is, sometimes you need to make your opponent dance around before you deliver the final blow, except this time there is no final blow. His ears sting, head could be split in two. Ribs, guts, legs, arms, hands…everything hurts, everything is tired, everything has given up.

His heart, too.

At least Katy won't see it coming.

At least that.

She'd thought the book might be able to help them, the book which carries half of her own heart. It hadn't. It only listens to the Wishmaster.

Walter shoves the dagger under Katy's neck. Nick closes his eyes.

The blade runs along her skin.

CHAPTER 46

"*WHAT?!*" Walter's voice is puzzled.

Nick opens his eyes.

Katy's neck isn't open. Walter runs the dagger across again, the flesh won't cut.

"What *is* this?"

It's Walter who asks the question, but Nick's thinking the same thing. Walter gazes at Nick and, for the first time, worry is etched onto his face.

Nick begins, "I- "

With an echoing boom, Walter is shoved back by a god hand. Sliding on his back, his tentacle uncoils from around Nick and Katy, leaving a sticky substance around them. Monster Walter looks up, a second boom pins him to the floor, only his tentacle can move, jerking madly. He's in line with the fireplace's mouth.

From Katy's lap the Liber Votorum floats to the ground, hovering just above the stone surface. Earthy, pale light spills from its pages.

"I don't- " Walter is cut off by firecracker explosions in his tentacle, starting at the tip and working their way up, taking sections of the arm away in bursting red coronas of blood and ichor. His scream is muted by brown filth boiling from his mouth. The stump is worse than before, the explosions have taken it away, hollowing out his torso. The stench of the brown stuff boiling now not just from Walter's mouth but any exit it can find is putrid.

Heaving himself and Katy up, cradling her, Nick backs into a corner, slumps back down on his behind. Though she is still unconscious, he tips Katy's head towards his chest so that, should she wake, she won't be able to see.

Walter is a nasty fuck, but no one should witness what's happening to him.

"Nick...?" Katy's voice is a tired whisper.

"You don't want to see this," he tries to convince her.

"I want...to watch."

He shakes his head, can't look at her. Nightmares are being branded into his psyche that will haunt his brain beyond death, a smell gluing itself into his nostrils that will overpower every other smell for the rest of his life. He can't possibly allow Katy to have that same treatment.

"I've seen...worse," she says.

And then he looks at her, knowing from her half-open eyes that it's true. If he peers hard enough, he can see in them the sights Katy has been subject to over her time in the hands of the society. A many-legged man...terrified of himself, the pain. The world.

Nick tilts her, and they both watch.

In front of Walter, a tall, muscular totem materialises from the ground. Darkness constructed into a man, wisps of smoke flail around its feet, shoulders wider than its hips. On top is a bowling ball head. Walter stares up in horror, as if he knows what it is.

"Apollo?" he asks.

The totem addresses Walter as a judge does a convict. The sound from its throat is closer to twisting steel than human. "Walter George, you have been found weak."

What the totem, if it is Apollo, has lost in its accent it has gained in height and muscle. It could be the devil's own bounty hunter. Perhaps it is, and maybe not just the devil's, but all of them, for isn't the Liber Votorum a collection of all the world's magics, its gods and anti-christs?

Glancing down, Nick sees Katy watching without blinking, breathing slowly. Everything is reflecting in her eyes, committing itself to memory. On her face the swelling has gone down, the bruising not so severe. On her chin the gash has closed itself, but will leave a scar. Seems being linked with the book has its perks. Two teeth, however, are still missing.

Walter argues with the totem. "I was so close! I had her! I- "

Both his legs break at the knees. He screams again, thrashing around on the floor, punching stone with his right hand until his knuckles break. Blood spills over his lips, mixed with the shit.

At the totem's feet, the Liber Votorum has become a spinning top, green sparks fling from it like an old toy gun Nick had and broke as a child.

The totem passes sentencing. "You had many opportunities, Walter George, and yet you could not supply. You have been judged…undeserving."

Wrenching more anguish from Walter, his right arm breaks, the bones in his hand crumble. The dagger falls from his now useless grip.

The totem figure drones on. "Incompetent."

Walter's back folds backwards, snapping spine and ribs. Any wailing he would have squawked is choked off. You can't scream when your lungs are empty. When the totem figure is finished, Walter is origami.

He wheezes, "You…how can you…only Schaeffer- "

"Simon Schaeffer's powers come from the Liber Votorum. As did yours, that which has been reclaimed. The book may do as it wishes when there is no Wishmaster," says the totem.

Apollo isn't speaking like Apollo.

The fireplace flares into white-hot life. Nick can't see the flames, but their ferocity is evident in the way the room is lit up. Heatwaves ripple over Walter, he shields his face as his body begins to smoke.

For a moment, whatever the totem figure remembers of its previous life comes back to it, and speaks with Apollo's voice.

"You were close…but it was a bad partnership."

"I am…" Walter manages a smile, finds Nick and Katy. He is full of hope and madness. "…the Wishmaster."

Apollo points at him, breaking the illusion that he is unmoving. "You are nothing."

With a flick of a finger, origami Walter goes sliding into the fireplace, the dagger with him, a patch of blood and shit left on the floor. The fire coughs flame at the arrival of its dinner. It spits, sizzles and cracks. It's a full ten seconds before Walter begins squealing.

"It's melting it! My soul! I can feel my soul melting! MY SOUL MELTING!"

Nick pulls Katy closer. She doesn't turn away, doesn't cover her ears. He tries to cover them for her, but she shakes him off.

The screams go on for some time. Any normal death would have ended long ago, yet Mercy doesn't seem to be in the building, leaving Death to its own devices. The totem stands with its back to Nick and Katy, the book at its feet spinning wildly, green sparks turning to purple, to red, to blue, back to green, a strong wind from it throwing up debris in the dining room.

"*MY SOUL IS MEL-* "

Walter George's death howls stop. The fire extinguishes itself, leaving not a trace of having ever existed. Not so much as a whiff of smoke...or charred flesh.

The totem remains, its job complete, but not its contract. Nick knows – but doesn't know how – that somehow Apollo was given to the book. No. Imprisoned in it, becoming its slave. How long the contract lasts, he can't guess at, though something tells him it's one of those forever deals.

The book drops to the cracked slabs.

Only now does Katy look away, her head flops against Nick's chest. She snores but isn't asleep, not really. He cups her head in his hand.

Over its shoulder, the totem glares at Nick. He stares back. Crazy, but he wants to thank it. The only thing that stops him is knowing if Apollo himself wasn't corrupted by the book or assigned as its personal soul harvester, Nick would be wherever those ghost fires took Walter as well. Apollo may no longer have his free will, but Nick can tell from his glare that he hasn't forgotten past vendettas. Soon enough, he will. The Liber Votorum will fully erase his human side.

Apollo knows this, bares filed teeth, then with a puff of mist that flows like dry ice, vanishes into the floor until the day comes when he is needed again.

The book is left behind, inanimate.

The dining room is in quiet desolation. A bomb sight replica from the war. Nick and Katy look as if they should never have survived. Puddles of blood pattern the floor like Dalmatian dots. An antler tumbles from the chandelier pile.

"I told you," says Katy.

Nick asks, "What's that?"

"That…the book might be able to…to help us."

"I wouldn't call that help."

She sighs as if coming home from a long day at work. "I would." She adds, "I'm sorry that I…tried to kill myself aga- "

Nick shushes her. "Don't worry about it, just…just rest."

She swallows, then asks, "Can we go now?"

Nick gawks at the destruction. "I don't think so. Not yet," he says, weary. There's someone else they need to see.

Katy yawns. "I'm thirsty."

"We'll have to hold on a bit longer," Nick tells her, realising that his throat, too, is a sand dune.

He stands up, she is still in his aching arms. He'll hold her for hours. Days, if he has to.

She asks, "How long…do we have?"

Perched precariously on a wooden beam, one small clock has survived, though the glass covering its face is smashed. The time is 11:53.

"Not long," Nick says.

"Is Pop Tart here?"

"No." Does she know about the cat?

Katy sniffs. Exhaustion finally takes its toll, she buries herself into Nick's chest, inhaling deeply of his smell. He can't smell any good, though he reckons it's a damn sight better than the shit that erupted from

Walter.

He goes to the motionless book. The Liber Votorum doesn't make him feel sick anymore. There's a brimstone aroma where the totem stood. Bending at the knees, which isn't easy with Katy in his arms, he's able to cover the book back up and take it in his left hand. It doesn't look like it had done minutes ago. It has no eyes, no anger, but Nick knows it's just dormant.

Because, really, you never can judge a book by its cover.

CHAPTER 47

The hallways of Crane Manor no longer go on forever, nor do they shift. There are no more doorways to oblivion, only those to other rooms.

There are no other working clocks, even though some of them persist with their ticking. After passing the third, Nick stops checking. When he moves by a bookcase filled with porcelain ballerinas, Katy asks to be put down. She walks with a slight limp, as if every now and then she steps on a hot coal. The wrapped book is in her possession, now. By choice.

They reach the hall in just a couple of minutes.

It's a grilled shrine of its former self, a plaque away from being a memorial sight, one that nobody wants to remember.

Society drapes are bundled up or burnt at windows with no outside, the triangular ceiling is a gutted carapace that drips condensation. Droplets hiss when they land on anything still hot from the fires.

"Are there snakes in here?" Katy asks, holding the book against her chest. Apparently, the book's sickness isn't getting to her either.

Nick tells her to be careful where she steps.

Grit crackles under their feet as they move around bodies, trying to not accidentally nudge one, or trip over a stray hand or foot. The blood and vomit and other bodily excretions have been boiled into tar, the smell scorched away. Small favours.

One chair covers a corpse with multiple limbs sticking out from underneath, resembling an overstuffed sandwich. When he goes to move it, Katy asks him not to. Nick leaves it be.

On stage the podium has capsized, the microphone dipped in blood. It looks like a candy apple. The spotlight, shining from nowhere, still works, though its brilliance has paled. All it spots now is a facedown…man?…woman?…with a hole in the back of their head, the brain apparently blown into ash except for the lumps caught in the short hair.

A steep series of steps leads off and behind the stage. The way is arrowed by a sword. It leads into an office room. It's in here that they find Ulysses Crane, lying on his back, his head in the lap of the bus woman. Her legs are tucked under herself. She looks down at Crane, stroking his grey hair.

"Nicholas?" Crane wheezes.

Nick goes first, followed by Katy. She keeps to his left, mistrustful of the woman.

A clock ticks too slow.

Tick...

...tock.

Nick stands over the dying man. Crane's suit is still immaculate, real gentleman's finery. It's faintly chequered, the legs starched, jacket creased where he bends his elbows. His pocket watch remains attached to its delicate chain. It's all ruined at the chest, where blood blooms across his white shirt, a flooded penny slot hole in his sternum.

Tick...

...tock.

"Nicholas?" Crane says again. "Where did it all go so wrong?"

"I'd say around the time you started killing kids," Nick answers without emotion. His damaged hand is caked in drying blood.

"Amusing," Crane looks away, a smile on his face. You'd be forgiven for thinking he hadn't murdered generations of children with that smile. "I pin it roundabout the time I met you."

"Agree to disagree."

"Yes." Crane tries a laugh but it comes out as a cough. The penny slot releases a bubble. "A fine saying. It gladdens my heart to see you alive, Nicholas."

Nick can't say the same thing. Yet still, after everything, there's something – a twinkle – about Ulysses Crane, the same way you feel affection for the grandad who'd read you stories by the fire on cold winter evenings. Nick never had that, but knows the fantasy.

He gets down on one knee, and it's now that he hears the woman. She is singing something, the movement of her lips louder than the words. Her eyes are open, fixed on Crane.

"You look a little worse for wear," says Crane.

Nick's injuries are plentiful. A split eyebrow and mauled hand are accompanied by many cuts, scrapes and bruises. The pains of each have morphed into a suit that dresses his body with a sting.

"Crane," Nick replies, "we need to know- "

Katy drops down on her knees. "What happens to me at midnight?"

"Oh! My dear." Crane sounds grandfatherly. "How the mighty hath *risen*. Forgive me for not seeing you, me eyesight…is failing me. My, you look a tad battered yourself."

Battered, yes, but Crane hadn't seen her even five minutes ago. Katy's recovery has been nothing short of miraculous. And…are those…have her teeth grown back?

Crane goes on, "And you have my book? May I…please hold it again, just this last time?"

Nick interjects, "You're never touching it again." He should leave it at that, though seemingly with an agender of their own, two more words pop from his mouth. "I'm sorry."

Katy leans closer to Crane, speaks with whispered authority. "Tell me."

Tick…

…tock.

Crane coughs again, a shoot of blood launches from the penny slot that Katy reels back from. With every weakening heartbeat, the pool of blood shudders. The old man is a sinking vessel.

"Did you…" He pauses. "…did you not study my countless books on the matter?"

Katy begins, "I didn't have time- "

"Ulysses." Nick gives the old man a stern look with a hint of pleading.

Crane sighs, his face not unkind. He regards the both of them, then tells her, "My sweet dear, it has already happened."

Afraid that he'll see a corpse instead of a girl, Nick glances at Katy in his peripheral vision.

She gasps. "*What?*"

"Yes." Crane takes a long breath. "The midnight hour has already passed us. You were there when the book rejected Walter George. That is when it happened, and now...now it is yours."

In unison, Nick and Katy ask, "What is?"

Gazing to the ceiling, Crane answers. "The great" – he rolls his *R*s – "Liber Votorum. It belongs to you."

Katy replies, "I don't understand."

Nick doesn't either. The woman continues to sing her silent song.

As if caught by surprise, Crane draws in a sharp breath, wind squeezing through a collapsed tunnel. His penny slot dribbles, releases several bubbles. For the old man, that penny slot is a countdown.

Tick...

...tock.

When he recovers, Crane says, "The ritual was not completed. Not by me and not by Mr George. The deadline was met without fruit. You and the book share a heartbeat because your blood was inserted into its pages, and when the ritual went unresolved the book sought its closest companion, namely...you. Now, you and the book shall be joined forever, until the day you pass. It can only be yours. That is your honour."

If there's anything to say to Katy, Nick has no clue what it is. He watches her look away, letting the information sink in, working out her future in a matter of seconds.

She looks back at Crane. "If it's mine," she asks, "can I destroy it?"

Good question, surely if it belongs to her she can-

"No," he splutters. The woman keeps stroking his head, looping her song, or is it a prayer...an incantation? "It is locked with your soul. Your blood still resides inside it. It is your heart's twin."

"Do I...*have* to keep it?" Katy says.

"You must. Parting with the book would be akin to parting with a literal, living, breathing piece of yourself. Can a heart continue to keep a body alive if only half of it exists? Soon enough, if you were to abandon the Liber Votorum, you would feel the effect, thereafter you would *see* the effect." Crane runs out of puff.

Tick...

...tock.

Nick joins in. "What about the magic? I mean, is it still dangerous?"

Crane chortles. "It never was, not for those who sought it."

"I don't seek it," Katy tells him, a tear running down her cheek.

Crane shakes a hand, the best he can manage to dismiss Katy's comment. "Even if you did, the book's magic is moot. It's being locked with you is as much its curse as it is your honour. Only when you die shall its potential be available again to those who would have it. Unfortunately, I will not be around to witness that day. I wish I could be. I wish."

"I don't feel honoured." Katy tightens her lips, wipes her tears. "I feel...I feel imprisoned."

"Oh, dear." Genuine sadness and bafflement fill Crane's eyes. "Please, do not feel that way. You are your own keeper now. You have a responsibility, the greatest there ever was and shall ever be."

Nick squeezes the old man's wrist, to which Crane sucks through his teeth. "You didn't answer my question. I need a yes or a no. Is the magic still dangerous?"

"Did I not just supply the answer?"

Nick glances at Katy. "The answer isn't important to me, I just need a yes...or a no."

Is it even important to Katy? What *would* she do if the answer was yes?

"My boy," Crane gazes at Nick with something like adoration, "the magic in that book is about as dangerous as a fifth printing of Huckleberry Finn whilst it lives with a piece of her inside it."

It's the closest thing Nick's going to get to a no. Crane, even in his final moments, cannot *not* indulge in his love of language. To him, yes and no are words of the imbecile.

Nick almost laughs.

"What do I do with it?" Katy asks.

"My dear, keep it close, keep it safe. Treat it as you would treat yourself. Once it was magic for others, now *you* are *its* magic, I suppose you could say. It really is an honour for you."

Katy hugs the Liber Votorum close, though now it's just a plain, unmagical book like the rest of them. Nick rests a hand on her shoulder. He guesses Katy is fed up of hearing what an honour it will be for her to have to carry that tome for the rest of her natural life. She keeps her lips zipped, tears patter with the speed of the clock to the floorboards.

Crane sighs, a rivulet of blood from his mouth fights through bristles.

Tick...

...tock.

Crane goes on. "Is not this house marvellous? I was able to conjure it with my memory. And, of course, the book. It took a lot, and I do not believe everything is as it should be. Of course, I allowed myself some artistic license. I think perhaps my father would have approved of this one thing I accomplished, to revive the old homestead. It is...a shame, that it shall disappear when I die."

Finally, the woman speaks. "No."

Crane continues. "It will not be terribly long now, now the book is bound to its fate." He looks down, his neck bunching into rolls as he takes in the sight of his penny slot. "Strange, taking a bullet, I have never felt so...young. That is a conundrum, is it not, Nicholas?"

"Yeah," is all Nick can think to say.

The woman sobs. "You can't leave me. Everything I have is because of you, I have dedicated my life to your beliefs. You can't die, you *can't.*"

Crane looks up at her, going ever so slightly boss-eyed when he does. "I can, Juniper, I can. Despite all we have been through, I do believe that I am ready. A little heavy-hearted, perhaps. I would have been nice to have partnered with the Liber Votorum, but alas," he looks back at Nick and Katy, "who more worthy to lose to than these fine people?"

Katy says to him, "*Are* you ready? For what comes next?"

Nick thinks she's trying to be cruel to the man, but Crane takes it another way.

He answers, "I am aware of the atrocities I have committed, the things I have done to strangers, friends and family, all in the name of the book, of secrecy. I know my judgement awaits on the horizon. Look around, both of you. Even in this room alone, I have surrounded myself with earthly and unearthly knowledges."

Nick looks, Katy does not. Her breathing is shaky.

Shelves that ring the office are packed with encyclopaedic volumes that go into the hundreds, bookcases are full of trinkets not unlike what Nick saw when first he spoke to Crane in the office at the back of the shop. A large desk is alight with every handheld puzzle box you can think of (the Rubik's standing out by colour alone), and the walls are adorned with religious symbols that care not for blasphemy. An upright cross lives in harmony with its upside down counterpart, wicker gods hold hands with gold ones, bird skulls squawk alongside lizard tails. All of these artifacts orbit the emblem of Crane's society, that odd circle with a diagonal line that cuts through it, a small triangle pointing down from the top. There are also three different versions of the globe in three corners of the room, all of them tacked with notes. Bird cages stuffed with flora and fauna dangle from the ceiling, mortar and pestle bowls leave no space on smaller tables, and a rickety collection of dated equipment for conducting experiments stands wherever their legs will fit.

"Whomsoever judges me," Crane smiles, "I will at least know how to converse with them."

"Then let me die, too." The woman straightens. "Let me die with you."

"Juniper, now is not your time."

"That is my wish," she says. It has impact. "And my punishment. I should have warned you, I should have- "

Crane touches her cheek, brushing away white powder. He tells her, "Would that I could. Would that I could a thousand times over, but I can no longer grant your wish. Perhaps Nicholas could be of some assistance?"

A mercy killing. Nick looks at the old woman. She doesn't meet his gaze. Anger pulls her face out of sorts. Tears clog in her powder, making a paste.

"Not a chance," he answers.

"Then I am sorry, Juniper. I cannot help you anymore. I have always loved you." A spout of blood shoots up from the penny slot, a water feature that won't turn on right.

A lone tear streaks Crane's face. The woman doesn't return the confession of love, only sits on her legs, breathing hard against her crying.

Tick...

...tock.

Nick starts, "How do- "

The woman bolts up, runs from the office with her face in her hands. The door slams behind her, faint footsteps thump on wood.

"She will be fine," says Crane.

"Don't care," Katy responds. There's a story between her and the woman, one that Nick doesn't think he'll ask about. Why fill in the blanks when you can erase them?

"Ulysses," says Nick. "How do we leave this house?"

Crane coughs, the blood spreads on his shirt. "When you leave the hall, you will see a new door. That will take you outside."

Katy stands then a there, the book heavy not only in her arms, but her mind. You can tell by the way her expression hangs on her face. "I hate you," she tells Crane, then goes and waits by the door.

Nick leans in. "Is there really no way to undo what's between her and the book?"

"Not a one. It really is not so bad," says Crane. The bubbles in the penny slot are more frequent.

"Some might disagree," Nick replies.

"Through disagreement comes wonderful conversation."

"I guess. Why're you helping us?"

"I am not a vengeful man. Things are the way they are. If I can aid you in any way now that the end is nigh, grant one last wish all of my own doing, then I shall."

"How? The book…"

"This house was conceived whilst I had the Liber Votorum" – there's those rolled Rs again – "and whilst it is no longer mine, the *house* is. Whilst still I draw breath, I have limited persuasion. Enough to create an extra door."

Nick can't keep the grin away. "You make it hard to hate you."

Crane smiles back. "The girl would disagree."

"Great conversations."

"Great conversations." Crane nods.

They take a second. Nick reminds himself of all the shit Crane has done so he doesn't leave with feelings of a warped friendship.

Tick…

…tock.

He asks, "Will anyone come after us?"

Drawing a rattling breath, Crane answers, "No. The society dies with me. Died when Mr George and my dear Apollo mounted their assault. Now, Nicholas, you must leave. Allow me to pass."

Nick gets to his feet, turns from Crane. He walks to the door through the scent of pinecones. When Katy sees him coming, she goes on ahead.

"I granted your wish, you know?"

Nick stops but doesn't turn around to Crane's voice. It has strength, one last push before the end.

"You saved the girl, Nicholas," the old man says. "You have it. You have your redemption."

Without another word, Nick leaves, closing the door on Crane.

Tick...

CHAPTER 48

Katy is by the stairs in the hall, holding the book – her heart's twin – in criss-crossed arms. She taps her feet on a moist section of carpet. Walking through, it really is like being in the shell of an insect, one that's been tortured and repurposed as a house for the fucked-up. Gone is the office's scent of the natural world and back flows the reek of the river Styx. All around Nick, the ceiling drops little snake hisses.

In a heap with her head buried in the ripped plush of a destroyed seat is the old woman called Juniper. She's crying. Nick doesn't feel a shred of sympathy. It had been different with Crane because he had known him first, before the madness, or before the madness was revealed, anyway. But not this woman. Is it a bit prejudiced? Yeah, maybe it is.

Thoughts of Danielle make an intrusion, steered to suicide by a society that used her. Driven to insanity, chewed up and spat out. It's obvious that Crane had command of that, and being at his side in some way the whole time, it was probable that this woman had orchestrated it with him.

Nick changes his mind.

He will help.

A gun, clutched in a severed hand, sits next to Nick's foot. He pries it out, approaches Juniper, who looks up at him with shimmering, desperate eyes. Nick knows eyes like that, has worn them, but at least he isn't a murderer. Of that, he is certain. Many things he is, but not that. Never that.

And yet…

What he's about to do is evil, the closest to being a murderer he's willing to become. He won't lose sleep, won't be on the lookout for a new figure following him. He won't feel any guilt. Sometimes, evil needs evil.

Dusting crumbs of burnt flesh from the gun, he places it on the seat. Juniper gawks at him, then the gun, then back to Nick, misunderstanding. Nick spells it out for her.

"Wish granted."

He sees her face change. Her mouth drops down, powder crumbles away, revealing wrinkles beneath. She opens her mouth to plead, but Nick walks away.

Taking Katy by the arm, they ascend the stairs, neither looking back.

"You shouldn't have given her the time," says Katy.

"I didn't," says Nick. "I took it away."

Sure enough, a new door awaits them at the bottom of the stairs outside the hall. A regular looking thing that's out of place. As long as it works, it doesn't matter. It does, creaks open.

It's night time. In front of them is a grass clearing that joins with woodland silvered by the moon.

When they leave, the door closes. A second after, they hear a single gunshot, as if from far, far away.

They turn around. The house is gone, a final magic trick. A few bricks of foundation remain where the building stood, most of it hidden in overgrown ryegrass.

The moon is full.

Wind rolls over the grassland, creating the illusion of a shallow ocean of knives. On it surfs a chill that has a cleansing quality, soothing Nick's hurts. Any dark mysticism the woods held is gone, though Nick knows – can feel – that just below the surface lies that residue, always here waiting to be tapped. Right now, the night is piano calm.

Nick didn't realise that Katy has already walked away. He sees her silhouette facing into the trees, her shoulders bobbing up and down. He thinks she's crying until he reaches her.

"Katy." He puts a hand on her shoulder.

She turns, crying *and* laughing. "I'm okay," she sniffs.

The trees rustle. All around them, abundant but unseen, crickets play their music. It's the soundtrack to the end.

"Do you wanna talk, about…you know." Nick nods at the book.

"No." She wipes her nose. Shiny with tears, the moonlight transforms her eyes into glittering coins. "Not yet. I want to enjoy this moment."

From a branch, a barn owl swoops silently, its crop not quite touching the grass. It's a ghost, so they say. The good kind. It screeches, and is gone.

Katy says, "Did you see that?"

"Yeah, I did," Nick answers.

"Night hunting. Means things are going well for him."

"Good."

"Do you want to name him?"

Nick would smile if it didn't hurt his face. The split eyebrow has only just started to reknit itself together. A pity his hand can't be as quick. "I think it's best I don't."

"Me too," she laughs, which turns to more crying. Nick hugs her.

He says, "Let's get you home."

They follow a dirt path into the trees. It's dark, yet somehow they can still see, as if the moon follows them like a bulb. Eventually, they come to the stone pillars that served as the estate gateway. Before, it had been a crossing from one world to the next, now it's just a ruin. When they pass, a small furry shape darts out from the bushes. Katy hunkers down, pops the book on the floor beside her, keeping it, Nick notices, close. Touching toes.

"Pop Tart!"

No! That's not a cat but a *thing*! Nick steps in front of Katy, meaning to see the beast off. "Keep away from it, it's not what you think it is."

The cat – more handsome by night – winds around Nick's legs, purring with enthusiasm.

Katy titters, "I know what *he* is. He's Pop Tart, and he's Solomon, or was."

"Solomon?"

She wiggles her fingertips, the cat races to her, then steps into her lap, pushing its muzzle against her cheek. It's aware of her bruises, showing its affection carefully.

"I don't want it around, Katy. I...shot it, but it lived. It belongs to Crane."

"You *shot* him?" Katy cuddles the cat protectively.

"He's how they found us. See the scar? He lived. Came back to life right in front of me."

"I'm glad he did." Katy ruffles the cat's mane. "Come back, I mean."

"Katy..."

"Look." She holds up the cat. "See his eyes?"

Nick peers into them. They are wide, of the predator, of the deceiver, the familiar spirit, and...they are blue.

"They're blue," he says.

"Yes, they are. Solomon was like this one's doppelganger, living in the same body, and Solomon's eyes were yellow. Remember?"

Nick does, yet still he has trouble accepting this animal, trusting it. It had integrated itself into his life, then acted as the tool to his betrayal.

He asks, "So what?"

"So, Solomon is gone now. This is just Pop Tart." Katy puts him over her shoulder where his paws begin to knead her back, purring for all the woods to hear. Her foot keeps contact with the book.

"Just...Pop Tart?" says Nick.

She nods, stroking the whole length of the cat. It looks over at him, blue eyes brilliant in the darkness. There is a difference in the animal, a change in its makeup that goes beyond the irises. He always had an intelligent human quality, now it's a cat quality, plain and simple. How it should be.

"Just Pop Tart," he repeats.

"Yes, and I'm taking him home, aren't I Pop Tart?"

Pop Tart meows.

Nick says, "If you're sure?"

"I am," Katy replies. "He has nowhere else to go."

"Well, okay. If that's what you want. Just…do me a favour and keep an eye on him. Just for a couple of days."

"I won't have to."

Katy plops Pop Tart down, picks up the book. A print is left in the topsoil. Holding half a heart is heavy business, Nick thinks. When they continue walking, the cat follows them of its own accord, keeping pace.

"Pop Tart," Nick chuckles. "You might wanna change the name."

§

He watched them leave the house, witnessed it vanish. He watched them walk into the woods. He watched it all from a dark alcove nature carved out of a fat tree.

The Fat Tree.

That could be the title of another rhyme.

Simon Schaeffer rubs the skull paint unsuccessfully from his face, then gets himself lost in the woods, taking himself in the opposite direction to the girl and Nicholas. He isn't sure why he's not dead, believed he would be should Master ever bite the dust. Probably best not to ask questions, yet still they type themselves out in his brainwaves.

Where will he go, what will he do? That, he doesn't know. What is there for him *to* do? Perhaps he will pay a visit to Mother's grave for a piss. Perhaps he will seek more than his power grants him. Oddly enough, it still works despite Mr Crane's failure. It's liberating to refer to him as mister instead of master. He always was just a mister.

There'll be much to discuss at his next therapy session.

Simon is alone, needs a friend. As he slinks through the forest, he summons a ghost. It walks beside him, slipping through the objects it doesn't have to traverse.

Maybe now they can be in love, he and Dani, against the world.

Together.

CHAPTER 49

It's five in the morning. Katy and Nick sit in the car Nick says belongs to the man whose pub they went to. It smells of old air freshener.

On the radio, Sam Smith sings about not being able to keep promises. Katy has never understood him. She changes the station to an oldies show with a band telling her to crack that whip. She turns the radio off. She and Nick sit in silence, listening to the birdsong. Better than any radio.

They're in a layby on a quiet road. Nature let loose on either side, a selection of houses lined up ahead. One of them, the one at the far end, is hers. It sticks out from the others because of the red garage door.

The sun is already up, yawning its rays on a clear blue sky, similar to the day she was kidnapped. She wonders how the tadpoles are doing. They're probably frogs now, ribbiting further downstream. Pop Tart is washing himself on the back seat, the book is in the footwell. If she only had to take one of them with her, the choice is obvious. And furry.

Katy is scared to go home, not because she doesn't want to, but because…how will she go back to normal life? How does she live with a split heart?

"Sure you wanna go on your own?" Nick asks. His hands are ten and two on the steering wheel, have been since they stopped. How he'd driven all this way with his pummelled hand, Katy doesn't know. Painfully, probably.

It's only a quarter mile walk, one she's made countless times, though today it looks longer. Longer than it ever has done.

She answers, "I'm sure."

They'd talked about it on the drive. It was the only thing they talked about. The rest of it, they listened to the radio, or the sound of the car, watching streetlamps zip by overhead. It was decided that Katy should return to her house on her own. With Nick would raise too many questions, not to mention suspicion. They'd never be able to fully explain themselves. It'll be much more simple – not that this could ever *be* simple – if Nick stays behind. Mum and Dad will already have a mountain of emotions to deal with, Nick said, and it's best to keep that personal. No one wants a stranger at a family reunion. Katy agreed with him, but doesn't like it. It feels like she's erasing something.

"What'll you tell them?" asks Nick.

"I don't know." She stares out the window, watching bees visit a honeysuckle plant. "I'll think of something. They…won't believe the truth, not all of it. No one would." She faces him. "I should tell them about you. I won't, but I should. You…you saved me, twice. You could have walked away, but you didn't. I'll never forget that. Thank you."

It's not something she ever expected him to do, but he blushes. "You're welcome."

"It's weird," she sighs. "I can hardly believe I'm back, that it's over."

"Believe it."

"Feels like I've been away for years."

"Treat it as if you have," Nick tells her. "Cram years of lost love into going home, into hugging your mum and dad. Cram it all in and believe you're home."

"In the cell," she says, "I drew pictures of the things I love. I didn't believe I'd ever see them again, so I made believe that they were there. But I'm really going to see them, they're in there now, I'm really still alive."

Nick smiles at her, letting her say everything she needs to. His hands slip from the steering wheel into his lap.

To her own lap, Katy says, "I don't know how I'm going to live with that thing."

"You feed it twice a day, make sure it has water."

She smiles, a tear drops. Pop Tart chirps, tries to grab at something on the other side of the window.

Nick goes on. "You'll figure it out."

"I'll start…" Katy stops to think. "I'll start by keeping it in my wardrobe. Right at the back."

"There you go," says Nick. "You're already starting."

They both say, "One step at a time." It'll be something she says all the time, like a mantra whenever life gets difficult.

"See how things go," Nick says. "You'll learn how you're s'posed to go about things. As long as the book's safe, so are you."

She gazes out the window. "I hate them all, Nick. All of them."

"I know you do, but try not to let that hate get the better of you. Don't be like I was, a sceptical, bitter person who only smiled when he had to. You've taught me otherwise. Continue being your own good example."

"I'll try. It'll be difficult, but I'll try," Katy says, then adds, "I like your smile, by the way."

"And I like yours. You should be proud of yourself, Katy."

"I don't feel pride," she replies. "I feel…exhausted."

"I'd say knackered."

"I had help from an inner voice or two." Gut and Survival, will they ever return? Maybe they don't have to, maybe they're still here waiting to help, if needed. She laughs, looks in the back at Pop Tart and the book. "I know I'm split in two, in a sense, but…" Back to Nick. "I can feel my heart beating. It's still mine, I still own it."

"Remind yourself of that every now and then," says Nick.

"And…I'll always be me. Won't I?"

"Yes, Katy. Always. Book or no book."

"Good." She looks back out the window, the meadow next to them begging to be ran through. "I like me."

"I hope so." He nudges her shoulder. "You're hard work."

"We have that in common." She laughs, then asks, "What're you going to do next?"

It's strange even asking the question. After everything, how is it that a next even exists?

Nick shrugs, peers out at the layby. It's clean, there's never been many litterbugs in this town.

"Home, I s'pose. Wherever that is. I'm sure there'll be some police interest. Like you, I'll figure it out. Might get myself a pet."

"Get in touch with me if you do, that animal should have a real name." Katy smiles.

Nick chuckles, "I will."

It feels good to laugh. She was worried it would be harder, or that she'd forgotten how to without crying. Both of them know they won't see each other again, not for years at least. Katy wonders if it upsets Nick as much as it does her. She hopes so, though hopes he isn't sad. Tonight, she'll dream of him. She prays the dreams outweigh the nightmares that are sure to be waiting, a place where all the bad people are still alive, a place where the spider man spins his web.

Nick reaches in his pocket, pulls out a silver device. "Forgot I had this," he says. "Everything from the house is recorded on this. Reckon I'll delete it. Some memories aren't worth keeping."

She sits up. "Don't you dare."

"Why?"

"A lot of kids have died because of those people. On there is evidence, *proof.* It needs to go to the police. I'm sure there are cold cases or something for missing kids, even ones that go back far enough that they'd be dead now anyway, but that isn't the point. That will at least point them in the right direction, maybe connect some dots."

"But it's over now, why drag it back up?" Nick asks.

She answers, "Families will need closure. That could give it to them. I know that if I...died...I'd want my mum and dad to know how."

Katy can't help but feel like a part of her *has* died, died and then preserved in the book. If she puts her ear to the pages, will she hear a heartbeat? A cry for help?

Nick looks at the recorder. "I'd have to give it anonymously."

"Just promise me you'll do it."

"I promise," he says after a few seconds, pocketing the device.

"Thank you."

They sit in silence for a while, thinking the same thing, Katy reckons. It's Nick who finally says, "Your parents will be missing you, Katy. I think you should go to them. You must be excited to get back."

"Yes." She smiles. She really, really is. "I think so, too." She looks at him. "Will I be safe?"

"You will," says Nick, a certainty in his voice she finds comfort in.

"I'm glad this happened," she says. "Not because of all the bad stuff, but because I got to meet you. I'm glad you were there."

"I never knew what Crane did until that night. You know that, right?" from Nick.

"I know."

"I'm glad I met you too, even though I didn't ask for it." He grins.

"I'll miss you," she says.

"I'll miss you, too."

She throws her arms around his neck, squeezing tight, burying her head into his chest. He smells of the house, of dry blood, but also of woodland, of nature, of all the things she loves. The tears come in a flood, the dam holding at bay the final goodbye finally broken. Nick pats her back.

"I don't want to leave you." Her words are muffled.

"You have to, and you'll be fine. Figure your story and stick to it. The police'll leave off before long."

"I will." She sniffs.

The hug lasts a little longer before they let go. It's the hardest hug Katy has ever had to finish. She doesn't think another hug will ever be as powerful as this one, not even the one she receives when she gets home.

"What about you?" she asks.

"What about me?"

"Will you be okay?"

He gives an answer that both ticks all the boxes *and* leaves them blank. "I'll manage."

And he will, she thinks.

"Time to go home," says Nick. Even under all his swelling and bruising, Katy can see his kind features.

She wipes her eyes and nose, rubs it off on the tunic that she can't wait to get out of. The thought of a long hot bath is almost too much to handle. By the time she's finished, the water will be toxic.

Reaching into the back footwell, she takes the book. An electric charge heats her body as she becomes whole again. After a deep breath that wobbles when she lets it out, she opens the door, field-smell hitting her instantly. Before getting out she looks back to Nick.

"Goodbye," she says.

"Goodbye," he says, smiling.

"Thank you for keeping your promise." She pauses. "You got me home."

He nods, lip quivering. Who would ever have thought that he was the sensitive type she's witnessing now. It's nice.

Katy sniffs, gets out, book to her chest. She likes it there for now, gives her the sense that her heart is singular again.

The smell of her town is everything green and everything sunny, permanently locked in holiday mode, like any seaside town. It's carried on the breeze. Before closing the door she calls Pop Tart. Like a dog, he leaps into the front then out by her feet, excited by his new surroundings.

Looking into Nick's eyes, she tells him, "You're my hero."

He says back to her, "And you're mine."

She never thought she'd have a hero, not in the literal sense, let alone *be* a hero. That stuff was for television, films and books. But here they both are, heroes to each other, though she isn't sure why Nick sees her that way.

She closes the door, and with a final wave, begins the walk home. It's a peaceful walk, the birds escort her, a fanfare of cheeps and chips and rings. Buzzing insects welcome her back, the grass on the roadside tickles her ankles. By her side Pop Tart follows, all the way to the house she thought she'd never see again, the one with the red garage door. Without knocking, she walks inside.

Home.

Nick watches Katy until she disappears through her front door. With a deep breath that stings his ribs, he dries his eyes, turns on the car and pulls away. It's a long drive back to the city. He'll miss this quiet town. It's better than Constable's Heath.

He imagines her running through the house, calling for her mum and dad, all of them falling on the floor in a crying pile, loving each other so much it hurts. What she'll tell them, how she'll explain her new cat and the book that she just *has* to have is anyone's guess, but he's positive she'll think of something, probably already has. The hardest thing for her will be dealing with the trauma. The reminders. She might have to see someone, but with the support of her family, she'll get through it. Hopefully, she'll have a normalish life when she reaches adulthood. Maybe when that day comes he'll pay a visit, or she might find him. That'd be nice, something to look forward to. Still, he doubts that day will come. The memories that connect them are too much, too distended by bad vibes. If Nick could wish for anything, it would be that Katy forgets everything, including him, and moves on.

If he can't see her, he can at least keep his final promise. In time, when the dust has settled, he'll drop the recorder off at a police station, perhaps with a small note detailing what it is, then let them make what they will of it. If Katy reads anything about it in the paper she'll know he did good, and then…then the tie between them will truly be severed.

Nick thinks he might drop by Frank's. Now the Georges are out of the picture, perhaps new management might be in order. It'd mean a job, a place to live. He and Frank could run a decent gaff, put on legit bouts, get all the proper licensing and what not. Nick's had enough of being enemies with the law, and there's always another fight, another night, always a punter ready to tank up and place a foolhardy bet. They could do something nice for lucky sods who win big, bottle of bubbly or something. Yeah, they could really make something of Estelle's.

There'll be a power vacuum with the Georges gone, a lot of muscle trying to stake a claim on available turf. Nick is ready for them. He won't let them take advantage, won't let them manipulate. As the old proverb goes: A baseball bat will see 'em off.

He pulls onto a dual carriageway, drives for a few miles, then decides, after little deliberation, to take the scenic route instead. Before he takes a left on a road he's never heard of, he stops at a service station to buy a can of whatever. His appearance draws a few stares, the clerk smiles politely when change slips from his mangled hand. The coppers have dry blood on them, much to the clerk's quiet chagrin. Nick says cheers, doesn't wait for anything in return.

Back in the car, on a blissfully lonely road, he thinks he sees a shadow in the passenger seat. He looks, and there is nothing. Old expectations worming their way in, is all. There'll never be anything there again, not in his car, not in a café, not watching him sleep. Not anywhere.

Through the quiet country roads he drives on clumsy, unorthodox routes. His face hurts, body, too. Might be worth paying a visit to the doctors for some pain pills. A tub of Savlon, that might help.

He's afraid of the things he'll see when he sleeps, the things that'll pop into his head when he least expects them to. It'll be a lifelong affliction. Unlike Katy, he's too old to forget.

Yes, he thinks, a cat might just be a partial solution to that problem, a friend to sleep with, keep him company. A set of eyes to talk to. Cornflake is a good name, he laughs to himself.

There's a lot to think about, a lot to process.

A person to miss.

None of it will be easy, but for now the drive is pleasant, the wind through the window is nice. The sun shines on a sky fit for a postcard.

It's nice, Nick thinks.
He feels it suits him well.

§

EPILOGUE

The prison cell is dark, as well it should be after lights out.

Tonight is unusually quiet. Everyone must be sleeping peacefully, or they all hanged themselves. Whichever it is, the prisoner treats the calm like a birthday gift. He'll have plenty of those coming his way. When will the system catch on that something's not right?

In his single bed with a hard mattress, he rolls over, clutching the thin duvet around his neck. He blinks awake, focuses on something in what is tonight the darkest corner of his cell, a corner than seemingly goes back into space.

Terror seizes his heart.

"Good evening," a voice says.

The prison's glassy silence is smashed to pieces as Phillip Crane's horrified screams echo across the landings, haunting the wings.

"HE'S HERE!" he cries.

"*HE'S HEEEEERRRREEEEE!*"

§

Afterword

This book has been something of an adventure for me (and – I hope – you too, but in a different way). It started with a simple idea and a title that I loved but promptly binned because it gave away the main plot twist. The title of 'Wishmaster' happened organically, as these things tend to, and actually aided in writing some of the story.

There was a time or two (okay…maybe more) where I became stuck, petrified by my omnipresent friend Self-Doubt, or turned the story over in my head thinking, "What's the point?" But I got through those, as is tradition, and after cutting a sizeable chunk of fat, here is the finished product. It is as good as it will allow itself to be, and as poor as I have made it, so if you find any junk, blame me, not the story.

As I stated in the front dedication, I was blessed with my baby boy during the writing of this book, which meant I had to step away from the words a while (happily, and probably necessarily). I believe this happened just as Nick is surrounded by Schaeffer's ghouls in the woods. From there, once I had settled into dad-mode (can we ever really settle in?), the remainder of the story was written in notes on my phone, then to be copied out over a number of weeks. I was worried the story would feel disjointed, but actually, I'm rather happy with the results.

I don't think I'll be returning to the characters of 'Wishmaster'. Though there are some open endings, I believe their stories have been told. I must admit, however, that I am intrigued as to what Simon Schaeffer will get up to next.

Thank you to all of you who purchased this book, I hope to see you all again soon. I shall leave you with what might be one of the world's finest cliché's, but one I think holds true:

Be careful what you wish for.

Acknowledgements

I would like to thank Kathryn for, as usual, putting up with me in times of creative stress. When I struggle to find the words or lose the plot (in more ways than one), she is always there to chase away the grumpiness, or join me in it. An extra special thanks to her for giving me the time I need to do this. It's not been easy with a little one, but we manage. I'm still there to change a nappy and wake up for night feeds.

Thank you to Debbie Laing, Alistair Hendrickson and Lynsey Hall for taking the time to read through the story, offering their insights, spelling corrections (I think we got 'em all) and honesty. Also, thanks is due to Caitlin Mapes for providing knowledge on injury detail. Anything medically incorrect is my fault.

Jorge Iracheta, your artwork for this tome is beyond awesome. Thank you so very much.

As in my last book, I want to thank the two writers who inspired me to join in the craft. You'll most likely never see this, but here's to you: Stephen King and Clive Barker.

Lastly, and most importantly, you 'orrible lot who hold this book in your hands. You are the reason I do this, and your support gives me the strength to carry on even when the plot falls off a cliff. I can't wait to see you all again. I have such sights to show you.

"She seems happy." Katy's dad observes her out the kitchen window.

"Whatever she's been through, she's handling it well," adds Mum.

They both have a cup of tea, watching their daughter play in the garden with that odd new cat of hers.

"Do you think she knows?" asks Mum.

Dad sips his tea, shakes his head. "I don't think so, it's been two weeks now. The police are satisfied."

"You're right," agrees Mum. "I just…I don't know how the offering could have gone so wrong."

"Shit happens." Dad sets his empty mug in the sink.

"With Mr Crane dead, where does that leave the society?"

"With us," smiles Dad. "We were only initiates, not full-fledged. Lucky us."

Mum thinks into her tea, biting her lower lip. "Can we…do it?"

"I think so." Dad undoes his top button. "We have the book in our house, and the key to unlocking its power again."

They both train their eyes on their daughter. She's rolling on her back, teasing the cat which waves its tail playfully in a bed of flowers.

Dad says, with the agreeing nod of Mum, "There has to be a Wishmaster."

Printed in Great Britain
by Amazon

27248817R00268